THE TWO MAGICIANS

BOOKS BY ZELDA LEAH GATUSKIN

Spiral Map of Time Trilogy
THE TIME DANCER
THE TWO MAGICIANS
THE TEN YEARS

Fiction
CASTLE LARK
WHERE THE SKY USED TO BE
DIGITAL FACE

Creative Non-fiction
ANCESTRAL NOTES
TIME AND TEMPERATURE
IF I COULD CONVINCE YOU OF ONLY ONE THING

Poetry
BUT WHO'S COUNTING?

Art
ZELDA'S COSMIC COLORING BOOK

THE TWO MAGICIANS

FROM NOWHERE TO FOREVER

Zelda Leah Gatuskin

sequel to "The Time Dancer"

Cover and book design by Studio Z, Albuquerque, NM

Printed in the United States of America
First Printing, 2017
ISBN: 978-0-938513-59-9
Library of Congress Control Number: 2017931499

AMADOR PUBLISHERS, LLC
Albuquerque, New Mexico
www.amadorbooks.com

in memory of Morning Star,
Esmarelda's biggest fan

THE TWO MAGICIANS

Contents

The Goathorn Mountains and the City of Ochersfeldt

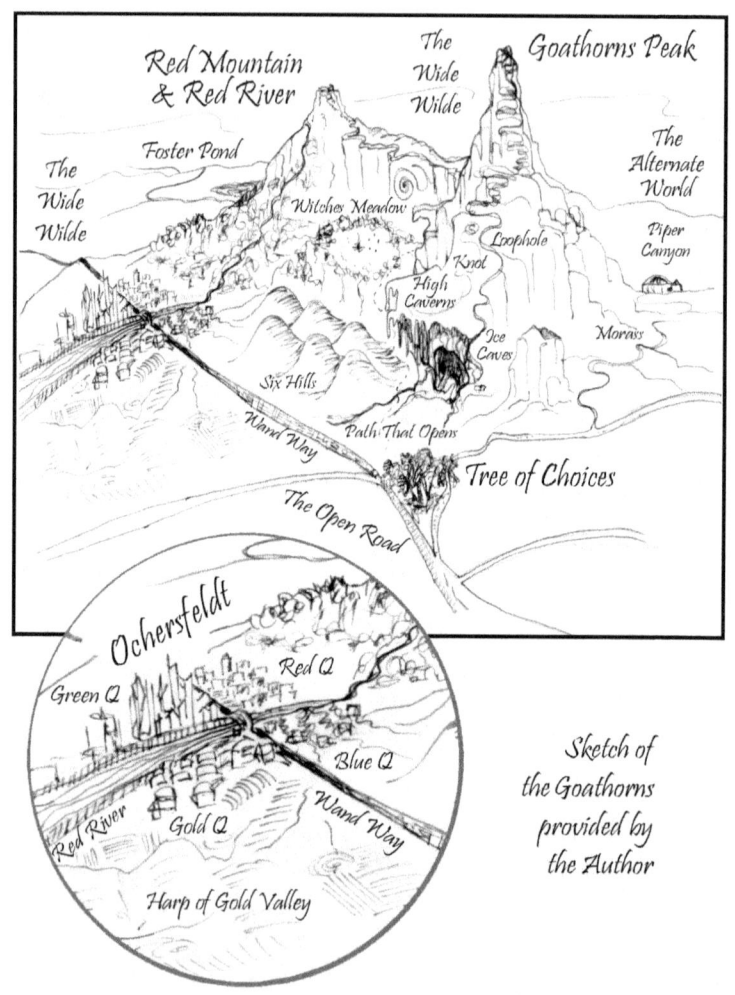

Red Mountain & Red River

The Wide Wilde

Goathorns Peak

The Wide Wilde

The Alternate World

Foster Pond

Witches Meadow

Loophole

Piper Canyon

Knot

High Caverns

Ice Caves

Morass

Six Hills

Ward Way

Path That Opens

Tree of Choices

The Open Road

Ochersfeldt

Red Q

Green Q

Blue Q

Red River

Gold Q

Ward Way

Harp of Gold Valley

Sketch of the Goathorns provided by the Author

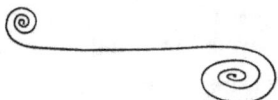

Prologue: Somewhere in the Rockies

PERSONALLY, I HAD NEVER BEEN OPPOSED TO THE HARMONY
Convention in Piper Canyon, which is the only reason it got to be
an annual event. I had the job of keeping an eye on the Loophole
and sending unwitting trespassers back to their side of the Spiral,
and so the other Minders allowed me the final say. I enjoyed the
convention, actually. Made for a busy week, but I had the most
interesting slice of the Alternate World coming right to my
doorstep.

That's where I went wrong. Allowing myself to be amused by
this "New Age" business. Dancing and drumming. Amateurish
fortune-telling and bogus, hocus-pocus spells. The participants
were like children to me, harmlessly playing at games they knew
nothing about. I loved them and pitied them. Poor souls had no
idea how many turns of the Spiral lay ahead before they would
turn the corner to reclaim this world of magic they vaguely
remember and deeply desire. They felt close to it in Piper
Canyon, and indeed they were. Uncomfortably close.

There are such places in the world where the thread of Time,
winding as it does in a continuous spiral into the center and then
out again—two alternating coils having no beginning and no
end—elaborates on its path with many offshoots and curlicues

1

that very nearly touch other, unrelated pieces of the Spiral. The sensitive ones feel out these places and gambol about in Nature hoping to magically cross over. They don't (that is, they shouldn't), but they benefit from mere proximity so that word gets around, and the next thing you know someone has put up a resort nearby with a sweat lodge and whatnot. And there is not a thing wrong with that, except when it happens right here in the Goathorns, one of the most magical of all the magical places in my magical world, where the five sisters took residence many a spiral-turn ago and have cast so many spells that the curlicues of Time have tied themselves into one big Knot on the one side and frayed thin enough to make a Loophole on the other.

In part because of my own knotty past, I was given the Knot and the Loophole to mind. It suited me—but, as I said, I was lax. Midway through the recent Harmony Convention, I realized that it would have to be the last in Piper Canyon. It wasn't anyone's fault, that's just the way the Spiral works around these parts. Every glitch and snag in the fabric of Time gets pushed along until it hits the Knot, where all lost and lapsed spells are trapped and teased out and hopefully tamed, or at least contained.

Wrangling old spells is the sisters' rent payment, you might say. Did they think they could appropriate the Goathorns for themselves without offering something in return? Not to mention that much of the magical flotsam that has washed in of late is the result of their own mischief. The chickens were coming home to roost, in other words.

Brunagwa herself created the Loophole by pushing her way through the merest small flaw in the Spiral at the outermost edge of a dead-end detour. And who espied her on the other side but young Robyn, shuffling around in the woods while on a family vacation. You might say that was the very beginning of things there in the Alternate World, and that the girl's life was changed forever and inexorably despite the sisters' memory-blocking spells, so that all things lost out of our world would land on

Robyn's doorstep ever after—the cat, the Gypsy, the fiddler, and finally the rugs—and it was only a matter of time before she, and all these others, found their way to Piper Canyon.

Round and round we go. Some things have happened twice already. Before we risk another doubling of the Knot, I take the unprecedented action, for a Minder, of recording the tale. Not that anyone stumbling into the Knot will be better able to follow the tangled thread safely out again on account of having read it. No, we won't even contemplate that. The only hope for this particular fraying strand of Time is to protect it from further strain of any sort, and that means keeping the New Age kiddies out of Piper Canyon henceforth and forever. For that I need cooperation and assistance from someone trustworthy in the Alternate World, and I suppose you can guess my choice already.

Charming girl, but she drives a hard bargain. Our agreement is this: She is helping to get the Harmony Convention relocated and this property sold to A.G. Brooks, who will forbid future trespass. I am supposed to be writing up my firsthand account of life on this side of the Spiral, everything I know about the Gypsy and her crew, and the true nature of Time. (Nothing to it, right?)

Robyn is looking for proof that magic exists. She has deduced correctly that I myself am witness to a tremendous amount of evidence, me being a Minder—that is, able to see and hear with great acuity even at great distances and even into the souls of living things. Add to that the Knot, with its repetitions and disjointed crossings, and the Loophole, that ratty passage across the Spiral—the whole of it lying within the circle of the Goathorn Mountains, where the five sisters corral broken spells from all Times and both worlds—and you may begin to comprehend how very many far-flung episodes and secrets I have been able to observe, one way or another.

Truly, now that I spell it out I have to agree that no one is more qualified than I to recount the circumstances leading to this fateful collaboration. It will be up to Robyn to convince the imaginative but skeptical Alternate World of my veracity (my very existence). I expect (indeed I hope) this chronicle will be perceived as fiction. Yes, even by those who have been here with us at Kestrel Lodge for the Summer Solstice Harmony Convention, Fifth Annual and about to be last, in Piper Canyon, in the Alternate World, somewhere in the Rockies . . .

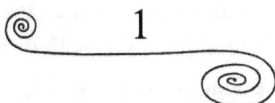

1

The Time Winders

THE LEAD DANCER OF THE TIME WINDERS TWIRLED SO FAST AND so long that she seemed to disappear. Some of those who were present for the elimination round of the belly dance competition at the Fifth Annual Harmony Convention at Piper Canyon claimed she had actually dematerialized. Yasmine laughed it off at the party afterward. She explained to a cluster of adoring young dancers and a few jealous competitors that a well-executed Turkish Drop will have that effect.

"First, there's the spinning, which creates the blur. Then, if you can keep it going long enough, the audience gets tranced out and sees all sorts of things. And when you drop suddenly, you really seem to disappear—only the first few rows see you hit the floor, and they're usually too surprised or distracted by the veil to notice."

So, maybe it was only a Turkish Drop, but it was still a hell of a Turkish Drop. Everyone wanted to get a look, and the crowd for the semi-final round on Thursday night was huge, as big as they had seen at past conventions for the Saturday night finale. The Time Winders were the last group on the program, and the women backstage—all relative beginners—were as irritable as the audience, wondering if the wait would be worth it.

Finally the stage manager gave the cue. The Time Winders

lined up in the wings with their props while the elegant Mustaphas took their bows. The curtain closed, the Mustaphas jogged off stage. Now the five costumed Time Winders and a male helper hurried to arrange six smallish oriental rugs into one big square of carpet in the center of the stage before the curtain opened again. The Time Winders took their places: four lined up across the carpet, their leader off to the side. The helper squeezed this one's hand, then hurried back into the wings. A techie cued up the troupe's sound track. Out front, the emcee quieted the audience.

"Ladies and gentlemen, thank you for your attention tonight. I am pleased to present our final contestants. A very *original* group. Please welcome, from Caliente, New Mexico, Alizia, Shanna, Ursula, Fatima and Yasmine— The Time Winders!"

Gentle music dubbed over the sound of ocean waves crashing to shore rose in volume while the curtain opened and the lights slowly came up. The four women center-stage swayed and undulated in unison. Their costumes were modest compared to others that had been on stage that night, consisting of harem pants with short vests and matching gauzy veils hemmed with sequins. Cheap stuff bought out of a catalogue and customized with strands of beads and feathers in kelly green, royal blue, crimson red and vivid purple. The tall leader, who had stepped forward to the emcee's microphone on the front corner of the stage, wore bright yellow. A few unkind snickers bubbled out of the audience. But if the troupe looked at first like a garish, dancing crafts project, their graceful movements to the snaky solo melody of a double reed flute, along with Yasmine's curious narration, quickly brought the audience under The Time Winders' spell.

"Imagine, if you will," Yasmine chanted, "that Time is a spiral." Her dancers began to circle, sweeping their veils behind them. "It winds in... And it winds out again..." The dancers spiraled into the center and then out several times in a hip-dipping line dance. "The center of the spiral is the place where the *Past* meets the *Future*. And the tail of the spiral, where it turns back and scrolls inward again, is where the *Future* meets the *Past*. And in between..." Each dancer began to turn slowly on her own while swishing her veil this way and that. "The two paths of the endless spiral lay side by side, creating *the alternating worlds of the Spiral Map of Time*."

Here, the music, which had been growing gradually louder and faster, broke into a heavily rhythmic Middle Eastern melody. The crowd seemed to take a collective breath and push forward in their seats.

"And if you know how to dance..."

The music escalated to an up-tempo rendition of an old Arabic tune, a favorite in the belly dance world, and the troupe went through a brisk choreography of shakes and shimmies. The audience clapped along softly, eagerly, waiting for Yasmine to complete the incantation and explode into dance herself.

"*Do* you know how to dance?" she challenged the auditorium, and a cry went up, "Yes!" then quickly faded to let her continue. Every word and pause was perfectly synched to the music and the troupe's precision camel-walks and belly-rolls.

"Then if you know how to dance," Yasmine sang out, "you can dance to any*where* and any *time*. You can dance your way *across the Spiral* and into the world *where Magic lives*. All you have to do is..."

The crowd buzzed with anticipation.

"Vibrate!"

The four women center stage lowered their veils and began to shimmy. The audience cheered. Yasmine seemed to fly on yellow wings to the middle of the carpet, where she led her dancers through the final drum solo. It was the standard fare—chest lifts, hip drops and belly flutters executed with rhythmic precision to a medley of drum patterns. With Yasmine front and center the troupe was more confident. Energy sparked between them. Their smiles inspired the audience to clap along. When the piece ended, they accepted their applause with a small bow and then took two more steps back to sway in a row behind their leader, creating a rippling rainbow backdrop for her with their veils.

Yasmine's routine began with a traditional *taksim* to the skillfully plucked strings of a solo oud, in which she showed off her control and grace with sinuous movements of arms and torso, and teasing flourishes of her veil. Next came a display of foot- and finger-work. Troupe members relieved Yasmine of her veil and provided little cymbals for her to slip onto her fingers. She clacked along with an Arabic orchestra of strings, horns and drums, performing a jiggly folk dance to a medley of standard four-four and eight-four rhythms—the walking *Wahadi*, hip-dipping *Beledi*, and bouncy *Chiftetelli*.

When the music changed again, moving north to Armenia with the addition of one quirky beat, Yasmine reclaimed her veil. Now it was the troupe's turn to don zils and click through variations of the nine-eight *Karshlima*. Yasmine swirled around the stage to the strange, urgent song. With each chorus, the tempo increased, and Yasmine's circles became faster and smaller until she was spinning in the center of the carpet. Yellow veil flying out like a sail as she whirled, and long blond ponytail snapping around her, Yasmine dervished into a golden blur.

The crowd was on their feet cheering. All eyes upon her, Yasmine twirled until the patterns in the carpets were set in motion, creating a whirlpool of color that expanded outward from her toes and lifted her above the surface of a fulminating cloud, a blur of yellow . . . that suddenly collapsed to the floor . . .

The audience gasped as one and surged toward the stage . . .
. . .

She was there. The yellow veil was, anyway, lying in elegant ripples on the patchwork of rugs on the very stationery stage. And then, with the crowd roaring, it took form, fluttered, and fell aside to reveal the trembling dancer. Yasmine slid up to her knees, did a few undulations, then reached back to her troupe, who danced forward and raised her to her feet. The audience collapsed back into their seats in wonder.

The final bit of The Time Winders' routine was anti-climactic. Once again they looked like beginners, and people began turning to each other to chatter about what they had just seen. Some got up and wandered out to the banquet hall before the performance was over, but most stuck around to give The Time Winders an enthusiastic ovation at the end.

Meanwhile, the man in the wings was beside himself. He'd nearly succumbed to the urge to rush out and tackle his wife before she could perform the Turkish Drop. His muscles were tensing to hurtle him on stage, but she became lost in a cloud of billowing yellow chiffon. Was it not even a second that she was gone? She reappeared before his heart had resumed beating. With the audience roaring, all he could do was pace frantically backstage until the routine ended. When Yasmine at last left the spotlight and came over to him, he grabbed her in a tight hug and almost cried.

"What the hell was that, Robyn? Where did you go? Don't ever do that again. I feel like I'm about to lose you!"

He spoke into her neck—she was almost a head taller than he—and the others couldn't hear. The women were too excited about their performance to notice anything unusual in Ramon and Robyn's embrace.

I noticed, of course, because I was there to see and hear for myself. Robyn wants to know where. She is impressed with how vividly I have described her performance, but is not so happy about my bringing Ramon into it. She reminds me that my task is to explain what *really* happened, so as to satisfy her own prodigious curiosity, and to supply the Alternate World with real and true evidence of the other side of the Spiral. (Even if no one believes it, and all the better for me if they don't.) It has come to this: Until this damnable chore is done, I have my own Minder, of a sort. Editor, she calls herself. Best to get on with it.

Are we clear that Robyn's—excuse me, Yasmine's—script was entirely correct about the Spiral Map of Time as consisting of my real and true world of magic and its mirror, the Alternate World, there where she lives? She had that right, having gotten all the details from Esmarelda (infuriating woman): Two worlds exist side by side in alternating coils of a Spiral that has no beginning and no end. The Gypsy's husband George Drumm will sing a song about it in a while, which may make it more clear, or you can act out The Time Winders' dance, or draw yourself a picture. The whole business is elaborated all too well in a certain publication that has recently come to my attention. I would like to figure out who wrote and disseminated that curious volume, which is (so far, fortunately) passing as fiction. Thus my account will be as thorough as possible not only to appease Robyn, but to tease out the secrets of this travesty called "The Time Dancer" and discover who is behind that preposterous *nom de plume*.

(Sorry, my dear, but I am at a loss. What now?)

Of course: *Moi*.

THE MINDER OF THE KNOT AND THE LOOPHOLE

I am a Minder. Minders are magical beings in a magical realm but we do not perform magic. No spells, no hexes, no charms. Were those methods available to me, I might not find myself in this predicament. On the other hand, even the best of our magic-makers—a Witch or Crone or Master Seer—would find their powers unreliable in the Alternate World.

Unlike those others, we Minders are not jealous for spells. It is magic enough that we transform our physical substance from one being into another, speak and think in several languages, hear and see with the sharpest senses of our multiple species. With no false modesty I state that I am exceptional even above all that, so of course my appearance is unremarkable. It is intended that no one will notice.

I cross through the Loophole by slipping between two sun-bleached sandstone boulders on our side and emerging into deeply shaded, thick pine forest in the Alternate World a mere mile from the Kestrel Kamp and Lodge. Typically, I stop at the boulders and lift a leg to mark the path before trotting through. That's right, I'm a coyote at that point. Small and rather mangy, I'm not ashamed to say. I work hard perfecting these appearances. I arrive in the forest as a small, wiry man in faded hiking clothes. I like to mark my passage here as well. The occasional hiker who encounters me thinks little of it when I step out from behind a tree pulling up my fly.

You'd have to be very observant to find me backstage during The Time Winders' routine, but I assure you I was there, picking up everything that was said with my sharp coyote ears, then following along with the dancers and crew on silent coyote paws when they attended the nightly banquet and party. Those who noticed me at all that week knew me as either a custodian or a park ranger, depending on whether they saw me indoors or out of doors. (Is it ringing a bell yet, Robyn?)

Of course, near the end, I had to get into a business suit and make myself known as A.G. Brooks.

Minders don't usually work up a big repertoire of forms. There's what we start out as—say, a hawk—and one other. We are most helpful to the Witches when we take human form for our second shape. They encourage that, but it leaves us little energy for anything else. That is to the sisters' liking, because then there are less ways we can spy on them. When the Witches find and adopt young Minders and train them to transform into human women, these individuals are called Familiars, and they serve the Goathorns Coven. (Note: The word "serve" is contro-versial. The Familiars and the Witches— Well, you'll see.)

I have always been independent like the Minders of old, back before the sisters came to the Goathorns. There were no human role models then, and Minders morphed freely from one species to another more in play than with purpose. The Firsts directed our actions in the way they made us. By instinct we guarded Red River, the high meadow, and all roads to The Top of The World and the innermost switchback of the Spiral, where the Beginning of Time meets the End of Time.

What I'm trying to say is that we are natural creatures of our locale. Any species here might produce an individual with Minder traits, the way Nature sometimes generates a pure white deer or a six-toed cat. The Familiars are different from me by virtue of the Witches' tutoring and charms, but we spring from the same stock. Over time there has been much confusion about the Minders and our origins. The sisters, who should know better, tend to treat us as if we are merely another product of wayward magic in need of taming. We Minders have not always been treated kindly by the Witches, nor, to be fair, have we always been kind to them.

The Coven asked me to take charge of the Knot and the Loophole, and I could hardly refuse. The job had to be done, and I was uniquely suited for it. I was a master of multiple forms, among them a human male, which is very rare. The Witches thought they had gotten me under control; and that misperception on their part sparked a deeper insight on mine: Their Familiars appear to submit because it makes the job of minding easier. One way or another, we Minders need to know what those gals are up to, so we play along. But do not be fooled, we are always prepared to act on our own when need arises.

(As some of us have done of late. Our most precious may already . . . No, let me not imagine the worst. My Editor requires Facts, and I applaud her. Facts she shall have. They can fill the space that would otherwise be occupied by foreboding.)

Fact: My original form, I swear on the First Weaver's bonnet, is a horned lizard. I learned to do the coyote next and then the man. But I found conditions across the Loophole in Piper Canyon strangely wetter than on my side. That's when I learned Frog.

Frog fared better in that climate; I am a frog there, and a horned lizard—or, as I prefer to be called, a horny toad—at home.

I also found that Man needed some adaptations for the Alternate World, mostly of the mind, and that took tremendous effort. It came down to this: I could bring some of my coyote traits into the Alternate World, but not Coyote himself. In Piper Canyon I would be either Amos G. Brooks the Human or Brooks the Frog, while at home in the Goathorns I must limit myself to H. Toad and H. Coyote. All of which was just fine with the sisters, because Amos has not been allowed near any of them for some time.

Yes, the indiscretions of my youth play into this. I'm a shady sort. I did not accept my assignment enthusiastically or take it very seriously at first. So, a fair amount of leakage had already taken place by the time I buckled down to my task as Minder of the Knot and the Loophole, which was not so long ago in the scope of this story—on the one side, anyway.

Fact: It is not possible to synchronize events between the two worlds at any given juncture, and especially here, so close to The Top of The World. The further my tale takes us into the Past, and hopefully into the Future, the less alignment there will be between the passage of time on either side.

I say "hopefully" with regard to the Future because here in the fifth and last year of the Harmony Convention in Piper Canyon—with rents and snags appearing all through this portion of the Spiral, and Time doubling up on itself in ornate detours on its way to Past and Future—the unfortunate leakage between the worlds has led to a semblance of synchronicity, at least in the places where everyone has been going back and forth. That is part of the problem I am trying to correct but not all of it, because, as it turns out, the Loophole is not the only way across the Spiral. Which brings us back to Robyn and The Time Winders, or, more to the point, the rugs.

Fact: It was the rugs, combined with the dance, that briefly transported Robyn/Yasmine off the stage at the Harmony Convention and into my world. The Loophole, my own method of crossing over, lay a mile north of Kestrel Kamp as previously described. Hikers found their way through from time to time and it was no big deal, Coyote quickly ushered them out again. But only in *my* world do Gypsies learn how to vibrate themselves along the Spiral through dance, and only here do Gypsies, Weavers and Witches—the most skilled of them—employ fiber-based conveyances such as magic satchels and flying carpets to skip across space *and* time. Once I'd gotten wind of The Time Winders' routine, I was bound by blood and duty to confiscate the carpets.

It would be tempting to lay all of the blame for this commerce between the worlds at the Gypsy Esmarelda's pretty feet, but my own role in the chain of events is inescapable. It is also a very long ways back. We will get there eventually (leap-frogging backward, if you will). For now, Editor permitting, we return to the scene in Kestrel Lodge last Thursday eve, when the boundary between the two worlds was weak and getting weaker. I believe we were on our way to the post-performance dinner buffet. The colorful affair is still fresh in my mind:

Robyn took a sip of homemade "ambrosia," passed the flask to someone nearby, and motioned that she was ready to get some food. A path cleared, and a young woman rushed ahead to get a plate and hold a place for her in the buffet line. Robyn's bangles tinkled gently under her caftan as she glided through the crowd, majestically tall, her silky blond hair glowing like a golden waterfall under the sconces of the convention's Great Hall.

"*Dios mio*," Ramon groaned, sitting with Faye at a linen-draped and ivy-festooned table they were holding for the troupe. "If you guys win, there'll be no living with her."

"We're not going to win," Faye assured him. "The judges hate our routine. We only got this far because of the buzz going around about Robyn. But the in-crowd here is pretty pissed. I overheard some of them griping about *beginners and their conceptual shit.*" Faye was sitting on the padded hotel chair with her knees tucked under her chin, unwinding the strings of bells from her ankles. Inwardly she longed for Zeek, the cats, and a home-cooked meal. "Besides, Robyn is not turning into a belly dance diva. She just happens to be really good. Especially considering she's only been dancing, what, a year or so?"

"More like two. She got into it right after we got married."

"After the business with Esmarelda."

"Yeah."

The two sat glumly amidst the swirl of gauzy, glittering, feathered, flounced, hooded, hatted, and be-caped fashion. The five-day Harmony Convention had attracted all manner of alternative types: healers and seers, musicians and artists, pagans and hippies, gamers and fantasy fans. This was exactly The Lost Unicorn's demographic, and the store's booth had paid for their trip already. By end of day tomorrow it would be so picked through that, were it not for the belly dancing, they'd probably just head home. But no, it was the dancing that Robyn came for and was determined to see through to the end. She'd gotten the bug, and her friends had been bitten too, swept up in the glamour and attention. For Faye, the novelty had worn off quickly.

Likewise for Ramon. The music and the dancing were great —he lived for music—but he didn't want this Yasmine creature taking over his Robyn. He had a band of his own and his own musical career. He didn't need to be a roadie for *the troupe.*

"Did you see it?"

"No." Faye didn't have to ask what he meant. "I was concentrating on my zils so I wouldn't screw up, and looking out at the crowd." She stuffed the ankle bells into a satin pouch she'd bought for her gew-gaws, and began pulling off bracelets and rings. "The funny thing is, *I* thought it looked like the *audience* was disappearing."

"Shit. I need some tequila. You think they got any, or is it all mead and crap?"

"What did it look like to you, Ramon?" Faye asked before he abandoned her.

"It looked like my wife twirled herself into oblivion and then reappeared under her veil on the floor." Ramon stood up and peered over toward the buffet, concerned that Robyn might disappear again at any moment. "Where the hell did she get to now? Okay, she's coming . . . I don't like it, Faye. I don't like it at all. What did she tell you about that Gypsy, Esmarelda?"

"Hardly anything. I actually met her twice, but she never had time to talk. You know, Robyn has a lot of friends like that. I mean, look around."

"Yeah, yeah, but that one was different." He said no more, seeing Robyn approach. She was followed by Paulette/Ursula, Alice/Alizia, and Sharon/Shanna. Everyone in the troupe had to have an exotic name.

Faye was Fatima. Two years ago, when the mysterious Esmarelda first dropped in on Robyn, Faye was a fairly new, part-time worker at the store. She and Robyn quickly became good friends, but Robyn never said anything more about the Gypsy to Faye. Apparently, she'd never mentioned her muse to the other dancers either. Strange, since clearly it was Esmarelda who'd inspired Robyn's fascination with belly dance. And Robyn had picked it up so brilliantly. Faye once found herself wondering if Robyn were possessed by the Gypsy . . . *Not possessed, obsessed.* Faye's pragmatic nature had prevailed. Even after a year of total immersion, she hadn't lost her skepticism toward the arcane projects of The Lost Unicorn's patrons. But the Turkish Drop was another matter. What was going on? Faye resolved to appear—*c'mon, and really be*—more open-minded. Maybe Robyn would finally open up to her.

Faye watched Ramon put his arm around Robyn's waist and squeeze affectionately before going over to the bar. The more

Alice, Sharon and Paulette bubbled forth about the performance and how much everyone had loved it, the more he wanted that drink. Robyn came over and took his empty chair. As she settled in next to Faye with her plate and goblet, the lights blinked off and on twice. Someone started tapping a microphone.

"Quiet please, everyone, we're ready to announce the winners of the belly dance semi-finals." The crowd fell silent and turned toward the little dais that has been set up at the far end of the ballroom. "Ms. Caper." The venerable Ms. Caper took the mic and read three names from a card to loud applause. As the clapping subsided, a few voices could be heard chanting, "Time Winders, Time Winders," and these were joined by others, "Time Winders, Time Winders . . ."

"Hush, will you!" Ms. Caper commanded. "I'm not finished. In addition to the three finalists who will compete for the grand prize, the judges are also inviting the Fourth Place winner to perform on Saturday night. That will be an exhibition dance only, but we want to acknowledge this new group's marvelous energy and originality. I think you know who they are, people, The . . ."

". . . Time Winders!" Everyone called it out together, and an even bigger cheer rose from the crowd. Yasmine, Alizia, Shanna, Ursula and Fatima waved to their admirers. Over at the bar, Ramon tossed back his shot of tequila and ordered two more.

Ramon had good cause to worry. His instincts warned him of circumstances his reason would never fathom. The twirling disappearance of his lady love bespoke the presence of a sort of funnel into a parallel universe that would swallow them all up. Or worse, her but not him. He had an uneasy sensation that the Gypsy was nearby. Like a latter day Pied Piper she would lure his Robyn away, and Faye and the others too. He had to find a way to keep them all safe.

Ramon downed the last shot of tequila, letting the liquor burn through the barriers of his ordinary thinking. He stuck a thin lime wedge in his mouth, bit down, winced, then spread his lips to form a bright green smile for the mirror behind the bar. *Don't mess with my Robyn, bruja!* He spit out the lime rind, shook his head like a prize fighter, and strode out into the night to take a leak in the woods before turning in.

"I'm telling you, Esmarelda," he spoke aloud this time while he marked a line in the pine needles. "Keep away from us."

That sent a chill so far up my spine that without thinking I let out a coyote howl. I surprised myself with how close I came, in my human body, to the real thing. Still, I had almost given myself away. I morphed into Frog to stay out of trouble.

Ramon, several tequilas to the wind, was neither suspicious nor frightened by the call of a coyote so nearby. He put his hands to his mouth and howled right back! He was answered by several wolf calls off in the distance. Ramon nodded with satisfaction and returned to the lodge. He would sleep a heroic sleep and wake in the morning prepared to deal with the impossible.

It was an admirable display, but I ask you: Can a reasonable man ever be prepared for the impossible? One of the purposes of this project is to prove the reality of things classified as impossible. Well, good luck with that. I can only state that what has in fact occurred must naturally fall into the realm of the possible, and I give you my word that this report is a real and true chronicle of my own memories and investigations. There will be no "and they woke up and it was all a dream" business at the end, I promise. (True, some will sleep and forget.)

(Sorry, sore subject.)

Ramon woke with a genuine hangover in the morning. The Time Winders suffered their own sort of letdown from the glitter and attention of the night before. Dawn broke with its customary precocious glory, and everyone rolled over and went back to sleep. Everyone but Faye.

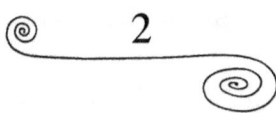

2

Converging on the Knot

FAYE WOKE UP FRIDAY MORNING AWASH WITH ANXIETY. TWO whole days before their "exhibition" performance, two whole nights before she would be back in Zeek's arms—how would she stand it? She was overcome by a feeling of dread. The Harmony folks were getting on her nerves, and her troupe-mates were causing her worry. They'd all had several propositions to hook up for the reputedly wild Solstice revelries to come. Some of the romancers were cute, others merely persistent. Some already had girlfriends and/or boyfriends.

Faye tried not to express disapproval. The scene was too loose for her taste, but who was she to judge? Mainly, she didn't want to get stuck working extra shifts at the Lost Unicorn booth because of her friends' self-indulgence. She would take today off and then pay it backward.

While the others slept off their excesses, Faye dressed quickly, grabbed a protein bar, and headed for the Lodge office. She got there in time to join two middle-aged couples and a family of five on a guided hike along the lower trails.

As Faye approached, she could tell that her companions were not seasoned hikers. She looked forward to a leisurely, low-impact walk in the woods. Joining the group, she heard several of them grumbling about the "hippie convention." She sauntered

over, stuck out her hand to one after another, and introduced
herself with a big smile.

"Fatima." She couldn't resist. "I'm with the belly dance
troupe, The Time Winders." Her fondness for the Harmony folks
had suddenly returned. At least they were colorful and creative
and open-hearted.

"Fatima, Fatima, Fatima," she pronounced for each of the
three children under twelve as she shook their little hands.
"Barry. Sherman. Roberta. So nice to meet you." After that,
they were hers for the duration. The parents appreciated this
unexpected break from minding the kids, while Faye thought the
children were better company than the grown-ups. It was going
to be a beautiful day.

Excuse me. Robyn thinks I should *move the story along
already*. She didn't appreciate Faye's taking the day off and
leaving her with the burden of the booth, and she's not keen on
me reiterating all the neat things Faye saw on her nature walk
while the rest of them were occupied at the convention.

Not to worry. I don't plan to describe all of that lovely
scenery again. But, maybe the things Faye failed to mention are
of some interest. The guide himself, for instance. So earthy and
unassuming, he practically blended in with the landscape. For
periods of time it was as if he wasn't there at all. And yet the
minute a question was asked—a flower pointed to, a bird
sighted—there he was, ready with the answer. Bill, his name
was. Or was it Bob? Brock?

Brooks, that's it.

Oh, yes. I was along on the walkies with Faye and the
common folk. I had to sniff out any new passages across the
Spiral and make sure that Faye, of all people, didn't slip through.
I tell you, the Witches are like magnets, the way they pull
everything into the Goathorns.

Haven't I said that all wayward spells and miscast charms

must land on the Witches' doorstep? Haven't I said that Brunagwa's chickens were coming home to roost?

Robyn is one of Brunagwa's chicks. Faye also because of her connection, through the cats, to Esmarelda, and all of the traveling that was done back and forth across the Spiral on account of Esmarelda—in *Brunagwa's* stolen magic satchel.

So, Faye goes for a hike and, right on cue, along comes Esmarelda on the other side of the Spiral. Exactly as Ramon feared, the Gypsy was nearby. While everyone lolled around the Harmony Convention recuperating for another night of partying, I was hard at it to patrol both sides of the Spiral down in the lower foothills of the murky divide between our two worlds.

Obviously, the Gypsy Esmarelda had to come to the Goathorns in order to return the stolen satchel and (try) to make amends with Brunagwa the Red Mountain Witch. (Esmarelda doesn't know Brunagwa.) She has with her George Drumm, who jumped ten years ahead on the Spiral Map of Time and never went back (so you know he's on his way to the Knot), and the cat Sylvestor that George brought over from the Alternate World (ditto). Just my luck, the Gypsies arrived in the Goathorns on the very day Faye was traipsing around nearby.

(You can tell I'm being facetious, can't you? Luck has no more to do with it than luck has to do with water running downhill, or with a cactus blossom closing up when the sun sets. The forces of Nature were at work, myself among them.)

It was a fine day in the mountains—but the wild irises, the butterflies, magpies, aspens and blue pine have already been faithfully observed and reported by Faye. At my Editor's request, I will now pick up the story on the other side of the Spiral (home to me), and describe the progress of the Gypsies thus far, both up to and beyond Faye's early morning hike. For those who are familiar with *The Time Dancer* (that is, Robyn, who is positively obsessed with the thing), and those who are not, what follows is a review and continuation of that (ahem) tall tale.

ESMARELDA AND GEORGE DRUMM

Esmarelda and George, with their cat Sylvestor, had traveled by
foot for several months in the leisurely way that Gypsies go.
Their route took them due north from Resthaven along quiet lanes
and through woodlands and fields. Sometimes it passed through
small villages where they could perform at a pub or country fair.
They were traveling north primarily, apace with the summer
season, so that spring dawned fresh at every turn. By the time
summer caught up to them, they would be climbing in altitude.
That was their plan. But, away from the confines of Resthaven,
the call of the road was strong. They took many detours,
dawdling along at a pace that was slow even for Gypsies.

Until recently, Esmarelda had been under a sort of self-
imposed house arrest. Her apprenticeship to Malcom the Master
Seer had proved disastrous. Long after she quit the magician's
company, he continued to stalk her. Her perceptual skills were no
match for the master of disguise. Once, twice, thrice—how many
other times?—she had made a new friend, only to discover that
it was *he*, the *fiend*, mocking, tormenting: "Take me back,
Esmarelda. I can be anyone you want me to be." Frightened and
humiliated, trusting no man, the Gypsy had retreated to the
abandoned cottage on the outskirts of Resthaven. The town's
orderliness and ordinariness, which the Gypsy would have
shunned in the past, made Esmarelda feel safe. But not even a
town full of gossips could save her from Malcom. The magician
had one more twisted plot up his sleeve. It would prove to be his
undoing, but not before Esma was driven to travel through Time
to seek the guidance of her Gypsy elders. There, in the ten-years-
ago, she met George Drumm. More leaps across the Spiral
ensued, including several forays to the Alternate World, where:
Esmarelda was befriended by Robyn; Malcom made his tragic
misstep; and George adopted the tiger-striped cat, Sylvestor.
How fortunate to have a home base amidst all of that. George and

Esmarelda finally did find each other in Resthaven, and they have been together ever since.

My point is, all of that having transpired, you can imagine how wonderful it felt to the Gypsy to get back on the road with George and Sylvestor—really on the road, in the natural way, on the proper side of the Spiral. Magical conveyances like the satchels they had used to go through Time are not meant for everyday use, and the outcomes of those journeys can have serious repercussions.

Which brings us to George. On Sumweir Isle, the dreamy lad had found signs that his own people were of Wanderer ancestry. He was inspired to set forth in search of the Wanderer bands who still crossed the great continent, for none remained on the island. Halfway around the world, George found the Traveler people. He proved his kinship to them with his music, and was taken in. Then, because he was intrepid and still in search of—he knew not what—he was passed from troupe to troupe to continue his journey in search of—whatever.

While George Drumm, the Wanderers' Celtic cousin, sought for what he sought, he carried their goods and messages from clan to clan. It was a nice arrangement for all. And when, by chance, George landed with a Gypsy caravan in time to witness Esmarelda's surprise drop-in from the Future, well, it didn't seem like chance at all. It seemed like Fate.

George Drumm was smitten with Esmarelda, the Gypsy dancer. So he followed her. He had crossed a vast sea and criss-crossed a continent, now he would travel through Time to be with his true love. He absconded with the Gypsy crone Huliyana's magic satchel to do it. Although our carefree fiddler was not in the habit of thievery, once he had fallen for Esma, and she for him, he felt that all of his actions were justified. Love would overcome all obstacles.

Including a ten-year stitch in Time? George had skipped over a decade of his own history. Was that also fate? Were those years, for George, a blank, a void? Or were ten years of experience waiting to be lived, a fold in the fabric of Time that needed to be ironed out?

The way the couple zigged and zagged to Red Mountain, you might think they were trying to cover enough terrain to make up for George's skipped years. If they did so, or thought so, the crazy idea was not spoken. On the surface they were simply young lovers who sought to please each other. Should Esmarelda wish to spend an extra day following a river bank instead of the road because certain herbs were in season and might as well be picked, George was more than happy to go along. He, in turn, was sure of getting his way when he wanted to stay on an extra night or two at a tavern where the tips were good and the bed comfortable. They had chased each other hither and yon across the Spiral, and now they were on this long walk getting to know each other. Why shouldn't they want to prolong the journey?

Still, their union had come with some breaking of rules, not only on George's part. Esmarelda was also in possession of a stolen magic satchel. It didn't matter that it had originally been Malcom's loot. It was hers now, and it was up to her to make amends with its rightful owner, the Red Mountain Witch. This unspoken but not unfelt fact tended to unsettle George and Esmarelda's blissful dalliance. Try as they might, they could not escape their journey's purpose. When they finally espied the peaks of the Goathorn Mountains wavering on the horizon, they agreed to push on in earnest.

The Gypsies set out across rolling and gently rising land. Rather than go the long way around on the cart path from town to town, they would travel as the crow flies. The fields here were no longer cultivated for lack of regulars rains, but in this season there were still mossy rivulets and grassy valleys hidden between the sun-soaked hillocks. When the trio stopped for the night, they rested comfortably, happy to have found some not-too-lumpy ground, and to be sheltered in a valley such that they could not see any part of Goathorns Peak, which had all day peered out at them through distant clouds like an inquisitive eye.

In the morning, our travelers ascended the low hill that had concealed them and confronted an expanse of flat, hot plain. This must be what the locals had referred to as Gumption Flats.

"Flats? What a joke," George cursed, while they struggled over the furrowed prairielands to the main north-south road. It took the better part of the day to reach Treasure Seeker's Way.

Setting their tired feet on smooth road with relief, the Gypsies began to march purposefully toward Red Mountain. They hiked through the long dusk and kept on all night, the pale surface of the road shining invitingly under a waxing moon while a cooling breeze refreshed them. In the small hours, a moistness in the air told them they were approaching the verdant, mystical valleys below the Goathorns where many byways converged.

Another day broke. Treasure Seeker's Way sloped steeply downwards, and the prairie gave way to pastures dotted with trees. Country lanes and farmhouses appeared to left and right. Soon they came to the hub where Treasure Seeker's Way crossed The Open Road.

Esmarelda and George Drumm, with Sylvestor the cat, turned northwest to follow this broad thoroughfare. The Open Road would take them through a busy town before rising up out of the valley again. Crossroads City was far bigger than Resthaven, bigger even than Fort Duty, which the Gypsies had hiked three days extra to avoid. This town had a friendly reputation, fortunately, but they were done with detours in any case.

In Crossroads City the music, dancing, fortune-telling, and gambling went on all night. George settled a ride with a farmer who had brought his produce to town and couldn't wait to get home to the quiet countryside. The man was hitching up his horses when the Gypsies were going up to bed. All they could do was grab their gear and tumble into the back of the wagon, where they slept at last.

The wagon bumped along. Esmarelda dreamed that a great tree was picking her up in its mighty limbs, getting ready to launch her into the air. She woke with a start and shook George awake. The farmer was calling "Whhoa!" to his horses. The team, which had plodded along so painfully slowly for hours, didn't want to stop. In fact, they were going faster.

"Better hop out quick," the farmer called. He berated his beasts until they had slowed enough for the Gypsies, with Sylvestor in the lead, to hop off into the tall grass beside the road. "Take care, ye..." The farmer's voice faded as his team of horses, seemingly of their own volition, took the wide westerly curve of The Open Road and broke into a trot.

George stared after the quickly receding wagon. "Did they take off like that because they can smell the barn, or because they are running away from *here*? Where are we?"

"We're at the junction of Wand Way," Esmarelda answered, steering him toward a narrower road that continued northward. Sylvestor trotted ahead of them. "This is the way to the magical places." Her demeanor suggested to George that she would also prefer to run in the opposite direction. He took her hand. With the Goathorn Mountains commanding the horizon, they marched bravely on.

At mid-morning, traffic was increasing on Wand Way, and people kept stopping to see if George and Esma needed a ride. They hoped to spare the strangers on foot an encounter with "the tree," little knowing that this was exactly their destination. Beyond the great tree, Wand Way would become a busy road pointing northwest to the legendary city of Ochersfeldt. Naturally, everyone thought the colorful couple with cat was heading for the magical city. The Gypsies politely declined all offers of aid. They sought out a lane that paralleled Wand Way but was hidden from the road by foliage. Once they were out of sight of nosy travelers, their walk went quickly enough, uphill though it was.

"Which one is the tree?" George asked. Wand Way appeared to be leading them directly into a grove of great, crooked, cottonwood trees.

"It is all one tree, the Tree of Choices."

"Truly? I hope it isn't really dangerous, because I'm eager to get into its shade."

"The danger is in Ochersfeldt, if you ask me," Esma answered cryptically. "But if you are *trying* to go to that city, you must keep to the left of the tree, which isn't always easy to cipher because of the shadows, and how that great limb curls down and over. It makes a sort of tunnel that is not the road but a trail for animals—and the likes of us."

Esmarelda led George to the Tree of Choices. It heaved upward in five thick trunks from a knobby thicket of roots that covered as much ground as Resthaven's central square. Massive limbs erupted from each main offshoot; they twisted and churned upward, outward, and back toward earth again in runic formations. Nearing the trunk, George found that the bark furrowed deep enough to hide his fingers up to the second knuckle. He felt encaged within the tree itself and quickly withdrew his hand, as if the tree might bite him.

"I had no idea you could get lost in a tree." George made sure Sylvestor was safely at their heels. "Now what?"

"This tree is not for getting lost, but finding the way."

Esmarelda began to lead George thrice clockwise around the immense trunks, within the ribs of overhanging limbs. Half way round, they encountered the obvious if dauntingly steep trail to The Top of The World, known locally as Goathorns Peak. There was even a marked trailhead with a sign that read, "THE Top of The World, straight up." Esma ignored it and continued on. When they rounded the tree again, and she passed by the marker again, George was ready to protest. But Sylvestor trotted resolutely beside the Gypsy, as though the cat also knew the way, so George kept quiet and followed along.

For a third time they stepped around to the north side of the great tree. This time, before they could pass by the trailhead yet again, a new path through the thicket appeared. Beyond the sweep of cottonwood limbs, the grasses suddenly lay bent as though walked on many times. A lane now traversed the briary slope up to a line of firs, and continued on up through a steepening canyon.

So, it is true. Esmarelda breathed a sigh of relief. All was exactly as Weaver Ehrte had described.

Her mentor had spoken at length about this legendary juncture. Ehrte claimed to know the lineage and location of every Weaver's pinnacle, all the way to Oshi at The Top of The World. Expecting that her pupil would continue her pilgrimage to these other wise women, Ehrte had described in detail the witchy Goathorn Mountains that bordered Oshi's summit. To get to Oshi, she told Esmarelda, one must take "the honest road" that was clearly marked and ascended the mountain in a series of exhausting switchbacks. The eerie "path that opens" would take one deep into the realm of the Witches, Ehrte warned.

Esmarelda stepped confidently onto the lane that had opened through the bracken. She was not going to Weaver Oshi this day. But she would use the knowledge she had gleaned about Oshi's neighbors, the Goathorns Coven, to reach the Red Mountain Witch and return the magic satchel.

Here my Editor intrudes (too bad, I was on a roll). She wants to know how near in time and space, at this point, Esma, George and Sylvestor are to Faye and the mild hikers of Piper Canyon.

All I can say is, "nowhere near," because it was my job to insure such was the case, and on this day I succeeded. Faye and the children were the only ones who complained about being kept on the lower, easterly trails rather than climbing up to a higher place with a better view. The others preferred not to strain themselves. And everyone was happy enough with the end point, where we found a view of the eastern plains stretching out like an ocean to the horizon. (I got lucky on the visibility, some days you can't see as far as the tip of your nose.) I had Faye and the others safely off the trail before they could stumble into trouble.

I'm beginning to see how this will get complicated. We have two worlds to keep track of here, two timelines, and multiple locations in each. Some of us are even two, or more, creatures. And for all of this I have your odd, inflexibly sequential language. There will have to be some jumping around, I warn you. I mean, what you have suffered so far is not the least of it. Still, I am not quite ready for the next leap of faith.

(I think what Robyn is really fishing around for is a *fact* about the proximity of Piper Canyon to the magical Goathorns. Unfortunately for her, there is no way I can convey this, given that in the Alternate World a hop, a skip, and a jump, not to mention leaps of faith, are not treated as actual units of measure.)

Now, Editor willing, I will return to Esmarelda, George, and Sylvestor the cat. They are finally entering the ring of the Goathorn Mountains. Pay close attention. They, and we, have much ground to cover both geographically and historically.

The Path That Opens was the shortest route to Red Mountain for our intrepid trio, who were approaching the Goathorns from the southeast. The trail ran between Six Hills on the west, guarded by Sestorina, and the Ice Caves to the east, at the foot of Goathorns Peak, guarded by Dremtessa. Then it skirted Witches Meadow, which was protected by Hesterluna. On the far side of the meadow, the ascent to Red Mountain began.

Since coming into possession of the stolen magic satchel, Esmarelda had taken it upon herself to learn more about the five sisters who made up Goathorns Coven. The more she learned, the greater her hope to avoid them all. The Red Mountain Witch was named Brunagwa—not very friendly-sounding—and she was said to be the fiercest of the five sisters. Maybe they could find a way to climb Red Mountain undetected, leave the satchel on Brunagwa's doorstep, and slip away.

The Gypsy's plan was to follow the Path That Opens between Sestorina's Six Hills and the Ice Caves of Dremtessa. Before they came too close to Witches Meadow, they would abandon the enchanted trail and climb up to the High Road. The detour would pay off if they could escape the notorious Meadow Watch Witch, Hesterluna, although for a short stretch it would bring them dangerously close to the fifth sister, Intuisha.

Intuisha, Dremtessa's twin, ruled the high outcropping that sat atop the Ice Caves. This mass of rock joined the foothills of Goathorns Peak at its northernmost vein, making Intuisha the nearest neighbor to Weaver Oshi. Having spent her season with Weaver Ehrte at Andarra, Esmarelda presumed to be wise in the ways of Weavers, and felt they would be reasonably safe there below Oshi's summit— Assuming they could ascend by daylight, quickly pass by the caverns, and reach the High Road before dusk. (Which was assuming a lot.)

George deferred to Esma's superior knowledge of the locale and its magical properties. Whereas he had been bold and intrepid along all the byways and through all the towns along the way, the seemingly idyllic setting they now traversed gave him the willies. The map he had studied at a shop in Crossroads City had shown a clear path to Red Mountain by way of Ochersfeldt. But Esmarelda would not hear of going out of their way only to come near "that place." George hardly dare imagine the horror of the town, if Esma considered this unknown, unpredictable, bewitched landscape a preferable route.

Up through a verdant valley still spongy from spring run-off, our Travelers followed the mysterious path. They ascended a downy hillock, and then turned east toward an apparently impenetrable mesa wall. Behind them, the Path That Opens was closing up. It quickly disappeared beneath a dense, waist-high bramble.

"I see there will be no backtracking," George pointed out.

"Never mind that. We need to get to the top of that mesa and then go north until we meet up with the honest road again," Esma said. "There is a High Road that runs along the escarpment overlooking Witches Meadow, it leads to Red Mountain."

The landscape was becoming barren, and the mesa loomed ahead, dark mouths of caves now distinguishable in its pock-marked surface. Esma had told George that *Ehrte* had told *her* that the caves and overhanging cliffs were patrolled by a cougar belonging to Intuisha the High Caverns Witch. This was serious business. George suggested that before making the final push for the High Road, they stop to rest and regroup. They had been hiking for what seemed like an entire day already.

Esma checked the sky. Not a cloud. The moist spring day had given way to crackling summer. The sun loitered high overhead. She hadn't wanted to bring up the bear, *Dremtessa's* Familiar. One had to get past Dremtessa's bear to even worry about Intuisha's cougar. But there was little danger either would be out in the heat of the day, and the heat was still rising. The Gypsy agreed they should stop.

George settled under a wind-twisted tree where a weathered boulder could serve as his makeshift desk. He would work on his songs to distract himself from thoughts of cougars and other dangers. He found several stones to weight the corners of his manuscripts, which wanted to curl back into the shape of the short leather tube he carried slung from a strap across his shoulder. He was pleasantly surprised to see that the tube had kept the papers dry.

Making up songs helped George make sense of his own story, which seemed strange even to him. For instance, his very first night with the Gypsies had been on an outcropping such as this, but far off to the northwest, on the far side of a distant ring of mountains. Was that but two short years ago? By the calendar, it was nearly twelve.

"The Chanties and Ballads of George Drumm and the Gypsy Esmarelda, Being the Recounting in Verse of Their Meeting, the Search for Lost Cats, Travels to the Alternate World, an Expedition to Red Mountain and Other Adventures," George read proudly from his scroll.

"You don't think that title is too long?" Esma spread her cape on the grass and began emptying the contents of her pack onto it. Everything was damp from splashing through fast-flowing streams further down.

"I think it's a good title. Descriptive. Tells exactly what's to be found within."

"We haven't even been to Red Mountain yet. And such adventures as we've had already perhaps ought not be told."

Esma began taking careful inventory of her belongings: her bells and beads, veils and vests, skirts and slippers, a crystal ball wrapped in silk, tambourine, hand-shaped pouch with all its compartments of powders and potions, and the magic satchels— the one that was rightfully hers that Ehrte had made for her, and the one Malcom had acquired that rightfully belonged to the Red Mountain Witch. The knots within the second satchel told Esma that it had been made by Oshi at The Top of The World. It was a powerful object still, despite its decrepit state. She was as eager to be rid of it as she was reluctant to meet its owner.

"Sylvestor, get away!" Esma forbade the inquisitive cat from padding through her colorful display. She quickly refolded the satchels.

"There you are, fella. Come along, Sly, leave the lady alone." The cat obediently trotted over to George, who bent down to pet him.

"My two redheads." Esmarelda grinned over at them. George's hair was sun-lightened almost to the tabby orange of Sylvestor's coat.

From his shady nook, George grinned back at his olive-skinned partner. She literally sparkled in the dappled sunlight, from her glossy black hair to her bejeweled toes. For many months they had traveled casually. They walked and talked, or walked and sang, or walked and were silent. Esma never found her feet so tired that she couldn't dance into the night, so long as George never found his arms too weary to lift his fiddle and play for her. This gentle, musical journey into each other's souls thrilled George in ways his previous adventures had not.

But now, watching Esmarelda's glittering form amidst her magical trousseau, George found his delight mingled with uneasiness. At the Tree of Choices, Esmarelda worked a spell to make the path open. It had reminded him of the magic that had brought them together and still defied explanation. Their happiness trembled on the precipice of impossibility. Had fate been cheated or fulfilled?

"You know, Esma, the more truth I tell in these songs, the less anyone is likely to believe them."

"You are probably right. Besides, I don't suppose I could stop you from writing songs any more than you could stop me from dancing."

"I wouldn't dare to try." George picked up his pen.

"It's just that writing them down—"

"Now, now, only one copy—before I forget any of the words. Or do you intend to help me remember all the verses?"

"Oh, no, not me. I already have to remember stars and herbs and magic names and musical rhythms—"

"Well then, you see the need to write this down. For everything you keep in your head, you still have much recorded on charts and maps."

"All right. One copy then. And I suppose the first entry will be The One Hundred Days At Sea?"

"Yes, that's already done, here we go."

George found the tightly written page—a few bars of musical notation at the top, the verses of the song carefully printed below. He appraised it with satisfaction for a moment, then he set it aside. He knew these lyrics well already. He commenced to sing them to Esma in a clear tenor range, not the gruff sailor's voice he used when he showed off for an audience:

> Oh, when all of John Cory's daughters were wed
> And not one of them to me
> I kissed me lovin' Mum on the cheek
> And then I took to sea
>
> From Sumweir to Else, the weather was rough
> And I thought of my late Great-Grand
> The last of the Drumms to board a ship
> And he never again saw land
>
> Oh, he never again saw land, boys
> He never again saw land
> The last of the Drumms to board a ship
> And he never again saw land
>
> My music and I could not stay ashore
> So teased by the ocean smells
> Me coat was wet but my fiddle dry
> On the rollicking voyage to Else
>
> "There is a continent in tales
> "Where mountains rise up to the moon . . ."

George faltered, realizing that he stood practically in the shadow of those very peaks. The voyage he sang of had seemed the adventure of a lifetime, but it was tame compared to where he'd been since, and where he was going. Esmarelda smiled at him as if reading his mind, and George sang out to the surrounding mountains:

"There is a continent in tales
"Where mountains rise up to the moon
"And its lands are vast as the oceans we sail,"
I mused in an Else saloon

"I'll take you there," an old Captain said
"But I won't take you there for free
"For a ship to reach those fabled lands
"Takes One Hundred Days At Sea!"

One Hundred Days At Sea, boys
One Hundred Days At Sea
For a ship to reach those fabled lands
Takes One Hundred Days At Sea!

Esmarelda never tired of the autobiographical ballad of George Drumm, bachelor fiddler from those high northern islands half a world away from anywhere. Watching the pulsing muscles of his freckled arm as he bowed the fiddle, the mop of red hair bouncing along in time to his music, her stomach fluttered with desire the way it had on their first meeting. Some would say this had been love at first sight, but Esma knew better. Such a love was too deep to be new, too familiar to be a first. Before he had leapt across Time to follow Esmarelda, George had crossed sea and land to find the Gypsies. His lilting chanty spun a spell that made Esma feel she had been there with him:

Parched from sun and sea and salt
Resigned to a watery fate
Seventy days and eighty gone
There was naught to do but wait

Then just when hope would perish
The wind once more did blow

And aft' One Hundred Days At Sea
We made Omanipinamo

Omanipinamo, boys, Omanipinamo!
Again our sails were pulling us t'ward Omanipinamo!

George's sudden silence jolted Esma back to attention.

"Excellent! How well I remember the first time I saw you perform that song. I played along on my tambourine."

"And coaxed your young cousins into doing the Time Dance, so that everyone nearly got seasick." George was also reliving that night.

"It seems a long time ago."

"It was."

"Hah! We met some years ago, but have known each other less than two. You're right, no one will believe it." Esma grew pensive. "George, do you ever regret jumping ahead in time?"

"To be with you? Never. And may I remind you that *you* had to jump *back* in time first, in order for us to meet, or *I* would never have jumped *ahead*."

"Yes, but I came back to where I belonged. And we might have met anyway, and fallen in love."

"Would you find me so appealing as a ten-year-older man?"

"Of course. But maybe, in those ten years, you'd have found a wife already."

"Had I stayed with the Gypsies, I'm sure your uncle would have seen to it." Esma frowned. "So of course I would have to leave, rather than wed a woman I didn't love, and that's how we'd eventually find each other." George felt certain he would have fallen in love with Esmarelda no matter when or where he met her, and none other in the meantime. Her expression remained dark. "You're not sorry I jumped ahead, are you, Esma? You've said yourself that Time is an illusion—the sequential nature of it, anyway. The Spiral Map, the Alternate

World, everything you have shown me proves that. It's all already happened, or happening, all at the same time. Past, Present and Future, inextricably connected and unalterable— Why are you looking at me like that?"

"You are a very good student." Esma smiled, though her eyes were troubled. She began polishing her crystal ball. It comforted her to roll it back and forth between her hands. "We've never spoken of Faye and Zeek."

"Can we? I assumed we shouldn't, because of what you'd said—that it was bad luck to meet yourself in the past. I thought we'd just pretend that we hadn't noticed that *they* were *us*."

"So they seemed. But not us in the past, us in the Alternate World. They are our future."

George grinned. "Then they'll be the ones with the bad luck, since we are *their* past."

"But I don't think they recognized us, as themselves. And they never saw us together. So, I've decided there's probably no harm done, so long as we never bump into them again."

"Well, that's a relief." George teased. "Tell me, how can harm ever be done if everything is always unfolding according to a perfect plan?"

"Don't think I haven't wondered that myself. My theory is that we don't ever see the whole of Time, only our own little moment. And within that moment, things can and do go wrong."

"Or right. Ever think of that? That maybe things are going right, not wrong. Faye and Zeek were, are—*will be*—so happy together."

"Yes, just like us." The crystal in Esmarelda's hand glowed pink when they spoke of their happiness.

"I think it was *good* luck to find Faye and Zeek as we did," George challenged.

"Of course you do, you always make the best of everything."

But Esmarelda still felt uneasy. She was sorry she had mentioned their counterparts in the Alternate World, especially so near the domain of the Witches. And she had an unpleasant itchy-tingly sensation all around her left ankle. She couldn't imagine how, but she was certain that wretched ankle bracelet would be coming back to her, or at least back to haunt her, because of her nearness to the city of Ochersfeldt where it was made. She stood up and rubbed her left ankle with her right foot.

"What other songs have you been working on?"

"Well, let's see..." George found another sheet and cast a defiant look at Esma. "I've nearly finished this one about the Spiral Map of Time."

Esma furrowed her eyebrows disapprovingly but kept quiet. George checked the tuning on his fiddle.

"Now, take a listen before you pass judgement. I've tried to make it like a riddle. Most people will think it but a clever rhyme."

"Then play away, my clever composer."

Perhaps it wasn't fair for Esmarelda to expect George to protect the Gypsy mysteries. Magical knowledge came so naturally to him, it must not seem secret at all. She listened intently to his new lyrics, while the mesmerizing raga that spun out of his fiddle caused her to sway, and then dance. She glided barefoot around the items laid out on her cape, making them part of the choreography.

George sang:

Oh, the Spiral Map of Time
Unfurls from Nowhere to Forever
And returns upon a mirror path
From Everywhere to Never

The coils of the Spiral
Trace a ceaseless path
And the End meets the Beginning
Where the First will meet the Last

Out and out the Spiral curls
From the point where All commences
And the Time it keeps is merry,
Full of Magic, spells, and da-an-ces

Winding in upon itself,
A second world created,
A spiraling of other Times
Where Magic is abated

These Alternating Worlds
of the Spiral Map of Time,
Are like phrases of a poem
It takes the two to rhyme

Each world's a shadow of the other
Within alternating rings.
Jump over in a Witch's sack,
See what the Future brings

Or dream your way across
On the psychic bed of slumber.
The spirit travels Here and There
Without body to encuh-uhm-ber.

Esmarelda struck an elegant pose with her right heel against
the inside of her left knee, and her arms up, framing her head in
a diamond shape, palms pressed together and fingertips pointing
toward the heavens. The air around her shimmered. Her eyes
were closed. The glow of her aura expanded to encompass
George. This visibly vibrating light appeared to flow into her
through her fingertips and then emanate outward, as though she
had made herself an antenna for transmitting the mystical energy
of the Goathorns. George seemed not to notice. He sang:

The coils of the Spiral
Trace a ceaseless path
And the End meets the Beginning
Where the First will meet the Last

Yes, the Spiral Map of Time
Unfurls from Everywhere to Never
And returns upon a mirror path
From Nowhere to For-eh-eh-ver

A long, final variation of the raga scrolled out of George's fiddle like a genie unwilling to return to its bottle. When George finally lowered his bow, he avoided looking at Esma. He busied himself putting away his fiddle and rolling up the manuscripts.

"It's a fine song, George. Every verse is exactly right."

With relief he turned toward her, but the look on her face did not reflect the enthusiasm of her words.

"What is it, Esma?"

"Jump over in a Witch's sack? I've been trying not to think about where we're headed. But we'll be within sight of Red Mountain soon, and then what? I'm afraid our Witch will not be pleased at the condition of her satchel, and now it bears my mark."

"But we're not the ones who took it from her, we're returning it. I'd think she would reward us."

George's words belied his own foreboding. They had two magic satchels to return, and the second bore *his* mark. He was no more anxious to confront the Gypsy Huliyana than Esma was to meet the Red Mountain Witch. He folded Esma into his arms and buried his face in her hair. *One way or another all things will be returned to their proper place*, he thought, but found little comfort. Some would say that his proper place was in the past. Yet he knew he had to be with Esma, here, now.

The lovers embraced, while Nee, drawn by the music,

observed silently. From the highest branch of the twisted tree, she prepared to attack. She did not understand how the couple had come to have her mistress's magic satchel, but, if she could take it from them, Brunagwa might never have to know about her foolishness.

Esmarelda pulled away from George and looked up. Nee froze. George crossed his arms and looked at Esma, refusing to follow her gaze.

"You keep doing that. If someone is watching us, how have you not seen them in your crystal? I think there is something else weighing on your mind, m'love. What lurks here is your conscience. Let's have it out."

Esma sighed and sank to the ground, noticing a faint shadow skip across her sparkling treasures. As she wrapped her crystal ball in its square of silk, she briefly glimpsed the striped feather of a red-tailed hawk. She was careful to turn her eyes to George, not skyward, as she patted the ground.

"Come, sit. I'll tell you what has been plaguing my mind, and you will have the answer for it as simply as you pluck out a new song."

"If you thought that, you'd've have told me sooner," George said, plopping down beside her. "Out with it."

"It has to do with Malcom the Master Seer," Esmarelda admitted. George tensed. If he noticed a rustling in the tree above he didn't show it, and neither did Esma. But this time a bit of white fluff drifted down into Esmarelda's lap. She picked it up and brushed her cheek with it, trying to feel the creature it had come from.

The creature who was interested in Malcom.

"I saw his grave," She said, in barely a whisper. Then louder, "I saw his grave. I found the note from his apprentice, Mark, who had buried the body with his own hands. I found the charmed ankle bracelet the Master Seer had used to enchant me."

Esmarelda suppressed the urge to rake at her left ankle with her fingernails. She said, a little too emphatically, "But the spell had been erased, the bangles were no longer etched with the letters of my name. I—"

"You what?" George asked sharply. His memory raced back to his confrontation with Mark, there in Malcom the Master Seer's house of spells. Esma had once been an apprentice along with Mark. It bothered him to think of them studying magic together.

Esmarelda could not admit what she had done with the bracelet, not when George was so irritable. Besides, she had to focus on this moment and the mysterious being who was present with them. She chose her words with care.

"I believe that Malcom, the man, is dead. But what of the Master Seer? He had powers. He put himself into the body of a cat and existed side-by-side in the consciousness of that poor animal, until the cat died in the Alternate World. And yet Mark left word that the black cat came back, alive, after Malcom was buried."

"I agree it's troubling, but lucky for the cat. They say cats have nine lives. Look at Sylvestor here. He's proven they can survive a trip across the Spiral."

"And what of Master Seers? Who knows what magic Malcom had mastered. Perhaps he poured his being into something else."

With that, Esma jumped to her feet and called up into the tree, "Come down here, you! If you are the Master Seer, come down here and prove how brilliant you are!"

George was on his feet as well, his walking stick raised, ready to strike the enemy.

This outburst was met with a silence deeper and a stillness steadier than even a slow, sunny afternoon can offer.

Esmarelda crossed her arms and tapped her foot. "No stick!" she scolded George through clenched teeth.

George lowered the stick and tried not to be angry at her tone. When he noticed that both Esma and Sylvestor were staring intently upward, he let his eyes follow theirs. A red-tailed hawk perched in plain sight on a weathered limb.

"Are you Malcom?" Esmarelda asked.

A gust of wind answered. The hawk ruffled its feathers— amidst them, a few reddish tresses also caught the breeze.

George gaped.

"George." Esma took his hands. They looked into each other's eyes; the tension that had been growing between them dissolved. Then Esma looked back toward the bird. But now a woman sat on the branch, a woman dressed in feathers.

"No, I am not Malcom," she said in a teary voice. "But I saw him not a day ago, there in Witches Meadow. You lie to say he's dead. And he's no Master Seer either. He's a thief, and he stole Brunagwa's magic bag from me!" The strange girl was becoming hysterical, and they feared her falling. Esmarelda raised a hand toward her. She shrank away and clutched the tree trunk. "But you are worse thieves. Look what you have done to Brunagwa's bag in just a day. It is ruined. Have you destroyed my Malcom as well? Give that! Give that! What am I to do?"

The girl's cry was a long "Kee-ahrr!" and in a breath she was a hawk again, diving straight down toward the Red Mountain Witch's beat-up magic satchel where it lay on Esma's cape, then veering off with another angry shriek as though she had hit an invisible barrier. The portal in Time that the Gypsies' song and dance had opened was closing. The hawk-woman vanished from their sight in a most unnatural way.

Esmarelda, shaking, still clutched the bit of down. "I have heard of this, I have heard of this," she muttered, stroking it.

George was trying to lock the images of the young woman and the hawk, and the sounds of their voices, into his memory. While he watched, Sylvestor sprang up into the tree and climbed as high as he dared, then padded out onto a thick limb.

"Esma, look."

Esmarelda looked up and gasped.

Before their eyes, Sylvestor was transforming into another creature. His ears twitched, laid back, then smoothed all the way down, while his snout stretched into a beak. His front paws turned into talons, and his fur to wings, while his tiger-striped tail flicked back and forth twice before fluttering into long, striped tail feathers.

"Oh, Sylvestor. . ." Esma moaned.

"Sylvestor, you're freaking us out." George spoke in the language of the Alternate World.

The hawk turned back into a cat. The cat skipped down the tree to sit in the grass blinking at Esmarelda and George. But before they could celebrate his return to normalcy, Sylvestor began to speak:

"Don't be afraid. Intuisha says I must be your Familiar until we pass through this place. Gather your things and follow me."

Esma immediately began to do as she was told. George was unable to move or speak for minutes. But the cat said nothing more, and in every way behaved like a typical house cat. Sylvestor circled George's legs, then stalked Esmarelda's cape when she shook it out.

"Come," she said to George. "Gather your music. You can work it through by making up a song while we walk."

"I can try. But it would help if you explained what a Familiar is, and why we should trust this Intuisha." George collected his gear. "Lead on, MacDuff," he told Sylvestor, again quoting something he'd heard across the Spiral.

Without hesitation, the cat led them a few hundred yards, aiming for a certain point at the foot of the mesa. When it seemed as if one more step would put their noses into solid rock, Sylvestor veered to the right and slipped into a stand of stunted juniper. His friends followed more clumsily. They burst through the scrub to find themselves standing in a wash recently wetted by summer rains and sprouting with desert plants. What had appeared to be a single outcropping was really two mesas, and

Sylvestor had found the canyon that ran between them, and the long treacherous trail that passed by Dremtessa's ice caves, then climbed up through Intuisha's high caverns to the plateau.

George and Esmarelda tipped back their heads, shielded their eyes from the sun, and gauged their ascent. Nope, they definitely would not reach the High Road before nightfall.

Here I must insert myself again, before we make one of those literary jumps I warned you about. Esmarelda has no idea that her carefully plotted course is taking her happy crew directly through the Knot. Ehrte hadn't told her about that, because Ehrte didn't know anything about the Knot, not all that way away on Andarra. Oshi herself didn't know about the Knot until very recently, even though it was right under her nose. When Oshi looked out across the cliffs and caverns toward Red Mountain from her high perch, her eyes weak from weaving, all she saw was a small stew of clouds. With no Familiar to inform her otherwise, these were no concern. She was above it all. And the sisters five weren't in the habit of telling Weaver Oshi about the trouble they got into, you can be sure of that.

So, Esmarelda, George Drumm, and Sylvestor the cat, unsuspecting, approach the Knot. Their experience of it will be different than that of others we will meet, since our trio is traveling naturally by foot—versus in a conveyance, or astrally, or crossing between worlds. They will traverse the Knot on the cliffs below the High Road, where its loops have been pulled out of place but are not entangled, and episodes past play out with vivid clarity. They are already under the Knot's influence, as you may have noticed.

Myself as well. The travelers' strange encounter with Brunagwa's Familiar has put me on high alert. I must investigate at once, and I must do so alone. Not even the tale I am telling can come with me now, for the encounters that occur from one moment to the next in my own chronology are the result of reverberations across many turns of the Spiral. Rather than plunge us unprepared into the dark jumble of the Knot, dear Reader (and Editor), let me carefully loosen the strands of my story from the outside in, until such time as we are able to bring light into the dark places, and to see even beyond them to the beginning.

Later you will learn where my investigations took me at this juncture. In a future chapter. (I can't say which one yet, but likely in the double digits.) Meanwhile, our next jump will be to the Alternate World—not back to Piper Canyon, but all the way out to Caliente—where Zeek is filling in at The Lost Unicorn.

Yes, it is certainly time to check on Zeek. He has the rest of our rugs.

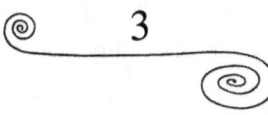

3

Summer Solstice

ZEEK SAT MOROSELY BEHIND THE COUNTER OF THE LOST
Unicorn. It was Friday afternoon. He had been babysitting the
store since Wednesday. His eyes came to rest on the peculiarly-
patterned carpets displayed near the front of the store, their
colors cast in an odd shade of orange under the late-day slant of
Caliente's blazing sun.

It all started with those rugs, he thought. *Where are they
from, anyway?* There were only about half a dozen left. Not quite
Oriental, not quite Navajo, each featured a radiating s-shaped
pinwheel pattern *à la* 1960s op-art. Perfect for a twelve-year-
old's bedroom. But it had been the belly dancers who'd snapped
them up—after they'd snapped up Faye. First it was a monthly
dance and drum party at Robyn's house behind the store. That
turned into a class on Wednesday nights, and before long it was
the accursed *troupe.*

The troupe idea surfaced soon after Robyn bought the lot of
rugs from Oscar Too. Faye said that the first night the women
spread them across Robyn's living room floor, everyone had
been giddy with the feel of them under bare feet, entranced by the
way the patterns seemed to come to life as they danced around.
They all had to buy one, and then Robyn raised the price way up
on the ones that were left and started trying to get in touch with

Too to see if she could get more.

'Trader of esoteric treasures,' my eye, Zeek thought. Robyn's old friend was incommunicado again. The first Zeek ever heard of the man was when Faye reported that some mobiles Robyn got from him hadn't lasted the week in the sunny store window—it was too bad, because everyone really liked them, and all the ones that were sold were being returned. When Robyn tried to get back in touch with Too, there was no response.

Months later, Too showed up with the rugs. He offered a big discount on them to make up for the mobiles. Robyn was more than mollified. She gleefully labeled the unique textiles "flying carpets" before she'd even touched a bare toe to them.

And the next thing Zeek knew, the whole crew was flying off to some new-agey Harmony Convention, Ramon included, and *he'd* been recruited to mind the store.

Yeah, that's just what I needed, to spend a week here at The Lost Unicorn serving the occult needs of Caliente's nut-cases—

"What the—"

A gust of wind bashed open the front door, and a large black dog lunged into the store growling fiercely.

"Hey! Get back!" Zeek reached for the baseball bat behind the counter, keeping stern eye contact with the animal. Not such a huge beast, but powerful, and frighteningly willful. It stared right back. *Doberman, probably, mixed with something huskier, maybe Rottweiler.* Folks in Caliente liked to breed nasty yard dogs, mean-looking mutts that often had the temperaments of cowardly lunatics.

"Back off, Cujo." Zeek raised the bat. Everything in the store jangled and flapped in the wind.

"Master, Master!" A disheveled scarecrow of a man ran breathlessly through the open door. "Don't!"

The dog lowered its head and began casually sniffing the floor, working his way over to a terra cotta urn that held colorful walking sticks. Zeek watched it warily.

"If he lifts a leg, you just bought that whole display."

"My sincere apologies for the intrusion."

Zeek turned his gaze to the shabby guy who spoke like a Charles Dickens character.

"Why the hell would you call a dog Master?"

At that the dog began scratching itself.

Its owner shrugged. "That's his name."

"Close the damn door." The wind was still wreaking havoc with the chimes and crystals. "And put the mutt on the other side of it. Those rugs will be yours, too, in a minute."

"Master" had plunked himself down on the stack of flying carpets. The man stepped over to take a closer look, pushed the dog aside with his foot, and feigned nonchalance.

"I may just want one," he said. The dog whined. "Maybe all of them."

"Yeah, well, I'll have to check with the owner. I think some are on hold," Zeek lied. The whole thing smelled fishy. "It's closing time. Come back tomorrow." He started around the counter, still gripping the bat tightly. "And leave the dog home."

"As you wish." The man began to urge the snarling dog toward the door. "What time will you open, good sir?"

Faye called soon after Zeek got home. She sounded happy and rested after taking the day off from the convention. This was a good time to talk, finally. Cheered by her voice, Zeek listened patiently while all of the details of her day spilled forth. When it was his turn, he told her about the weird encounter at the store.

"I'm not kidding, he actually said, 'Good sir.'"

"And I'm not kidding, either. When Robyn danced last night, it was like those rugs swallowed her up. That's what she said— like the pattern came to life, became a sort of whirlpool that took her to another dimension. Ramon and a bunch of other people swear she disappeared."

"Well, what did *you* see?"

"I was standing on the rugs, the very edge, behind Robyn. And I felt like I was going *with* her."

"Too weird, Faye—" Zeek became distracted by Dash, who was readying herself for a leap to the windowsill. The cat was suddenly frantic to get out, the way she had been as a newly adopted kitten. When Faye had finally relented and let her outside, the kitten went missing for ten days, and then returned just as mysteriously. After that, and until a minute ago, Dash had been perfectly tame—coming and going with her sister, the ever-docile Dot, and their protector, Felix.

". . . Zeek?"

"Dash is going crazy. As soon as I picked up the phone, she started agitating to go out. We haven't seen that behavior in a while." Dot and Felix remained curled up comfortably against Zeek's hip. Without thinking about it, Zeek was petting them for comfort. The cats soaked up his warmth; they all missed Faye.

"She must be sensing something from me, something unusual going on here."

"Yeah, like everyone around you is licking toads and chewing peyote."

"You know it's more than that," Faye said softly. *She* did, in spite of her skeptical side.

"After what happened today at the store, and after what you just told me, I know that something funny is going on with those rugs. Is Robyn there? I want to talk to her."

"Yeah, Robyn's here and she wants to talk to you, too . . ."

"What?" Zeek recognized the you're-not-going-to-like-this tone of Faye's voice. He got up and started pacing. All three cats scattered.

"She's in the other room with Ramon and two old friends who showed up at the booth today. One of them is Oscar Too."

"No."

"Yes. And he has this big Indian with him—you know, Native American—named Black Star. He's related to Ramon somehow, though they don't seem to be on very good terms. It seems to me like, like Black Star is pressuring Oscar to get the rugs back from Robyn. I only heard a little. I could tell they didn't want me to hang around. When I came into the sitting area, Robyn jumped up and steered me back to my room. She asked me to ask you to watch the store tonight."

Zeek stopped his pacing. Faye moved the phone a few inches from her ear. "Now you want me to sleep at the damn store? I've been there all day—all week!"

"You're right. Maybe you should call the cops to watch."

Zeek shook his head, defeated. "I'll go, I'll go. This sucks, Faye. Tell Robyn to call me. I want to know what to say to this character when he comes in tomorrow."

"Yeah, sure."

"And come home, will ya?"

"Two more days, honey. I love you."

"I love you, Faye."

"Oh, and don't let the cat out this time."

This time. The words rang in their ears after they'd hung up. What exactly was about to happen again?

Zeek was in no rush to return to The Lost Unicorn. It was the beginning of the weekend and the longest day of the year. The store would be safe with so many people still out and about enjoying the lingering light. He took his time washing up, getting a sleeping bag, blanket and pillow, his backpack, laptop, camera, tripod, and cables. He'd have to drive, even though the store was only a couple blocks away. The cats watched him anxiously, and Dash had to be put in the bedroom while he loaded the car. When he was ready to leave, he opened the bedroom door and poured out the nightly portion of kibble in the kitchen. Then he slipped out while the trio gobbled hungrily.

The Lost Unicorn after hours was eerie. Headlights from the cars going by on Fourth Street briefly illuminated feathered masks, twisted driftwood sculptures, craggy crystals, and a panoply of statuettes, then dragged their ragged shadows across the store. Zeek kept the overhead lights off and found he could see well enough by the repeating, overlapping streaks of head-lights and the glow of his monitor. He huddled at the counter with his laptop and forgot his surroundings entirely for an hour. He was back to programming, and liking it again now that he no longer worked from a cubicle.

Robyn finally called, but there wasn't much to say. She wouldn't make a decision about selling the rugs. Which meant to Zeek that she didn't want to sell them, but she didn't want to argue with him about it. She sounded stressed. He almost felt sorry for her—until she said she was going to ask some friends to drop in tomorrow to help him protect the store, should the man with the dog return and seem "ill-dignified."

"I told the guy not to bring the dog," Zeek assured her.

"Just in case."

"Whatever." Zeek sighed, thinking, *I won't get a thing done tomorrow with her friends coming around.*

After the call, Zeek glared at the small pile of "flying carpets" that had ruined his life. The least they could do was cushion his sleep. He laid his sleeping bag on top of them and placed the pillow and blanket nearby. He set up the camera on the tripod, plugged it into his laptop, and focused it on his nest. Then he started a couple of programs—one to operate the camera, and one to play six hours of soft music to help him sleep.

Zeek checked the doors and windows, turned off the laptop monitor, and lit a single candle in a green glass globe that had clearly been used before. With the baseball bat at arm's reach, he stretched out on the floor—on the thin stack of rugs and a sleeping bag—and felt surprisingly comfortable. He tested the camera by taking a picture of himself with the remote clicker. The flash was brighter than he expected. He clambered back to his feet and helped himself to a lavender eye pillow from one of Robyn's displays. Then he wearily eased himself back down into his bed. He lay on his back with the scented pad of soft silk over his eyes.

Several minutes later the camera clicked off its first automatic shot. Crystals, beads, glittery scarves and sparkled posters burst out of the darkness for an eye-shocking instant. Zeek was already asleep.

Every ten minutes throughout the night, the clever device captured an image of Zeek's twitching form. Let the record show that he was always there. The rugs would not be carrying this galoot anywhere. He did go far on the astral plane, thanks to Robyn's candle flickering on the counter, the dream pillow covering his eyes, and the lingering breath of magic places that blew in with the strangers earlier. They are the ones who led him to his unpleasant dreamland.

Did you think that "scarecrow of a man" was me?

He was not. Nor was the dog. If you were paying attention earlier, you know that. Nowhere did I mention being a black dog.

It is true that these two (or three, it depends how you count) were working for me that night, with some self-interest as well, to get those rugs back into our world where they belong. It is through their eyes and minds that I know what went on at the store. Combined, of course, with A.G. Brooks' mastery of Alternate World technology. The devices have become for me something like the Familiars of the Witches. I train them to gather information, and they report back to me from places I could never reach myself. Faye's phone, Zeek's cloud—I've hacked everything. Oh my, it's *better* than the Witches' magic. (Yes, Madame Editor, now you know why certain passages will not be edited out of this text no matter how many times you press that delete key.)

There on the shortest night of the year, the scarecrow man and the black dog were having an unpleasant time in the Knot while they waited anxiously for day to dawn in the Alternate World,

when they could try again to get the rugs. Having wormed their
way back through the all-new gap they'd worried into the Knot
(*not* what I intended when I sent them to get the rugs), they did
not know exactly where they were. Fearful of losing their place
in Time, for a time they lost their place in Place.

Zeek, dreaming his way across the Spiral, followed the man
and dog to No Place. In this nightmare world, he felt that *they*
pursued *him*. He ducked and dodged through the strange
landscape all night long, while his supposed pursuers cowered in
the shadows. From time to time Zeek would stumble toward a
sliver of light, fall to the ground, and find himself looking down
through a crevice—like looking through the gap under a door—
into a slice of someone else's life. In the way of dreams within
dreams, he would enter that world as an invisible observer, with
no thought of the logic of it, and become immersed in the new
scene. Then, with a jolt, he would find himself stumbling
fearfully through a dark place, the noisy gasps of his pursuers
coming closer and closer. He was certain that at any moment he
would feel the sharp fangs of a dog sinking into his leg, after
which he would be pulled to the ground and devoured.

The photographs would reveal only an uncomfortable man
having a bad night's sleep. And Zeek, simple soul, would not
remember his dreams; he rarely did. As you can imagine, he was
not in a very pleasant mood come morning.

But I'm getting ahead of myself.

I suppose you (my Readers, let's say) will want a detailed
account of the scene back at Kestrel Lodge with Robyn and
Ramon, Black Star and Oscar Too, for the purpose of further
explaining the rugs. I can describe the doings generally, but there
were no revelations about the rugs. Oscar Too, at this juncture,
had no idea what he'd sold to Robyn, and was fishing around for
hints. The fact that Black Star wanted the rugs so badly had
stoked Oscar's curiosity and greed. The visit of the two to Ramon

and Robyn in their suite at Kestrel Lodge was strained, despite Robyn's former friendship with both men from her time in the city, when she worked for Too.

Ramon was trying to be nice because, for one thing, Black Star was family, or at least had been raised as such by Ramon's Uncle Sylviano. Plus, it was Black Star who first encountered Robyn at Oscar Too's Crafts Of The World shop and advised her to visit the Southwest. Black Star pointed Robyn straight to Caliente. Eventually she went, and wasn't in town a month before she met Ramon at a concert. Ramon felt he owed the man for that if nothing else. He didn't like him much, no doubt because of the family bias against Black Star—Salvador—who was a rotten kid of questionable lineage according to some, but already off on his own before young Ramon ever heard mention of him. By the time the men met as adults, Salvador had become Black Star, and Ramon could judge for himself if his cousin was a serious spiritual seeker and teacher or a smooth-talking con man. Ramon leaned toward the latter, but if any of those talents would help Black Star and Too get the rugs out of Robyn's life, Ramon was more than happy to cooperate.

Robyn had no intention of parting with the rugs. It wouldn't take a Minder to notice the tension in the suite that evening.

The presence of Oscar Too at the Harmony Convention should be no surprise. His Crafts Of The World booth was in the busy foyer, while The Lost Unicorn booth was crowded into a little side room. Had Robyn gotten a moment to do any shopping for herself, she would have found him as easily as he found her. Oscar had helpers to work his booth while he scoped out all the others. He also liked to watch the belly dancers. Surely he knew Robyn was there at the Convention. But the constant presence of Ramon made Oscar afraid to approach her until he had Black Star at his elbow. (As we have observed with some trepidation, it is no accident that Ramon's closest pals call him "Lobo.")

(Once again my Editor protests my inclusion of Ramon in this chronicle. Seriously, Robyn? I don't see how I can avoid it.)

Black Star was a fixture at these conventions, I'd seen him every year. You'd think I'd have had him pegged, but that was the problem—I did. I had him pegged as a complete fake, not worth my attention. I had it wrong, in other words. I left Black Star alone to ooze around giving his workshops and mesmerizing earnest, earthy young women. I knew that game well, believe me, so I didn't give it another thought. (Minders can and do get lazy, okay? I've admitted it already.) Black Star will have something to teach us down the Spiral, to be sure, but not on this night. It was Summer Solstice, and numerous celebrations were about to start in the campground. Soon the canyon would echo with drums, chanting, singing, laughter, and squeals of sexual delight. When the pair was evicted from The Time Winders' suite, Oscar Too hurried back to his own room to guard his cashbox while his helpers were out cavorting; and Black Star went his own way, presumably to join the festivities.

Despite Faye's fears, The Time Winders were models of good behavior amidst many temptations. Alice and Paulette attended a serious Druid ceremony, and Sharon settled into bed to read a book and rest her feet. In the small, furniture-filled room she was sharing with Alice, Faye savored her solitude and kept herself busy fixing up their costumes for the Saturday night exhibition. Robyn came and found her after the visit from Black Star and Oscar Too, and they called Zeek.

When Robyn rejoined Ramon, she related Zeek's story of the strange man with the dog. They worried over it until it started to seem ridiculous—hardly real at all. They had to laugh. Ramon got out his guitar and sang a song. Then the happy couple reverenced the Goddess with matrimonial love. Afterwards, Ramon fell into a deep sleep.

Robyn slept more lightly, then lay awake thinking. She got up and took a steamy shower. When she came out to the sitting room, Alice and Paulette were having a nightcap. Faye and

Sharon had joined them to hear about their night. They all looked up at Robyn in her frumpy robe and slippers, with her dripping hair spilling out of a floppy terrycloth turban—their glamorous leader.

"To Yasmine!" Paulette saluted, holding up her glass of wine.

"*Yiyiyiyiyi!*" the others trilled.

Robyn gestured for them to keep quiet. They had forgotten about Ramon. The women held a collective breath, and then dissolved into giggles at the muffled sound of snoring. Robyn plopped down onto one of the little couches, Sharon poured her a glass of wine. The midsummer night's party continued in whispers. Someone opened another bottle.

(Now Robyn is even more discomfitted. My recounting of these private doings in The Time Winders' suite has turned the tables on her. She does not care for being minded herself, though she delights in hearing all the intimate details of everyone else's life. Once again: we Minders read minds and hearts, and with them memories, and we pick up on other clues, so that we come to have our own picture of events. I assure you, we do not watch everyone all the time in the way of your Alternate World surveillance. The sequences preceding and to follow are significant to our story, and I would be remiss not to report; but with respect to all activities in the troupe's quarters, I have been a complete gentleman, and that's a fact.)

Faye was still at work with needle, thread, and beads. She liked listening to her friends' chatter as she sewed. She liked having something useful to do to take her mind off how badly she wanted to go home. The next day was destined to be long and pointless and hung-over—watching people pick over the last dregs of the booth, and feeling guilty about leaving Zeek to babysit The Lost Unicorn—

"Wait, what?"

Robyn was saying that her family had vacationed at this very place when she was a child. Her father was stationed in Colorado

Springs, and they had visited many parks around the southwest. She was so young, the memories tended to blur together. But since arriving in Piper Canyon, she had begun to remember details of one of those family trips.

"So, on a whim, I called Mom this afternoon, and she actually remembered. I was surprised, but apparently it was really an emotional episode. She said we'd spent a week at Kestrel Kamp when I was four years old, and she would never forget it because of the scare I gave her. We had been on a walk, and my parents had stopped to look at the view, when I wandered away from the trail. I didn't go very far, she said, but, *You might as well have fallen down the rabbit hole.* Those were her exact words. She said it seemed like I'd just disappeared and then reappeared again, after they'd searched the same area over and over."

Robyn looked meaningfully at each of her drowsy friends, but only Faye was awake enough to register the significance of this event.

"That's pretty weird, all right. What do you remember?"

"I have a vague memory of going around a tree and almost bumping into the knees of a beautiful tall blond woman in a long gown. She was unlike anyone I had ever seen, but I can't explain why. I mean, my mom and aunts were tall and blond."

"As are you," Faye said, smiling. Robyn seemed not to hear.

"Anyway, this woman looked startled to see me at first, then she held out her hand. I think she asked me where she was. And then a big bird flew straight at me and knocked me over, and I started crying. But mostly I was upset because I lost this pail I had. I think it had mermaids on it. Hmmm." Robyn wrinkled her brow. "Anyway, the part Mom described has come back to me pretty clearly—me crying, and her running over and making a big fuss. She was hysterical like I'd never seen her. I think that's probably why I blocked it out."

"And why she can't forget." Faye felt a chill go up her spine. It was very late, nearly dawn. She put aside the sewing. Her wine glass was still half full, but she couldn't stomach it so close to breakfast time. "Do you think you could find that place where you got lost?"

"Ye—es," Robyn said slowly, getting up to help Faye carry glasses and bottles to the kitchenette. "I think I probably could."

"So, you wanna take a walk? I could use some fresh air."

Without another word, the two sleep-deprived but willful women began to dress for the brisk dawn air of Piper Canyon. Their dance practice proved useful here, in the way Robyn and Faye moved with the quiet, cat-like grace of Yasmine and Fatima, so that Ramon never woke, and even Paulette, Alice and Sharon, stumbling back and forth from the bathrooms and into bed, did not register what the inquisitive duo were up to. (What they were up to, as we well know by now, was working their way toward the Knot.)

The women tumbled out into the metallic blue light of predawn, which meant no rest for Yours Truly. The extent of my exertions will yet be told. Here I had to deal with these two traipsing up the canyon. Once I got wind of them, I could taste the inevitability of their crossing into my world like you taste the burp that precedes horking up a hairball. I supposed my will to prevent it would sooner or later be overcome by my desire to just get it over with, but meanwhile I followed like a good Minder.

I am taking a deep breath here because my Editor is relentless. I mean, she was actually part of the upcoming scene and seems to remember it well. Yet she insists on a detailed recounting from my perspective. We are back to proving things.

I do wonder why Alternate Worlders are so determined that their magical experiences be verified. I mean, it's either magic or it isn't. You either surrender yourself to it or you don't. Alternate Worlders experience everything retroactively, as this project itself demonstrates. You surrender to magic in the moment and then take it back later on with a hypothesis or some kind of evidence that proves it wasn't magic, it was science. Either that or fiction. This treatise isn't going to prove anything, but I will vouch for Robyn's experience nonetheless. (Have I a choice?)

Now then, Faye finally has a chance to ask Robyn about . . .

THE GYPSY AND THE BLACK CAT

"Do you ever hear from that Gypsy woman, Esmarelda?" Faye asked Robyn casually. "I half expected to find her here. Doesn't it seem like her kind of crowd?"

They were circling around the campgrounds, where last night's Solstice celebrants slept with the abandon of a weary army that has vanquished all foes. A dawn fog pressed down into the clearing, as if it too were subject to the leaden heaviness of spent revelries.

"No, I don't think so," Robyn mused, noticing litter, smoldering fires, and crumpled figures in dusty finery sleeping in the open. "Real Gypsies have nothing to do with sloppiness. They're very disciplined and private. Our idea of Gypsies comes from Hollywood, and the act they put on because that's how they make money. They dance and sing and tell fortunes and pretend to let us into their exotic world precisely to keep us out."

"Oh, sure, I get it. So, uhm, anyway." Faye tried again. "You say you haven't heard from Esmarelda?"

"No. The last time I saw her was right after Ramon and I got back from our honeymoon."

"She never wrote to you or anything?"

"Uh uh. I think of her a lot, though. I mean, obviously."

They had reached the trailhead. Robyn stopped to drink from her canteen and gaze out at a spectacular sunrise. She was thinking that there would be no troupe were it not for Esmarelda.

"What about that guy, George? I often wonder if I did the right thing, letting him adopt Sylvestor."

"Ramon has heard from him," Robyn lied impulsively. "George and Sylvestor are fine."

Robyn was afraid she might let slip what she and others had noticed, how Zeek and George Drumm looked very much alike. So did Faye and Esmarelda—at least she and Ramon thought so; hardly anyone else had seen the Gypsy. But the possibility of Faye being Esmarelda in a past or future or alternate life was something Robyn preferred not to think about. Faye was uniquely Faye; even when she dressed up as Fatima, there was little chance of confusing her with the glamorous Gypsy dancer.

"Did they know each other, George Drumm and Esmarelda? Somehow I've got it in my head that they were connected."

"Yes, yes they were." Robyn felt off her guard and dizzy. (Attribute it to altitude, lack of sleep, and proximity to the Knot.)

"And the stray cat? The black cat?" Faye prodded, as the two started up the trail.

"Right, the cat."

The women could walk side by side here. Neither had forgotten that they were on their way to the place where Robyn had "fallen down the rabbit hole" as a child. Robyn knew she must tell Faye about the Spiral Map of Time before she fell through again.

"I know this is going to sound crazy, Faye. I've thought a lot about it, but I have no other explanation. There are witnesses. Ramon saw some of it, and so did you. If I tell you that the script of our dance routine is based on what Esmarelda told me, and it's all true, will you laugh?"

"I'm not laughing," Faye said. While Robyn paused to recite the lines about the alternating worlds—a world of magic existing alongside their world of the mundane—Faye used a stick to trace the Spiral Map of Time in the dusty trail. She listened intently and nodded as though she understood. In a corner of her mind, Zeek was laughing his head off. But he hadn't been at their performances when Robyn disappeared.

"Do you think that's where you went when we danced? To the other world?"

Robyn resumed walking up the path. "I'm certain of it," she said, relieved that Faye was receptive to the idea. It was the first time either had acknowledged that Robyn really had been transported from the stage.

"And do you think that's where you went when you got lost here as a little girl?"

"What else would explain that?"

"Lots of things." Faye took a deep breath of forest air and looked around in wonder. It was easy for the senses to get confused in nature. Easy for children to hide, and for grown-ups to be blinded by panic. Easy to be converted to magical thinking. Who could walk amidst such scenery and not imagine elves and sprites, animal guides and sentient trees? "This is awesome. I'm so glad we're out here."

Something caught Faye's eye as she savored their surroundings, a movement on the trail where they had recently stopped: A frog was hopping back and forth across the dusty path, mussing up her drawing of the Spiral.

"That's weird." Faye turned to Robyn, but she hadn't waited. "So, what about the cat?" Faye called, hurrying to catch up.

"I can only tell you what Esmarelda told me. If you can believe there's an alternate world full of magic, you'll have to believe this as well."

"Okay, let's hear it."

"There was a magician named Malcom. A really good one. They called him a Master Seer. More like a wizard, I guess. Esmarelda sort of, uhm, lived with him. They weren't lovers. They were attracted to each other but didn't trust each other. They each had their own kind of magic and wanted what the other had. The Master Seer wanted to travel through time like the Gypsy could, in a magic satchel."

"A magic satchel?"

"Yeah. She showed me one. It's like a net that expands and expands—and there are bits of thread and beads and things sewn into it to mark different places and times. She crawls inside and comes out in a different place."

"Really?" Faye bit back a smile.

"Anyway, I guess the Master Seer's magic was more powerful and sinister than the Gypsy's. She realized he was trying to trap her and keep her with him. She managed to break away, but he kept turning up in her life—as different men. He was literally a master of disguise. He, like, stalked her, and she went into seclusion and stopped traveling around."

Robyn risked a glance at Faye, whose brow was furrowed in concentration. She forged ahead.

"So, Malcom tracks down Esmarelda, and takes her cat—she thought maybe he had sent it to her in the first place, you know, set her up. But when he tried to get away in a magic satchel, he ended up in Caliente. The cat freaked out and ran away, but it must have been snagged on the satchel and dragged it along for a while. The cat was gone and the satchel was lost. Malcom's prank was a disaster, and Esmarelda had to come and try to clean up the mess."

(One moment, please, while I cross off Robyn from my list of suspected authors of *The Time Dancer*, which chronicles this episode. Clearly she didn't know enough to have written it, nor had she read it at this point. While we pause to let Faye digest what Robyn has told her, I will correct the record: The black cat was Malcom *himself*. The magician had found a way to insinuate himself into the Gypsy's affections after all—by becoming her pet. But he did not intend to remain a cat. Following Malcom's twisted plan, his apprentice Mark came to Esmarelda's place in Resthaven to steal back the cat, make a quick get-away in the magic satchel, and return Malcom to his human self. But instead of transporting back to the Master Seer's laboratory, Mark blundered into the Alternate World, where the cat ran off, et cetera. Now that I think about it, it was probably just as well that this remained unclear to Robyn, so she did not have to broach the subject of human-animal transmogrification at this juncture. As it was, Faye was having a hard time digesting the account.)

"So, that stray black cat came from the other side of the Spiral?" Faye asked finally.

"Yes. His name was Audy. Esmarelda came to Caliente to look for him, but she gave up and left before George Drumm showed up looking for *her*. George stayed because I told him Esmarelda wanted to catch the cat—and then it died in that weird way, and he sent its body back, and then he went back."

"So, when George Drumm offered to take *our* Sylvestor with him when he left town, he was really taking my cat to the other world? What if Sylvestor runs into trouble on the other side, just like the black cat did here?"

"Oh, gosh, I hadn't thought of that!"

Faye had been half-kidding, being only half-believing. But when she saw the genuine alarm on Robyn's face, she wondered if she'd better take this seriously.

"Well, Sylvestor kind of adopted George first. And you guys couldn't deal with so many cats," Robyn was busy rationalizing. "I'm sure George has taken good care of him."

Faye frowned. "Ramon never has heard from George Drumm, has he?"

"No."

"Then why did you say—?"

"I just— My instinct was not to tell you any of this. Think about it."

Faye thought about it and concluded, "This is crazy shit."

"But it's real, Faye. I swear. I know you don't buy into a lot of stuff we deal with at The Lost Unicorn. Frankly, I'm dubious about some of it myself. Things get commercialized, people start believing in their own fantasies. But underneath all of that is the truth of the universe, and it is beyond our wildest imagination. Gypsies and cats, and me, and who knows what else, are slipping through the cracks all the time."

"Like Dash," Faye mused, remembering what Zeek had said about their skittish foundling.

"Yes. Your kitten got tangled up in the magic satchel that was lost in Caliente, and it carried her to Esmarelda in the parallel world. You know, if we guessed right that the stray black cat—Audy, *from the other world*—was the father of those two kittens you took in, then Dot and Dash might be predisposed to time travel. They'd be half-magic."

"Really? You think Dot and Dash are predisposed to time travel? For sure, Dot is not going anywhere."

"But Dash went all the way across the Spiral Map of Time. After your kitten went to Esmarelda in the magic satchel, Esmarelda brought Dash back to you. Hey, maybe Dash got all of Audy's magic, and Dot's just normal like the mother cat."

Faye shook her head. "Crazy shit."

"Anyway, that was the last time I saw Esmarelda, the night she came back with Dash and I showed her where you lived." The memory came back to Robyn vividly: The Gypsy had taken her hand and pressed the charm bracelet into it for the second time. *Take it. My name has been erased. The spell is broken.*

(Wait—what?)

"And Esmarelda and George Drumm ended up back in the parallel timeline, where they've been living happily ever after?" Faye pressed on.

"I like to think so, with Sylvestor."

"And what about that creepy magician?"

"I got the feeling Esmarelda was done with him, but she didn't say how she managed it. I guess I assumed George scared him off."

"So, what you're saying is, even in a magical universe relationships get all screwed up," Faye grumped.

"Maybe even more so," Robyn mused.

She had tossed the ankle bracelet into the magic vessel at Ramon's insistence. But when Esmarelda gave it *back* to her, supposedly de-charmed, Robyn had kept it; she just never told Ramon. The secret weighed on her.

(Have I mentioned that Esmarelda is an infuriating woman—and I am an idiot?)

Robyn and Faye had no breath for conversation on the last steep leg to Piper Spring and the wood where Robyn remembered being lost as a child. While they labored on, I nipped over to my side. Coyote's nose was telling me that something important was afoot. We had already entered a kind of twilight, in-between place—No Place or Every Place—the Knot. I crossed right here without doubling back to the Loophole.

Foolishly, I thought I would be able to monitor both worlds. But within the Knot, Time was in too much of a jumble. I crossed over to find that it was still *the night before* on my side. I was unexpectedly swept into an eddy of Time (as I shall describe in due course), and, to see it through, I had to leave Robyn and Faye to the care of the High Caverns Witch. Intuisha had strung out a line for them, just as she had for me, and she would reel the two Time Winders in and out as she pleased.

(Isn't that right, Robyn?)

Robyn is not in a laughing mood. She was shocked and appalled when she learned that the black cat Audy *was* Malcom the Master Seer, and she wants to know what the cat's death meant for Malcom.

Well, setting aside how shocked and appalled *I* was when I realized the Gypsy's bracelet was back in *your* possession on the wrong side of the Spiral, I will review:

We know from Esmarelda's earlier prattle that after George sent the lifeless body of the black cat back across the Spiral, the deceased body of the Master Seer reappeared in his laboratory and was found by Mark, the apprentice. The black cat also returned—alive. Mark buried the Master Seer and kept the cat.

By the time Esmarelda arrived on the scene, Malcom's house

was abandoned. Mark had left her a note detailing all, along with the ankle bracelet once inscribed with the letters of her name but now no longer. For both apprentice and Gypsy, a chapter had come to a close. They were apparently free of Malcom the Master Seer.

As we have seen, however, Esmarelda was still haunted by Malcom, even after ridding herself of his gift by regifting it to Robyn (twice). There was reason for this, for a Master Seer does not give up the ghost easily.

Where was the magician's body while his consciousness inhabited the black cat? What happened to Malcom's spirit once his body was deceased? Can you guess? One and then the other ended up here in the Knot, where all lost souls and broken spells wash ashore from the great sea of Time. The magic is beyond me, but I can tell you that the twins, Dremtessa and Intuisha, cooked it up together. It is typical of them to take pity on the cat, but I have yet to learn why they dealt so gently with the presumptuous magician who has been nothing but trouble in a place that doesn't need any more of it.

I am beginning to appreciate this method of storytelling. Each episode may be pinned down with paragraphs and chapters, until bit by bit the mind is cleared of all the clutter of remembering and can contemplate the connections. I have had a long life and accumulated many observations. Each one that I empty into the word processor makes room for more. And so I write another and another.

Written down, I may hold my memories at arm's length, as it were. Turn them this way and that. Position them in relation to each other like gems in a necklace. Whereas the way they are collected in my amphibian-canine Minder mind is more like the way little Robyn would pick up small stones, acorns, pine cones and snail shells, and plunk them into her plastic pail. She would stir through her treasures with her dirty, pudgy hands, take out one and then another to examine, and then drop it back into the mix. It's really quite amazing, thinking back, that she ended up with such a disciplined, systematic mind. But then, I know very little of human children and how their scatterbrains develop into such precise tools. Robyn was a toddler when last she entered my world, and her thought process was no more advanced than that of Brooks the frog.

Too much information, Robyn? I'm sorry, but you may not delete. You were an adorable thing. And by the way, you were right about the the blue bucket with the mermaids, weren't you? Your family photos show a yellow one with butterflies and bees. But that one was hastily bought at a gift shop after the other was lost on that fateful day in Piper Canyon.

You see why we dwell on the details. I see, now that I write them down. This has always been a story about lost things.

The star of lost things is Brunagwa's magic satchel—the satchel stolen from Nee-Reta by Malcom, later lost in the Alternate World, and then recovered by Esmarelda with the help of the kitten Dash.

Esmarelda and George Drumm were on their way to return the satchel when Nee found them and attempted to take it back to Brunagwa. Had Nee succeeded, she might have saved the Gypsy couple much trouble. But poor Nee-Reta was impossibly out of Time, both too soon and too late. In order to explain, my narrative must also skip a spiral-turn. Hang on, dear Reader. The written word is about to take us through time in a page-break.

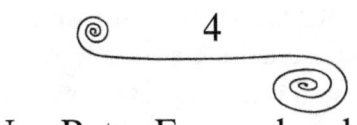

Nee-Reta, Forward and Back

NEE WHEELED OFF TOWARD THE MEADOW AND MADE A WIDE
circle around the area. When her heart had quieted, she returned
to the place where she had seen the Gypsy couple. There was no
sign of them. No mark of any kind on the path, behind or ahead.
They could not be seen within the walls of the canyon, and, more
tellingly, they could not be heard.

Nee allowed that one or the other of these Humans might
possibly evade her sharp senses, but two together never would.
She flew back to the twisted tree where she had perched above
them, then fluttered to the ground. Not a blade of grass was bent,
not even where the big man had sat. No strand of the woman's
black hair or the cat's orange fur could she find. It was as if they
had never existed. But Nee had seen them, and *they* had seen *her*.
She and the Gypsy had actually conversed. Yet there had been a
gulf between them that Nee could not cross. When she dove for
the magic satchel she had come close enough to see clearly how
faded and worn it was, as though it had been in use for many
years; then a force like a blast of air had turned her away.

Nee flew to the high ledge that marked the final ascent to the
mesa top. There was a deep cave here—not Intuisha's, but her
cougar's. Yau would be sleeping in the heat of the day. Should
the cat wake and detect a hawk perched on her favorite boulder

overlooking all the canyon, her first instinct would be to attack.
But if she saw Reta there on the ledge instead of Nee, Yau would
slip into her own human form, Yani.

Nee shivered herself into the woman Reta. She was not
frightened of Yau, for her hawk senses were sharp and her
reflexes quick. And she did not especially want to visit with
Yani, who was so much more adept at her womanly shape that
she made Reta feel awkward and ugly. But Human was better at
thinking than Hawk, and the upsetting events of the past two days
had given Nee-Reta much to think about.

Reta settled into the shady nook under an outcropping of rocks
where she could not be seen from the mouth of Yau's cave. It did
not offer the vast view to which Nee was accustomed, and it
forced her into her own thoughts. Uncomfortable in every way,
from the sensation of her skin on the sandy ground, to the painful
emotions of Malcom's betrayal, Reta called up the charm
Brunagwa had given her for focus and clarity. With her eyes
closed, Reta made herself remember the white candle. She
visualized it in the brass sconce above Brunagwa's hearth.

"Mind of Woman, fear not the light," Reta whispered to
herself. The flame, which so frightened Nee, danced invitingly.
"Mind of Woman, do not take flight." Mentally, Reta tucked Nee
safely away within a great cottonwood tree. "Mind of Woman,
kindle your second sight!" Reta squeezed her eyes shut more
tightly, then opened them. The small slice of canyon that was
visible from her niche—in which Nee would have noticed every
breath of dust dislodged by every burrowing creature—offered no
distractions. It was but a silent, blurry background to her
thoughts, which were suddenly as clear as her memory of the
flickering candle.

To Reta's relief, for she was reluctant to think about Malcom,
her thoughts were on Brunagwa—on the Witch's obsessive urge
to travel, which had driven her to acquire the magic satchel.
From the moment she was brought into the Coven, Nee-Reta had

been picking up hints that the one she minded had wanderlust. Brunagwa was not content with the Witch's ways of traveling on an astral plane or seeing far through her Familiar, she wanted to get up and *go*. The first to speak of this openly to Nee-Reta was Sestorina . . .

WHEN THE FIVE SISTERS FLEW AS CRANES

Young Nee was playing on the updrafts that burped out of Six Hills one windy day, when suddenly Flame came galloping along below and playfully herded her toward Sestorina's ranch. Nee did not know the sisters very well then, or their Familiars. When Flame waded across the rushing stream that guarded Sestorina's land, and stepped out on the other side as Mari, clothed in a dripping mane of chestnut hair, Nee began to understand her own destiny—and to welcome it. She flew from tree to tree, following the beautiful Mari through Sestorina's woods and orchard, watching the graceful way the woman plucked a leaf or flower as she walked.

Between the orchard and Sestorina's log cabin lay a tangled garden of vines and shrubs. Here Mari paused and turned to look back at Nee, who perched in a cloud of apricot blossoms. "Come down, Nee," she said. "My mistress wants to see your progress. Come, Reta, walk with me." Mari reached out her hand.

Nee fluttered to the ground, plopping down clumsily into a female heap at the last instant. Mari didn't laugh or rush over and make a fuss. She simply stood with her hand outstretched until Reta had risen, composed herself, and come forward to take it. This was the first time Reta had ever touched a human hand with her own, and again she felt a sense of acceptance wash over her. It would not be so bad to be a Human, she thought, so long as she could have a friend like this. Even more reassuring than the touch was the feeling of oneness, of communing as one Minder to another, Nee to Flame, even as Reta and Mari walked hand in hand through the overgrown garden to Sestorina's cabin.

Having gone to the trouble of making tea, the Six Hills Witch paced her front porch impatiently, her boots clacking across the worn wooden boards. The three elder sisters all looked very much alike, though nature and time acted on them differently. Sestorina was brown as a nut, and her long hair was bleached nearly white by the sun. She was the only one of the sisters who wore trousers and a buttoned blouse like the villagers of Ochersfeldt. Brunagwa had instructed Reta to be careful to meet Sestorina only on her ranch, and to fly fast away if ever she should see her beyond its bordering stream. "The stream cools Sestorina's heat," Brunagwa had said of her younger sister. "If you see her alone in the forest, fly fast and raise the alarm, for when little sister walks abroad, fire quickly follows."

Recalling this, Reta settled in a chair by the porch railing.

But now it was Sestorina's turn to tell tales on Brunagwa. She and Mari took seats in the shade and began to gently coach Reta on the drinking of warm tea. It had a sweet flavor that made Reta want to gulp eagerly, but when she did, it burned her throat.

"Just a little sip," Mari told her.

"No more than you would drink as Nee," Sestorina added. And then she went on to say, "*I* have been a bird, you know."

"No, I did not know. How is that possible?" Reta squawked. Her voice was still unfinished, and she startled herself each time she spoke. She was glad that Sestorina's aim was not to make her practice conversation. No, Sestorina intended to do the talking. This is why Mari had brought Nee to her. Nee-Reta was Brunagwa's Minder as well as her Familiar, there were things she needed to know. Sestorina commenced:

"In the beginning, my sisters and I would meet in the meadow every night, not just on the special nights as we do now. We were forming our Coven, following the path that had been revealed to Dremtessa under the instruction of Master Seer Varluft. Brunagwa saw to it that we followed his recipes exactly. By moonlight we administered the potions and balms then danced around our fire in the center of the meadow. When exhaustion overtook our limbs, and our bodies fell to the ground in slumber, and the flames dwindled, our dream bodies would awake on another plane where we would meet with others of our kind. They welcomed us and gave us further instruction, so that we learned to find other Witches and other covens there on the spirit plane, and everyone's magic was strengthened. Once we had made Goathorns Coven known to the others, Witches Meadow became an astral meeting place as well. Or, I should say, this place of great magic was revealed, through us, and joined to the network of cosmic pathways."

Reta understood very little of all this. She had seen the sisters dance around their fire under the full moon and then collapse to the ground to sleep the night away. They claimed they traveled to other places while they slept, but Reta still could not fathom it, nor could she see what it had to do with herself, the sipping of tea, or Sestorina once becoming a bird. As Sestorina rambled on about the Coven's rituals, Reta tilted her head in the way of Nee when listening for the sound of something hiding.

Noticing this, Mari made a snorting sound and tapped the ground with her foot impatiently. Sestorina interrupted herself mid-sentence and looked at Mari with fiery eyes.

Reta cowered, prepared to revert to Nee and take flight should the place suddenly burst into flames. But the Witch fluttered her lids, and a cool, sage-scented breeze swept across the porch to refresh their moods. Mari stopped stomping the floor under the table, and Sestorina resumed her tale:

"We were all of us still making camp here at Six Hills back then, if you can imagine. All but Brunagwa. You see, Hester-luna, Brunagwa and myself were all women of the world before the twins called us home, and fate cast us into these hills. Brunagwa had come home to Ochersfeldt dutifully when called, thinking she would go away again in time, but then we came to the Goathorns and our destiny was sealed. Nothing held her here but the place itself. *We* did not insist—we were all in the same boat—but she blamed us, especially the twins, and she blamed Varluft, and she blamed the strange beings that were responsible for our coming here.

"We still did not know their ways or powers, or even what to call them. Could they be the ones our cohorts hinted at during our astral travels? For we were frequently asked if we'd encountered any 'others' in these mountains—beings who could transform one body to another—they were said to dwell right here, but perhaps they were only of legend. While some of us set out to find and befriend these others, Brunagwa shunned us all. She staked out her place on Red Mountain and busied herself making her own camp. She caught and cooked food for us, protected the potions, and took her place dutifully in the Coven's circle, but her spirit was troubled and angry. We allowed our sister her solitude, such as it was . . ."

Nee-Reta watched warily as an unhappy memory flickered behind Sestorina's smoky eyes. She asked no question that might spark what smouldered there. (Nor will you, Robyn, one story at a time, please.) Mari stamped her foot again, and the two women shook their long tresses with an identical flip of the head. Sestorina continued calmly:

"Sitting atop her mountain, Brunagwa daydreamed of transforming herself into a bird so that she could soar across the landscape, alight in a distant place, revert to human form, and cavort in the flesh with those friends we'd made on the spirit plane. She devoted herself to this magic. She chanted and prayed and conjured there in her aerie, then brought her spells to our nightly meetings, where the circle of five magnified her magic. We began to feel we were coming closer to her goal.

"One night, Brunagwa was flushed with excitement when she ran to the meadow to meet us. She told us that a man had boldly come into her campsite by day while she rested under a tree. When she jumped up to protect herself, he transformed briefly into a coyote; then he rose up on two legs, and in the blink of an eye stood before her as a man again! Thinking she was dreaming, Brunagwa treated all as natural. She brought the man drink, and they sat together as friends—just as we sit here."

Sestorina interrupted herself to encourage Reta to practice the sipping of tea, for Reta sat frozen in fascination, holding her teacup in mid-air.

Reta sipped and put the cup down. "Do go on," she chirped.

"In the course of their conversation, the man, who would give no name, explained that he was with the circus in Ochersfeldt. His talent was of illusion, and he had mastered the art so well that he could venture through the forest safely with the appearance of a coyote.

"'Ah, an appearance, but not an *actual* transformation?' Brunagwa pressed, convinced that the entire episode was a vision through which she would obtain the secret knowledge she desired.

"'Below the magic circle of the Goathorns, my act is mainly acrobatic and hypnotic,' the man confided, 'but once I began climbing your mountain, I felt a *becoming* that I have never felt before. My senses became sharp, my hunger a craving for something freshly killed.' He leered at Brunagwa; she salivated for his power. 'Then let us hunt,' she declared, for that is often the way of the animal vision. He became the coyote again and bounded into the forest. She followed with bow and arrow, nearly as fleet of foot as he. They returned to her camp with a brace of hare, which she quickly skinned and trussed while the man made a fire. Brunagwa poked stems of rosemary into the meaty bundles and cooked the game very lightly on a spit. Seeing the man's appetite, she took but a bite for herself and gave the rest to him.

"Over this meal, my sister and the man spoke at length about his experience of becoming the coyote. Brunagwa stated her wish to fly as a bird, and she readied her mind to accept the wisdom this vision was no doubt sent to convey. The visitor carefully described several laborious techniques by which she might accomplish the difficult feat. Brunagwa was not satisfied, because each method was more exacting and time-consuming than the last. 'Is there no way you can simply convey your power to me?' my foolish sister asked. The man said that there was, in fact, though it required certain intimacies."

Here, Sestorina and Mari snorted in unison, but their joke was lost on Nee-Reta. Sestorina continued:

"And so, by the light of day, Brunagwa dreamed up a lover for herself, seemingly in much the same way we conjured our lovers by night. Afterwards, she felt certain that a knowledge had been conveyed to her, and that with our help she would be able to transform from woman to bird, just as she had seen the apparition change from man to coyote and back into man.

"The next morning at dawn, following a night of magic and meditation, we commenced the spell by holding hands and dancing around the embers of our fire. I shall never forget what happened next: The five of us lifted as one into the air, a ring of Witches with hair and caftans flapping, and then as one we let go our hands and watched each others' arms become wings. I felt my neck reach forward and my legs reach back, as if Nature herself were pulling me into a new shape, while around me my sisters also flowed into the shapes of sandhill canes. We flew in widening circles higher and higher, and then soared above the meadow, then Ochersfeldt. We nearly reached the clouds of Goathorns Peak! We flew out over Lady's Way and all the way to Foster Pond, where the Crone ran out from her hut and hurled hexes upward. But her curses could not touch us.

"We flew, my dears, we flew. There weren't many who recognized us as anything more than a stray flock of cranes, but the Master Seer Varluft surely did, as did the Crone of Foster Pond."

The Master Seer. Hadn't the Gypsy referred to Malcom as a Master Seer? In her shaded niche above the canyon, Reta clutched at the words she remembered from Sestorina's story. There was a Master Seer in Ochersfeldt named Varluft. Malcom must either be his student or his rival.

An idea came to Reta about how she would explain the loss of Brunagwa's satchel, and she shivered with pleasure at the sensation of her cleverness. But she still had not solved the mystery of the disappearing Gypsies and the impossibly aged magic satchel. What else had Sestorina told her that day that should be important to her now?

Sestorina had said that the sisters never again became cranes, or any other animal, after that. The far-sighted Master Seer Varluft had seen the cranes from his compound in Blue Quarter, but he only cast doubt: Was the experience genuine or shared dream? He himself had mastered the form of an eagle and, like the circus illusionist, found his abilities enhanced when practiced within the ring of the Goathorns. But to say the sisters *really* became cranes that *really* flew was self-deception.

If the Master Seer's aim was to constrain the Coven's power to fly, he succeeded, for doubt is the enemy of magic. The Witches never again turned themselves into a flock of cranes. Yet, important knowledge was gained, and after this the Witches trod more respectfully o'er the Goathorns, which allowed mutual awarenesses to bloom.

And what of this man who had turned into a coyote? He did exist. Varluft easily discovered his identity—Amos Goathorn, circus trickster.

Brunagwa ventured down the mountain to find Amos Goathorn. His surname indicated he was descended from the oldest human inhabitants of the region. No wonder he had such earthy and magical ways. No wonder she was attracted to him, and he to her mountain. Setting aside the strangeness of their first meeting, Brunagwa determined the man to be worthy and, by good fortune, physically real. A passionate affair ensued. Amos often traveled to Red Mountain. The sisters were not pleased, but what could they do? It kept Brunagwa content and the Coven intact. No, it was not the sisters who evicted Amos from Red Mountain, Sestorina insisted. The circus people shoved off and he with them, without even a farewell.

Brunagwa went a litte crazy. She was plagued by suspicions about her lover. At first she accused others of driving him away. Then she worried that he had fallen victim to a malevolent spell. Or perhaps he hadn't gone away at all—for everywhere she looked she found coyote tracks. To demonstrate their good faith, her sisters undertook a thorough search for Amos Goathorn. They already had an inkling about the man's true nature, for while Brunagwa had been preoccupied with him, they had been getting to know the Minders, and sometimes enlisted their help with their witchy business. The Minders cooperated in the hunt for Amos, because they were as displeased with this Man as the sisters were.

Now the coyote came no more. The tracks disappeared. Brunagwa roamed farther and farther in search of Amos, for sometimes she could hear the sound of bells and singing wafting across the northern plains, and she thought the circus people would return.

One day, in the course of following the deceptively close-sounding jingle-jangle, Brunagwa wandered far along the High Road that spanned the distance between Red Mountain and the foothills of Goathorns Peak. Glimpsing a strange sliver of green within a dark shadow of rock, she skittered down the far side of the ridge and followed the mirage into a lush glade. For surely it must be a mirage, with this pretty blond child shuffling through the leaves in a land that was suddenly cool and moist. Brunagwa walked toward the child, but before she could touch it, the great hawk Ti swooped through the rift, brushed the girl back, and circled round Brunagwa thrice, binding her with an invisible thread, then led her back up to the sunny ridge.

From that day forth, Ti became the Red Mountain Witch's Familiar. Ti's job was to hold Brunagwa within the circle of the Goathorns. The only way Ti could keep Brunagwa in check was to fly far and wide as her spy, then transform into the woman Wyan to sit with Brunagwa and report every detail that Ti the hawk had observed. Eventually Sestorina and Flame found young Nee, and they sent her to Brunagwa so that Ti could have some rest.

Brunagwa was delighted with her young Familiar. Almost immediately she set the hawk on the task of negotiating with the Weaver Oshi for a magic satchel. Not knowing any better, Nee had complied. She flew all the way to The Top of The World on two occasions to see the job done.

Remembering all of this after her encounter with the Gypsies, Nee-Reta was troubled. Ti's job, and then her own, was to keep Brunagwa close to the Coven. Shouldn't one of the other Minders have prevented Nee from ever helping Brunagwa to get the satchel? Or was this expected, or in some way required—that Nee would bring the satchel to the Goathorns, then take it from Brunagwa? The magic satchel had traveled far and wide since yesterday, when the charming stranger had flattered Reta into letting him touch it—and then her—only to steal both her prize and her heart. Perhaps the satchel had its own destiny, which could not be circumvented by Brunagwa or her Minder, or Malcom or his Master.

That is why I had to take the magic satchel from her! It was my duty, Nee-Reta concluded with surprise. It hadn't seemed like the reason at the time. Reta simply wanted to play with the strange thing herself, for Brunagwa hadn't let her touch the satchel even once after Nee's exhausting flight to fetch it from the Weaver.

Nee-Reta's head ached from all this cogitation, but she had settled on a plan. She would tell Brunagwa that Malcom had put a spell on her—on Nee—to make her steal the satchel. For all she knew, he had. And for all she knew, the Red Mountain Witch had already destroyed him for doing so, for the Gypsy had spoken of his death.

The thought of Malcom's demise so disturbed Reta that, without intending, she was suddenly Nee again, lifting off into an updraft above the canyon to soothe herself with flight. She would fly to Brunagwa and tell her about Malcom, and how she, as Nee, had already been out searching for him so that she could get the magic satchel back. Brunagwa would be angry at the magician, and Reta would be angry along with her. And the other womanly feelings would recede.

Nee dipped into the canyon then soared upward again to fly over the plateau. She zig-zagged her way to Red Mountain ever on the alert for movement—for any sign of the Gypsies or Malcom. She caught the blur of a bird in the distance, then was thrilled to recognize old Ti. No sight could be more welcome. Brunagwa's original Minder would instruct Nee, and all would be well. Nee flapped toward her old friend with all her strength and speed, then wheeled around in confusion when the other hawk suddenly dropped out of sight.

What now? What now? Nee shrieked in dismay.

A cry came back to her. Ti's voice. Not an answer, but an alarm, a single long, "Kee-ahrrr!"

Nee began a spiraling glide downward, searching for Ti. A mist appeared, like the thread of smoke from Brunagwa's pipe. Nee followed to see its source, and found a deep cut in the canyon wall where moist atmosphere from another world leaked out into the Goathorns. The scents of pines, ferns, and a myriad of scuttling things attracted the hawk. Nee was irresistibly drawn to the densest part of the mist, and the canyon wall gave way to receive her. She flew through the cloud and found herself in a wet, wooded place where Ti's shriek still rang in the air—and a small blond child cried in the arms of her mother.

Again! Before!

Nee flew off quickly, following the echo of Ti's voice up through another cloud and out into the blue sky of the high desert. She emerged in time to see Ti winging powerfully toward Red Mountain, and then receding quickly to nothing—a hallucination—while Brunagwa trudged angrily up the High Road after her, until her form also wavered into thin air. Ti and Brunagwa—*young* Brunagwa—were gone without a trace. Just like the Gypsies.

So this was the Knot. Nee had seen the Gypsies in the Future, and then Ti and Brunagwa in the Past.

And what of Malcom? He had been present. She had touched him. He had taken the magic satchel, he really had. It would go to many places but it would be returned, one day, by that Gypsy. By then Malcom might be dead, or he might not. The Gypsy thought he was dead, but then she thought he was not. And what happened in between? What was supposed to happen next? It was up to Nee-Reta to make the next move.

I know, I know, I know. It has not slipped anyone's attention that a sort of villain emerged in the last sequence. A coyote who could turn himself into a man, and as a man seduced a certain Witch. And then all the sisters were angry at him, and all the Minders, too. Boo hoo. Oh, such trouble. Oh, what a cad.

But did you also notice that, as a result of my misbehavior, the Minders and the Witches began to forge their bond? A little credit is due there, I think. And the tale of the women turning into sandhill cranes and winging their way around the Goathorns is a doozy, you have to admit. The stuff of legends. Believe me, it made the Coven's reputation. The sisters owe me, and they know it, for they have held the memory of flight within their breasts ever since, and it has strengthened their powers tenfold.

All of these events are well past, let's not forget. Nee-Reta had made a very brief foray to the Future, where she found

Esmarelda and George Drumm just days ago (depending how you count). She then returned to her own Time and reflected back to her own Past, when Sestorina had told her about events from an even earlier period. (Clever, no, how I covered all that ground?) Lots and lots of water under the bridge.

Yet still the sisters scorn me and treat me like their dog. I do my chores and accept their scraps. For the most part we leave each other alone. I honestly don't understand what they find so appalling about me. They were all full of the hanky panky in their day. Brunagwa was hardly seduced in the sense of having been chaste up to that point. She was my willing playmate.

We were all young and feisty in the Time before the Time before the Time before. The sisters were positively glorious. Probably fortunately for me, the others were beyond my reach. Hesterluna was too chummy with Varluft, and too smart by half, to be taken in by any of my tricks. Sestorina I admired from afar but forbade myself to go near—I did not want to be set afire literally. And with the twins one risked the opposite—to sleep in the arms of Dremtessa might mean to wake in her ice cave frozen to death. As for Intuisha, she was simply unapproachable in the flesh. By now I am used to encountering her. Early on, though, when her chill visage surprised Coyote on the cliffs, I would be so shaken that I'd immediately turn into a horned lizard. As H. Toad I would follow her like a smitten fool.

The High Caverns Witch has the power to attract yet never be taken. Thus she pulls the string that sends us hither and yon. If we can turn away from my youthful indiscretions, I will tell you about one of Intuisha's best stunts ever.

(Robyn says fine, we will come back to my indiscretions later. More likely, they will come back to me.)

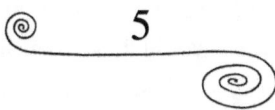

The View from Intuisha's Cliffs

INTUISHA IS COMMONLY REGARDED AS THE OLDER OF THE TWINS, though Dremtessa disputes it was Intuisha who came out first. The mother of these women, when asked, would always say that they were both so slow to emerge that she was near death after the delivery, so for all she knew Dremtessa was really Intuisha and Intuisha was really Dremtessa, but for certain Intuisha came out first. Make of that what you will, it cannot be disputed that the twins were inseparable. They were boisterous children, but became reclusive as they matured, seeking out dark and quiet places as if craving a return to the womb. They would ultimately establish separate hiding places but, being twins, they remained in close mental communication. Thus, the important thing you need to know about Intuisha is that you are never dealing with her alone. Dremtessa is there too, in spirit; and Dremtessa's Familiar, the bear Roth, minds both twins vigilantly. This makes up for the fact that Yau the cougar only does half her job.

George and Esmarelda worked their way up to the mesa top behind the agile Sylvestor, and Esma finally confided that they had a bear to worry about as well as a cougar. They picked up the pace, certain they felt the presence of one or the other—but it was really H. Coyote.

The Gypsies were passing directly through my turf on their

way to Brunagwa's mountain, and I was following their movements closely. Which brings me to another of Intuisha's qualities:
She is revoltingly soft-hearted. She cast a spell giving the house
cat the powers of a Minder while he was in the Goathorns so that
he could become a bird and fly out of reach. She knew that one
of us—Yau or Roth or I—would make a meal of him if we could.
Minders have to eat too, you know. But we are loathe to eat each
other, even if we could be caught. Intuisha knew I had my eye on
that cat, and she fixed it so I wouldn't take him.

Intuisha had her own plans for Sylvestor and Esmarelda and
George—and for me too, it turned out. Also for the stranger with
the black dog who had surprised Zeek at The Lost Unicorn. Even
for Zeek, I suppose, though he wouldn't remember. Her desire
for all who found themselves, one way or another, on her cliffs
that Solstice night was that we would watch certain bits of history
play out again in the loops of the Knot. She had been waiting a
long time to tug the thread that would unveil the murky past of
the magician who took Brunagwa's magic satchel out of the
Goathorns. Sylvestor would be her agent, leading Esma and
George up the escarpment with such intensity that he seemed to
be following an invisible string. And so he was.

The Gypsy and her lover struggled to keep up, not daring to
stop to rest. Strange sounds issued from the caves and crevasses
they passed. As the sun dipped low, Esmarelda thought she
glimpsed a ragged man and a big dog peeking out from behind a
boulder up ahead—but they found nothing when they reached the
place. Not long after, George called out that he had found a pool
of water. However, by the time Esma caught up to him, he was
shaking his head in dismay.

"It must have been a mirage," he told her. "But it was the
damnedest thing—I looked down into it and saw my own
reflection looking back."

Esma shuddered. The light was fading, and every step was
more treacherous than the last. "We'll have to stop soon," she

said. "Maybe once the the moon rises—"

Sylvestor suddenly let out a long wail. They raced after the sound and arrived at a patch of scrubby vegetation in a small wash hollowed out by spring rains. Sylvestor, fur raised and eyes gleaming, had sprung to the top of a dwarf oak, too short to offer him much protection. As soon as he saw George and then Esmarelda stumble into view, he changed into a hawk and flew off with a cry, "Wait for me!"

Esma slumped to the ground and wept from frustration and exhaustion. George dropped his gear beside her. In the waning light, he quickly gathered kindling and built a small fire to keep whatever had frightened Sylvestor at bay. Esmarelda soon rallied to the flickering light and pungent smoke—for a campfire is home to a Gypsy.

Foiled by Intuisha's spell, I retreated into the brush for a brief time. I emerged as H. Toad to sit companionably with George and Esmarelda. A banquet of insects was attracted to, or scuttling from, the flames.

The couple brought out food and ate. Gradually their anxiety faded. They sensed animals all around and understood why Sylvestor had fled. Yet they had no fear for themselves. They let the fire dwindle so they could look out at the stars that floated above the canyon. George sat close to Esma, a protective arm around her. Did they doze off and dream? If so, they dreamed as one.

"What am I looking at?" George asked. "Do you see that?"

"It looks like daylight on the canyon floor, though it is pitch black night up here," Esma observed. "How can that be possible?"

"But that's not the canyon floor anymore. It's green like a meadow, and I swear I see a city in the distance."

"Oh, George, look, the whole scene seems to be levitating. It's coming closer, I swear. Or are we falling into it?"

"Did you ever go to the movies in the Alternate World? It was just like this. The theater got dark, and then a screen lit up, and a new universe unfolded. Only, where is the screen? When did we come into a theater? How is this possible?"

They were terribly dense. I would have liked to set them straight, but imagine the spate of stupid questions *that* would have provoked. I recognized the period of time that was about to be replayed, and it was of some interest to me. I started scraping the ground loudly to drown out the pair's doltish exclamations, and I succeeded in startling them into silence.

Esma clung to George. Night had fallen and obliterated everything beyond the glow of the embers at their toes. Now they felt a disturbing absence of substance. The little oak tree was no longer simply cloaked in darkness, it was *gone*. They no longer shared the sensation of a comforting mass of rock behind them. Night itself was being disbursed by a strong wind as fingers of blue sky brushed aside the stars. Their own bodies seemed no longer . . . relevant.

"This is not like the movies," Esma breathed.

"I feel like I just crawled out of the magic satchel," George whispered. "A giant magic satchel."

"Yes, the very fabric of the Spiral Map of Time."

"We're in a another *time*?"

"Seeing it. I don't think we can change it. Weaver Ehrte had a word for this. Oh, what was it? A splash or a swirl . . ."

I hopped closer to them, thinking to give a quick explanation of the *eddies* before their prattle provoked H. Coyote into lunging for someone's throat. Before I could give myself away, Intuisha conveyed sufficient understanding to each mind so that they quieted themselves. I presume she enhanced their natural psychic connection as well, so that they shared their perceptions of the event without speaking further. Or perhaps she gifted me with deafness to their speech.

In silence, then, under Intuisha's protection, we three plunged into an eddy of reflected Time, a spin-off from the Spiral in which a sequence of events is preserved and replayed over and over—Time's memento but not Time itself. There are many such souvenirs of Time preserved in and around the Knot. I have learned their nature and how to distinguish them from segments where the actual Spiral is still in flux. *That* is truly dangerous territory, where the sisters ply their magic to keep order. George, already displaced in Time, was surely on his way, but we were not there yet.

This historical lookback on the life of Malcom the Master Seer had to be for my benefit, I figured. Ochersfeldt, after all, was the place Esmarelda least wanted to go. Although she still had concerns about Malcom, it was not for her that these scenes of his early days unfolded. No, it was all for me. Esma and George, with their delicious-smelling cat, were merely the bait.

It stirred me deeply to live those times again from Intuisha's enchanted cliffs. I will try to tell it all to you exactly the way it played out for us in that eddy of Time. Esmarelda, George Drumm and I were as dreamers within a dream, observing from the inside and outside simultaneously, from as near or as far as our minds required. I could make better sense of Malcom's story than the Gypsies, for I knew the chronology well. By the calendars on the walls of Ochersfeldt's taverns, I saw that twenty-five years had passed since I first became *persona non grata* in the Goathorns. H. Toad and H. Coyote still made their homes in the mountains, but the randy Human was consigned to town. And I was good with that (as you say). There were many diversions, much to learn, any sort of companionship I craved. Ochersfeldt was where I had learned to be a man, after all. I don't believe anyone knew my secret, except perhaps Madagascar at the circus, where H. Coyote originally stood on his hind legs for his supper and secretly studied the human attributes of ringmaster Gunther Storm.

Well, Varluft knew, but that goes without saying. We might have been allies, had I been wiser, but I did not want him to be my master. The only words he ever spoke to me were at the circus, early on, when he scratched my head and said, "Minders can do their work anywhere. Do not neglect yours." I nearly bit the Master Seer's hand off, and Gunther Storm nearly had a heart attack.

In Ochersfeldt, no one troubled over who I was, or what I did. It's easy to blend in there, or be lost there. My forest home, when I craved it, was only a hop, a skip and a trot away. For twenty-five years I had gone back and forth at will—years that passed in a blink. Witches and Minders aged little, the other denizens of Ochersfeldt, the Meadow, and the Forest only slightly more. Time in and around the Goathorns can be kind when the Spiral is becalmed.

The coming of Malcom to Ochersfeldt coincided with the beginning of the disturbances. We have aged a good deal more in the years since. And sobered up, some of us. The eddy that floated into view while I sat with Esma and George showed me things that ought to have caught my attention at the time. But my attention was turned elsewhere. By the time the young magician came to town, I had long quit the circus and wasn't minding anything more on my visits to the magical city than where the next ale was coming from, and the next female.

It is only because of my recent front row seat to Intuisha's theater on the Past that I can conjur Malcom's story now. Was there a personal message for me? If so, let it come out in the telling . . .

MALCOM ARRIVES IN OCHERSFELDT FOR THE FIRST TIME

Malcom stood on the highest point of Ochre Bridge, in the center of Ochersfeldt, and surveyed his future kingdom. He intended to possess it all. No, not as a ruler or a rich man. He would not own or govern anything. But the magic would be his, all of it—the secrets, the spells, the signs—it was only a matter of time. The enchanted waters of the Red River splashed along below him and laughed merrily. Even this river would be under his dominion one day.

Ochersfeldt was a city that traded in occult secrets. Its craftsmen were all magicians in their own right and belonged to guilds that passed down specific formulas for specific spells. The glassblowers knew how to lock up a dream so it would never come back, for instance. The flute-maker knew how to implant a dream so it would never go away. Wizards, Witches and Wanderers poured in from all the world to shop for such wares. The locals, Malcom learned, also exchanged another currency, gossip, in order that no practitioner of magical arts could gain so much power as to rule the others. In this way, the flow of secrets was self-regulating. One who reached too far would be found out and disciplined. But Malcom felt he could beat the system. With enough disguises, he could evade the gossips while making his fortune. And with enough gold, he could buy all the secrets he wanted.

The attraction of Ochersfeldt for an up-and-coming magician like Malcom, aside from its deserved reputation for premium spells, was its sheer size. With his talent for disguise he could ply his trade at numerous locations around the city without fear of being exposed. His opportunities seemed limitless. The city teemed with pilgrims, tourists, merchants, apprentices, and artisans year round, situated as it was so near The Top of The World. Indeed, Goathorns Peak was so close in the east, as the crow flies, it was hidden behind the nearer Goathorn mountains that spilled down to the high plain on which Ochersfeldt perched. The Goathorns raked the town with chill, jagged shadows each morning, but by mid-day the city glowed like a gem on its grassy plateau, and the vast Harp of Gold Valley unfurled below, a shimmering carpet.

The Red River gushed down from Red Mountain, the most northerly of the Goathorns, lost its fury in the long descent, and crossed the plateau as a reasonably contrite waterway. As the

town had grown up around it, the river was further civilized by
generations of talented architects and bridge-builders. The old
north-south road across the plains, named Wand Way in these
parts, spanned Red River in the very center of Ochersfeldt,
creating four quadrants, each with its own unique character.

Malcom had amassed a great deal of knowledge and lore
about Ochersfeldt on his long journey, but the scale of the city,
now that he had resided in it for a week, continued to take him by
surprise, for it defied logic. From his vantage on the bridge, all
appeared exactly as it did on the postcards and leaflets he had
collected along the way: To the northeast, the Red Quarter
sported handsome rows of three- and four-story red brick homes
fanning outward from a cluster of taller, turretted buildings of
ornately sculpted pink granite. The southeast Blue Quarter
consisted of low, shapely buildings following the snaky loops of
a man-made canal system that drained off overflow from the
river. On the west side of Wand Way, the Gold Quarter provided
a jumble of inns, eateries and shops lining cobblestone roads,
then a cluster of quaint thatched-roof houses overlooking the
valley, dwindling down to a few farmhouses on the slope above
the valley floor. To the north, Ochersfeldt's Green Quarter lent
a stark backdrop to this pastoral scene, its spires of glass and
crystal erupting into an eerie, mirrory cityscape as modern as any
on the planet.

Distinct as each quadrant was, they packed up against each
other and into the foothills of the Goathorns very economically.
From the bridge, Malcom could make out Lady Way, the long
road that skirted Ochersfeldt's northern border; the Red River
exiting town on the west; and the Wand Way Gate, which
impressed tourists arriving from the south. It was all as clearly
and neatly laid out as in the pictures. Yet, when Malcom stepped
off the bridge and ventured into any of the Quarters, he felt that
the streets were branching off endlessly. He was lost for long
hours, and then would suddenly turn a corner and be back on one

of the broad main roads shown on the maps, not a block from where he'd first turned off. And if he tried to keep track by counting storefronts or alleys or canals, he quickly reached a number that defied belief. How could a single block contain so much real estate?

Malcom had performed an experiment soon after he came to town. First, he sat in front of the Hedgerow Cafe on quiet little Tulip Lane in Gold Q and counted passers-by from ten 'til noon. He did not reach triple digits. The next morning, he again arrived at the Hedgerow at ten, but instead of sitting, he set forth on a counter-clockwise loop up Tulip Lane, around a minuscule plot of land called Old Golden Green, down to Peddler Street, and back over to Tulip. It should have taken no more than twenty minutes, going slowly and counting everyone he passed along the way. But he walked for two hours and counted over two hundred people—and those were only the ones coming toward him—and somehow he still hadn't gotten around the Green. Or had he passed ten or twelve such parks? In which case he ought to have come out far, far away from the cafe. Not so. No sooner had he heard the twelve peals of the Gold Town Clock, than he took a turn and found himself on Peddler Street, where he could see the Hedgerow Cafe up ahead at the next corner. It boggled the magician's mind—and even at his young age, Malcom was a man not easily boggled. Ochersfeldt must be breaching a dimension or two, he figured. And why not, with so much magic being made here? But the possibility of such a thing had never occurred to Malcom until he'd arrived. And even here, among Ochersfeldt's many crafty denizens, he could find nary a one who would acknowledge it. Where was the mentor who could enlighten him? He hadn't a clue.

Macolm turned his back to the river to watch the parade of carts and pedestrians crossing Ochre Bridge. Some people on foot began drifting over to him; he felt exposed, and wondered why his spell wasn't working. But these tourists were not interested in the medium-sized man with the medium-length, medium-brown hair and nondescript clothing. They pressed against the bridge railing to peer at the river, which had turned flame red in the setting sun. Malcom did not turn to look. He felt the sun on his back. He watched his shadow lengthen and stretch across the paving of the bridge. He wished he had the magic to make his shadow live independently of him. How convenient would that be? To have a silent, secret, other self. But even as he watched and wished, his dark twin merged with the dusk and abandoned him.

One by one, the tourists sighed and shivered and pushed away from the railing and continued on over the bridge, south to Gold and Blue, or north to Green and Red. Malcom remained either unnoticed or ignored. He needed no disguise to disappear. He was invisible and alone. In all of Ochersfeldt, he had no place to call home. He had a long-range plan, but nothing for the present. The magician stood in the dark wondering which color to choose, which direction to turn. Calling out for random magic in such a place could be disastrous. He must wait. *It's only a matter of time*, he thought again, and forced himself not to want, to take comfort within his solitary spell.

Thinking nothing at all, he followed his feet across the bridge to the south side, turned onto River Road, and followed it out of town and into the forest, until the road came to an abrupt end. Here he had his choice of continuing up a scrabbly mountain trail to, presumably, Red Mountain, or picking his way down to the river and along its banks. Or he could simply sit in indecision where many an uncertain soul had sat before, on the low stone wall that finished off the road like a bookend. It had a layer of smooth slate on top, placed there not to protect visitors' posteriors, but to carry a warning.

Do not cross the Red Mountain Witch, Malcom read. He shrugged, then stretched out on his back across the words that had been crudely etched into the slate. He put his hands behind his head and waited for an idea. The forest held no fear for him, the Witch's words no threat. With the cocky confidence of one who has made many a dark crossing, Malcom dared the spirits of the wood to enter his dreams and instruct him. But before sleep could take him came the sound of a man running—a man who seemed to be burdened with bundles and belts and his own weight. With much huffing, rattling, and thrashing of foliage, the fellow was descending quickly down the narrow, forbidden path in the deepening dusk. Malcom rolled off the wall and crouched against it.

A large figure barreled toward the clearing, leapt over the wall, and loped down the road with long strides, dust and bird down filling the air in his wake. Malcom followed easily with silent speed all the way to the outlying hovels of Gold Quarter, until he was at risk of overtaking his prey. The man had slowed so as to quiet his approach to one of these poor structures. He stood outside it for a moment, looked either way, then entered.

Malcom wondered at this precaution, for the fellow quickly lit lamps inside the domicile, making himself and his loot visible through the thin curtains. Malcom thought long about the appropriate disguise in which to approach. Once decided, he waited until the man had put out the lights and put himself to bed. Awakened harshly from his slumber an hour later, this poor soul was no match for Malcom and his tricks.

By the time morning dawned, Malcom, as a candlemaker who had lost his way, had been rescued and befriended by Avalon the feather merchant. It took but another day for the beguilingly forgetful "Wicks" to draw out Avalon's secrets. Before a second day had passed, the candlemaker had slipped away, to be absorbed into Ochersfeldt's throng and never heard from again.

Now Malcom commenced a week of hard work, keeping at bay all thoughts of the true object of his desire. If an actual Master Seer resided in Ochersfeldt, as Avalon had said, he would quickly ferret out any mind turned too eagerly in his direction.

Malcom confined himself to Green Quarter, where the money was good and the crystal towers deflected charms. He told fortunes with dice as a clown-like figure on the Palisade, hypnotized giggling youths as Sir Irwin at a pub on Lion's Lane, and sold medicinal remedies as Chan on Chandler Place. The next time Malcom strolled across Ochre Bridge, he was a dark-haired, barrel-chested street musician who enjoyed the attention he attracted . . .

"Tenorio" hummed melodiously as he walked. Sometimes he interrupted himself to cluck to the monkey who hopped along with him on the end of a leash. Madagascar, festive in his yellow bow tie and jacket, shook a tambourine to cover the sound of coins rattling in the singer's pockets. It was a service he performed now and then for the right price. (As the saying goes, "In Ochersfeldt, pockets pick themselves.") Beyond the bridge and around the bend, the two went their separate ways. That is, Madagascar bolted out of sight by prearrangement, and Tenorio, who was supposed to feign distress and rush off in the opposite direction, simply turned away and disappeared. Strange doings, anywhere but in Ochersfeldt.

A muscular, tired-looking man continued down the road. He carried his coat rolled up in a tight bundle in his arms. Limping slightly, like a hiker returning from the tourist trails, he turned left at the first wooden footbridge and crossed the main canal into the heart of Blue Quarter. Each time he came to a little bridge on his left he crossed it, until he had lost track of how many left turns and crossings he had made. There would be no end to it at this rate. The Master Seer of Ochersfeldt must be on to him.

Malcom paused, took a breath, and put on his jacket, letting several coins fall to the ground. Not a soul was in sight, not a single urchin rushed forward to grab them. He stood as if on an island, the canals having somehow joined to become a moat penning him in on an earthen mound. *Nice*, Malcom thought approvingly. He made a sweeping bow, allowing more coins to fall, and called out:

"It is I, Malcom the magician, at your service, Master Seer Varluft. I am a worthy apprentice with the means to pay and the talent to learn. Have I not proved myself by finding you?"

An eagle shrieked high above. Malcom looked up. Coins fell from the sky and pelted him like rain while the eagle laughed. Malcom shielded his head with his hands until he felt the barrage stop. When he lowered his arms, he stood in Varluft's study, his pockets turned inside-out, the floor littered with his gold.

The great magician himself sat thoughtfully at his desk plucking at his beard. "You are not the one I expected," he told Malcom. "I must be getting senile."

Malcom kept his head bowed slightly, more to hide his thoughts than out of respect. Varluft might in fact be senile, for he was old as the hills, as Avalon told it. And Malcom caught a faint whiff of death in the air despite the sorcerer's heavy perfume, and saw the wrinkled geography of age despite the Master's make-up.

Many times had Malcom imagined an encounter with a great Master Seer, but in none of these fantasies was the star attraction a spindly, womanish type like Varluft. Malcom reminded himself of the spectacular eagle that demonstrated Varluft's powers—this odd character might be only a facade. Yet he, Malcom, had special powers as well, and he intuited that it was indeed Varluft in the flesh behind the desk. Malcom felt certain that the Master Seer had dispensed with illusions when he had emptied his pockets of coins.

So, here was the great man: A petite figure in a purplish caftan. Silver-gray hair parted down the middle from front to back, gathered at the sides behind his vast ears and braided into two rat-tail plaits that draped over his shoulders. Many strands of silver and gold, beads and amulets around his neck. Gold hoops in his long lobes, rings with great stones that dwarfed his pale fingers, bracelets jangling on his wrists. Eyelids dusted with peacock blue powder, cheeks lightly rouged. And a beard, pure white, fluffed out over chin and neck, then brought into a braid from sternum to belly—a belly that was round and bulging beneath the caftan in a way that mimicked the early months of pregnancy. All in all, of all the strange characters Malcom had found in Ochersfeldt, Varluft was the strangest. Which, when he thought about it, was as it should be.

Malcom's spirits lifted. Here he was, he had made it! And, to all appearances, Varluft had no apprentice or helper or heir to receive his secrets before death, which might be imminent. The hand of fate was upon them. Did Varluft feel it? He'd said that Malcom was not the one he was expecting. Was it Death itself the old sorcerer awaited? Had Malcom come—been sent—in time to receive the wisdom that Varluft would otherwise take to his grave?

It must be so, Malcom told himself. *Surely this has always been my destiny. Every step, and even every apparent misstep, has led me here. I have kept my appointment with fate!*

"Malcom always thought that everything that worked out well for him was fate," Esmarelda whispered to George at this point. "And anything that went against him was a spell that could be broken. He wondered, and so did I, how a man could have such strength and power as he without being specially blessed by some force, for some purpose. But he never knew his purpose, as far as I could tell. And I think we both had fears about the force that empowered him."

"Whether it was good and natural?"

"Yes."

"Which is why you couldn't love him?"

"Yes."

The couple clutched each other, and I felt my fur bristle. Their words upset me, and without thinking I had become Coyote, hackles raised and nose twitching. Why was I angered by this exchange? My instinct was to slink away and watch no more of Malcom, but a low growl nearby told me that Yau stood guard for Intuisha. I could not have overheard had the High Caverns Witch not willed it. Now, though I could see the couple's heads tucked close together while their conversation continued, Coyote's ears caught nothing.

My nose was another story. Bad cat breath wafted toward me. I reverted to H. Toad and put out a poisonous belch of my own. We Minders settled. Esma and George stopped whispering. Malcom's meeting with Master Seer Varluft continued.

MASTER SEER VARLUFT QUESTIONS MALCOM

Varluft kept Malcom standing in silence for many minutes. Stalling for time, he took off pieces of jewelry and laid them on his table to see what they would tell him about this impertinent visitor. It troubled him that Malcom had amassed so much wealth without anyone in Ochersfeldt informing him, until Madagascar gave it away at the last minute. Malcom had not arrived in the city loaded with gold, of that Varluft was certain. Money flowed only one way in Ochersfeldt: out of the pockets that came to the city full, and into pockets that entered the city empty. That was Varluft's own spell, and he was quite proud of it.

Varluft never did care for gold, and he especially didn't care for Malcom's. He was planning to die and was all dressed up for it. His magic had been doled out to a variety of students and colleagues over the years. He did not need to take yet another under wing. He did not need this Malcom or the puzzle he presented. But, in spite of himself, the old Master Seer felt the flame of curiosity flicker—a tickle, an itch, a memory or a prophecy tugging him toward engagement.

At the same time, he was mildly repelled. Something was missing from the young man. That is how he was able to sneak up on the great Varluft. That is how he was able to pass through Ochersfeldt and not make an impression on anyone. Varluft held up a bracelet and looked through it, framing Malcom's round face with the silver hoop. Quickly he flipped it with his fingers while speaking Malcom's name backwards. "Moclam!"

Malcom winced. Through the silver hoop Varluft caught a glimpse of a black dog, then nothing. It was as if he looked into an empty bowl. When he flipped the bracelet again, Malcom's face reappeared.

"Sit!" Varluft commanded Malcom. A chair rushed forward. Malcom sat as if this were the most normal thing in the world. He looked Varluft in the eye. They did not have much of a staring contest. Varluft's gaze was penetrating, Malcom's merely masklike. The inquisition would begin. Master Seer Varluft would be asking the questions.

"Who are your parents?"

The gems indicated this was unknown, but Malcom did have an account of his origins at the ready. Varluft's talismans deemed the tale truthful, so far as it went:

"A couple named Frederick and Destiny Wing adopted me when I was a tiny baby. My little years were spent with them on Belinda's Bluff, in the north country. I was a difficult child, so I was told, and was given over to the boys school at Galeside, where the Brothers of Compliance employ mind-magic to manage their troublesome orphans. When I was sixteen I was pushed out the door with a full education and not a single memory of my boy years. I cut patterns for two years after that while the fog cleared. One day, a man came to the tailor with a pattern for a special cape. The tailor did not know what he was making, but I did. In secret I made a cape just the same for myself. And I have been on the magician's path ever since. See how far I have come in only five years?"

"In what town did you cut patterns?"

"In New Bonnet, not far from Galeside."

"Then I will agree that you have come a far distance. As to your skill, that has yet to be proved. Where is this cape?"

"With your permission?"

Malcom indicated his wish to stand, and Varluft nodded. Malcom stood, twirled on his toes like a dancer, and when he stopped, stood wrapped in a black cape.

"What is it made of? Let me touch it." Varluft reached across the table.

"I'd rather you didn't." Malcom removed the cape in one swift motion and cast it toward the ceiling. It did not come down again—it was gone.

"Sit!" The gems on Varluft's table went dark with his mood.

"Will you replace your lucky-guess cape with one made here in Ochersfeldt by one of our fine artisans?" Varluft asked when the atmosphere had lightened.

"No, I don't think so. My cape— You're right that I knew nothing of magic things when I made it, except what I learned from the magician's pattern. And yet my fingers knew, or something knew, and so the cape nearly made itself. I still do not know as much as my cape knows, or my fingers know, or my feet must know to have carried me here."

"So, you are not here to learn what I know, but what you know?" The trinkets began to get cloudy again. Varluft shushed his pride. The great Varluft, standing next to death no less, had no need to compete for honor against this fool's self-esteem.

"I want to know what everyone knows!" Malcom exclaimed passionately, winning a drop of empathy from Master Seer Varluft, who had come to Ochersfeldt with the same desire.

"Oughtn't you to have apprenticed yourself with an artisan or two before leaping ahead to the Master Seer?"

"But, Master Seer, you were waiting for Death and not for me."

Varluft looked at Malcom sharply. The young magician seemed genuinely hurt that Varluft might have quit living before making his acquaintance, in some way defying providence. Yet Varluft was fairly certain that providence, in the sense of blessings, was not Malcom's keeper.

Under Varluft's drilling gaze, Malcom continued his story.

"The fact is, I intended to do just that—work with one tradesman and another until I had gleaned the secrets of their magical wares. If the sewing of the cape had come to me so readily, perhaps I would find other talents within myself. But when I got here, and began wandering the Quarters to gain an income and discover the best of the craftsmen, I found a mystery that distracted me from my plan.

"There was something about the city that defied explanation and even description. No one but me seemed to notice it, or none would acknowledge it. It was beyond crafts and spells as best I could tell. Only a true Seer could enlighten me."

"Of what do you speak? Enlighten you as to what?"

Varluft made two loose fists and stacked the right on the left, as if to make a telescope of his hands—but he put them up to his forehead and not his eye. He was focusing his second sight on Malcom's mind to make it easier for the lad to describe the indescribable. He felt the young man—proud and defensive one moment, sincere and respectful the next—respond like a puppy to his firm lead by mentally rolling over on his back and showing his belly. All of Malcom's inklings, observations, suspicions and burning questions about Ochersfeldt's dimensions lay exposed for Varluft to examine, while Malcom summed it up like this:

"I speak of the other dimension. Of the *expandability* of the space here. Like your canals. There are more places in this town than the physical space allows."

Varluft lowered his hands to the table. "This is so. I am impressed that you saw it."

He was also distressed. Now he was committed to guiding the man in some way. His elite guild required it. To find the rare person with the vision to be a Master Seer and not offer guidance might have dire consequences. And to find it in one such as Malcom . . .

"Will you teach me, sir?" Malcom asked contritely, touching his own forehead with curiosity, and then scratching it roughly, irked by Varluft's ability to make him submit.

"I might." Varluft fell silent and observed Malcom's struggle to contain his emotions, which flitted from impatience to anger to hope to awe, and around again. How much did the young magician know of his own nature? Very little, Varluft guessed. Had Malcom known himself better, he would not have this talent for shedding his identity so readily and donning a new one so convincingly.

More minutes passed with Malcom's question in the air. Varluft commenced to handle first one trinket and then another. He was reviewing Malcom's exploits in Ochersfeldt. The sapphire ring revealed "Tenorio" and Madagascar crossing into Blue Quarter, then Malcom's dogged approach across the canals. The gold and silver sun medallion tattled on Avalon as he unburdened himself to "Wicks." The turquoise beads enumerated Malcom's appearances in the Green Quarter. Varluft pawed through his gems, aware that his guest, behind an expression of utter impassivity, was paying close attention. Nowhere in the collection could Varluft find the key to the young magician's soul. The circlets came up empty, empty. A great sadness filled Varluft. A sadness tinged with fear.

"Do you not wonder about your parents? What do you know of the circumstances of your birth and adoption?" Varluft asked, suspecting that this was Malcom's weak spot.

"My adoptive parents were rich, and my birth parents were poor, I suppose."

"There on Belinda Bluff?"

"No. The Wings had been traveling when they took me. I remember very clearly what Mother said when she put me in the carriage to Galeside. She said, 'Do not cry for us or for this place. You are not of us or of here. This is why we have all been so unhappy. It was a mistake. I'm sorry.'

"I had not noticed being unhappy, actually," Malcom added.

"And it does not make you unhappy—you who seek every occult secret—it does not make you unhappy to know nothing of your family to this day?"

"No, I am not an unhappy sort," Malcom averred.

"No. Nor fearful," Varluft observed.

"No. But why are *you* fearful, Master Seer Varluft?"

Angrily, Varluft swept all of his baubles into his lap and began to put them back on. They had given him away! This Malcom was a fast study. He would get what he wanted with or without Varluft's cooperation. And the old magician, like it or not, and whether or not he cooperated, would be responsible.

"Incomplete things are dangerous," Varluft told Malcom, "they are always searching for their missing parts."

"I am not incomplete," Malcom answered. "I told you truthfully that I have no curiosity about my parents."

Varluft arched an eyebrow at the gap so large that Malcom could not see it. "And yet you have come all this way. First to find spells, then to find me, and next to find—what? Or whom? I am not the end of your journey, young Malcom. I say you are incomplete. And an incomplete man cannot be trusted—not with secrets such as you desire. Have you come this close to the center of all mysteries to take the knowledge second-hand from a dying man? Will you not go on your vision quest, perhaps all the way to The Top of The World, to look about objectively and to search your deepest soul?

"Here is my challenge to you, Malcom, to us: Go into the mountains and find your missing self. In the Goathorns all manner of lost and unclaimed and unimagined things reside. Even I cannot penetrate the secret of your birth, but I sense it calls to you—called you here, and calls you beyond, up to the meadow of the Witches.

"Yes, that is a place for one who has no fear. Go to the Goathorns—to the Six Hills, Witches Meadow, and Red

Mountain. Or venture into the Ice Caves and up through the High Caverns. Go all the way to Goathorns Peak if you dare. Prove yourself to yourself first, and then to me. Fill that void within yourself, and you will be fit material for a Master Seer. Perhaps you will even learn the answer to your question about the dimensions. I promise to persist to see the results of your quest and, *should you succeed*, to fend off death so I may tutor you until you are satisfied.

"But, *should you fail*, and return to me with the same stunted soul that stands before me today, you may have the moat and nothing more. My secrets are not treasures but good deeds. I am content that they be done when I am dead. It is what I intended.

"You are not the one I expected." Varluft shuddered and rested his head in his hands, exhausted.

Malcom hurried around the table to put a half-full cup of something into the old man's hand.

Varluft sipped his cold tea. "Thank you," he sighed, and felt the paternal tug he had so wanted to avoid.

"I'll go," Malcom said, "if it will keep you alive."

The questioning went on for an entire day more, even after the agreement was reached. Varluft probed into everything that Malcom knew about the Witches of the Goathorns and the routes to The Top of The World. At least he offered some instruction while he was at it, intentionally or in passing providing much information to his eager student. Malcom, wanting to prolong his time with Varluft, spun out clever, misguided answers so that the Master Seer would either correct him or in some way reveal where the truth lay. They began to enjoy the game.

Malcom thought that Varluft might relent and allow him to postpone the vision quest indefinitely, or perhaps Varluft would die before it came to pass. Malcom had little confidence that the Seer would fulfill his promise to live to see him return from the mountains. But maybe that was unnecessary. Maybe Varluft had already dispensed with physical existence. For, while Malcom required a periodic walk around the gardens—gardens which had been nowhere visible on the day of his arrival—and an occasional bite in the kitchen, where fresh food and drink always awaited, the Master Seer would take nothing but the magic tea with which he staved off sleep—or death. Or perhaps he was already dead.

"My life is like the city of Ochersfeldt," Varluft had said, reading Malcom's mind. "There is more of it than would seem to fit." And then he sent Malcom out to the garden to select a stone. The Master Seer of Ochersfeldt would tell the young man's fortune for his trek into the Goathorns.

One moment, please, while I quarrel with the Editor. She thinks this chapter has gone on too long and we need a break here—just for the math, I guess. I say it is absurd. I have taken us into the very warp and weft of Time to reveal significant historical events only recently revealed to *moi*. In order to make it all fit—for our tale bears the same fractal qualities as Ochersfeldt and its Master Seer—I am attempting to include these backstories within the existing framework. *Capiche?*

(She acts as if she is acquiescing to me, but I know better. She's thinking that she'll take my opening chapters—which I have so conscientiously composed from the confines of this stuffy room in this wretched lodge—and rearrange them later on. But I beg her—I beg you, Robyn—not to risk it. I am knitting you a story here, and if you pull the wrong thread, it will unravel before you have even seen its shape.)

Now, If I may . . .

MALCOM GOES TO THE GOATHORNS

Malcom fingered the stone in his pocket and frowned, angry that the Master Seer of Ochersfeldt had gotten the better of him. He was climbing an alpine trail that skirted Red River and its woods for a short distance, then continued due east through a high valley running between Red Mountain to the north and Six Hills to the south, and from there rose straight up to Witches Meadow. He had always intended to go up into the Goathorns. He knew their legends well and had gleaned more in Ochersfeldt. But he had hoped to get more instruction from Varluft before making the hike—not to be sent immediately on a journey of self-discovery. Malcom was a good magician, a natural, but still unschooled. He did not feel prepared to match wits with the Witches. Varluft must be either cruel or senile to send a willing companion on this fool's errand while himself on the verge of death in his solitary domain.

Malcom did not see the value of soul-searching as pertaining to his quest for spells. Magic required an iron will and complete confidence. If those doors on his inner being were shut tight—as Varluft had said—then this served as well to keep evil influences out as to stifle the power held within. "Find the lost self." "The danger of incomplete things." It was nonsense, an old man's babble. Malcom's core was neither bad nor good—it was curious, determined and pure. He would acquire all the occult power he could and perfect it like an art. Then he would be complete. The rightness or wrongness of his feats would be for others to judge.

Soothed by these thoughts, Malcom busied his eyes and ears with his surroundings, and put his mind to work reviewing all he had pieced together so far about the Witches of the Goathorns. Perhaps he was watched even now. Every chirp and twitter of nature might bespeak their animal spies and Familiars.

The hawk is the Familiar of the Red Mountain Witch, Brunagwa, he recited to himself. *Sestorina of Six Hills tames the wild horse. Dremtessa and Intuisha rule the caves and cliffs that guard the western approach to The Top of The World. Dremtessa has the brown bear for company in her ice caves; Intuisha and her cougar prowl the high caverns and cliffs above. And ahead of me, at the end of this trail—* Malcom stopped and shaded his eyes, but he was still far from his destination, and the path rose steeply so that he could see only sky beyond, *Witches Meadow, center of the five-spoked wheel of power that is Goathorns Coven. Protected by the Meadow Watch Witch, Hesterluna, and her Familiar, the badger.*

Malcom fully expected to meet one or both before the day was done. Hesterluna was known to be the only sociable member of the sisterhood, since her meadow was frequented by tourists and pilgrims. Elegantly dressed in a tight, satiny gown, she beguiled jewelry and other treasures from them, and especially desired gossip from Ochersfeldt. If she was not crossed, her tricks were benign. The badger, when unleashed on the unwitting traveler who lingered in the meadow at dusk, was meaner with her pranks. Once night brought forth its stars, not even Hesterluna could be counted on for protection.

Still, it was Hesterluna and her Familiar in whom Malcom placed his hopes for a speedy and successful vision quest. He too was a trickster and master of disguise. He would willingly allow himself to be beguiled, even seduced by Hesterluna. What danger was there in the Witch's lust? Perhaps Varluft's idea of a vision quest amounted only to a young magician's rite of passage—a night in Witches Meadow satisfying Hesterluna's legendary carnal desires. He would pour himself into her—what matter how she looked by day if she appeared as a young nymph at night?—and her power and knowledge would flow into him. This was Malcom's plan. He would make love to Hesterluna, befriend her badger, and take their secrets back to Varluft as his own. No missing pieces of the self, no empty holes. He would fill up every part of himself with magic and let Varluft pick his pockets again. The old man would stay alive just to hear the tale.

While Malcom was occupied by these thoughts, the sun crossed its zenith and morning gave way to afternoon. Malcom became aware of a shape moving along silently beside him only a few paces away. Turning sharply, he caught sight of a large, sleek, black dog. The surprise of it sent a jolt of fear coursing through him such as he had never felt. How had the animal come so close without him noticing—in broad daylight, in open scrubby country where most living things hid themselves from the sun? How long had it been following? Malcom was frozen in panic, saturated by a cold sweat.

As Malcom stood gaping, the panic gradually subsided, and so did the vision. The black dog proved to be nothing more than his own shadow. Malcom cursed his stupidity, vowing to be more alert to the spells and charms that filled the Goathorns. The game was on. He was in the dominion of the Witches.

There was no way he could forget about the enchanted nature of his surroundings now that the black dog moved with him. It appeared again and again as the afternoon wore on. Malcom became convinced that there was some sort of entity literally shadowing him. But no matter how much he put his second sight on it, he could not fathom what it was.

A Familiar? he asked himself, while he made his progress up the steepening trail into an experimental dance—slowing down and speeding up, stopping suddenly, or crouching quickly behind a rock—to see if he could catch the creature off guard. The thing seemed only to exist in the corner of his eye.

Back in Ochersfeldt, there was some disagreement about whether the Witches' Familiars were real animals magically imbued with human qualities, Humans enchanted into animals, a completely unique breed of being, or apparitions with no physical substance at all. The last of these theories was falling out of favor lately, with increased tourism in the area producing much anecdotal evidence to the contrary. When a badger, a bear, a cougar, a hawk, or a charging horse attacked a Human, that was very real. The victims returned to Ochersfeldt with the wounds to prove it, yet never mortally injured. The animals who attacked but did not kill had plenty of physical substance, though their behavior was unnatural. How could they be merely apparitions?

The commonly accepted notion was that Familiars could be

the result of enchantment either way—Human to animal as a punishment for some wrong, or animal to Human as a promotion for service. The particulars of the transformations depended on the spells and varied widely. It was to the Witches' advantage to have helpers of animal body and human mind, so this was primarily the form Familiars took. The Familiar could scout for the Witch and report back to her, scare off intruders, and marshal its animal kin to carry out complex plots and spells. Such was the prevailing theory.

Malcom's meeting with Varluft had given him another idea—that a Witch might have the power to appear in animal form, in the same way Master Seer Varluft had become the eagle. If this were so, then, where legend had it that there were *two*—Sestorina and her horse, for instance—in truth there might be only *one*, and it was Sestorina herself who galloped down from the hills to terrorize hikers who had strayed too far. This possibility held some appeal for Malcom. First, it meant he only had to worry about the five Witches (albeit in multiple forms), not five Witches plus their Familiars. Second, it suggested another kind of power he might strive to acquire. When asked, the Master Seer would neither confirm nor deny this theory. He only reminded Malcom that liking an idea was not proof of it.

There was one last explanation for Malcom to consider—that the Familiars were their own species of changelings. Hardly any-one gave credence to this. Mainly, it bothered people to think it so, so they cited many reasons it could not be, and generally convinced themselves and each other. The only strong defense of the theory had come from Madagascar. Madagascar was not a Familiar. He was a talking monkey bred by a circus supply company on the outskirts of Red Quarter, and set free to retire there after his tour of service. They had been sitting together on the porch of the monkey's red brick house when Madagascar explained to Malcom that Familiars called themselves Minders and had inhabited the Goathorns long before the Witches moved in and began to train them.

"Now that's a fine fantasy for a talking monkey!" Malcom had told Madagascar. And they'd clicked beer mugs to seal their deal for the bridge escapade, laughing heartily.

What else would a talking monkey dream of, but to be wild and untamed and able to transmogriphy at will, Malcom told himself now, collapsing in the shade of a tall tree. His manic dance up the hill had exhausted him, and nothing had come of it but dizziness. The black dog still flitted in and out of his peripheral vision at unpredictable intervals. If it was a Familiar, whose was it? Was there a sixth Witch in the mountains? Or was it merely the trick of a weary mind—or a trick placed in his weary mind by a cunning Witch? He was acting like a maniac. He needed to regroup.

Malcom drank some water from his flask, then produced his cape from its hiding place. Wrapped in the cape, the magician himself disappeared for a five-minute catnap. He woke to the sensation of being watched by many eyes.

"It's only the trees," he muttered uneasily. He should have noticed when he entered the stand of aspens—or had the trees crept up around him? Their silvery bark was banded with dark, eye-like buds, all turned to the young magician. While the trees' shivering leaves whispered his secrets, Malcom lowered his head and proceeded stealthily but decisively to Witches Meadow.

Nee swooped from tree to tree. She had been half hunting and half minding while watching the man's progress. She was not really trying to evade his notice. A hawk was not an unusual sight in this valley. The clomping approach of the magician—though he imagined himself treading lightly in his charmed leather booties—was causing small animals to scurry out of their burrows and roosting birds to take wing. Nee glided silently above the scrubby wood beyond the aspens, careened suddenly to take a dove right out of the air, and proudly carried her kill to the twisted branch of a cottonwood tree up ahead. By the time the intruder came even with her, she was cleaning her beak on the rough bark and combing her wing feathers. She would let the man pass, then follow secretly. Should he notice, she would give him the great pleasure of observing her, but only from a distance.

Nee's likeness had been captured once by hikers carrying memory mirrors they had bought in Ochersfeldt. Brunagwa was furious and forbade her ever to show off like that again. Later, when she was allowed to accompany Brunagwa to the Witches' circle, Nee learned that the sisters were upset about the new inventions out of the city. Silent slippers, memory boxes, spell finders, and dream snares were being sold to curious tourists hoping to experience a close encounter with Witches on their trip to the Goathorns.

Although most Ochersfeldt artisans had long been banned from the higher elevations because the feathers and bones they pilfered too often cost the lives of mountain denizens, and sometimes ended up in laymen's hands, the sisters had tended to ignore casual hikers. Innocent intruders were left to the pranks of Hesterluna, which reinforced the Goathorns legends. The three older sisters sometimes conducted business with a select few in Ochersfeldt, and everyone was able to make out nicely without giving away secrets or violating the Witches' sacred rites. But things were changing as Ochersfeldt grew. The Witches were getting less respect, you might say, and the Coven was close to severing ties with Ochersfeldt completely. The Familiars had been instructed to treat all passers as potentially dangerous, to drive off local scavengers, and to report any tourists who carried contraband goods.

But the man coming quickly up the path so late in the day was neither a tourist nor a scavenger. Nee observed that he was not overly burdened with packs like the hikers and campers, and he was not interested in scouring the ground for collectible bits of bark and stone, or plucking specimens of leaves and wildflowers to press into a notebook, or capturing insects in small jars. He was on the lookout for more mysterious things. She had seen this type before. The sisters would decide whether to welcome him, toy with him, or expel him.

Nee wondered whether to tell Brunagwa, finally, about Dark. She had never mentioned the ghost dog to her mistress. Dark was a secret she treasured. He was a being unlike any other, who seemed to have no master. He came and went as he chose, but he was often near Nee when she was alone, and he was protective of her. More than once he had sprung up in her defense, and the feather hunter had been scared off. To the Witches, Dark was but a legend—a fantasy invented by the rubes of Ochersfeldt along with all their other misapprehensions about the Goathorns. Could Nee-Reta be the only one with whom Dark communed?

Until this intruder. Nee was used to Dark following along with her, but now he shadowed this man. What could that mean? Nee perched on her limb, so focused on the black dog that she didn't stir when the man approached, stopped, and looked directly at her.

"If you were Varluft, you would be an eagle and not a hawk."

Before Nee could react, the man said something in a magic tongue. She did not understand, but it frightened her. With a single angry cry she flapped off in the direction of Red Mountain.

Nee was relieved to see that Dark followed her and did not stay with the man. When they came out into the open, she dipped low and batted the tip of his ear with the tip of her wing. What she felt was not fur or fiber but a crackling energy that seemed to reach out and touch her in return. No, she would not tell Brunagwa about Dark—not now, not ever. She would not tell anyone. She made this decision many years ago and had held to it all this time, she would not waiver now.

They reached the far edge of the meadow, and Nee began to work her way up through the treetops. She paused frequently to watch for the stranger, who eventually became visible as he crested the rise to the plateau. Dark did not follow the hawk far into the woods. Nee sensed when he turned down a side trail. She knew by now that if she looked back she would see him disappear, as though he were stepping into and being enveloped by a thick fog that dispersed as quickly as it gathered. Her only comfort was knowing that her friend would reappear with equal ease when the time was right. She continued on.

Beyond the treeline the tall conifers dwindled to stunted oak, the oak melted into a tufted tundra, and the tundra gave way to pale, bare rock, like a fringe of hair around a bald man's pate. Nee fluttered down from the last stubborn limb of the last stubborn pine and arranged herself as Reta in order to approach the Witch's retreat. She hoped that the concentration required to maintain her female form would drive away any thoughts of Dark through which Brunagwa might perceive him.

Speak only of the stranger, Reta told herself, hurrying against a stiff wind to Brunagwa's mountaintop chalet. She gave a ladylike tap on the unlatched front door, slipped inside, and called out, "If I may, Brunagwa, I bring news," as she glided toward the Witch's study. Her voice was hardly chirpy at all.

An eerily similar voice sang back to her, "Well, well, Reta. Perfectly done. By all means, come tell me."

And now, Robyn and Readers, you finally get a chapter break. I must collect myself before we encounter Brunagwa.

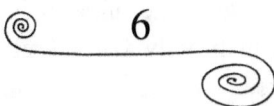

6

Brooks Considers Brunagwa

BRUNAGWA. SUCH EMOTION WHEN I SAW HER AGAIN—AS SHE was back then. It is still fresh with me, for not many days have passed since this recapitulation on the cliffs of Time. And the entire scene doubled by memory, as I shall explain.

Brunagwa. Magnificent woman. Malcom was wrong about the sisters. They were beauties by day the same as in their dreams. Time had only burnished them so they shone more richly. Even consigned to the edges of this reprise of Time— which was centered on Malcom, after all—the Red Mountain Witch walked in her own riveting aura. I heard Esmarelda and George gasp when she appeared with Reta in the distance. In the eddy of Time, Malcom the young magician trudged toward his fate, but the Gypsies pushed their senses to reach beyond him in order to observe the ways of Red Mountain and she who rules it. They greeted Brunagwa's appearance with pleasure and relief, as if gracefulness of form might indicate a gentleness of nature. (Who can blame the fearful for taking refuge in misguided hope?)

Naturally, Esma and George were fascinated by Nee-Reta as well. Here, it seemed, were the events immediately leading up to their encounter with the hawk woman. No need to repeat their whispered calculations—how their encounter was but yesterday, yet the theft of the satchel was many years in the past, and so the hawk must have been caught up in the jumbled threads of Time back then, just as they were at present. I will only say that the obsessive chatter of Humans does not always aid clarity.

Let us press on.

As I've explained, after the initial upheaval resulting from Brunagwa's affair with the wily Yours Truly, there was a period of adjustment between Witches and Minders. I laid low in Ochersfeldt, and stayed out of trouble when in the mountains. H. Toad visited Brunagwa often, though she didn't know who I was. She spoke to me sometimes, suspecting I was a Minder. I minded her very well. Nee's predecessor, the hawk Ti, minded me, and never let on my identity.

Ti kept a good many secrets. The creature Dark, for instance. I cannot imagine it eluding the Witches, Familiars, and me all those years without an assist from someone in the forest. Nee's own feelings for it might have given it away at any time, for, as you have seen, she was not well disciplined. Someone helped, and if it wasn't Ti, then who was it?

I respect Ti, and I reminded myself of this while observing Dark from our overlook on the Past and feeling the same confusion I had felt on encountering this canine for the first time only hours before. The displeasure was not lessened by the knowledge that even now it lurked nearby. And so I plunged into my memories to prove to myself that I had not known Dark then, that there had been no mention of him when Reta told Brunagwa of Malcom's incursion into Witches Meadow, and that Reta had not given away the slightest hint of the dog's existence by her demeanor.

The truth, I discovered, is that I noticed nothing and no one but Brunagwa. If there were clues about Dark to be found in the newly minted Reta, I might have easily missed them. My lady sat languorously at a cloth-draped table nibbling from many plates of food and taking sips from three different goblets. Her long fingers plucked glistening bits of cheese, fruit, and honeyed breads, and raised them unhurriedly to her glistening honeyed lips. I saw little else from my perch atop the clock case, though I occasionally shifted my gaze to the tangle of long blond hair that flooded over her shoulders and across her bosom. I had been waiting many hours for Brunagwa's return and would have preferred not to share these minutes with Reta.

Brunagwa and I listened to Reta's report about the man who could disappear under his cape, who had scared her away with a magic name, and who now strolled the meadow as if intentionally looking for trouble. In the course of this, Brunagwa ate a great quantity of food, and her interest in Reta began to wane.

"You have done very well, Nee-Reta," she crooned sleepily. "Well observed and well described. I wish you could have remembered the magic word and not been intimidated. We'll have to work on that. But I do not feel concerned. Hesterluna will deal with the impertinent fellow. This is nothing out of the ordinary."

Then Brunagwa actually tilted her lovely head toward me for validation, and naturally I blinked in agreement, having no more to go on than she did, since I had been on Red Mountain waiting for her all afternoon. Reta gave me a sharp look, and I thought I saw talons flash from her fingertips for the merest instant.

Brunagwa said, "I am weary, for I have been practicing traveling in my magic satchel. I have been out to Mount Shanama for a ritual with the Monshanama Coven that lasted fourteen days. And yet, here I sit not half a day since I left. I plan to sleep for a week before I leave the house again. My dear Reta, go watch how Hesterluna handles the stray magician. It is bound to be entertaining. Then return to guard my hilltop while I rest. I am done in."

Brunagwa retired to her chamber, leaving Reta ruffled. This is how it had been with the Red Mountain Witch ever since she'd gotten the magic satchel—the Witch had less and less companionship and instruction to offer her Familiar. I had some sympathy for Nee-Reta. I also missed Brunagwa's vitality. Even when the lady was present, she was distant, depleted, as though she had left her life force elsewhere.

Reta felt poorly used. She paced the study, then stopped in front of Brunagwa's mirror to practice expressions, but found she had no patience for it. She saw me watching and fluttered back into the hawk Nee to perch uncertainly at the window that was always left open for her. Now that Brunagwa had retired, I was able to give my attention to the Familiar. I could tell that the hawk Nee felt less offended by Brunagwa's indifference than the woman Reta did. In fact, Nee felt liberated. For a week she would be free. Already Brunagwa's soft snoring filled the chalet. Nee the hawk and H. Toad exchanged a look, passing an idea back and forth.

This was the moment, the meeting of two impish Minder minds (and even here, I swear, no whiff of the black dog) that set in motion the chain of events that brought Esmarelda and George Drumm to their overlook on the Past. The import was not lost on the lovers as they clutched each other and leaned far forward over the chasm of the Spiral, willing the distant scene to come into focus:

Nee glided silently to the Witch's bedside. She knew the hiding place of the satchel. Without hesitation the hawk snatched up the woven bag in her beak and flapped clumsily but quickly out of the room, back through the study, and out the window. The object was heavier than she'd expected. Brunagwa had sewn in several small beads as place markers since Nee had brought the satchel to Red Mountain, which made it weigh noticeably more to the small animal. Nee would not be able to carry it far.

H. Toad followed Nee's tipsy flight unobserved. When, once more below the treeline, Nee fluttered into Reta, I bristled myself into H. Coyote and kept close but hidden.

The young woman twirled Brunagwa's magic satchel and pranced about in delight. *So there*, she thought, skipping down the path. She would consult with Brunagwa's sisters and their Familiars about this strange object, but first she would get to know it. It fairly tingled in her fingers. From a compact little bundle of woven twine, the magic satchel had unfurled into a big sloppy netted bag. Reta sniffed it. She turned it inside out and waved it over her head, and swirled it like a lasso near her ankles and hopped over it. She tossed it up in the air and spun around once, twice, and caught it again. In this way she frolicked down the mountain. She was taking it to Sestorina, who had given her good advice about Brunagwa in the past. But before Reta had reached the path to Six Hills, a man appeared on the trail and blocked her way, hands on hips, laughing at her antics. It was the crafty stranger—the stray magician, as Brunagwa had called him.

"Come," he said in a seductive voice. "What have we here?" He reached out his hand.

Reta gave over the magic satchel without a thought. "It's a magic satchel. The way we Witches travel across Time, or from place to place without time passing. I used it to travel all the way from Mount Shanama in the blink of an eye, and I shall return home before the moon rises."

"What a marvelous device. And how fortunate the timing. I am on a mere one-day excursion myself." Then the man put out his other hand, and, again without a thought, Reta put her hand in his.

"And it was just that simple!" Esmarelda erupted, looking away from the scene in distaste. She did not want to see Malcom make love to poor Reta, or think about the implications. George cuddled her affectionately and continued to watch with interest.

"It's okay," George finally said. "He wasn't a complete cad. I would say he left *her* wanting more, but went away satisfied himself—all he really wanted was the satchel."

In my own view, the young magician's restraint was sufficient to cast doubt on his earlier boasting about making love to

Hesterluna. My suspicions seemed to be borne out by Hesterluna's failure to appear. Neither she nor her Familiar, the badger Snip-Edie, interfered with Malcom's progress across Witches Meadow. They left him entirely to Reta. Perhaps, like me, they watched the magic satchel being passed off to Malcom with a secret satisfaction.

At any rate, George was right—Malcom wanted that satchel badly, more than he wanted Reta. Once she had told him everything she knew about it, which wasn't much, and lay pliantly in his arms, melting under his petting and nuzzling, he brushed his hand lightly over her eyes as if to shade himself from her adoring gaze. Her lids fluttered closed, she slept. Malcom took the satchel and sprinted for Ochersfeldt on the same path Reta had been following, but instead of going on into the Six Hills, he skirted around the west side of the meadow and followed the river trail. Wild horses did not run him down. The black dog did not show itself. A coyote stalked him for a short way and then returned to the woods. Malcom wrapped himself in his cape, and we all pretended he disappeared.

This is how Malcom was able to steal Brunagwa's magic satchel—all of us who might have stopped him let him take it. He would take it to Varluft; either Varluft would keep it safe or the two of them could have the trouble of it. Better them than us, we thought. That was before we fully understood that every trouble with Time inevitably gets pushed along the Spiral and ends up back with us anyway. We let the satchel get away, and we're still paying for it.

Hindsight is not nearly as pleasant as cocky inexperience, is it? *Farewell to the satchel*, I thought happily at the time. And perhaps farewell to Reta, too. I trotted back up to Brunagwa's chalet and reverted to H. Toad to watch over my lady's slumber, taking some rest myself in preparation for the excitement to come. Thus my infatuated younger self missed much that might have been useful, such as Reta skipping ahead on the Spiral and meeting Esmarelda and George Drumm, and then her calculations about Brunagwa while resting on Intuisha's cliffs. By the time Brunagwa awoke, Nee-Reta's story was unassailable. It went like this:

As instructed, Nee went to spy on the interloper. The man said his magic word again, and this time it caused Nee to turn into Reta. He put a charm on her and questioned her about the satchel. Then he let her become Nee and fly home. But the charm was still upon her, for she took Brunagwa's satchel and returned to him in the way of one who sleepwalks. The crafty fellow made love to Reta, then stole the satchel while she slept.

When Reta was finished telling the tale, Brunagwa was more outraged at the misuse of her young Familiar than the loss of the satchel. Reta had made herself the victim, and Brunagwa would be extra kind and patient with her ever after. Which is not to say that the Red Mountain Witch's overall character softened. She swore revenge on the mysterious magician and his master, whomever that might be. She doubted it was Varluft, but would start with him and destroy him if necessary, old friendships notwithstanding.

It was too late for that, her sisters informed her when they met in their circle that first night after Brunagwa's waking and raging. She had slept a full week, and the young magician was long gone. Not only that, Varluft the Master Seer was dead two days now. They had hoped to bring his body to Witches Meadow for rites, but when the Sprites of Blue Quarter laid the old magician in his coffin, his body burst into flames. The casket was set in the canals, which took it swiftly away.

"I heard that dear Varluft is aflame still, and halfway to the sea," Hesterluna reported with sadness and pride for her old friend.

Her sisters' refusal to attach Varluft to any part of Reta's unhappy episode, or even to affirm or deny what had actually happened while Brunagwa slept, or to take the disappearance of the magic satchel the least bit seriously, came as a bitter blow. It was added to several other grudges that had accumulated over the years. To this day, Brunagwa resides in haughty solitude on her mountaintop and only comes down to attend the sacred circles. (Which is exactly as her sisters and the Minders like it.)

So, it was not Reta who was evicted from Brunagwa's life, but me. Soon after these events, H. Coyote was summoned to the Loophole and made to mind it. Brunagwa's original Familiar, Ti-Wyan, who has been like a mother to us all, had noticed the slippage—Nee in the Future with Esma and George, then at that long-ago scene with Brunagwa and little Robyn in Piper Canyon. Ti-Wyan gathered all the Minders and invited each of us to try to go through to the Alternate World at will. When I was able to do it, I was given my assignment and paid with flattery. Intuisha and Dremtessa participated in this snow job. I'm not complaining. They would reward me with their company from time to time, and while we exchanged pleasantries they would allow me to catch glimpses of their sister Brunagwa in their minds.

That sounds pathetic. I would like to delete that last. Why does this tale keep coming around to me?

Robyn says it is a common pitfall, but she is not critical. She is as curious about me as she is about all the others. Still, she reminds me, I have left Esma and George on the cliffs above a replay of time; and Zeek in a nightmare with the black dog and scarecrow man; and Robyn and Faye hiking intrepidly toward the Knot; and, somewhere back along the Spiral, Malcom is on the lam with a stolen magic satchel, while the Master Seer Varluft is suddenly dead!

Yes, so many thoughts and memories reside together in my mind like a pile of squirming pups, but the words come one by one in relentlessly singular sentences. (I'm glad I haven't got to smell a trail or hear the forest in this way.) I must continue doggedly on.

Solstice night wanes, there on Intuisha's cliffs, and the last scenes in the eddy of reflected Time spin through with increasing momentum like water swirling down a drain:

... Varluft's deep disappointment with Malcom and the magic satchel. "The stone told true!" the Master Seer roars at the upstart magician. Whereupon the young man reaches into his trouser pocket and hurls a small rock, no bigger than a dollar coin, at Varluft's face. It is Varluft's rock, from his own rock garden, and stops in mid-air not an inch from the spot on the old man's forehead where, had it struck, it would have killed him. Varluft takes two steps back to peer at Malcom's fortune stone—a dark gray, triangular bit of limestone creased and pitted to resemble a frowning face. "The stone told true," he repeats sadly as he takes it in his fist. The young man storms out, to be seen no more in Ochersfeldt—but then, he was only barely seen before.

... A montage of Varluft pacing his study over the course of several days muttering, "Not the one I expected, not the one I expected," and, "The stone told true, the stone told true," then dropping into his chair wearily and rubbing the spot on his head where the stone had not hit.

... Varluft lying dead on the floor of his study, his limbs and garments neatly arranged, expression stern and eyes wide open, the frowning stone balanced on his forehead over his third eye.

... The canal sprites buzzing all over Blue Quarter with the news, then bringing the Master Seer's trusted friends to him. They find Varluft's body out in the open. The study, the house, everything has disappeared from the little hillock where the magician staked his claim so long ago. No structure impedes the view of the snaky pattern of canals unspooling to south and west. There is but one object remaining out of Varluft's vast estate—his coffin.

... So slight a man. It only takes six sprites with gently flapping wings to lift him. He has shrunk over the years. The

Master Seer no longer fills his custom-fit box. On contact with it, he ignites. The Sprites fly off in panic while the others rush forward, shielding themselves from the flames, and push...

...Flames spew into the air from the depths of the coffin, but the wooden box does not burn. It slides down the grassy hillside and into the canal, to be carried south and west and south and west until the waters rejoin Red River in the valley below Ochersfeldt.

...The Witches dance crazily and wail like madwomen in their grief for Varluft—not together, but each in her own small, hysterical circle. And the maddest of them all is Brunagwa. The Familiars—Bear, Cougar, Badger, Horse, and Hawk—have taken positions outside of the circle to guard the sisters the way they always do, but they are perturbed by the especially strange, wild shape of their ritual.

...Suddenly, in the center of the circle of dervishing Witches, a colorful spiral-within-a-spiral shimmers into view, a swirling rainbow mirage, at the center of which is a fluttering yellow shroud. The brown bear Roth lets out a roar, the cougar Yani-Yau howls. The Witches leap back and pose with their arms raised and arched forward, splayed fingers aimed in the spell position. Nee dives toward the intruder, but the swirling current of air deflects her. The yellow veil is lifted gently by the disturbance, then settles again...

...And the entire scene spins into a blur and collapses back into the canyon below.

"Robyn! That was Robyn under the yellow veil! Did you see her?" Esmarelda had caught the gleam of silver bangles encircling the dancer's ankle. What on earth had possessed her to take the charmed bracelet *back* to Robyn in the Alternate World? She felt ill.

"Robyn, from The Lost Unicorn? I thought she looked familiar."

George slipped his arm from Esma's shoulder to her waist and held tight as she strained forward to see into the canyon.

"Yes, that Robyn. That would be very bad!"

Very bad indeed. I was already racing toward my slot to the Alternate World. (Thereby missing, again, the Gypsy's guilty thoughts about having foisted Malcom's malicious love token onto Robyn.) I was after magic carpets. Something had to be done about those rugs, and quickly.

"Robyn, do you see that? That's you! That's where you went. Do you remember any of that?"

Faye had grabbed Robyn's arm. They stood in a fairly flat lea, its size indeterminate, for the mist that met them at the end of their climb was so thick they could hardly make out the ground beneath their feet. As they had shuffled forward uncertainly, the scene at Witches Meadow emerged.

"I see it," Robyn breathed, grateful for the solidity of Faye's touch. "But no, I don't remember any of them—"

Before she could finish, the vision had swirled back into nothingness. And now, not only could the women not see the ground they stood on, they couldn't feel it.

"I don't like this," Faye whispered.

"No, I don't either," Robyn agreed, linking arms with Faye.

"You don't? I thought this would be right up your alley."

Faye was still speaking in a stage whisper, and Robyn found herself doing the same.

"No, I hate mysteries!"

The women dissolved into giggles, clutching each other and the small sense of normalcy that remained. With effort, they composed themselves.

"What now?" Faye asked in an almost normal voice.

"We should be able to find the path again if we turn *exactly* one-eighty degrees and start retracing our steps. You have a compass?"

"Yeah, right."

There was a solemn silence while the women realized they had ventured into the unknown without either of them bringing one of their magical devices, or even so much as a watch.

Faye rallied. "Hey, let's do it like the choreography to *Desert Queen*. You know, the part with the quarter turns."

She started humming and snapping her fingers. Robyn joined in, slowing down a little. Once they were in agreement on the tempo, they sang their way through the first half of the song, slowly letting go of each other but staying very close, feeling the beat in their knees, and swaying their hips in unison. Now came the first quarter-turn. Each woman stepped with her left foot across her right, swung her hips around clockwise, then straightened. They knew they were facing exactly ninety degrees to the right—they'd practiced this move a hundred times. Another repetition, and they would be in position to descend the trail. But the view that emerged through the mist when they lifted their heads froze them in their tracks once more.

"Oh my gosh, that's me," Robyn breathed.

"I know."

It was the scene from Robyn's childhood, exactly as she had described it to Faye a short while earlier—the intrepid little girl, the glorious robed woman walking toward her, and then the hawk diving at the child before chasing the woman away.

"I don't remember that part," Robyn mused as the scene faded back into the mist. She strained to see the moment when her mother came and scooped her up—she would have loved to see her mother young again—but it was not to be repeated now.

"What part?"

"The hawk chasing the woman up the mountain."

"Like in that other place with the dancing—the hawk was trying to chase you away, back to the stage at the Harmony Convention."

"I wish it would show up right now and send us back to the lodge."

"I don't, thank you. C'mon, one more time." Faye began the tune again. They calmed themselves by getting into the rhythm, then made one more perfect quarter-turn.

"Oh, cripes, that's *them.*" Faye immediately recognized the shabby man with the fierce black dog as the pair Zeek had described over the phone. They emerged through the thinning mist, distant yet in focus, and the street they walked along was all too familiar.

"It's Fourth Street."

"They're on their way back to The Lost Unicorn."

"Shit. And I never called anyone to go help Zeek today."

The mirage quickly faded, and the mist began to clear.

"At least we found the trail." Faye pointed. They could now make out the top of the path that had brought them to this strange place. They jogged toward it and skittered down to the still-sleepy campground, then hurried back to the suite . . .

Where no one was even awake yet.

Ramon woke to a lonely bed. He heard Robyn's voice and staggered out to the sitting room.

"S'up?"

Robyn held up a finger for silence—she was still on the phone.

"We went for a morning walk," Faye piped up from the kitchenette. She was making hot chocolate. "We saw a wolf!"

I know, Robyn, you tried to tell her it was a coyote.

At any rate, now that I have gotten you and your friend safely away from the Knot and the Loophole, we are going to resume the story from the point where Varluft has been mourned, and Malcom has disappeared with the satchel, and Nee-Reta has learned far too much about human frailty far too quickly.

To be absolutely clear—take note Robyn, there may be a hint here for you—we are going back to the first time Malcom came to Ochersfeldt, and the satchel was stolen, and Varluft was mourned. The original time, which the Gypsies watched replayed from Intuisha's cliffs, in which your yellow-veiled self appeared in the Witches' circle.

Robyn detects some ambiguity. Am I saying that she went *all the way back* to this original time during her dance, or that she simply crossed the Spiral to appear in the eddy/illusion?

Excellent question. Well done, my dear.

The rugs carried you across the Spiral more than once, Robyn, as you well know; but the *first* time was *the* first time, and necessarily so. It was the Coven's first clue that something strange would be coming round the Spiral. Your visit was too fleeting for the Witches to determine what exactly, or when. Nee-Reta's further adventures would soon enlighten them.

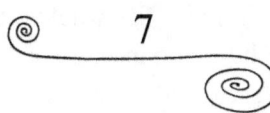

7

Nee Follows the Magic Satchel

NEE HAD BEEN THROUGH A GREAT DEAL IN THE PAST FEW DAYS. She had perfected Reta, been wooed by a handsome magician, learned to lie, stumbled into the Future then the Past, and seen true sadness for the first time when the Witches grieved for Varluft the Master Seer. Even Brunagwa mourned, who had recently threatened to kill him.

When the rites for Varluft were finished, Nee flew from her perch, circled the meadow twice, then winged hard in the direction of Foster Pond. This is where the young magician was thought to have headed. Sensing her resolve, none tried to interfere. Brunagwa returned contritely to her chalet without need of a Minder.

Safely beyond the Coven's second sight, Nee wheeled around. To follow Malcom she needed to understand the workings of the magic satchel. She had fetched that satchel herself from Oshi, and now she would return to question the Weaver about it. As she doubled back, she caught sight of a dog-shaped shadow below. It was Dark. He was sitting still as a statue, all of his attention trained on a distant marker—a signpost at the junction of two country lanes. Which road had Malcom taken? Nee was certain that Dark had watched him go, yet the shadow dog had not followed. Why? Was he unable?

Nee flapped loudly, briefly blocking the sun as she crossed overhead. Dark bristled, then leapt up at the sight of her. Together they began working their way up to Goathorns Peak, but there were places on the barren north side of the mountain where Dark could not follow. Nee would see him slip back into the woods, then later he would meet up with her again, running into the open so that she could glide low to bat his ear with her wing. At the treeline, Dark sat at attention, the way she had found him looking into the distance for Malcom. He would go no further. She bopped him affectionately one last time then glided up through the mist that always surrounds Oshi's perch at The Top of The World. Nee-Reta was not free to go just anywhere, but why was Dark held even more closely to the Goathorns? And why, being held so closely there, was he invisible to the other Goathorns denizens?

Nee paused frequently to rest on her long flight. The prey she needed for energy were growing scarce, the air felt thin. Her trek was so much longer than those first visits, when she had launched herself from the peak of Red Mountain. An updraft had carried her along the cut of the canyon wall to the high ridge above Intuisha's cliffs, from whence she flew easily to Oshi's loft. This trip was requiring great exertion just to reach the treeline, for the wind gusted unpredictably. It charged at her from one direction then another as if intentionally hindering her. She tried staying within the thin canopy of crooked trees that marched up the mountain with bent backs, but a sudden strong blast sent her crashing into a limb. Feeling lucky not have broken a wing, Nee ascended once more into the churning currents of air. Eventually she came to a place where even scrub oak and pine surrendered to the beaten verticality of Goathorns Peak, and only mosses and squat, clumpy flowers of the high desert survived.

Weary to her hollow bird bones, Nee shivered herself from the large red-tailed hawk into a smaller variety, a trick to conserve energy that Ti had taught her. Now she could maneuver closer to the ground to hunt, and make do on small rodents.

At last Nee detected a waft of smoke. Oshi's cabin was near. Nee fluttered to earth, then gracefully rose to her feet, smoothing her feathered frock. The chill mountain air refreshed Reta, and the smoke, which choked the hawk, smelled delectable to the woman. She ran with long, light strides the way Yani-Yau had taught her, and was soon within sight of Oshi's camp.

"Weaver Oshi, it is me again, Nee-Reta! Reta—Brunagwa's helper—remember?"

Oshi's ancient figure, folded nearly in half, toddled out of the beehive-shaped structure.

"What's the matter?" the old woman called back. "Is your Witch dissatisfied with her satchel?"

Reta loped forward and quickly closed the gap between them. She presented herself to Oshi on bended knee, less out of subservience than to allow the crippled elder to look at her without strain.

"The magic satchel has been stolen, Weaver, and I confess I played a part. The question is, is it meant to be or not? Some would say that Brunagwa oughtn't ever to have had such a thing. But if that was so, why would you make it for her? What troubles me most is not that she doesn't have it, but that none of us do. The thief has left the Goathorns. It is lost in the world with one who does not know the ways of it."

Oshi rubbed her knotted hands, taking this all in.

"Oh, and do you have something to eat?" Reta added.

"Hah!" the feeble woman erupted with surprising strength. "And now you know why I have to sell the magic satchels to any and all, even foolish Witches like Brunagwa. Everyone arrives here hungry. Come with me."

Reta followed Oshi. She had to duck as they passed between two heavy rugs that hung across the opening of the hogan-like shelter, but she could stand upright once inside. She went directly to the fire, which glowed invitingly in the center of the one big room, and plopped down onto another thick rug. She felt like she had landed in a soft nest. Oshi brought her a bowl of tuber mash with a crust of bread.

"You are too kind."

"I only want to keep you silent while I think," the Weaver groused. She shuffled out again, leaving Reta to her meal.

When her bowl was empty, Reta curled up on the marvelous rug Oshi had hand-tufted from yak wool, pulled a light blanket over herself, and fell sound asleep . . .

Now we are presented with a question: Is what happens next but the dream Reta dreams, there by the Weaver's fire, or did she wake and partake of Oshi's knowledge "for real" (as you Alternate-Worlders like to say)? Put that way, the question is ridiculous on its face, isn't it? "For real" Reta learned what she needed to know—little matter if Oshi instructed her through dreams or in the flesh. Trust me on this, and take the scene to come at face value. At The Top of The World there is no separation between anything—Past and Future, dreams and waking, your world and mine. Once Reta eats and sleeps in Oshi's place, she might as well be Oshi herself. No separation, I tell you—any vision that is available to Oshi may easily permeate the mind of Reta as well. And if, while Reta digests the information to which being Oshi entitles her, Oshi chooses to fly free as the young hawk Nee, that seems only a fair exchange. You see how it works at The Top of The World, at the place where the paths of the Spiral are joined? Everything is everything.

(Yes, Robyn, you are catching on—even fact and fiction are the same. You thought you were making a joke, but you are absolutely correct. See, you have proved my point.)

But we need not speak only of opposites. Even things of slight distinction become the same here at The Top of The World. A near truth is the same as the whole truth, noontime is the same as three p.m. Oshi is the same as every other Weaver who ever sat at a loom and sorted out the strands of Time...

Reta woke and heard the Weaver working at a loom. Oshi's voice seemed to come from above her head:

"Go outside, Reta, and climb up on that boulder that I have built my house against. It deflects the force of the north wind. If you brave that wind to climb to the top, you will have an excellent view. Go there and watch how the satchel travels and where it goes, with whom. Then come tell me. We'll work out together what is for good and for ill, and what you must do."

Obediently Reta rose and did as she was told, wearing Oshi's blanket over her shoulders.

"The boulder" turned out to be a good-sized hump of mountain, the peak of the peak, and the wind that was being channeled around and over it nearly blew Reta off her feet. She scrambled up the bulwark of Oshi's peculiar cabin—a cross between a yurt, a hogan and a castle keep—and found shelter in the rocky hollow between the building and the mountain.

As Reta shivered within Oshi's blanket, she noticed its unique properties—its clinginess and weight, how it could bunch up into tight ribs or expand into a loose netting. The blanket practically held on to Reta of its own accord. It gave her confidence. The slight but well-muscled woman sprang upon the rock and climbed to its flat summit against the increasing strength of that rushing airstream. She arrived at the place where few people have been—even the ones sporting a souvenir poncho proclaiming, The Top of The World.

Reta found room enough on the rock slab to sit cross-legged facing directly into the wind. She pulled Erhte's blanket over her head and shoulders like a hooded cape. It fit close to her ears, neck and bosom to keep her warm, with a fringe that protected her eyes yet permitted her to see, then fanned out around her with a porous weave that allowed the air to pass through instead of filling like a sail and carrying her off. Reta gently pulled this magical cloth—its resemblance to the magic satchel did not escape her—across the front of her lap and the rock she sat on, so that she was tented within it. She watched with amazement as the fringes on the bottom ends of the blanket grabbed the edges of the boulder in a tight grip.

Feeling anchored and secure, warm within the blanket and yet refreshed by the air flowing around her, Reta breathed deeply and put herself in mind of her encounter with Malcom, the last moment she had seen him. His face had been very close to hers as he held her cradled in his arms. She could taste his cinnamon breath as his lips hovered near hers. And then he'd drawn away and passed his hand over her eyes. When she woke, Malcom and the magic satchel were gone.

Reta opened her eyes and saw exactly what happened next, and then what was about to happen, and what would happen after that. It all made her exceptionally unhappy, from Malcom's inexcusable scene with Varluft, to his crooked path to Master Seerdom via every scoundrel in every side show he came upon, then his hideous stalking of the Gypsy Esmarelda, and his unconscionable experiments on his trusting apprentices. All the while, the satchel was with him, growing frayed and faded. Malcom brought it out often to examine and contemplate. He never actually used it, as far as Reta could see, though he got in it now and then. Every time Malcom brought the magic satchel from its hiding place to find it a little more tattered than before, he would rage and accuse whomever was at hand of having tampered with his things. They hadn't, though, as Reta perceived it. The magic satchel was wearing out due to natural, or perhaps supernatural, forces.

By now Reta was peering years into the future. Based on the satchel's state of wear, lying hidden there under Malcom's floorboards, she felt she was close to the time that would bring it back to the Goathorns. But there were more horrible events yet to transpire:

Malcom would find a way to put his consciousness into the body of a cat, and in this form he would go to Esmarelda, and in this form he would later be taken to the Alternate World in that worn-out satchel by his apprentice Mark. There the cat would be lost along with Brunagwa's satchel. At that point, people from the other side of the Spiral who had no business being involved would get involved, and one of them Reta understood to be the girl of the scene with Brunagwa and Ti, now grown up. The Gypsy and her man would go hither and yon trying to get back the bag, the cat, each other, et cetera.

Reta, having already seen the satchel in the hands of Esmarelda, found that she did not care so much about its upcoming adventures in the Alternate World. She was riveted to the saga of Malcom, and she feared that if she turned her attention away for one moment he would be lost. This was the magician's primary skill, after all—distraction, diversion. While one part of him was plaguing the poor black cat, and everyone chased after that unhappy creature, where was Malcom—the body of Malcom—and what sustained him? It was clear that Malcom the Master Seer had no intention of vacating his physical person for good. So, where might he stash it? Reta strained forward into the gale and fought to keep her concentration on Malcom, on his body lying within a woolen wrap on the table in his laboratory, and then simply melting away . . .

"Oh my! Stop!" What was happening? "Kee-ahrrr!" Without willing it, Reta was becoming Nee. The wind would tear the bird apart. She shrieked in panic. But she was transforming again, to nothing, no body, like Malcom. In order to know what he would become, she must become like him. And so she did, there at The Top of The World, where everything is everything.

He will discover the state of being that I take when I am between shapes, and a way to remain there. But I am whole, Reta thought, finding her substance had returned, *and he will be in pieces. When his body takes shape again, it will not be able to reunite with his spirit, and so it will perish.*

Reta looked into the future to see the apprentice Mark laying Malcom's remains to rest in a white ceremonial robe; then the black cat returning, quite alive absent Malcom's spirit; and Mark and the cat going on their way, freed from the Master Seer's service.

Reta closed her eyes and concentrated on the comforting weight of Oshi's blanket. She felt the fringes let go and swirl the empathic textile close around her in a warm hug. Imbued with the wisdom of Oshi, Reta found she could live with this outcome— that Malcom, having always lacked a moral compass, would later lose his mind, then the satchel, and then his life. The satchel would cause some trouble, but nothing terrible, and come back to Brunagwa in due course, safely in disrepair.

Reta nodded. It was resolved. The winds seemed to abate along with her fear and confusion. She had learned as much as she needed to know, and would go back to Brunagwa and wait patiently for the Gypsies to return the satchel. And she would think nothing more of Malcom—

"Malcom! No, no, it can't be! Stop! Get away!"

A blast of frigid wind pummeled Reta. She pulled her arms and knees to her chest, clutching the blanket tightly as the gust sent her tumbling backwards down the knobby hill in a tangle of textile and feathers. She skidded around and down to Oshi's cabin in a panic, stumbled inside, and collapsed by the fire.

. . .

"Were you frightened, child?"

Reta woke to find Oshi sitting nearby. The Weaver had pulled half of the blanket across her own lap, and was combing through the tangled fringe with her gnarled fingers.

"I thought the magician was dead. I saw him buried. I no longer loved him because I had seen his wickedness." Reta's mind echoed with roaring wind and unpleasant scenes. She trembled and inched closer to Oshi. "It was done, I thought. But then the spirit still lived, I felt it rush towards me. It wanted a new body, it was trying to steal mine!" Reta sobbed. Oshi continued to smooth the fringe impassively.

"It did not succeed, and it will not."

"But now I care for him again!" Reta wailed. "I hate him, I loathe him, I am ashamed of him, but he is torn apart and he suffers. And he wants to make others suffer too." Reta held her head in anguish. She had seen it all . . .

MALCOM ARRIVES IN OCHERSFELDT FOR THE SECOND TIME

The irony of being incorporeal, the Master Seer quickly learned, is that while you can know everything, you can do nothing. There can be no mixing of potions, no hypnotizing gaze. The all-knowingness itself is a hindrance. But Malcom the Master Seer had always been a persistent man in life, and after death—that dubious death—he patiently worked his way through the layers of knowing to arrive at a semblance of his former self, ego-wise. His own memories were the worst of it, as they kept pulling him back into the fear and confusion of his last days. Over and over he braced himself for the pain, but it would not come, would never come again. The anticipation of pain was the torment he willed himself beyond. Then he entered a state of contentment that was even more unendurable, for to be content—to be passive, to relax at all—was to come dreadfully close to the void. No body would wake him, no itch of desire would spur him to act— Act? He couldn't act. He shouldn't want to. He should subside, surrender.

Malcom the Master Seer did not intend to surrender. A victim of his own ill-conceived magic, he would not admit defeat or error. The concept was not even present once he had wound his way back through the fear, confusion, and that perilous content-ment, all the way to desire.

He wanted and so he lived.

Now he wanted a body. A body to want with some more. To want and to get. Because with the things he had learned, with the discipline he had attained, he was certain he could get whatever he wanted. But first he required a body. And he knew exactly where to get one.

Varluft removed his jewelry so as to be more comfortable while he napped at his desk with his cheek resting on his forearms. He did not expect the young magician to be away for very long. The fortune had told that the quest would not be successful. The Master Seer of Ochersfeldt would be free to go to his final slumber. He was eager for it. Was there any point in waiting? True, he had promised. Varluft had never failed to keep a promise. So, he merely rested, allowing his life force to seep away slowly in preparation for the last.

This sleepy emptying of the Master Seer Varluft's soul made room for Malcom's dislodged spirit to usurp the body. The transfer was far easier than Malcom expected. His only difficulty was quelling his excitement at again being embodied. Even the decrepit person of Varluft was a thrill after what he had been through. Malcom knew it would not satisfy for long, but it didn't have to. This was only the first step.

Varluft offered no resistance when Malcom gently roused the body and prepared to meet his younger self. He adorned himself in Varluft's jewels, bracing for the wily Master Seer to spring his trap. But even the amulets seemed to be drained of life. Malcom had a fleeting moment of sympathy for tired old Varluft. He decided he was helping the old man by accelerating this last act. He composed himself. Any moment now . . .

The young magician came crashing in with the stolen magic satchel, to be met by his bitter older self in Varluft's body. The voice was Varluft's, the lines were Varluft's, repeated word for word as they were seared into memory.

"The stone told true!"

Young Malcom hurled the stone.

And Varluft, instead of stopping the stone with his magic, stepped forward and was killed. He crumpled to his knees and fell hard onto his face. Young Malcom dropped down beside the broken body in shock, and in that moment of confusion the soul of his future self escaped the withered body and swarmed into the young one.

All in a rush, they were one. Everything the older Malcom knew, the younger did too. How could he resist? Why should he want to? All of the hard-won knowledge and power of accumulated years had become his in a blink. Not only that, he knew what to do with it. Young Malcom suddenly had a clear objective, something more solid than his broad ambitions for occult power. He wanted the Gypsy Esmarelda. He could woo her properly now, as a young buck. He could use Brunagwa's satchel to find her in the right Time, to anticipate and control every event to make her fall in love with him. No misunderstandings. No mistakes. He would leave nothing to chance.

"Feathers are not meant to get so wet," Oshi chided the sobbing Reta. "And my poor blanket. Stop sniveling into it." Oshi gave a tug; the blanket slithered out of Reta's hands and curled up in the Weaver's lap. "Is that the end of your dream?"

"No."

"Then why do you stop?"

Reta hugged herself, pouting. "He's supposed to love *me.*"

"Do you love *him*?"

"He's awful."

"Well then?"

"Esmarelda doesn't love him! She's supposed to love George Drumm!"

"What if she never meets George Drumm?"

"Oh!" Reta beat her fists on the ground in frustration.

"Stop that. My poor rug." Oshi petted the yak hair.

"Oh, the rugs! Wait 'til you hear this part."

"I would prefer not to wait any longer, child."

Here Reta continued her story. I will go on retelling it in my own words, because typing is wearying enough without having to transcribe all that blubbering.

The second time around, Malcom himself called the Sprites and announced the death of Varluft, declaring himself the sorcerer's heir. He felt confident that he would be able to defend his claim if it were contested, for he had the strength of a young man combined with the knowledge of a Master Seer. But no one came forward to challenge him. The estate, with its structures, gardens, canals, and invisible servants all submitted to him. Malcom the new Master Seer of Ochersfeldt took residence in Blue Quarter and commenced his project.

Unfortunately, the magic satchel did not bend to Malcom's command. He could not decipher its secrets, and dared not seek answers from any Witches or Weavers who might discover his own. Not to worry, he told himself, a Master Seer could concoct his own magic conveyance there amid the magical artisans of Ochersfeldt. Malcom's disastrous adventures with the cat had come to seem like success, or at least something to build on, now that he had a second chance.

Finding his way out of the Blue Quarter and Varluft's maze was young Malcom's job. He proceeded jauntily across the canals, taking only right turns, while the new Master Seer muttered fretfully in his head:

"A weaver, a weaver, my boy. Find us the best of them down in the valley, and don't even think about going up the mountain. Find me a witchy one. Or better yet, a genie—one who's been with the caravans, or out and about with the Ethalees, those nomads Esmarelda spoke of." The two magicians shivered with double delight at the mere mental utterance of her name.

This backseat driving ruined young Malcom's concentration,

and he had to go across twelve footbridges instead of the usual six to get out of Blue Quarter.

When he had finally crossed over to Gold Quarter, Malcom decided to start at the feather merchant's house, since it had brought him luck before, or luck had led him to it. He soon discovered that the hand of fate was still upon him, for there where the feather merchant had lived, three hovels had been gutted and redone into one big workshop, freshly plastered and whitewashed. The door was propped open, and there was some traffic in and out under a sign that read E. ARAP, TEXTILE TRADES.

Malcom, now two magicians in one, did not exactly talk to himself. There were two inner voices, both aware of the other. The older was the stronger and could have drowned out the younger, but he needed his younger self, and gave him free rein as much as possible to keep him cooperative. The instant this younger persona became disinterested or daydreamy, the Master Seer took charge to urge them onward with his schemes.

Upon encountering the establishment of E. Arap, the inner response of the Malcoms went something like this:

'Look, look, here where the feather merchant was. Exactly the sort of place we need. Though I don't know what Textile Trades means. Do we need a textile to trade for the sort we want? Perhaps an "r" was left out and it means "Traders"—but then, perhaps the trades could be such as weaving and fringes and felting and whatnot. I do wonder—'

'Walk inside and ask the old man if he makes flying carpets.'

'It can only mean trades, just as it says. Why else would it be here? Fate dictates it should be. This is how I become great. I will simply go inside and ask if they make flying carpets. That is what I require, that is what I will ask for. This is Ochersfeldt. No one will blink.'

'Ask the old one.'

'But, to be safe, I will make sure to look for the old master of the place. Arap himself. The elder. Yes, that will do it.'

'Then do it already. (I do not remember being such an ninny at this age.)'

Malcom crossed the street and strode into the shop. The old man of the shop—there is an old man in every shop—shuffled over to greet them.

"Arap." He put his palms together and tilted his head in a token bow. "How can I help you, sir."

Malcom, a head taller than Arap, scanned the room before lowering his eyes to the old man. Arap was completely bald and clean-shaven, lacking even eyebrows. He was dressed in loose trousers and tunic of excellent gray linen. His only adornments were a pair of thick glasses with finely filigreed silver frames, and a pair of bright red slippers with long, pointed toes that curled upward. He also had a bright white hankie with which to pat his perspiring brow.

"Magic!" Arap exclaimed, noticing Malcom notice the hanky. To Malcom's annoyance, the two other customers in the shop turned to watch.

"Never dirties. Look, I blow my nose into it," he honked wetly, then held up a pristine square. "Nothing!" He turned the fabric this way and that.

"You just made a noise with your mouth," Malcom accused with good humor.

"So you think. Show me your shoe."

Malcom bent his knee and showed the bottom of a damp boot. Arap wiped it clean of mud and bruised grass, clasping Malcom's ankle and really applying some pressure.

"Ta da!" The bottom of Malcom's boot was clean, and so was the cloth.

"Amazing!"

"Remarkable!"

Both spectators asked the assistant for some magic hankies and turned back to their business.

"Very impressive," Malcom agreed, growing more impressed as he handled the product. "This is proof positive that I have come to the right place—presuming your magic extends to something bigger than a handkerchief."

"Indeed it does, good sir. What do you have in mind? No, no, not here. Come to my office for tea."

A long afternoon of tea drinking and negotiations ensued, but there was never any doubt that a deal would be struck. Arap guessed Malcom's identity as the sorcerer Varluft's heir. He was an old friend of Varluft's. Had not Malcom seen him at the funeral? They laughed at that, for nearly everyone in attendance except the Sprites had been in disguise. By end of day, a partnership had been forged, and young Malcom's first real friendship in Ochersfeldt.

The Malcoms returned to Blue Quarter quietly. The Master Seer Malcom was troubled by something but he could not put his finger on it, and he did not want to disturb the other's peace of mind. He rested. The younger one entertained fantasies of the Gypsy Esmarelda.

They launched the first flying carpet only two weeks later. It was small, more like a kite, with a bright rainbow spiral pattern. Arap showed Malcom how to wave his arms over the colors to make them swirl to life. The fibers of the textile vibrated, and then the rug levitated—higher, higher—circled slowly above the shop, and then fell with a heavy thud onto Malcom's head.

"You're going to have to work up some magic on your side, my friend, if you expect to make my flying carpets do your bidding," Arap chided.

"Of course. Now I see what you have in mind." The Malcoms were pleased despite being knocked over onto the dusty road. Malcom rose, brushing off his trousers. I'll work on the spell. You work on making a rug large enough to hold me."

Arap had Malcom step on a scale, and then told him not to eat any cakes until their job was done.

A month passed, or was it a year? Hard to tell in Ochersfeldt. The carpets were now of good size and could circumnavigate all of Gold Quarter. With a passenger who knew how to control them, they would fly straight across Blue Quarter to the eastern edge of the city. Yet time after time Malcom was dumped into Far Last Canal. At first, the carpets fell with him. He dragged each one back to Arap, furious.

"Make me a flying carpet that will leave Ochersfeldt!" he demanded.

The next flying carpet dumped Malcom in the canal and flew off without him. Arap said this was progress. They kept at it.

After a year, or maybe after ten years—so hard to tell in Ochersfeldt, and neither Malcom nor Arap appeared to have aged a day—a couple of dozen flying carpets had escaped into the world without a rider. The Master Seer was in no condition to judge objectively how time passed, or if they were or were not progressing at a reasonable rate. He fed his younger self's imagination with vivid memories of Esmarelda, trusting that the young man's natural urges would drive them forward.

Frustrations began to grow all around. The Malcoms were relentless and sometimes abusive to Arap. Arap said that it was obvious by now that the flying carpets could not leave Ochersfeldt—they either fell or flew off into nothingness.

"Nothingness? What makes you say that?" Malcom sneered. "How do you know they are not lost in the mountains, or sitting in someone else's shop, or shuttling the Witches around? How do you know they haven't gone to the Gypsies without me, dammit?"

"In all this time, you could have found the Gypsies twice or thrice over on your own, couldn't you? Why haven't you done it? Why haven't you gone into the Goathorns to find the rugs, if you think them lost? I'll not go—an old man like me would never withstand the lust of the Witches—but I would've thought a young starter like you would be game. Why, you haven't even been around Ochersfeldt to look for the rugs. If you don't think they dematerialize once they get away from us, why aren't you out looking for them? I know old Varluft was a recluse, but did he make you into one as well? Maybe the trouble isn't with my flying carpets so much as with you," Arap goaded.

Young Malcom had nothing to say to this. An alarm went off in the mind of his other—Arap was right, the Malcoms' behavior had not been normal. For the first time in the year or the decade since they had been working on their project, Malcom the Master Seer spoke to Arap in his own voice.

"I agree. We must gather our things and continue the work on the outskirts of town. We should go to the far side of the Goathorns and launch from the High Road. Then I can fly straight across the plains without interference from the Coven."

Arap responded to the new authority in Malcom's voice. The plan was clearly not to his liking, but he resolutely began to gather his supplies. "We will need a cart," he said over his shoulder, not meeting Malcom's eye. "And you are in charge of getting us past the Witches."

The Malcoms stormed out. The Master Seer thought that something was very wrong, and his young self was agitated by his suspicions.

"You *don't* want to go anywhere, do you?" The older spoke his thoughts directly to the younger. "What happened to you? You're not the man who turned into *me*." It was a cruel joke. He had entered his young self and then stunted him . . .

The word, "stunted." Varluft had used it when he sent Malcom to the Goathorns the first time. And here they were going back. The young man was inadequate, clearly. Varluft had been right. Well then, the Master Seer would take another body. Arap was not young, but he had talent and gumption. He would do for the interim. Somewhere on the trail, away from his magic workshop, Arap would let down his guard, and Malcom the Master Seer would take him. Then they would get the job done, once the two elders put their heads together, literally. As for the young body with which to woo Esmarelda? If the Master Seer's timing was right, that would be provided by none other than George Drumm. Brilliant. It could only be fate.

"You frighten me, child. What are you thinking?"

Reta's tantrum had stopped as suddenly as it had begun; her fists hovered above the yak hair rug, the tears dried on her cheeks. She lowered her hands to her lap and fingered the feathers of her dress thoughtfully.

Of course Oshi knew what the young Minder was thinking, but it would have to be spoken aloud in order to be refuted. Reta complied in a cajoling, sing-song voice.

"Oshi, could I not go back and prevent all of this from happening? Here I am at The Top of The World seeing all that was, is, and will be, while you weave Time into being. What would be the harm of unraveling just a tad and giving me a re-do? I needn't have stolen the magic satchel from Brunagwa. Had I not, I would still have met Malcom. I could help him on his vision quest instead of letting him return to Varluft with the satchel only to disappoint and be disappointed. Both he and Varluft could be spared; the world saved from a bitter, powerful man; Esmarelda and George saved from—"

"Ever meeting?" Oshi asked pointedly. "If the satchel is not stolen, then likely Esmarelda never meets Malcom, and so she never goes back in Time to flee him, and never meets George Drumm either. And George never goes forward to find her in her own Time."

"But that is not to say they would never meet." Reta had overheard the lovers' own conversation on this matter. "George would be an older man to Esmarelda, but only ten years, not so uncommon. If their love is meant to be, age is not a hindrance. And it would sit better all-in-all with the sisters. George's jumping ahead in Time looks like a flaw to them. Won't they try to fix it, if I don't?"

Oshi nodded. "I am impressed with you, Reta-Nee. You have been buffeted about in Time in recent days, yet have kept your wits. You have taken in strange experiences to become wise beyond your years, where a lesser soul would recoil. How shall I instruct you, Reta-Nee? I can give my assent to your unraveling the Past. And then I need not say more, for the Future will unfurl again differently and, whatever is to come, all of us must ride it out. Or, I can forbid you to skip backward to re-set the Spiral on the grounds that too many strands are already in motion— Esmarelda and George Drumm being but one tiny pattern among an infinite number—and many lives hinge on the Now going forward, come what may."

"You are saying that if I choose to go back and do things differently, you will give me no guidance."

"I cannot give what I do not have."

"But you wouldn't stop me."

"No. You are a Minder. You must do what you think best."

"And if I think it best *not* to re-do this past week?"

"Then the Future will be coming at us exactly as you have seen, and patience will bring you to the time of Malcom's return to the Goathorns and the creation of the rugs, and the Gypsy's return to the Goathorns with Brunagwa's satchel. And, having tasted these events already on the wind that blows across The Top of The World, we might discuss how you can be prepared when they come to pass, and put to rights all that appears to be going so very wrong."

Reta thought this over carefully while absently petting the yak fur rug. Having seen the Future, how would she ever find the patience to let it play out? What would she do with all the intervening years before the satchel, and Malcom, came back to the Goathorns?

"Reta-Nee?" Oshi prompted, for the shadows grew long, and the Weaver had her day's work to complete.

"Nee-Reta!" the Minder corrected sharply—and the question was answered. Reta might be troubled by such thoughts as this long day had brought, but Nee lived for the seasons, the wood, the breezes, and mountain life. And for Dark, her secret friend. She would never want to undo Dark. So long as he was there, she would not be lonely or impatient. All this time that she had seen ahead—throughout the future exploits of Malcom, Esmarelda, and George Drumm—where had *she* been, Nee-Reta? Right there in the Goathorns, of course. With Dark, with the Coven, with the Familiars. It was her home, her family. There was no need for undoing. The things that would happen on the *outside* were not her concern. All things lost would return to the Goathorns in time, and Nee-Reta need only make sure that she and her friends would be ready.

"Well, Nee-Reta?"

"You know my answer, Weaver." Reta fluttered briefly into a feathery state of hardly-there before returning to her human form. "I am neither a weaver nor an unraveller. My task is to mind."

Oshi was pleased at how much the young Minder had learned in her short stay at The Top of The World. She took Nee-Reta to her spinning wheel and loom to reward her with a story.

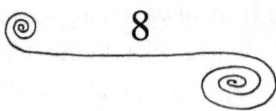

8

The Weaver's Loom Remembers

ROBYN WOULD LIKE TO KNOW MORE ABOUT TIME AND THE TOP of The World. She rightly surmises that this is where the Spiral turns in on itself, where the one of our alternating worlds that flowed in, flows out; and the other, which flowed out, flows in. But so what? The snake is biting his own tail, and everything is everything. All it amounts to is chaos. Not really a nice place to visit. Not always or very enlightening, and sometimes downright deceptive.

For instance, this Dark. Nee-Reta has thought of him in the Weaver's presence, but there is no indication that Oshi knew of the creature. I certainly didn't, and wasn't I there with them all that time ago when Reta thought those thoughts? Yet they have only come clear to me now, with this word-by-word sweeping away of cobwebs. And I watched Nee-Reta for all the years that were to come, and I never saw this dog-shadow she doted on.

What did make an impression, at the time, was the lookback to the sisters whom the Familiars served—how they came to settle in the Goathorns and form their coven. This was the fragment of history that Oshi chose to reveal to Nee-Reta. Witnessing this as I did, I was profoundly affected by my journey to The Top of The World. I would return from Oshi's hilltop a willing servant to the Goathorns Coven, whereas up 'til then my cooperation had been grudging and lackadaisical.

Reta was also moved by the Coven's story. From this time forward, she too undertook her duties with a deeper respect for the Witches, and a greater sense of the honor of being a Familiar. Yet, in all the while Brunagwa's magic satchel worked its way round the great wide world, Nee-Reta never spoke of what we had learned about the Redfern family. And I, being an outcast, had no one to tell.

But now I have you, my Readers. (We can pretend, anyway, can't we, Robyn?) Settle in. I have had a change of venue since writing the above paragraphs, and my Editor has suffered a suspenseful gap in my correspondence while still laboring on for A.G. Brooks in the Alternate World. I warned her that I was going to be "off line" for a while, and there was no way to predict how long. She would have to trust, like I was trusting, that the forces of the Goathorns were intent on closing the Loophole, and therefore would aid me in fulfilling our plans.

As it turns out, "aid" would be putting it strongly, but here I am, regardless. I will reveal exactly where in due course. Robyn's wait has been a tad longer than expected (alright, days— sorry) because, apparently, we are no longer synched up. I have returned to my side of the Spiral to find Time running differently here. I'm counting this a good sign. There have been some positive developments whilst I dallied at Kestrel Lodge, but too much is still all knotted up—and too much of it to do with *moi*.

Well, my predicament is to my Editor's benefit. I find myself with untold time in yet another distasteful location, with my fate in limbo, during which to keep my promise to spill all of the magic beans. (You see, I am making it up to you.)

We left off with Nee-Reta lingering at The Top of The World, watching Oshi's spinning wheel go round and round and round and . . .

Night fell. Nee-Reta would not be able to start her descent from Goathorns Peak until morning. The Weaver dozed in her rocker. Reta continued to read the threads of the Past like a book, and I was able to follow along mind to mind. If she sensed me nearby, she was as circumspect as I.

Herewith is the knowledge we gained that night, which is the origin of the five sisters, one of whom owns my heart.

DEANNALISA

The arranged marriage of the milliner's daughter to the taxidermist's son was a happy match for all. The fathers sometimes transacted business around fancy feathers and small decorative rodents and birds that the milliner bought from the taxidermist to use on his hats. The bride and groom had thus known each other and each other's families from childhood. Pushed toward romance, they found it easy to fall in love. All of Ochersfeldt rejoiced.

Ochersfeldt was a small town then, or really two. On the north side of Red River was Appleton, today's Red Quarter; to the south and west was Harp of Gold, a farming village above the valley, not much changed from then 'til now. Today's Blue Quarter was a marshy floodplain where a few industrious pioneers were attempting to channel the water's flow and create dry land to build on. The Green Quarter, once a dense primordial wood, had been gradually cleared for pasture lands. Instead of the great crystalline city glimmering on the northwest shore of Red River—as has become the iconic image associated with modern Ochersfeldt—lay a rolling swath of green and gold grasses framed by a dark, dense backdrop of immense trees.

(Remember how Malcom discovered that Ochersfeldt has more streets than would seem to fit in the available space? Well, we are up against the same problem with the town's history. The creation of the Quarters shall have to remain—I beg you, Editor—a tale for another day.)

The young couple, both from the Harp of Gold side of town, were married in the new red brick courthouse in Appleton, with its view of majestic Red Mountain. Afterwards, a festive picnic was held on the bank of the Red River to get the pair off to a good start. Bride and groom were loving, the marriage harmonious, and both families prospered. But after the first, second and third daughters were born, the groom's family grew worried for the inheritance of the taxidermy business, and the bride's family were equally worried for their millinery.

One might think that any young woman would be amenable to learning the hat trade, but Deannalisa found the environment unhealthy. She would no more allow her daughters into her father's shop than into her husband's. The taxidermy business was loathsome to her, though she did not blame her husband or his family. She kept far from it, and she used the little girls as her excuse—the foul odor of the preserving agents and glues was surely poisonous to their small bodies, the aura of death would sicken their souls.

"Then give me a hearty son," her impatient but not unkind husband demanded.

Deannalisa wanted to please and be loved, she wanted to obey and contribute. When a caravan of Gypsies came to town, she went to their fortune-telling wagon and found a woman of untellable age with a knowing sparkle in her eye. Soon, several colorful cards were laid out. They told the young mother's story with frightening accuracy.

The cards told so true, in fact, that Deannalisa was afraid to see any card turned on the Future.

"No, do not tell me what will be, as though I have no say in the matter," she begged the Gypsy. "I've come here for advice on how to make my fate come out right."

"Brave girl, ask away." The Gypsy scooped up the cards and hid them in her sleeve.

"You have seen my plight. The next child must be a son. Tell me how to make sure it *will* be."

"You need to make peace with your husband's work so you can welcome the son who will carry it on. Do not trouble your small daughters, but go into the taxidermy shop on your own. Let it be a time when your husband is away but returning, so he can find you there. Look at his work, see how skilled it is, how lifelike the animals. Think not of the sorrow of their deaths, but the honor of being able to look upon their beauty, to admire their purpose and each attribute that—were they alive—would prevent you from being near them or even seeing them at all. Would you walk right up to the moose to rub his nose? Would you draw near to the bear to study his mighty paws and claws?"

Deannalisa shook her head and shivered.

"And the owl," the fortune teller went on, "shall never pose for you on a low limb in the light of day while you contemplate the patterns within patterns of her feathered breast. These are the gifts of your husband's craft, and good fortune awaits his son. Accept all that is the man you love, including his work. If he is capable of giving you a boy, he will." The strangely knowing woman rummaged something out of her deep skirt pocket. "This might help as well. Put it in the wine or mead you will both drink before making the baby."

A tiny, corked vial half-filled with bluish liquid was passed across the table. Deannalisa pulled a small cloth sack from her cleavage, removed some coins and put in the vial, then returned the purse to her ample hiding place. She thanked the Gypsy, leaving the coins. When she was well away from the Gypsy camp, Deannalisa took out the vial and threw it into the river, because she had not liked the woman's funny smirk at the end.

Poor Deannalisa, she followed all of the Gypsy's other advice—it was good advice for a woman who loved her husband—but disposed of the one thing that might actually have increased her chances of giving birth to a son.

The Redfern family's business employed everyone who could

call themselves a relative, and it encompassed a small compound on Redfern Lane. There was the collectibles shop streetside, adjacent the workshop for preparing furs, hides, mooseheads and complete specimens; across a small courtyard were the barracks and kitchen. Knowing her husband and his kin to be away to the High Road on rumors of a herd of bison grazing in the plains beyond, Deannalisa went directly to the taxidermy shop. The men had left before dawn and would be back for midday meal, which Redfern's mother and aunts were busy preparing in the kitchen outbuilding. Deannalisa had the workshop to herself, as she had hoped and feared. She found a grotesque scene in which a variety of animals lay at all stages of being gutted, stretched, stuffed and sewn. She forced herself to look carefully at each completed and in-progress specimen. She was especially upset by one of these beasts, which she felt still shimmered with energy as if its soul had been captured up in an aura that floated warily above its abused physical form.

Yes, there were Minders among the poor creatures under remodel, and Deannalisa was able to perceive them, though it would be years before she knew their name or nature. She only knew that certain of the animals possessed a life force more tenacious than the others. Could the Redferns not see it? She had to know if those who worked in the shop really failed to notice how some of the animals still had souls that lived and suffered.

The men came back from their hunt with their massive prize. Young Redfern greeted his wife delightedly, and she made much of the great bison. To her relief, it was quite dead. It did not show any signs of the lingering second life of the newly mounted brown bear, which would soon be moved over to the store. When she complimented her husband on the completion of the bear, watching him carefully, he gave no indication that he noticed anything special about the bear, or that there had been any trouble working with it. She felt he was sincere, and that the others were innocent as well.

Puzzled, Deannalisa Redfern hid her concern for the family trade behind dutiful attention to her husband and in-laws. She was still willing to provide a son to work in the business—she would secretly train him to recognize the special animals, so he might eventually help her to free them...

Deannalisa grew and grew for ten months. She and young Redfern were certain to have an heir of heroic proportions. Even after the first girl child came out, there was hope for a son. But after more long hours of agonizing labor, the twin was a girl as well. Deannalisa sensed that her married life was doomed, but she did not curse the Gypsy—the demands of caring for the twin girls would save her from dealing with the taxidermy shop for the time being. Still, the peculiar animals haunted her.

Over time, several more such creatures were slain by the Redferns. (This feat indicates some magical qualities on the paternal side, but second sight was not among them. Perhaps being dense about the souls of others was itself their special talent.) One by one, the animals were prepared and then moved into the store. But they were never sold in all the years that passed while Deannalisa raised her daughters. When the girls were old enough not to need so much mothering, Deannalisa went to work in the gallery, and these animals were still there. They spoke, and she was the only one who could hear them. Their spirits cursed the petrified forms that could no longer house them, and huddled possessively close. Deannalisa was at a loss as to how to help, but she kept them company and watched over them, and she made sure they were not discarded. She swore that she would not rest until they were released and made whole. A troubling amount of time would pass before she could keep her promise, but keep it she did.

In her determination not to let go of the special animals, Deannalisa became a successful saleswomen for the other pieces. Soon she was put in charge of the whole retail operation. She taught her kinswomen how to make clever leather and felt costumes for some of the more common species, and these—such as the Ochersfeldt Owl in liederhosen—sold well to the tourists.

With the family members busy making crafts, Deannalisa needed help in the store. Hesterluna, Brunagwa and Sestorina were grown and were off to other places. (Between them, the elder daughters would have a great many experiences, as we shall learn.) And so the twins were recruited to work in the taxidermy gallery. Their mother was glad for the psychic assistance of her twin girls, whose propensity for second sight had begun to show. Plus, they were big and strong, which would be important.

You see, given the speed with which Deannalisa sold the "standard" pieces, and the stubborn unpopularity of the others, the proportion of specimens on display was leaning more and more heavily toward those freakish ones. The spirits were beginning to interact and draw strength from each other. More than once, Deannalisa had been startled out of a quiet reverie by a shocking vision of the animals that surrounded her coming to life and destroying the store, the shop, and all of her relatives. She brought Intuisha and Dremtessa into the store and begged them to help keep the creatures in check.

The twins had already perceived the hidden half-lives of the animals on their occasional visits to the store. Daytime visits. They had also been sneaking into the shop at night, when they encouraged the living forces to persist and organize. They didn't tell this to their mother. They did confess that they had consulted the local magician, Varluft, and he was eager to help free the animals. His first suggestion was to bring home the other sisters, so that there would be five to make a Witches' coven that could marshal the powers of the forest to take back its lost souls.

It was barely thought, and it was done.

The sisters came home, worldly and wild. Varluft, still hearty in his late middle-age, had a time of it keeping them and himself focused on the task at hand. There was never any question that the Redfern daughters had the right stuff (as you say) for magic.

Deannalisa devised a way to protect her husband's family from the upheaval to come. To start, she brought all five daughters into the store as clerks. The robust young women were irresistible. In the space of a week, every single item that they were willing to sell was sold. Deannalisa presented the proceeds to her mother-in-law, and recommended that the Redfern clan repair to their mountain camp for the hot month ahead. The men could hunt. They could all clear their lungs of glue and sawdust.

The matriarch, suddenly enamored of her granddaughters, was itching to begin matchmaking. Before assenting to the vacation, she made Deannalisa promise she wouldn't let any of them "get away again." The sisters had a good laugh over that, and then plunged into their preparations.

On the night of the Summer Solstice, with the Redfern clan safely away, the five sisters gathered to perform their first ritual together. They enacted their rites under the guidance of a modest magician named Varluft and the watchful eye of their mother, Deannalisa. It was not long before a brown bear, a cougar, a wild stallion, and others came meandering through the streets of Ochersfeldt.

These were all simple, mortal animals of the mountains and foothills. Submitting readily to the Witches' magic, they accepted the homeless spirits from the taxidermy shop into their bodies. But it was not a gentle scene. The animals became wild upon being enlivened by the Minder spirits. They tore up the place and came near to killing each other. Residents of the area gathered round, and more came hurriedly from farther away. Things were quickly getting out of hand.

Varluft brought the riot to a standstill by hurtling into the air like a rocket and bursting into the shape of a giant eagle. He dove into the crumbling compound and shielded the women with his massive wings as they fled. Then he harried the animals with beak and claw and wing to get them moving quickly over the cobblestones, out to the river, and up toward the mountains. The last to go was the stallion. Shooting sparks from his heels, he set the Redfern compound ablaze. While the townsfolk shrank back from the inferno, aghast and unwilling to intervene in such supernatural events, Varluft shrieked at the women. They understood his magic language and followed his instructions.

The twins, giantesses even then, bundled up their stricken mother like a babe and took turns carrying her through dark, narrow back alleys and along quiet country lanes to Wand Way. The older sisters stumbled along behind, barely able to keep up. Then the women struck off from the road and commenced slowly upward toward Six Hills. It was a long up-and-down journey on a night strangely devoid of animal sounds or even rustling leaves, as though Nature held its breath while the women fled.

In the first light of dawn, the dark silhouette of an eagle crossed the sky. They followed it through the valleys of the Six Hills to a place with shelter and pasture, an overgrown orchard and a charred ruin of a summer camp. When they fell exhausted to the ground at the edge of the orchard, they found ripe fruit at hand with which to replenish themselves. The eagle flew off, and in time Varluft came to them.

Deannalisa begged the magician for a potion to end her life. She had destroyed all that belonged to the Redferns, and even deprived them of potential heirs. Varluft refused; her daughters pleaded with her. But Deannalisa said it would be done with or without their help. All she wanted now was to know that the restored ones were safe.

"Safe and near at hand even as we speak," Varluft told her.

"Yes, they know to be near, because we have made a pact, they and I. When those poor souls felt their fate was sealed, and they must expire to put an end to their torture, I promised I would set them free. But I could not promise when; and all I had to offer day after day, year after year, was a promise in the midst of more suffering. They pleaded with me to let go of them, and I pleaded with them to persist. And all the while they watched the

others that had been killed and dressed—often very disrespect-
fully, on my instruction—come and go. A sad compromise, for
which I knew I must someday do penance. A stronger woman
would have put an end to the entire operation as soon as she
discovered—"

Here Deannalisa was cut off by her daughters' protests.

"Have it as you will," she continued when they let her. "But
I have done all that I set out to do except this: to die, and to give
my body to the Minders for their first sustenance. This is what
we have agreed to, and I am ready. You cannot know how tired
these years of secrets and sorrows have made me."

There was no more arguing with her, for she had spoken with
her last breath. She fell heavily into her daughters' arms even as
they reached out to comfort her. A great keening rose from them,
and was joined by the groans and howls of all manner of forest
animal.

Varluft raised his voice above the ruckus, "They are gathering
in the meadow. Come, sisters, we must fulfill your mother's final
wish."

Brunagwa lurched toward the magician and took him by the
throat. "I think those beasts will find you just as good a meal as
this poor woman."

A test of wills ensued, with the sisters and the magician
challenging each other back and forth with spells and mind
puzzles. Varluft soon prevailed over the five novices. He broke
free and became the eagle, whose voice they could not deny.

"Hear me, women! You must surrender the remains of
Deannalisa to set her soul free. Did she ever break a promise in
her life? Will you be the cause of her breaking one now?"

Falling back in despair and grief, the women saw the great
eagle clutch the bundle of bones that had been their mother in its
talons. It flew with Deannalisa's remains toward the meadow that
capped a small plateau standing halfway between Six Hills and
the High Road. The sisters regrouped and quickly began to climb

to the crest of the northernmost hill, joining their lament to that
of the howling animals. Soon they stood above the meadow
where they could watch what transpired.

The eagle cautiously deposited Deannalisa's body in the center
of the meadow, now ringed with predators of all kinds. The
animals had grown quiet with his approach. When he flew off,
the meadow became completely silent. The blankets had fallen
away from Deannalisa. She lay there as gracefully as one asleep.
It was all her daughters could do not to run to her to try to wake
her. They held each other back and gazed upon her, appreciating,
perhaps for the first time, her beauty and gentility. She was not
so old, after all. Her cares had aged her beyond her years.

The animals had not moved. The sisters could not tell which
were the re-enlivened animals from the shop, or which were the
common animals from the woods. They understood that a spell
had been cast. Something more was yet to happen. What was
Varluft up to now?

But the new shape against the dawn sky was not Varluft's
eagle. It was a red-tailed hawk. The twins in their superior
second sight immediately recognized it as a "special one"—kin
to those they'd just released—but one who had always been free,
who had not been crippled by the torment of the taxidermists.
Dremtessa and Intuisha rejoiced in the creature's power. They
told their sisters to shed their anger and fear so they might help
with the magic.

The hawk glided high over Deannalisa's body, and a pale
thread of something like smoke spiraled out of the lifeless form
and into the breast of the regal bird. Then the hawk flapped hard
away. A long cry sliced the silence in its wake.

"Kee-ahrrr!"

The beasts that had been ranged around the meadow sprang
toward the form that was no longer Deannalisa. The sisters
bowed their heads in awe and horror. For better or worse, they
and the Goathorns were forever changed. Their mother's spirit

had been taken into the heart of a unique being, and her body was being taken as nourishment for the magical mountain life. They themselves had been transformed into a coven of Witches. And Varluft, who had been just one of many corner magicians in Ochersfeldt, would, when word of his doings spread, become the town's Master Seer.

Sad to say that despite Deannalisa's precautions the Redferns were not spared. Their mountain camp, off to the southeast in the foothills of the slopes that lead to The Top of The World, suffered a devastating fire in those same dawn hours when Varluft's eagle was leading the women to Six Hills. Those who weren't suffocated or burned to death did not fare well in the forest, where an unusual number of predatory animals had gathered.

No need to be sentimental, Robyn. The events described are far into the Past. Ti the red-tailed hawk was ancient even then. But the taking in of Deannalisa's vital force at once renewed her life, gave her a protective spirit toward the Goathorns Coven, and led to her eventual mastery of the human form (all on her own, I might add, after she saw that Brunagwa *must* have a Familiar). In no way did Deannalisa, that broken woman, take over Ti; but the woman whom Ti created, Wyan, might be said to be a product of them both. Ti-Wyan is the embodiment of creative forces imbued with boundless love. Her successor, Nee-Reta, exhibits similar qualities—but then, one would have to, to tolerate Brunagwa.

(Am I suggesting that I myself have those qualities? Robyn asks. Unclear. I may only be trying to talk myself out of my obsession.)

In any event, I hope this episode has been edifying. Nee-Reta and H. are going to descend from The Top of The World during this chapter break. To continue our history of Goathorns Coven, we must return to Witches Meadow.

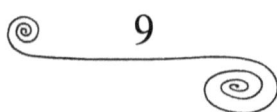

9

Nee Returns to Her Own Time

NEE-RETA WENT BACK TO THE COVEN AFTER HER VISIT TO THE Top of The World. She reported that she had seen the future of the magic satchel, and was satisfied that it would not cause great harm in its travels. It would hardly be used, and eventually it would be returned to Brunagwa—so they must wait for it. The sisters didn't find this very exciting, but there was a new seriousness and maturity to Nee-Reta. They did not doubt that she had ascended to The Top of The World, or dispute her authority.

Nee had returned to them in the form of the smaller Cooper's hawk, which had served her well on her trek to The Top of The World. Now that she had seen Time all in a jumble, both in the Knot and atop Goathorns Peak, she thought it best to distinguish herself from the venerable red-tailed hawk Ti-Wyan. Whereas her original desire, on taking over for Ti as Brunagwa's Familiar, had been to be just like Ti, now Nee was confident in her own qualities. The Witches complimented her on her refinement, having immediately accepted and understood the change. Nee-Reta had come into her own.

"When the satchel nears, all sorts of lost things will start showing up in the Goathorns. You'll really have a lot of work to do then," Nee-Reta promised. "And there is something we can do to prepare." The sisters perked up. "We must learn to do a certain kind of dance."

Nee-Reta reminded them of the fleeting appearance of a yellow-veiled dancer not many nights past, when the Coven had mourned Varluft. It bespoke of wrongful and misplaced magic that would be woven in the Future in the form of flying carpets—rugs that were operated like the magic satchels, with dance and music. The Witches must learn those Gypsy arts so they would be ready to deal with the rugs when they appeared.

This pronouncement settled matters. The Coven and the Familiars would manage the Goathorns in their usual ways while keeping their magic sharp for the heroic feats to come. The sisters would learn how to do the magic dance of the Gypsies. They loved a project. This is how they would pass the time between Then and the Future.

It proved to be more challenging than any could have thought, this training of the Witches to dance the Time Dance. Nee-Reta had seen it in person only once, and only a semblance of it at that—when Esmarelda danced to George Drumm's song and opened the way for Nee to enter the Future. She would glimpse it again from her Top of The World vantage overlooking the travels of the magic satchel, but only in the periphery of her attention. Still, her memory of George Drumm's song was vivid and mostly accurate; she held on to this as a constant, and taught it to the sisters as faithfully as she could.

Now, the way that Witches normally dance is to dervish. They spin until their souls fly off, and their bodies are left vacant and strewn any such way, like seaweed washed ashore. Getting these women to do steps, like the village folk dance, was an exercise in futility. The sisters knew exactly one step, and they could not, for love or money, for curses or flattery, move rhythmically in a straight line one after the other, unless they were also spinning. Well, imagine it. They'd topple over or go into trance in spite of themselves.

Week in and week out they worked at it, adding dance

practice to the traditional rituals whenever they gathered. Week in and week out, Reta finished the lesson, reverted to the hawk Nee, and flew away discouraged, almost too weary to flap her wings. There was progress, but so very slight. And here she had worried that the project would not occupy them for all the long years they would have to wait for the rugs. The way it was going, they would be lucky to be ready in time.

Periodically, Nee flew to the High Road and listened for the Gypsy caravans in the distance. She often heard them, for their jingle-jangle carried far across the Wide Wilde, but they rarely came close enough for her to observe them. When she did have a chance to watch the ways of the Gypsies, she noticed that they never did the Time Dance for fun around the campfire. (Esmarelda's earlier escapades had seen to that.) Nee-Reta supposed that the Time Dance was only done in secret, like the Coven's rituals.

The regular Gypsy entertainment was a different sort of dance, one that did not evoke the shifting of spiral-turns, but instead all manner of personal feeling and memory and unusual experience, like a story without words. This is similar to how Minders know the world and share their observations with one another in our special language. Nee-Reta quickly came to understand the workings of this other Gypsy art form—the Story Dance—with its vocabulary of gestures, steps and rhythms. She saw that the young Gypsies easily learned this style of dance from their elders. Maybe one had to master this form before moving on to the Time Dance, in which case this was a better place to begin with the Witches. She would give it a try.

With the introduction of the Story Dance, the dance lessons took on new life. They also became more interesting for we Goathorns denizens, for they yielded new knowledge about the five sisters. The Witches took up story dancing enthusiastically. When they had mastered the basics, each of the sisters performed her own autobiographical sketch for practice.

I shall relate what the sisters conveyed in their presentations as best I can, but let me first clarify that, Reta's flawless logic aside, the project did not meet its essential objective of teaching the Witches to dance. While the women smartly took in every subtlety of the theory and language of story dancing, they were incapable of picking it up in practice like those limber little Gypsy children. Their muscles and minds were long set in the witchy way, and the best the older sisters could do (no small feat, though it frustrated Nee-Reta tremendously) was to enact their dances via auric manifestation while they slumbered in their usual travel-trance state.

No kidding. On her chosen night, Hesterluna administered a standard potion to her younger sisters, and herself downed a different brew. While the women sat around her swaying drowsily, Hesterluna twirled herself to collapse.

Nee-Reta stood apart, arms folded disapprovingly, and you can be sure that I was nearby. To our surprise, Hesterluna's illusion was visible to us, just as it was to her mesmerized sisters. Perhaps we saw it through their eyes, as Minders may sometimes do. At any rate, we all followed Hesterluna's story dance with ease and fascination.

Over the course of several full moons, each of the three elder sisters told her story in this fashion. Somewhere in the depths of their muscle memory, perhaps this aided in their effort to actually, physically dance. But that business aside, the revelations of their hearts and souls into the heart and soul of the Goathorns was a transformative experience for all.

We begin with the eldest Redfern daughter's memoir, so ingeniously conveyed by the shimmering, slightly translucent emanation of Hesterluna the Meadow Watch Witch in the gesture language of the Story Dance. Converting this to the written word will take some ingenuity on my part as well. Fortunately I have benefit of a short autobiography that Hesterluna herself penned in the time since—

Oh. Now that is intriguing. Could Hesterluna be our novelist? I wouldn't put it past her. With respect to her memoirs, she was more detailed in the writing, but more honest in the dance.

My account shall be definitive:

HESTERLUNA

The first child of young Redfern and Deannalisa was welcomed and beloved by all. She was a happy girl, energetic and curious, at ease in nature, obedient around adults despite her natural high spirits. She was greatly spoiled, as you might imagine. But by the time Hesterluna reached her twixed and tween years, she had two sisters younger by two and four years, and her mother was fat with another (two, as it turned out). Along the way, the girl had been demoted from being esteemed as a welcome herald of her parents' fertility to representing an unfortunate trend toward female offspring. The loving generosity of doting grandparents dried up, to be replaced with chores and more chores.

Once Brunagwa and then Sestorina were walking and talking, Hesterluna might have been given some choice between outdoor work or indoor work, work in the house or work in the businesses. However, as we have seen, Deannalisa kept the girls busy in the house and family garden, away from both the millinery and taxidermy shops.

When the second daughter, Brunagwa, was old enough to work, it became harder to justify having both girls at home. Rather than consign her eldest daughter to a gluey workroom, Deannalisa quietly found a position for Hesterluna as a shepherd on those green, rolling plains on the far side of Red River. (This was before the crystal towers went up.)

For several years Hesterluna spent most of her time outdoors with a large flock of sheep and several well trained dogs, unencumbered by human society. She bunked at the farmhouse, where she was included fairly if not warmly in the lives of a farmer and his wife. The wife was much younger than the man but aging fast from the load of work that fell upon her, now that her husband had become old. Their own children had flown the coop long ago. Two nephews with neighboring lands plowed, planted, and reaped for the couple in the course of tending their own acres.

Hesterluna was paid at the end of each sheering an amount based on how much weight in wool was gathered, since this represented the number and size of the sheep she had managed to keep in the flock. She was a good worker and loyal, taking every penny back to Deannalisa that was not needed for her clothes, shoes and other modest sundries. From a sparkling, ebullient babe, she matured into a rather scatterbrained and sometimes sly woman, there amidst the sheep. No one taught her to read or write, or bothered with her education in any way. Out in the pasturelands, Hesterluna frolicked and sang, studied the ways of the land and weather, of the dogs and sheep, birds and insects. She laughed and was merry. Around people, she watched warily and tried to understand what made them so inconstant.

On those rare occasions when Hesterluna crossed the river to take her pay to her family, she avoided both the millinery shop and the taxidermist, as well as the school that her two younger sisters now attended. She visited only her mother, a woman who seemed sadder and smaller on each meeting. Hesterluna never guessed that Deannalisa hid a weighty secret in her breast, for it was apparent that taking care of the twin toddlers—outsized physically but mentally underdeveloped—would sap the life of any woman. The family on both sides shunned the household, fearful of contracting whatever had so cursed it with two more daughters, and deformed ones at that.

Dutifully, Hesterluna offered to give up the position at the farm and come back home to help her mother. Her mother would not hear of it. Deannalisa had prevailed upon her kin to let the middle daughters attend the newly opened school, claiming it would serve the family businesses well in the long run. But Hesterluna was already too far behind in that regard, and the girl was used to running free; it would be harsh indeed to bring her back only to keep her in service to a family where, through no fault of her own, she would never be properly respected.

"Keep this money for yourself," Deannalisa told Hesterluna on what would prove to be the last of these visits. "The shops do well, we have no shortage here. Buy nice things for yourself next time you are at the market, and pretty yourself up, my daughter. You could love a man and be loved, I know you could. When a couple is suited to each other, there is nothing better. Your father and I have not set a very good example, though we started out so well. You and your sisters shall do better, you'll see. The open sky will always be there for you, but hearth and home are precious." She said this even as she all but banished Hesterluna from her own.

Poor Hesterluna. She had offered valiantly to do something she'd rather not, which was to stay, and been told to do something she wanted even less, which was to go. The love and caring in her mother's voice and her long embrace only added to the girl's heartache when they said farewell.

Hesterluna went to the only other person whom she could remotely call friend, her employer's wife, and asked what she should do.

"Marry my nephew," the woman said at once, seeing a way out of her own misery. "He lost his wife in childbirth last winter, as you know. We had planned to give him the farm and flock entire, and go into a small cottage with our small savings, and quit our toil. But without a wife, that man can barely handle his own property. I fear both his and ours will go to the brother, who already has his nose so high in the air, it's a wonder he doesn't drown when it rains."

Hesterluna laughed and acted grateful for the offer, but she was dying inside. *Oh no*, she thought to herself. *And become old before my time like you, with a husband much older, and another woman's brood? Oh no no no no.*

She went at once to the market to find some good-smelling soaps and nice clothes, then returned to the farmhouse to bathe and dress in all new things. The farmer and his wife assumed she had accepted their plan, and they indulged her. While the old man went off in his dilapidated buggy to fetch the widowed nephew, and his wife began preparations for a festive meal, Hesterluna stuffed her meager belongings in a straw basket and slipped away.

Striking out on The Open Road in a southerly direction, Hesterluna felt surprisingly comfortable in her new dress and cape, shoes and cap. The road shot like an arrow into the distance. It focused her mind. How different this was from roaming this way and that on a wide pasture beneath endless sky, tending to movements of sheep and dogs instinctively with nary a thought. A remnant of Hesterluna the bright little child sparked back to life.

There were more but smaller towns in these parts back then. Hesterluna skirted the first one she came to, then circled back to The Open Road to resume the following of a single thought: Survival. Though she had made herself look civilized, Hesterluna knew she was not. Until she could read and write, she would be at the mercy of strangers for directions, decisions, and advice. A husband was not the worst idea. She could remember the times of her parents' happiness; and even after the twins came, and disappointments she could hardly understand poisoned those warm feelings, the couple still pulled as one when it came to duty. Yes, a husband might be helpful.

Hesterluna passed through or around one little town after another as unobtrusively as possible, looking for a place where she could blend in on arrival and remake herself before moving on. She found what she wanted in Crossroads City, a bustling place then as now. She asked after and was directed to a schoolhouse. The children coming out were young indeed, but they were a mix of girls and boys. Their exodus was swift and boisterous. Hesterluna ventured into the small building and called out a greeting.

"Come on in," a woman answered.

Hesterluna was pleased to discover that the voice belonged to a girl not much older than herself, pretty and confident—exactly the kind of person she wanted to become.

"I've run away from home to avoid being married to an old farmer," she told the young woman at the big desk in the front of the room, while she plopped wearily into a little bench at a little table and set her basket on the floor. "I've been walking for four days now, hoping to come upon a town such as this. I am a good worker but cannot read or write. Won't you please let me take class with the children, and find some work I can do in exchange?"

Hesterluna's straightforward appeal touched the young teacher, who could only imagine the barbaric place this poor girl had escaped. If it was true. In proportion to the sympathy such a story evoked, the teacher responded with severity in order to test its teller.

"I suppose you have no money meanwhile."

"I have my last pay from the farm where I herded sheep." Hesterluna tossed the small purse with her remaining coins onto the teacher's desk.

"Have you a name?"

"Hesterluna."

"Goodness."

"Redfern. Hesterluna Redfern."

"From?"

"Harp of Gold, near Ochersfeldt."

"Aren't you afraid I'll send you back to them?"

"They don't want me back. Besides, you wouldn't do it."

"What about the old farmer?"

"He'll find someone else. He's not young, but he's not poor either."

The young teacher smiled and peeked inside the coin bag. "Can you read what's on the board behind me?"

"A, B, C. I never got any further than that. I know that those are words underneath. And I know the numbers—well, maybe not so much written down. But I can tell the numbers from the letters."

The woman shook her head sadly and removed two coins from the purse before tossing it back to Hesterluna.

"That's for what's left of the school season. You have enough more for a couple of nights in the lodge. Maybe they need a housekeeper or a cook, and you can stay on for hire. If not there, someone will take you in if you are handy. You seem to be honest enough. You're right that I wouldn't try to send you back. Now, do you want to get right to work? A private lesson to get you off to a good start?"

Hesterluna tried to match the admirable woman's calm poise, though she wanted to cheer. Even if it meant a return to housework or farmwork for a time, at least by going to school she would be advancing herself. She said, "Excuse me. I know that is your name on the placard on your desk, but I truly can't read it. What shall I call you, Miss?"

"I'm sorry. How rude of me. My name is Agnes Newell. If you are going to take class with the children, I think you should call me Miss Newell. I will call you Miss Redfern."

"Thank you, Miss Newell. So nice to make your acquaintance. I will never forget your generosity." Hesterluna leaned forward to rest her arms on the table, put her head down, and was instantly asleep.

Agnes Newell left her desk and stood over the sleeping girl for a moment. She leaned forward and took a good sniff. Yes indeed, this Hesterluna had been near sheep more often than near soap. Shaking her head, the shaper of young minds hurried off to see who might have a room and a job for the unfortunate soul.

And so commenced Hesterluna's formal education and

coming out into society. She proved to be a quick study. In no time at all she graduated from the grade school, and then the middle school, and she and Agnes progressed to a first name basis. Agnes had a beau, of course, and soon Hesterluna did too. The young men were friends, in the usual way that these things go, and so both romances progressed apace. In due course, Agnes, and then Hesterluna, was married.

But Agnes was true and Hesterluna was not. Agnes was already pregnant by the time Hesterluna and that soon-to-be-jilted lad Soren stood in the center of the wedding circle.

Not to be outdone by his buddy, Soren talked about having children with increasing frequency and urgency following the wedding, and Hesterluna used all of her wiles to prevent it. She liked Soren, and enjoyed his company and his lovemaking. But all he wanted from her and for her was children. Did he not see that such a life of responsibilities would keep the couple apart more than it would bring them together? Maybe he didn't want a lover, an equal, any more than she wanted a sire and provider. You see, with her new found power of literacy, the husband had become optional. She could fend for herself.

Hesterluna had seen what married life is. Though her mother had told her it could be different, Hesterluna did not think several years of wedded bliss at the start was worth decades of disappointment thereafter. It had been her intention right along to go her own way when the pleasure of having a husband faded, but she didn't think that moment would come so soon.

Yes, it was a cold and calculating woman who emerged on the other side of Hesterluna's makeover. Spoiled while a babe, then (she felt this keenly) cast aside as a child, given little guidance growing up, and again cast aside on the brink of womanhood, Hesterluna had made up her mind that *she* would be the one doing the casting aside in all future relationships. She presented a principled and honest front to all, but kept always in mind a tally of grievances with one person or another that might justify a breaking off of dealings at any time. This included the man she would marry and abandon. *She'd* had the best of intentions, she told herself, *he* was the one pulling away. She would skip out before he could.

She packed only what would fit in her old basket. She told Soren that his oppressive demands for children and obvious disregard for her own desire to continue her education were intolerable. Soren begged her to stay—he would help with the children while she pursued her studies. But her mind was made up. Maternal love would be the end of her will and her wherewithal. Motherhood was not for one such as herself, who aspired to so much more. Soren insisted they go to the town Judge to have the marriage officially annulled before she left.

(Not long after the annulment, Soren married a local girl. Some of their progeny eventually found their way to Ochersfeldt, allowing our diligent gossips to record that there had been fourteen Sorenson offspring from that couple. By now there are well over a hundred descendants in Ochersfeldt alone. Imagine the havoc if they had all been Redferns! No, the union of Soren and Hesterluna was a match that Fate could not permit.)

Hesterluna was not proud of herself, but she was relieved to be free and moving beyond yet another unsatisfactory experiment in how to live. In explaining to her husband why she had to leave, she had clarified it for herself. From this time on, she sought out all of the big cities and their institutions of higher learning. Through force of will and a discipline for study that was only rivaled by her exuberance for play, she attained some notoriety as an eccentric but innovative modern thinker. There are some places where Hesterluna Redfern is still remembered as a brilliant scholar (as she is ever quick to remind us).

Thus our shepherdess continued her process of traveling as far as she could from the Harp of Gold valley, the fecundity of the pasture, the dark mystery of the primordial forest it bordered, and the mindless meandering of sheep on rolling hills of plenty.

In other words, as far from her primal nature as she could get. But that didn't mean giving up her womanly pleasures. As an academic and a freethinker, she did as she pleased. She supported herself by tutoring bright young women who wanted an education, often enlisting civic-minded sponsors to foot the bill. She had indeed remade herself.

By the time Hesterluna was called back to Ochersfeldt, she had to admit that even this life of her own choosing was weighing her down. People—and she mingled with so many now—were still more inconstant than not. A succession of lovers was exciting, but a succession of breaking-offs was not. The students began to tire her. She rescued one after another and then, when they were strong, she gave them a pat and sent them on their way—not unlike tending the sheep. She was comfortable and respected. But she realized with chagrin that she was not satisfied. And so she was already ripe for making a change when she felt the summons, "Hesterluna, come home."

Here, Hesterluna's solo career comes to an end, and her story rejoins that of her sisters. I think that went rather well, don't you? Now, Editor permitting, I propose to combine Brunagwa's and Sestorina's reminiscences. Their auric Story Dances were performed on different occasions, but I am not dancing. Plus, you know how easily I get sidetracked with respect to Brunagwa, so I beg to take this liberty. (Good, she agreed.) Onward, then, to the second and third Redfern daughters:

BRUNAGWA AND SESTORINA

Brunagwa and Sestorina grew up almost as close as twins. They went to school, helped with their baby sisters, and shared a longing for their older sister, whom they imagined to be vastly successful even while she was still a poor shepherd. Together Sestorina and Brunagwa formed a kind of cabal to defend against the demands and expectations of their adult family. The status of the parental relationship did not permeate their awareness, and the nattering of relatives had no effect whatever. There was a newly cosmopolitan feeling growing in Ochersfeldt, which was becoming known as a center for the occult, and the pretty young women observed all with fascination.

Though Brunagwa was the elder sister, she usually went along with whatever Sestorina wanted. In general, Brunagwa had a tendency to seem remote. There was a day-dreamy quality to her, but she could also be quite perceptive. She paid more attention to what was below the surface than to what was in plain view.

Sestorina, in contrast, was pragmatic about external circumstance and unhindered by inner turmoil. She looked at her family and saw that they prospered but did not enjoy. In her mind, the twins were not so bad, and the shops were not so bad. Yes, there was a witchiness about certain of the lot—some of the stuffed animals, and certainly those pudgy babies, and all in some way connected to their beleaguered mother. But magic was in vogue—it was going to put Ochersfeldt on the map—and the Redferns needed to get on board.

No one could resist Sestorina's energy. To start, she insisted that she and Brunagwa be enrolled in the new school. It proved to be an ordeal for them at first, because they weren't used to using their minds in that way. But once they got the hang of study and practice, they kept up easily. Every so often they played hooky, and Sestorina led Brunagwa on an adventure around the growing city to meet some of the colorful newcomers to the area. Sestorina had decided that she and Brunagwa must collect as much arcane knowledge as they could with which to make the most of the Redfern inheritance. They would take the family trades to new heights.

Sestorina's appetite for life knew no bounds. She tackled her academic studies with zest and her social explorations with equal zeal. She was strong and competitive physically, and, before long, very sexy. Brunagwa watched over her little sister vigilantly, suppressing her own strong desire and curiosity as best she could. But these were romantic times in a romantic place; both young women were in love with the idea of love and looking for worthy suitors.

Sestorina found her man all too quickly. He literally charged into town on a muscular gray steed of the type traded by the high country Ethalees. After winning three of four racing competitions at the annual Harp of Gold Farmers Fair, and swaggering around Ochersfeldt for a week flashing his expensive gear, he galloped away with Sestorina in his arms.

No one doubted it was true love, but they hated to see her go, and none more than Brunagwa. Finding a husband was one thing, but leaving Ochersfeldt had never been part of the deal. Why spend all that time spying out the ways of the magical artisans, if they were only going to abandon their claim and run away to places and people who likely feared such things?

It was a blow, but Brunagwa was resilient. Before long she forgave Sestorina for leaving, and she began to enjoy a new feeling of liberation. She did not feel tied to anything now. She continued her studies and dutifully helped Deannalisa, while trying to ignore her vague insights and intuitions. The big baby sisters, freakish in their ability to read each other's minds and blurt out the secret thoughts of others, never betrayed those of their mother. Brunagwa was left guessing about the nature of Deannalisa's clandestine dealings at the taxidermy shop.

All in all, the second daughter felt her loyalty was wasted on such a fractured family. They looked cohesive from the outside, but the ties that bound grew frayed and thin. The last thread snapped for Brunagwa when she wandered into the taxidermy showroom one day and found her mother alone there, rocking in her chair, humming quietly. Separated from Sestorina's frenetic energy, Brunagwa's second sight had been lately on the rise. Suddenly, she became aware of the Minder spirits that her mother sought to soothe. It was beyond grotesque! She felt the entire foundation of her life slipping. Had she really been raised by heartless hunters and forest thieves?

"The Redferns can't see them or feel them," Deannalisa whispered from her place in the shadows. "Don't blame your father, blame me for letting it go on."

Brunagwa sensed the truth of it, but found blame enough for all. But what was to be done? How could she fix any of this now? Must she? She was terrified of having to act decisively in this matter that was so new and distressing to her. She hastened home and gathered the young ones.

They giggled at first, seeing that their big sister was only now learning something they had long known. But when Intuisha and Dremtessa felt Brunagwa's despair, they reached out to her and nearly smothered her in comforting embraces.

"Don't be sad, sister. It only makes them sadder. We are going to help Mother save them."

"I believe you, you strange pair. But I am sick to the center of my heart and cannot abide it here, knowing what I know."

"We're big girls now. And Brunie is all grown up. We'll cry when you go away, but do it anyway."

"Do it quick before they make you marry cousin Wolfgang," Dremtessa chimed in, for she had dreamed it.

And so the last of the elder daughters would soon make her escape. Brunagwa was perhaps the best prepared of the three. She had finished school, she had worked diligently for the household, and she had held a job keeping accounts for the new Magic Fabric Mart. (It was ahead of its time, and might have made it, had Brunagwa stayed to make sure the magic fabrics were not so easily spirited away by the cunning customers.) She even belonged to a club of young ladies who had graduated school with her. It was to their small office that she went for guidance on how to make a respectable exit from Ochersfeldt, being that she had no beau to carry her off on a gray stallion.

Brunagwa kept her mind steady on her plans while they came

to fruition, and did not let her emotions give her away. She was packed and had a carriage waiting when she announced that she was taking a job as an assistant for a tailor shop several towns over. The trades could always use someone who could measure and add.

"And nothing like that here in town?" her father shouted after her, outraged. But there really wasn't at that time, not for that kind of pay.

Brunie was all grown and off to make her fortune. The twins cried, but only briefly. Deannalisa breathed a sigh of relief. Others thought her strange to let the three oldest daughters go so easily, especially with the twins to raise.

"My two babies eat for five as it is," she would point out, correctly. "I wish the older girls would keep in closer touch, but I think it is grand that they are reaching for the stars."

She told the twins that in her heart she knew the girls would come back if they were needed.

The twins readily agreed with her. In their secret, psychic way, they knew they could contact their older sisters at any time.

Brunie Redfern's new job took her way out west to the prosperous town of Copperfield that overlooks Homestead Lake. She'd heard about Hesterluna's exploits in Crossroads City, and knew she would not fare well there, even with a different name, for her resemblance to her older sister was unmistakable. In Copperfield she started afresh and met with success. She was soon persuaded to leave the tailor's shop and take a position at the hotel, where her well-rounded experience earned her rapid advancement.

Of all the doings in the hotel, the work of the kitchen interested Brunie the most. The hotel restaurant was known for its gourmet menu and talented chef, a woman. Brunagwa decided that she wanted to be a chef also; it delighted her that the "women's work" she had been consigned to at home could be elevated to an art form and lucrative profession. She immersed herself in work and study, but she could not easily put aside the moral confusion that marked her departure from Ochersfeldt. After all, she spent hours learning to butcher everything from wild boar to baby quail; and in her assigned task of keeping the shopping lists and accounts for the entire hotel, she saw the sacrifice of pulsing life reduced to cold hard figures for profits and losses. Not so very different from the taxidermy shop, after all, she worried.

(In Brunagwa's defense, I shall insert here that the Minder phenomenon is one of place. Out from the shadows of The Top of The World, creatures are what they are and for the most part no more. No doubt other power places come with their own brand of local magical beings, but Brunagwa was rightly confident that the game and such she prepared as food was quite killed and dead—in some cases she'd killed it herself after probing it carefully with her second sight.)

Brunagwa shared her crisis of conscience with her mentor. The feisty old chef put her hands on her hips and shook her head disapprovingly.

"You'll make the food taste bad with such thoughts," she chided. "From time immemorial the species have fed off one another, and though individuals do not survive, the species do. Who are you to reform Nature? Your task is to live, love, eat well, and rejoice that you are *stirring* the pot, not *in* the pot!"

Brunagwa took heart from her teacher's mirthful confidence. Besides, she loved to cook and eat anything, there was no denying it. One day, her teacher gave her a white cap and a white jacket with "Chef Brunie Redfern" embroidered over the breast pocket.

"Bless your heart, love, I can finally retire. It'll be easier for the Mr. and Mrs. to find someone to take over the hotel accounts than to keep up the quality of the kitchen. It's all arranged. I told them you could do it near as good as me, and would be better than me as soon as you could stop working yourself to death.

Your new job and your higher pay start next week."

"You mean, all I have to do is cook and manage the kitchen, and they'll pay me more than I make now?"

"They already got double their money letting me train you for free after your office work. This is how it's supposed to be—hard work rewarded. I am very proud of you, and relieved for us both. My back is killing me."

Brunie gave her such a bear hug that the chef's back popped three ways and she felt better immediately.

Another Redfern sister was making her mark in the world.

And what of the sister who was swept away by love?

Sestorina's exotic prince really was the master of a country estate—or, more accurately, a vast untamed nightmare of tundra and steppe. The family lands were spotted with yurts and manmade reservoirs for collecting water, so that the natural herds of wild horses, yaks, llamas and reindeer could multiply and be culled for trade.

The prince's own yurt was a vertitable palace, if more sprawling than soaring. But although the scene was more exotic than Sestorina's home in the Harp of Gold valley, the activity was fairly much the same. Out in the wilds, men herded animals to shear for wool, to breed for their milk, or to tame and train for transport. In and near a low, labyrinthine fort, women and children engaged in the many crafts that would convert these animal materials into cash commodities—butter and cheese, blankets, rugs and decorative textiles.

Sestorina's in-laws were polite and welcoming, but not a demonstrative people. They were pleased that the young heir had sought and found someone from a different tribe who could match him in spirit and wit. Sestorina was given her pick of what she would do—it could be something different every day if she wished. Just so long as she provided heirs.

There is a familiar theme here, is there not? The pressure for the wife to have children. Yet this did not trouble our zestful

Sestorina. She was ready, willing and able to bear children. In the case of this couple, it was the happy husband who was unwilling to see his wife grow big and milk-laden, to share her with demanding little ones, and surrender her to the society of matriarchs.

So be it, Sestorina thought. *The children will come in time, but there is no need to rush.* She taught her husband the moon magic that would keep his seed from sprouting, and they reveled in their lusty union. Riding from one remote outpost to the next, the pair savored their freedom and passion. When they galloped side by side under a blazing sun or a full moon, they felt at home in the vast landscape—attuned to their horses, akin to the wind. They were the very inventors of romantic love, the first and last couple on earth.

"Beware your happiness, lest the gleam of your smile attract sorrow." This is a saying of the people of the steppes, and the reason they never show their teeth except in anger.

One day Sestorina was riding fast beside her husband, laughing into the blue sky. The next she was a widow, no children at home, and none in her womb. They said the husband died of a burst heart because his love for his bride was so great. He died in his sleep without a mark of violence or illness.

Negotiations immediately commenced for Sestorina to be given over for marriage to a relation on the prince's father's side. Through her tears, Sestorina detected an exchange of victorious looks among those doing the negotiating. Sorrow was bringing forth Sestorina's second sight. She woke next morning in the certainty that the family had figured the prince to be infertile, and so had plotted to replace him.

"I will take that mere child as my husband," she announced when the dickering resumed around more pans of yak butter tea. "But as you may have noticed, I am barren."

"You are not, and I know it," one of the elders sang out. "Look at you!"

"The prince pretended he was postponing children, but really he couldn't have them," someone said cruelly.

Such disrespect—they had barely buried the man. Sestorina felt her broken heart take cover from her rage.

"Hateful people! Betrayers!" she exploded. And she grabbed the skinny youth by his throat, lifted him out of his seat, and brought his gasping face close to hers. "Be grateful I haven't got you by the balls," she growled into his ear. "Or you would be their next victim." She flung him aside, gave an ear-splitting whistle, and slammed through the shocked gathering and out to the paddock to claim her steed.

Did our Sestorina flee to Ochersfeldt? Oh no. The loss of her true love caused her natural fire to burn with bright, steady clarity in place of its previous passionate abandon. She rode at lightning speed from one outpost to the next to report the murder of her husband, their prince, and exact from those who had hosted the couple warmly an oath of loyalty to herself as legitimate heir and overlord of the late prince's lands. When his kin arrived to make their own claims, it was too late. The enclaves were armed against them, and their sellable goods were already heading to market at Sestorina's instruction.

She ruled that principality from its northernmost camp with steely confidence until her call came, "Sestorina, come home." The wealth she brought back to Ochersfeldt was only matched by that which she left behind. All but the prince's immediate family made out very well under Sestorina's governance.

And so we come to the twins—

Sorry, but my Editor is rapping me on the knuckles again. She doesn't think that I ever finished Brunagwa's story. *Didn't Brunie ever fall in love, or get married or have children?* Robyn wants to know.

Well, what do you expect me to answer? If she loved, it was not her true love—I should say, none of them were. She enjoyed her culinary profession too much to crave married life. Frankly, I wandered off during the part about "Brunie's" romantic exploits in Copperfield—such an undignified name and life for such a magnificent woman. I wasn't interested in the pale shades of male who may have won her favors. If they sought her heart, they were unsuccessful.

As for this moment, I beg permission to again wander off, in a literary way, from the subject of Brunagwa's love life. So far as I'm concerned, she hasn't got one and doesn't deserve one. I am not a namby-pamby romantic sort who will claim his love is so deep and devoted that all he wants is happiness for his beloved, even if it means she must be with another. No and no. Brunagwa spurned me and continues to spurn me, and I wish her nothing but loneliness and regret to the end of her days—for such will be my own lot if our reconciliation does not come to pass. If we cannot live happily ever after together, then I say let us live parallel lives of misery!

Heard enough, Robyn?

That's what I thought. Let's get back to the facts, they don't make me want to bite someone's face off.

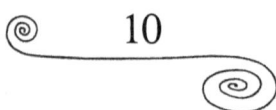

10

A Remarkable Event in the Goathorns

WE NOW COME TO THE TWINS' STORY DANCES. TO START, I HAVE been asked to clarify exactly how large the twins were and are. I have described them as giants, and in other mammoth terms, so this does bear some explanation.

Intuisha and Dremtessa were larger than average babies, and even larger than large babies, which was initially attributed to their extra month in the womb. They developed "ahead of the curve" as people of science like to say—large for their age at every stage, and increasingly so. They were nine years younger than Sestorina, their next older sister. They caught up to her in size at around the time of her elopement with the dashing prince; she was seventeen and they were eight. Brunagwa, who stands more than six feet by your measure, still had several inches on them a couple of years later when she set out on her own. But the twins were about to undergo another growth spurt.

By their twixt and tween years, when their mother finally involved them in her secrets, the twins' growth had become more a matter of magical powers than chronological age. They had an eerie way of physically enlarging themselves when exerting their gifts, at first involuntarily, and then reverting to their usual large but human proportions. Once they made it to the Goathorns to stay, they were free to expand to the limits of their need and desire, and they have done so. I have seen them in phases when their dimensions are downright geological. But for participation in the Coven's activities, and conversing with things of average size, they politely contract back to the scale of, say, one of your larger male athletes.

Intuisha and Dremtessa are both beautifully proportioned, by the way, at any scale. Mighty women. Surprisingly, they danced their story dances in actuality, not via auric emanation. Perhaps they felt the need to practice with their abundant bodies, or were showing up their sisters with their relative youth, but that was a night to remember in the Goathorns, to be sure. The meadow literally vibrated. The elder sisters moved back to make a much bigger circle and provide sufficient distance for the great gesturing arms and pounding feet.

Intuisha danced first and then Dremtessa, but they alternated frequently and also danced at times simultaneously but separately and sometimes together. Since they did not have the same sort of adventures out in the world as their sisters—they had just turned fifteen when the Redfern women fled to Six Hills—they elaborated instead on their time in the Goathorns, both before and after the liberation of the taxidermy shop, and including the time of finding and training the Familiars.

Intuisha and Dremtessa

Deannalisa blamed the strangeness of her youngest daughters on that visit to the fortune-teller. Something unwholesome had been imparted by mere proximity to the Gypsies.

(An aside, if I may: I once heard Esma tell George that she used to think her people only *existed* to take the blame for others' misfortunes, such are the misconceptions surrounding their kind. I mention this to remind Robyn that even here, in my magical world, magic is suspect.)

Most likely, it was the upset of finding Minder spirits in the taxidermy shop that set Deannalisa's pregnancy on such an unusual course, beginning with its depressed, lethargic pace. The natural psychic abilities of the twins would only have grown stronger from that extra time together in the womb. They themselves acknowledged this in their Story Dance, when one and then the other demonstrated how she remembered herself and her sister communicating in their embryonic states, and then the almost psychedelic experience of each birth itself.

Being oversized, and twins—that is, having each other—led to a childhood that lacked the level of supervision of ordinary children. Deannalisa seemed to be the only adult who could keep in mind the twins' actual age and care for them suitably. Others were fooled by their size into treating them as though they were older. And everyone observed that they communicated in a secret language and learned doubly fast, like a single person with a double brain. People were a little afraid of the twins; they excused themselves from minding the children by asserting that "they keep each other company," which they certainly did.

(Here, Intuisha petulantly gestured something rather close to neglect, whereas Dremtessa's dance conveyed a welcome freedom from oversight.)

Lacking sufficient human companionship, the twins kept company with all variety of birds, animals, insects, flowers and trees. Long legs carried them away from the village for delighted play in the countryside, and strong prescience brought them home again the moment anyone began to miss them. When they played dress-up in their mother's clothes, the clothes actually fit them. And so they might roam around interesting areas of town pretending to windowshop while eavesdropping on people's thoughts. This is how they would eventually find Varluft.

By the time they reached the age where even a typical child would start getting some freedom to go out a little bit on her own, the twins were already setting their sights on the looming Goathorn Mountains. They loped into the Six Hills at every opportunity, until Dremtessa had the idea—in a dream, of course—to circle around and look for a faster route to that high meadow they had espied from the top of Fourth Hill

By age ten, they had found the Tree of Choices and the Path That Opens, as well as the posted trail to The Top of The World. They had even met some Minders though they didn't know it, because they assumed that all of nature spoke—to everyone, not just themselves.

Intuisha and Dremtessa might never have approached the magical Varluft, had they not found him in the very place that had been their goal, and which they finally attained. He had been going up to the high meadow to practice his transformation into the giant eagle. (Emanation might be a better word, though to be absolutely accurate I should call it an illusion. But it is such a dandy illusion, and was even back then, that the thing is truly felt to be real.)

When the twins at last crested the last hill to the meadow, the giant little girls were just in time to see a giant eagle landing there. It quickly melted away, to be replaced by the man they recognized from the corner magic shop. They ran to him delightedly, as happy little girls will do, and you can imagine his alarm as they grew near. The magician readied himself to launch the eagle apparition again, if only to compare to these moppets in size, but was stayed by a prescient vision.

The Witches, Varluft thought, standing in the very place that would one day be called Witches Meadow, in the shadow of The Top of The World, and his thought bounced back toward the girls, so that they stopped with eyes wide and smiles even wider upon hearing it.

The Witches. They saw what was in the magician's second sight—an image of a Coven of five mighty women marking the five points of a pentacle there in the center of the meadow.

"And he didn't even know that the other three were our sisters!" Intuisha, then Dremtessa, and then the two together danced with delight.

Allow me to emphasize again what a remarkable event this was in the Goathorns, the night that the normally hermetic twin sisters danced together in their real bodies under the full moon in Witches Meadow. It felt like every living creature within the ring of the Goathorns was being drawn to the scrubby fringe and woods surrounding the meadow, and that a benign spirit stayed our natural instincts for predation or flight. (My assumption was and is that we were under the influence of the sage Ti-Wyan.)

The three elder sisters settled to their haunches to clap or pat the ground in rhythm as it suited the story. Nee-Reta looked on from her place in the treetops, gratified that two of the sisters had actually learned to dance, and the others to clap time.

But wait—

It had to have been *two* nights that the twins danced. Because once their story progressed through the wretched scenes of the Minders in the taxidemy shop and their eventual rescue, mother and daughters' escape and the strange end of Deannalisa, and then the demise of all the other Redferns, all five sisters went a little wild from the remembered anguish. The twins stopped gesturing in dance language and simply held their arms straight up toward the stars while they cried out for their mother, and the three older sisters sprang to their feet and followed suit.

The women turned slowly at first, then faster, and then the uncontrolled dervishing came over them. I remember how the tears flew from their faces and pelted us like raindrops in the wind. Yes, that memory is very clear now. They spun themselves to exhaustion and fell to the ground. There would be no more dancing that night.

So, the Familiars' stories must have been told on another night. Was I even there? Were any of us? Excuse me, but I must back up and review the preceding scenes before we move on:

As I search my memory of those three nights when the older

sisters' emanations were made visible to us, I can see clearly the five Familiars ranged in an outer circle around the Coven's circle. Remember that the Witches all slept, the way they do when they dervish and drop, including the one who told the story. The Familiars guarded the slumbering women, and together we watched the ghostly dance of an auric emanation.

(Have you got all that, Robyn? Care to give it a whirl?)

But things went differently on the night the twins danced. I was in my usual place in the shadows. Nee-Reta had flown to the safety of the trees to watch. All of the Minders were present at the start, along with many others from the forest who were drawn by the quaking and shaking. We followed every gesture and thought with ease, feeling at times as though we ourselves were dancing. At other times, it was as if the mountains around us danced.

When the twins began to mime how they had carried their mother into Six Hills, and the tale of Deannalisa was hurtling toward a conclusion that would take place on this very ground, the form of the dance failed them. A gathering of ghosts surged out of the earth to swirl upwards in an icy mist. The simple animals of the wood fled, and even some of the Familiars could not face the grief and power of the sisters' memory. But I was transfixed. Here was the answer to how those once irrepressible girls had matured into the chill, stoic queens of the Ice Caves and High Caverns. For on the night of their greatest sorrow and strangest magic, the twins had dervished thus.

Now, as the remembered grief and fright were spent, the twins' shrieks and curses calmed into a wordless song. Their turnings slowed, and they ritually wound up the sparkling thread of their mysterious girlhood as onto a spindle, and it has never been spoken of—or danced—again.

I suppose we all slept when the Witches did, our senses shattered from their twirling and crying into the cold night sky. What I remember as a sleeping and waking, like the turning of a page, was surely a passage of days or weeks or months. Allow me to continue in an actual page turn, because the scene is coming back to me, and I am counting on this word process to make it come clear.

It was probably on the next full moon that Intuisha and Dremtessa resumed their Story Dance . . .

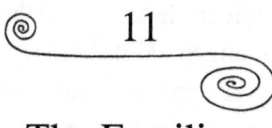

11

The Familiars

ANOTHER FULL MOON CAME ROUND. THE TWINS DANCED AGAIN
in Witches Meadow. The traumatic events that had destroyed the
Redferns of Ochersfeldt were behind them, and they picked up
their story with gusto from some point after the women had fled
to the Goathorns. Intuisha and Dremtessa and their sisters were
settling in, and some of them were about to find their Familiars.

FLAME-MARI

As you may imagine, the three older Redfern daughters came
home with many skills that would serve the Coven well. The one
who was best prepared for life in the wilds from the outset was
Sestorina, princess of the northern steppes. She and the twins
quickly built a lodge that would house herself and their citified
older sisters in the relatively gentle valley between Third Hill and
Fourth Hill. They did not attempt to build a place large enough
to house Dremtessa and Intuisha. The twins preferred to camp
out—they picked a place around the corner, as it were, on the
slopes of Fifth Hill.

Sestorina set out to tame a small herd of wild horses that ran
freely within the ring of the Goathorns and frequently wandered
into the valleys of the Six Hills to forage and find water. She
soon had them in her thrall, and they carried the three elder

189

sisters hither and yon around the Goathorns during the time in which they explored and made this place their own. Brunagwa was able to scout out Red Mountain, and, with the twins' help, relocate to the sort of lofty perch she preferred. Hesterluna staked out her claim in the milder climes below the meadow.

Now Sestorina had the Six Hills lodge to herself, but she was not satisfied. There was a spirited mare that she wanted for her own, but it was staying separate from the herd, as though willfully shunning her. When Sestorina confided to the twins that the animal had clearly communicated to her that it would never be ridden, they told her that her perceived failure was really an achievement.

"You have found a special one," Intuisha said. "You mustn't ride her, ever. Be content to ride the one who has submitted to you."

"But do not abandon Flame," Dremtessa added, giving this special horse a name. "She has spoken to you. Ask nothing of her but her trust. Maybe she will show us the special power of her kind, the one that makes their spirits fly above."

Varluft had told the twins what little he knew about the unique breed of Goathorns inhabitants that had been trapped in the taxidermy shop. They had powers that increased the closer they dwelled to The Top of The World. Even though he didn't fully understand it, he found he could draw upon the same energy to expand his manifestation of the Eagle.

At this point, none of the Humans, not even Varluft, recognized that the Minders' apparent separation of body and spirit was actually a stage of transformation from one complete being to another. We Minders employ our ability to transform as a way of knowing. The majestic wild horse Flame, and later Ti and the others, would learn what was in the hearts of the sisters by becoming like them. Sestorina had tried to "tame" Flame, but the horse was unwilling to be controlled (to put it mildly). Still, Flame was interested in these new arrivals to Six Hills, and ready to make friends. To do this, she would learn to mirror Sestorina's physical form first, and then her mental state.

When Sestorina saw what Flame was attempting, she retreated to the ranch and orchard, and the equine Minder stayed nearby. Sestorina went naked for days on end. Finally she saw the beautiful Mari take shape in her own image.

The mental aspects of becoming a Human proved more difficult for Flame-Mari. Fortunately, Intuisha and Dremtessa were able to act as amplifiers and translators for everyone's thoughts. It helped that Sestorina, from her time on the steppes, already knew how to think like a horse.

And so Sestorina became the first of the sisters to befriend and then be copied by a Minder, and Flame-Mari became the first Familiar.

At this juncture in part two of the twins' Story Dance, Flame-Mari actually led the herd in an equine dance into the circle and out again. When the horses dispersed, Intuisha completed Flame-Mari's story to ululations of approval. Sestorina, the co-star of the tale, took a few bows herself and blew kisses to her ponies, until Intuisha shooed her next-older sister back to her place and presented her twin.

Everyone quickly settled and looked on eagerly, knowing which chapter of the Goathorns Coven's story was to come. It appeared that Dremtessa would play herself, and Intuisha would play the bear.

Nee-Reta wisely kept to her tree. As H. Toad, I was also staying well out of the way of the dancing giantesses, the prancing ponies, and the clapping, chanting trio of older sisters. I wish I could place the other Familiars in this scene—Snip-Edie and Yani-Yau—but the badger and cougar are not coming clear. Of course, at the time, my attention was alternately on the twins and their bear.

Roth-Thea, officially Dremtessa's Familiar, was a hulking

presence sitting halfway between the two points of the pentacle that Intuisha and Dremtessa would occupy were they not the stars of the show, and several paces back so as to be in shadow rather than moonlight. I remember envying her ability to settle comfortably midway between Human and ursine. She watched stoically while the twins danced her story, which I shall recount herewith, after I dispel a common misconception.

A rumor has built up around Roth-Thea in which she is related to the first Minder spirit that Deannalisa encountered in the taxidermy shop, was stashed as a pup in the Ice Caves to save her from the hunters, and then propitiously found and adopted by Dremtessa. Such is the flattering glow with which we imbue the Past. Truth is, the bear had long been a menace to any living thing that wandered into her extensive territory, and Dremtessa had to literally wrestle it into submission in order to claim those caves for herself, and the caverns above for Intuisha. Here is the story of that epic confrontation. You must try to imagine the hefty but strikingly rejuvenated twins enacting this saga in dance. My narration is but the subtitling to their dramatic ballet.

ROTH-THEA

Intuisha and Dremtessa, resting against the slope of Fifth Hill, turned their sights to the east and the great wall of pockmarked rock rising up toward Goathorns Peak. Their twin thoughts dwelt on the ledges and caves, the icy interior and the cooling heights that the imposing outcropping would afford. As they watched the moon and stars dangle teasingly above the massive silhouette of stone, they bounced their single thought back and forth. Like a dried gourd in a game of catch, it sometimes rattled one way and sometimes another, but it was always the same thought, destined to land in the same place at the end of their friendly play.

And so it was decided, and they told their sisters. The eastern rim would be theirs. They had looked about with their second sight, and found vast chambers within the rock in which to make their apartments. In the cool, they could conserve physical energy and consume less food and water even as their bodies expanded with psychic power.

Hesterluna, Brunagwa and Sestorina had reservations:

Hesterluna, who felt most keenly the severing of the Redfern lineage, did not like that the chosen place was so near where the Redfern family had met their demise.

Dremtessa reminded her eldest sister that it was only near in the sense that it was on the opposite side of the mountain. To travel there directly would require boring through a great length of solid stone. Otherwise, one would have to walk a long way down and up again to get to the far side; going up and over the mountain would be an even longer, harder hike.

Brunagwa complained that the terrain beyond the meadow was far too rugged to cross on a regular basis. How would she, Hesterluna and Sestorina keep tabs on their little sisters?

Intuisha's sarcastic retort immediately flashed across all their minds, and they laughed off further concerns on that score.

Sestorina posed the most serious objection. She had learned from Flame-Mari and the wild horses that the place was already inhabited by an animal force with great powers. Hadn't their second sight told them that? She challenged Intuisha and Dremtessa, knowing that not only the twins, but all of them had perceived a threatening presence within those caverns.

The twins insisted on their ability to prevail over whatever dark force ruled the formation. Intuisha would take it on soul to soul. If need be, Dremtessa would capture and contain it until they could commune and reach a truce. The twins spoke confidently, but were quick to accept help from their sisters, since that had been part of their plan right along. They would need everyone's willing involvement to extend the Coven's eastern boundary. When they framed the project as an acquisition of both land and power for the Goathorns Coven, their sisters could not resist.

To begin with, Brunagwa asked practically, what exactly were they facing? Firsthand reports were hard to come by, for the beast of the cliffs and caves was ravenous and left both plant and animal life devastated. Based on this, she supposed it was a bear. They had better prepare themselves.

In the following weeks the Witches learned what they could from such living things as had managed to survive near the area. They heard tell of a variety of ravaging bears that roamed there, from a small but speedy black bear, to the larger brown bear, to the immense grizzly bear. Was "it" actually "they"? The sisters enlisted the Master Seer of Ochersfeldt to send his Eagle sight to soar above and count bears. Varluft reported only one—one that shifted shape as it ranged over diverse terrain. A Minder!

Now the five sisters combined their second sight to reach toward the menacing animal directly. At their next circle, their vision touched on something lost and frightened, capable of deadly rage but not willfully malevolent. To subdue it, even by force, would be a kindness. There was little question that force would be required, and that the task must fall to Dremtessa.

For the next many days, the sisters worked together to make a thick wool jumper, gauntlets and high boots—extra extra extra large—to protect Dremtessa from the sharp claws and teeth of something potentially the size of a grizzly. The sheepskins were turned outward and made stiff with a concoction of sap and sand, and the thick wool padding turned in. When the uniform was complete, another psychic call was sent to the Master Seer of Ochersfeldt.

Master Seer Varluft returned to the meadow with the new moon. This time he participated in the Coven's rituals. At dawn the Eagle flew aloft again to track the wild Minder's movements.

Now Dremtessa waited with her sisters between Next Hill and Third Hill, trying to stay cool in the shadows, and as small as she could make herself within her massive sheepskin armor. At last they heard the screech of the Eagle. Soon after, Flame-Mari galloped into the canyon with Varluft's message: The black bear had temporarily sated itself on berries and was resting on a ledge above its den.

The sisters chanted urgently. Dremtessa sprang up, instantly filling the huge garment so that it fit like her own skin. She loped out of the valley and up to the crest of the witchy trail known as the Path That Opens, which became a mini-meadow below Witches Meadow when the path did open, but otherwise was a tangle of stickery bracken. Here she planned to have her encounter with the bear well away from those treacherous, rocky cliffs. Her sisters raced to the top of Third Hill to watch from a safe distance. Sestorina sat astride her large steed, with the mare Flame at her side, ready to race to Dremtessa's aid if needed. Intuisha actually "watched" with her eyes closed, the better to tune in and add her strength to her twin's labor. The Eagle circled above.

That angry, confused, hungry-for-meat bear took the bait. The combined smell of the sheepskin and the women was unfamiliar but tantalizing. Thoughts of giant prey, while an eagle squawked menacingly overhead, perturbed and goaded the animal even more. With terrifying speed the bear sprang down the rocky cliff and out into the shifty landscape.

Dremtessa braced herself. The changeling was transforming from a black bear into a brown bear before her eyes. When the bear's front paws struck ground just paces from her, and then its back paws caught up to them and flexed to spring again, she spoke a word, and the Path That Opens closed suddenly. The animal howled in pain as long thorns stabbed through its fur, and a viny growth entangled its limbs.

Dremtessa strode across the unwelcoming mat of groundcover in her thick-soled boots. She pulled the bear's front paws out of the painful thicket, quickly pressed them against each other, and bound them that way to render them harmless. This was no easy feat with the animal snapping deadly teeth so near, but Dremtessa kept her wits. She managed to finish with the claws, and then clamp shut and wrap the menacing muzzle. At this point, she might easily have kicked the bear's back legs out from under it and let the beast fall with the full force of its weight into the prickly patch. Instead she hoisted it over her shoulder, braving its flailing hind legs and knife-like back claws to save it further pain.

"Open!" She commanded, and she heard the rest of the Coven echo her from their perch on Third Hill, "Open!"

The Path opened again, and the exhausted woman sank onto soft mossy earth, tumbled the bear off of herself, and then kept it pinned to the ground with her superior size as she carefully rested her forehead against the bear's panting flank. The terrorized animal calmed. Dremtessa gently shifted her weight. She placed her forehead on that of the bear. An entire night passed with the woman and the bear seemingly frozen in this position, while the others stood watch.

When morning came, Dremtessa unwrapped the bear's snout and jaw. Brunagwa, also in a sort of armor that she used for hunting, came down to them with a large hare that she had prepared in a raw style she thought a bear would like. The others followed: Sestorina on horseback, wearing a colorful woven serape from the steppes over her everyday garb; Hesterluna, tripping along in her distinctive university robes that flapped around her noisily, the deep sleeves weighed down with several small volumes of lore and wildlife manuals; and Intuisha in a billowing wool caftan and long linen vest, starting out from behind but quickly overtaking them all with her great strides. She took the aromatic basket from Brunagwa and presented it to the hungry animal at her long arm's length.

While the bear devoured the food, Sestorina motioned for her Familiar to come close. The smell of the horse caught the attention of the appetized animal; the bear looked up from the now empty and half-eaten basket. The moment their eyes met, Flame-Mari demonstrated her ability to transform into a woman.

The bear watched warily but did not rage.

"Her name is Roth," Dremtessa said.

Roth melted gently into a figure resembling a woman, which released her paws from their bindings. Her new Goathorns family began to move closer to lend comfort, she looked so confused and vulnerable. But the twins, attuned to Roth's desperate thoughts, issued a sudden warning.

"No! Get away!"

Everyone backed off quickly, and the almost-woman surged into the shape of a massive grizzly bear. This bear was much larger than Dremtessa could possibly have matched in strength had *it* been the version of Roth to come down from the cliffs. Now Dremtessa stepped back and locked elbows with Intuisha. The twins stood tall and fierce while the beast raised itself to two legs and roared until the mountains shook. Sestorina shielded her older sisters with her mount, while her feisty herd, with Flame-Mari in the lead, circled wide round the bear and took turns rearing up and screeching threateningly. The Coven trembled but did not run.

Roth expelled her years of anguish and frustration. The terrible sound rose up and up, was amplified, then rained back down to earth doubled in volume, and doubling again. When it seemed the very ground would shatter from the force of her roar, the grizzly quieted, shrank back into the form of a black bear, and, with a brief backward glance at Dremtessa, bounded up to her caves.

"Roth says thank you." Intuisha spoke for her twin, who had quickly diminished in size once the threat was passed. The oversized armor crumpled to the ground, and Dremtessa crawled wearily out from the stiff shell to collapse in the fresh air.

"You have done well, sister," they all commended her with relief. Then they carried her up to Witches Meadow, parted to fetch provisions, and returned to celebrate with a rare noontime ritual and feast.

The next time the black bear showed itself on its high ledge, Dremtessa and Intuisha went to it together, and they began to forge their bond.

Once Roth had mastered her form as the woman Thea, she and the twins began to make regular visits to Witches Meadow, where they cleared the bigger rocks away to make more space for the Coven's sacred circle. These rocks were used in the building of Hesterluna's small fortress in the foresty area that runs between the meadow and Red River to the west and south. The home of the new Meadow Watch Witch was made comfortable and civilized within, while looking like a natural tumble of rocks from the outside. And it was Hesterluna, with her worldliness and superior education, who took in hand not only the once wild bear Roth-Thea, but also the grossly neglected twins themselves, so as to provide her youngest sisters with some education.

Roth-Thea, in her new womanly form, took to the lessons eagerly, and gratified Hesterluna with her hunger for knowledge and interest in the life of Humans and the world beyond the mystical Goathorns. Long after the twins retired to their hideouts and abandoned any attachment to "reality" such as the rest of us, on either side of the Spiral, might know it, Roth-Thea continued her studies. Though Roth-Thea never attained as fine a female figure as the other Familiars, her elegance of mind surpasses all.

(A pause here, while I jot down the name of another suspect in the case of that mysterious publication, *The Time Dancer*.)

As the twins told it, the sisters had worked as one to rescue the bear, and so the bear was adopted by the whole Coven. That said, Roth-Thea did model herself loosely after Dremtessa, and she was always most loyal to the twins. She shared their space, after all—or, more correctly, she shared her space with them. The other sisters were finding their own Familiars. Sestorina had the mare Flame-Mari, as we have seen. And Brunagwa, now atop Red Mountain, would attract the attention of the old hawk Ti before too long, and become the first of the sisters to actually *require* her own Minder-Familiar.

As for Hesterluna, who had experienced a highly intellectual life out in the great cities, she had some difficulty leaving civilization behind and bringing her witchy talents to full fruition. Tutoring the twins and Roth-Thea was hardly the mental challenge she craved. She relied heavily on Varluft's mentorship and company, and she made frequent trips to Ochersfeldt. Witches Meadow fairly bustled as the new gathering place for the sisters now that Sestorina had booted everyone out of Six Hills. It would be some time before a Familiar was found to join Hesterluna in her busy domain. But there was more to this than just the distressing level of activity in the meadow.

To whit, the once Professor Redfern made no effort to adopt any sort of woodsy ways or wardrobe. Hesterluna had started out as a shepherdess in rope sandals and smelly woolens, and she had no intention of reverting to those rough ways. Though her domicile was camouflaged, Hesterluna was not. When the original purple and orange robe of her highest academic function went to tatters, she fetched more of the same fabrics from Ochersfeldt, and insisted that Brunagwa assemble another just like it. Over time, this costume has been made more form-fitting and low-cut in front, while the satiny purple panels and orange linings remain, so that our voluptuous Meadow Watch Witch stands out starkly against the glade. She haunts the dreams of many a Goathorns interloper.

Obviously, our regular denizens prefer to be more circumspect. It would take a uniquely obnoxious critter to hold her own with Hesterluna in Witches Meadow. One was found eventually, but, as I recall, the twins did not dance any part of the story of Snip-Edie. Perhaps they were unclear on the details of how that had been settled, since by then they had retreated into their caves. Or maybe they didn't want to take the liberty, because Snip-Edie wasn't present. . .

Yes, back to this puzzle. Now that I think about it, I did *not* see Badger in the meadow that night. I assumed she was there, because she is the Familiar of the Meadow Watch Witch. One assumes she is always there—or one ought to, so as not to be surprised by any tricks. Snip the badger is a sulky thing, and nasty if you should ever see her, so she is not much missed when she chooses to stay under cover.

The other one I'm missing on the perimeter of the twins' second performance is Yani-Yau. I'd assumed that she was also lurking out of sight but near at hand should Intuisha call for her. Like Snip-Edie, Yani-Yau was a latecomer to the Coven, and she seems to have been omitted from the Story Dances. It didn't mean much to me at the time. Who could have foreseen how Badger and Cougar would come to the forefront of our tale as events unfold, leading to the mix-up with the flying carpets? But come to the forefront they will, and to learn about *their* pasts we must first catch up to them in the Present.

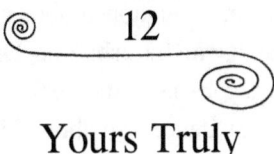

12

Yours Truly

NOT SO FAST, SAYS ROBYN. (FIRST SHE TRIES TO RUSH ME, NOW the opposite.) According to her, although I have recounted in detail the histories of the five sisters, I have said the least about the events that concern *me* the most. My Editor figures that I have told the story of Brunagwa from her Familiar Nee-Reta's vantage, and from her sister Sestorina's. I have narrated the Story Dance of Brunagwa's own auric emanation, and observed Brunagwa on Red Mountain by looking across the eddy of Time from Intuisha's cliffs. And I have exposed my "love/hate relationship" with her (Robyn's words, not mine—when did I ever use the word "hate"?) but I have yet to explain *myself* or convey the lurid details and peculiarities of my affair with the Red Mountain Witch from my own perspective.

I would have thought this would be the area of least curiosity for my magic-obsessed Editor, because Romance is the one form of magic that transcends the Spiral and is very much the same from one side to the next. Besides, who among the Witches could have told the story of Yours Truly in the language of dance or any other? Only Sestorina danced of love, her own true love. But it turned so quickly into a story of love lost that she was bitter by the end, just like her older sisters. No, there were no sympathetic tellers of men's tales in this women-only club.

Brunagwa's auric autobiography ended with the twins' summons and her return to Ochersfeldt. She revealed nothing of her subsequent life on Red Mountain. The twins skipped over every bit of that as well—even the turning-into-cranes incident, in which I might have made an appearance at least by reference. With respect to Brunagwa, Intuisha and Dremtessa were only interested in Ti-Wyan, for she would be the next Familiar to join Goathorns Coven. They danced all about Ti, up to her bringing Brunagwa back through the Loophole after the encounter with little Robyn—and even here they did not refer to the reason for Brunagwa's meanderings, which was her wish to find *me*. I had been expunged from the record. How do you like that?

At any rate, it will be more efficient for me to tell my own story than to tell about someone else telling it—which I would rewrite anyway if I didn't like it. So we might as well get to it directly. Herewith, the story of Yours Truly, the authorized version:

H. TOAD, H. COYOTE, AND AMOS GOATHORN BROOKS

Horned Lizard guarded the trail that led to Red Mountain. Hard to say how or why or when. I may have existed from the beginning of Time, or at least from the beginning of the Goathorns. But I think if I was a First, or had been, I would know it—don't you? I hate to think that I could have been a First and then fallen this far. Still, I do go back quite a ways, I know that. If I have to put myself together in any way with the Firsts—and these things do come to mind, especially here in this odd limbo awaiting Fate's fancy, not to mention having actually been *asked* (more like commanded) to state my origins—

Where was I?

Right. The Firsts. Most probably they existed umptymillion spiral-turns *before* my time. *But*, if I *had* to speculate on some *possible* direct link between me and the Firsts oh-so-far-back, the most plausible scenario would have to be this: that a First, in performing some heroic deed like they were always doing, sacrificed a toe—in a landslide perhaps. In gratitude to the toe, its First owner granted the toe, with its thick, jagged, protective nail, a life of its own. And this new offspring (as it were) of the Firsts became the Horned Lizard or Horny Toad.

You know, the more I think about it, the more I like this theory. And if that toe-turned-Lizard *wasn't* me (really, you'd think I'd remember that), it could have been the old Horny Toad before me, or one before him. (Though I don't remember a Paw or Granpaw any more than I do the Firsts. Plus, as I explained earlier, Minder traits are not typically passed down through generations, although we have been reminded recently that exceptions do occur.) At any rate, I am quite convinced, now that I have given it some thought, that the first Horny Toad came from the Toe of a First.

(Well, you asked, Robyn. You're welcome to posit other theories, but I think mine is quite promising. When this is all over, I will ask Hesterluna to give it some academic study— assuming we are still on speaking terms.)

My point is that H. Toad *was* even before my memories began. He was on guard, although there was little to guard against for time uncounted. Eventually things in the foothills below the Goathorns changed, which led to things in the Goathorns changing; and as things changed, H. changed with them.

For instance, as the town of Ochersfeldt grew, Humans began to venture up the trail that H. guarded. Sometimes they hunted. We all hunt. They did not offend H. Toad. I could not speak their language but I could read their hearts. At first they did not trouble me. But over time what I began to read in the hearts of Humans was less about hunger or warm coverings and more about desire. That is how I perceived it—a hunger not for food, not for mating. I have since learned to understand this as a desire for wealth, which includes power over others, and that this kind of desire is called greed.

My own desire to understand these things caused me to begin to experiment with other animal forms. The coyote was useful because the people did not hunt it for its meat or pelt. Coyote frightened them. He could track them and keep up with them in the woods. He could howl a warning to the forest when they stalked around at night.

Eventually, Coyote followed the Humans down the hillside. Coyote had begun to have desires too, cravings for certain foods. My nose and belly led me to the camp of the circus people, down the hill from the municipal circus grounds. Even back then, the town kept up a big lawn ringed with simple structures to provide a space for vendors and performers. The itinerants themselves camped near Red River, where they were comfortable in their own tents and wagons.

As I observed, so I was observed. A clever character trapped me and took me to the circus to be in his show. He fed me well, and I performed. I had a very mysterious trick: I could get out of any cage. I bet you know how I did it. Since it only worked when no one was watching, even my keeper didn't know the secret. He put me in a pen, draped it with a dark cloth, and soon after I was stalking him from the other side of the ring. Like I said, he fed me well—his health depended on it.

There was no point anyone trying to chain or cage me after hours. Eventually even the most devoted watchman would shift his attention, and in that moment Coyote could run away if he chose to. Naturally, my keeper and others figured out that I hadn't been trapped at all, I had allowed myself to be caught. My secrets made them uneasy. When the group left town, they happily left me behind, even though I had made good money for them.

The circus troupe thought they had given me the slip, but in truth there is only so far I can ever go from the Goathorns. I have never traveled with the circus, it has always come to me. After some number of circuses, between one group and another, H. gave up being an animal act and presented himself as the man Amos Goathorn.

The question arises as to what I knew of the Redferns and their taxidermy business, the wife, the daughters, and all of that. Once again I can only speculate, because memories such as they were for H. Coyote, just as for H. Toad, lacked solidity and sequentiality all the way until A.G. mastered the human mindset, and that only came late in the game (from my perspective, stretching perchance as I may all the way back to the severed toe of a late First). H. Coyote was far advanced from H. Toad in some respects, like communications with other species, but not so swift intellectually. His only thought was of food.

One is hard pressed to pin down exactly when things changed, but I will venture to suggest that the Redferns themselves had much to do with my evolution from H. Toad/Coyote to the man Amos Goathorn. Each encounter sparked my curiosity and propelled me further toward my human form. These especially vivid memories from my transitional period reveal the significant moments at which our paths crossed, and suggest that exposure to the Redfern women had a cumulative influence on me:

—A distraught wife consults a Gypsy fortune-teller in her wagon at the edge of town. Nearby rests the animal act in the Gypsies' traveling circus—a coyote with sharp hearing and the ability to receive people's thoughts.

—A very smart young shepherdess and her well trained dogs frustrate a hungry coyote who stalks the flock during lambing season. The predator begins to take more notice of the unique qualities of his opponent.

—Fresh dancing horses are acquired by the lucky circus troupe that is playing Ochersfeldt when the Prince of the Steppes rides into town with his equine wares. Because of the appealing woman who takes up with him, the exotic man's manners are closely observed and catalogued, along with those of the circus

men and the local male sorts, by one who is considering a change
of image.

—Giant little girls are espied in the foothills. Their thoughts
are so probing, H. Coyote quickly reverts to H. Toad to escape
them. The Minder is alert to them thereafter—their psychic
abilities act as a bridge to the human language.

—Word around town is that the taxidermy shop is full of
glorious women: "You have to see it to believe it."

And now the truth comes out. However and whyever I first
chose to add a human male to my Minder repertoire, it was my
awareness, as Man, of the beauty of Woman that drove me
onward in my task. I decided to practice my new trick one day by
sauntering into the Redfern shop to take a gander at the sisters.
The twins made me nervous and I didn't stay long, but I have had
my eye on Brunagwa ever after. In fact, I can safely say that
there has never since been an accidental meeting between
us—myself and Brunagwa the Red Mountain Witch. She has
always been the object of my attraction.

(If you were to press your dear Ramon, my dear Robyn, I
expect you would find that not one of *your* "coincidental"
encounters early on was really accidental. A man in love does not
leave things to chance.)

Have we established that I was well aware of the Redfern
women both before and after the taxidermy shop inferno? I left
the sisters to their own devices during the time they stayed in Six
Hills and explored eastward toward the caverns. I was working
diligently on my male form. Once the Witches started roaming
north and west above the meadow, H. was obliged to take more
notice. Soon I caught wind of the sumptuous smells issuing from
Brunagwa's cook fire up on the mountain, and I worked harder
than ever to achieve Amos Goathorn.

First it was her beauty, then it was her cooking, and finally it
was her stormy soul. Everything about Brunagwa attracted me,
and I spared no wile or deception to gain her favor. I began by

gleaning secrets from Ochersfeldt's magicians and circus tricksters in order to play to the Witch's fantasies while disguising my true nature. My approach was dishonest—I knew no better—but my love was true. And hers was too, or she could not have accepted me for so long without suspicion. We were a happy pair for a moment in Time. Atop her mountain we created our own reality.

What changed?

Something sparked her curiosity about me. Love itself played a part. For the more we love, the more we need to know—to *own* in some way—the beloved. Add to that Sestorina's discovery of Flame-Mari, and you can see how the pieces of the puzzle may have been starting to fall into place for our infatuated Witch. When Brunagwa finally turned her second sight on me, there was nothing I could do but flee. I did not feel worthy of her judgment, I was in no way ready for her wrath. I had come to know Brunagwa well by then—her critical eye and her demanding nature. I expected her to be outraged at my deception, and I would have been disappointed were she not.

I cut my losses and dropped out of sight, which meant retreating deep into Ochersfeldt and staying there until the thing blew over. The growing Green Quarter was as far as I could go. Amos picked up a lot of skills there. The crystal skyscrapers were going up, and they generated a new kind of magical energy. But then my Minder link to the Goathorns began weakening. I felt sick, like I was aging, and I worried that I would never again roam the foothills of Red Mountain as H. Toad or H. Coyote. What if I were consigned to be a Human for the rest of my days? It would be a living hell.

(Excuse me. I need to think about that for a moment...)

The prospect of losing my Minder abilities drove me out of Green Quarter and back to the Goathorns side of Ochersfeldt, and gradually back up Red Mountain, closer and closer to Brunagwa's lodge. When they finally noticed me, Brunagwa, Ti-

Wyan, and later Nee-Reta accepted H. Toad as a forest friend and possibly a Minder. If they connected me to a lover that Brunagwa once dreamed up, or a clever coyote, they tactfully did not let on.

After Brunagwa's satchel was stolen and Nee-Reta—and I—had been to The Top of The World, Ti-Wyan, our unofficial Minder of Minders put me—that is H.—in charge of the Knot and the Loophole. The Witches and their Familiars and I made our peace. Everyone seemed willing to live with H. Coyote, so long as I restricted the man Amos to the other side of the Loophole. Periodically I took the long way down to Ochersfeldt to snoop around. Nothing much had changed there. It seemed that we were into another of those chunks of quiet, uncounted time that we are prone to in these parts.

The doings on the other side restarted the clock. There was a First Annual, a Second Annual— I was bolder each year. In between Harmony Conventions, I began to establish my identity in the Alternate World. It made it easier to linger at Kestrel Lodge. I took the last name Brooks, the name I had given to my new Alternate World creation, Frog. The man Brooks is also a new creation, a refinement over Amos Goathorn. Not that Brunagwa and the others have noticed. (Perhaps I comply with this documentary folly only to demonstrate my evolution.)

Amos G. Brooks became a Harmony Convention regular. If anyone ever thought to ask, he was attending on a work scholarship. He might have mingled more and been welcome, but he preferred to sit with a book in a quiet niche when he had completed his work. The lodge had accumulated an extensive collection of classics. These novels taught Brooks a good deal about human nature across the Spiral (not to mention how they prepared me for this epic effort). And so by the Fourth Annual Harmony Convention I was, in my own nebulous way, a fixture. Very unassuming and helpful. Everyone called me Bro. By the Fifth—and last, so help me—

Ah, we have finally caught up to ourselves. Or have we? No, not yet. I pray, not yet. There is a tumult all around me, and I much prefer the orderliness (attempted, anyway) of my narrative. I will forge ahead with Robyn's growing list of questions. Perhaps some clarity of mind on my part will help clear the air here, and when I lift my head again things will not be so unpleasant. (Seriously, when it came to instilling their Familiars with womanly traits, the sisters did not scrimp on temper. My present confinement with just two of them will haunt my dreams for many a spiral-turn.)

But where was I?

Where indeed. Robyn says I have yet to explain where I am as I write, who I am with, or what brought me to this place. I might remind her that it was she who insisted I backtrack to my own biography—

Right. I had been writing my way to the two Familiars who were left out of the Story Dancing, the badger Snip-Edie and the cougar Yani-Yau. If you should surmise that these are the creatures who now torment my peace, you would be correct. Our location will be made clear in due course. As for the *why* of it all, the answer to that has always been: the rugs.

Yes, we will need to circle round one more time (you know how we dogs like to do that). I have one more layer to scratch away before I can settle into anything like sequentiality. But before you turn the page, kind Reader, you may want to flip back to Chapter—

No, I take that back, it will only encourage Robyn to try to shuffle things. Read on. I've got nothing better to do, I'll explain as we go along.

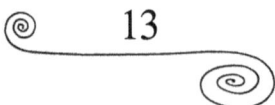

13

The Mystery of the Rugs

THE RUGS HAVE BEEN MY MAIN CONCERN RIGHT ALONG, HAVE they not? Since The Time Winders brought them to the Harmony Convention, I have been trying to figure out how to return them to my side of the Spiral where they belong. The mystery of how they got away from us has been equally perplexing.

By my estimate, it was around the time the Witches performed their Story Dances, and well before the Harmony Conventions accelerated the leakage across the border, that Malcom the Master Seer flung himself back in Time and started going around again. Strangely, he was not perceived by the Coven. Stranger still, he was not perceived by *me*. How could that be?

Fortunately, my forays into Piper Canyon as the man Brooks have provided me opportunity to indulge that unique variety of reasoning Humans possess. As Brooks, I hearkened back to Nee-Reta's adventure and her visions, which I originally observed as H. Toad and Coyote. Hadn't I followed Nee-Reta to Oshi all those years ago and observed her observing the Future from The Top of The World? Yet I had never since detected the return of Malcom to Ochersfeldt and the second version of events that had been portended—the creation of the rugs and the experiments of this E. Arap. How could all of that have happened under the very sensitive nose of H. Coyote? And how had the rugs eluded me on their way *out* of the Goathorns—and ended up in the *Alternate World*?

I replayed in my mind's eye Reta's overview of Malcom's destiny, which took her all the way to his epiphany about his inadequate younger self, leading to his resolve to launch the flying carpet from outside of Ochersfeldt, so as to ultimately occupy the body of George Drumm. Her distress at such a prospect cut short her vision. I presumed that this was the point at which Oshi was allowing some leeway in her weft for Reta to configure a happier outcome. Perhaps the rug business had been avoided.

Then I learned that a number of Arap's rugs had *already* escaped into the Alternate World. Robyn twirled herself across the Spiral on them two nights in a row. And imagine my horror when I overheard Black Star hounding Oscar Too about an additional stash of rugs residing at The Lost Unicorn many miles away. He was plotting how to buy them back from Robyn so they could bump up the price and make a handsome profit in the last big days of the convention. From all of this, I concluded that we were well past the return of the disembodied magician and quickly approaching the time of the Malcoms' revolt.

What had Reta said? That Malcom believed that, using Arap's body, he could fly a magic carpet to the Gypsy caravan of Esma's clan. There he would find George Drumm, transfer into the young man's body, steal Gypsy Huliyana's magic satchel, and go to the Future to find Esmarelda. Malcom, in George's body, would win Esma's heart. The unhappy circumstances of Malcom and Esmarelda's previous encounters need never occur...

But, how long *had* the Malcoms been working on the rug project with Arap? The magician was clearly mixed up about Time. His flying carpet would have to do more than carry him across the plains of the Wide Wilde to achieve his end, it would have to transport him back a decade. Add to that how completely shielded Malcom's been from me on my occasional forays into Ochersfeldt—how unchanged I found the place on every visit—- and there could be only one explanation. The answer was literally right under my nose. The Malcoms were not in Ochersfeldt, they were in the Knot, spinning out a self-contained mini-timescape, not altering Time itself.

That is, they *shouldn't* have been altering the whole of Time. And yet they were.

I promised to eventually account for my whereabouts at the end of Chapter 2, and we are coming to that at last (into the double digits just as I predicted). Do you recall my playing Piper Canyon tour guide for Faye, so as to keep her from encountering Esmarelda and George Drumm? I know it seems like lifetimes ago, but it was only the day before the day before—hmm, uhmm—let's say yesterday (once again, it depends how you count). In the bracing early morning air of the rational Alternate World, I was able to reason out the puzzle of Malcom's second time around in Ochersfeldt.

After making sure Faye was safely off the trail, I returned to my side of the Spiral to search for the spot where the consciousness of Malcom the Master Seer would attempt to leap from the body of his younger but doltish self into that of the elder but spunky Arap. I didn't get far before I witnessed the Gypsies interacting with Brunagwa's Familiar, Nee-Reta—Nee-Reta *out of the Past*. It was that long afternoon of the Summer Solstice, midway through the absolutely last Harmony Convention that will ever be held in Piper Canyon, and I was already determined to venture into the Knot, which I had previously avoided as much as possible. As it turned out, *I was already there.*

Not surprisingly, time does get murky here. My literary leaps have not helped, so let me place this bit in sequence on either side of the Spiral: In the Alternate World timeline, we are talking about Friday afternoon following Faye's morning jaunt in the lowlands (not to be confused with her hike up the mountain with

Robyn at dawn the next day). On my side, we are between the Gypsies' odd morning encounter with Nee-Reta, and their odd evening overlook of Malcom's past.

In my personal chronology, I simply track this episode as the afternoon I saw Dark for the first time.

DARK

I saw him, and yet nothing of him registered save his size. He was a big house pet, as best I could tell, exuding no magic, clearly anxious for someone to appear and take him home. Strangely, he seemed not to register me, not even a whiff of my fearful musk. So I figured he had come through the Loophole and hadn't the senses for our side. His owners were probaby camped in Piper Canyon and would be looking for him. I would return him after my work was done.

Without hostility, the black dog and I waited below the High Road for something to happen, each hunkered down and panting in the shade of a rocky outcropping. Our attention was focused on a wide turn of the sandy trail just below us. In the glare of the full force of the sun, the air shimmered with heat. Our canine ears had picked up the distant sound of trudging feet and cartwheels grinding over the path. Our hackles raised when the sound had become so clear and near that the travelers would surely be rounding the corner at any moment.

But those we awaited did not appear and advance toward us from behind the cliff wall—they took shape right out of that thin, shimmering air. Malcom strode ahead arrogantly. Behind him, an elderly man labored to push a two-wheeled cart loaded with skeins of wool, wooden loom parts, tools, provisions, and one complete rug. The cocky young magician burst into the splash of sunshine and into solid form with an ugly leer shaping his lips. His attention was focused on his companion, not on the sleek black dog and the mangy coyote who were both silently shifting weight and tensing haunches to leap.

"Come along now, you old sluggard!" Malcom chided, turning his back to us.

Having also emerged from a blur into substance, the once-elegant merchant looked the worse for wear. His frame hollowed out, his garments faded and tattered, Arap watched Malcom grimly.

"Come out from behind that cart," Malcom commanded.

Arap slowly lowered the handles of the cart and stepped around it.

While the older man retained his form, the younger was losing his as quickly as he had gained it. Malcom could see this himself when he reached out forcefully toward Arap—how his hands and arms were becoming wavery and translucent.

"No! No! You devil! You betrayer!"

The raging magician threw himself at Arap.

In a beat I could have lunged forward to stop him, but there was no flesh to fell, for the young man had dissolved into a white hot blast of energy. As quickly, the old rug maker rose up into a giant eagle and used its massive wings to corral those angry sparks into a glowing orb.

"Iyeeee!" The eagle's shrill call repelled the orb of light—it changed its path and came toward *me*. Now I reared up, expanded to my greatest size, and howled with all my strength to deflect this frightening force. The black dog, meanwhile, was on the attack. Beyond the fiery orb, I could see the beast bearing down on me—one more leap and it would have my throat in its jaws. I twisted out of its path and rolled to the ground, readying myself for the fight. But when I lifted my head, I saw that the dog had not changed its direction. It was lunging for the orb, not me, and when the two collided it was as though the dog devoured the light, and it burned and churned in his belly. He bucked like a wild horse for long minutes before collapsing into a panting heap of half-dead dog.

I sniffed my way over to it, keeping one eye on what was now a regular sized eagle perched atop the load in the wagon. I half expected the dog to smell burnt, but it didn't. It smelled of the forest—my forest. How could that be? I had never seen it, heard it, or smelled it before.

But the eagle was familiar, as were the scents around the cart and the ground where the old rug maker had stood. I was working my way around the whole clearing now. Though the heat was draining, I didn't dare transform into H. Toad within range of that murderous eagle beak.

"Not to worry, Coyote." The eagle spoke to me in the language of the Minders.

"Of course not, 'tis just another day in the Knot," I growled suspiciously.

"You'll have to trust me, H. If I change back into Varluft, we won't be able to talk in this way. Your Brooks is not viable here; we would need to cross the Loophole to speak together in human tongue."

"Master Seer Varluft?" I was shocked, of course, though I had little emotion for the man, unlike the sisters—or Malcom. When the name Varluft was passed between us on our thoughts, the black dog raised his ears in recognition. He hadn't the strength to move any other part of his body.

"Who is he?" I asked, reverting to my horned lizard form to better bear the heat. Varluft's Eagle was the stuff of magic and hadn't the appetite of a bird of prey.

"Why, that's Malcom—Malcom the Master Seer. All grown up, grown wicked and greedy, got dead on account of it— physically—but powerful enough to keep his spirit going to try to put into the bodies of others, and not quite ever succeeding. Now he's ended up in this unfortunate dog."

"You don't know the dog?"

"No. He's from the other side, don't you think?"

"I thought so, but he smells like here."

"Well, you would know. But you didn't give him a good sniff

'til Malcom had already joined with him. And Malcom's definitely from here. And who knows how long that dog's been lost on this side."

"He looked like he was waiting for the two of you to appear," I told Varluft. *"And then like he wanted to, well, consume that ball of spirit. And by the way, what happened to the young Malcom who was walking ahead of you, who had been housing the spirit of the older Malcom?"*

(See how quickly I catch on, Robyn, even as a horned lizard? Are you keeping up?)

"That man was not young Malcom himself, only his reflection in the spur of Time that I created after I faked my death."

The dog whimpered. It still lay in the sun. Varluft ignored it and continued:

"As soon as we crossed the boundary of the spur, the body lost substance, and Malcom had to relocate to another. He had intended to do so anyway, and he had intended to take me first and then move on. We are lucky the dog was here."

"Then we shouldn't let it die," I chided. Varluft was in my domain—in fact he was the cause of my labors. It was time to exert my authority as Minder of the Knot and the Loophole. *"Do as I say."*

And he did. Human again, he lifted the dog into the cart and prepared to push. H. Coyote led him to a spring, beside which he set the dog to take water and recuperate. Then we two went through the Loophole, where we could talk man to man.

Arap—Varluft—was delighted to be back in Time, back from the dead, and already on a grand adventure to the Alternate World. But he quickly sobered when he learned that he had been making real magic there in his spur of Time, real rugs, which really escaped across the Spiral, and now threatened to warp the careful coils of the Spiral Map of Time.

"You two are going to have to help get the rugs back."

I referred to Varluft and the dog that housed Malcom. They

were Master Seers, after all. They would have to go where I could not and get the rugs out of The Lost Unicorn in Caliente, while I focused on getting those that had been brought to the Harmony Convention. To Varluft's credit, but not to mine, he returned to the dog and made it comply.

Let us remember that the two magicians had spent some while in an illusory spur of Time, the one so ancient as to be half dead, and the other only half a being to start with, housed in a mandrake charm. In my frustration, I unleashed this madness on the Alternate World and the very fragile place I was charged with protecting. I had thought they would use magic to reach Caliente in astral form and work a charm to call the rugs back, but instead they thrashed right into the Knot and out again, making a dangerous new passage. And all the while Malcom was close to ripping out Varluft's throat. Who could blame him? He'd already had a bad time of it as a black cat, and now found himself trapped within a black dog—and back in the dread Alternate World. He made the pair so fearsome that Zeek resisted selling the rugs. They had to lurk in No Place and wait for another day to dawn in Caliente, while I looked out over the Past with Esmarelda and George Drumm, and reflected on the errors of my ways.

When Esma and George and I watched the escapades of young Malcom, I knew we were seeing a reprise of actual events that had actually occurred, for I had experienced some of those events firsthand. In contrast, no part of Reta-Nee's long-ago Top of The World vision of Malcom's *future* ever did come to pass in all the time I watched for it—until recently, when I learned that it had all *already* occurred within a spell concocted by the great Varluft. It was supposed to be a self-contained spell, but some had leaked out. As the eddy of Time swirled away, I realized that whatever was to come of the rugs, I mustn't risk sending the two magicians to the Alternate World a second time.

Yes, H. Toad was clear-headed on that score, whereas Amos G. Brooks, for all his supposed rationality, had not acted wisely.

Now, where was I?

(Seriously, Robyn, I have gotten all in a muddle.)

Ah, my Editor proves her worth. I went back to the end of Chapter 2, she reminds me, to reveal what I had been doing leading up to the Gypsies' overlook of Malcom's life from Intuisha's cliffs. In the last page or so, I caught up to that scene, which means we have arrived at Solstice night *again*.

I don't like her tone, but her irritation does underscore the nuances of this saga. We have two sides of the Spiral to account for, after all. In the Alternate World, our story has progressed beyond Friday night, when the Harmony crowd celebrated Solstice elaborately while at The Lost Unicorn in Caliente Zeek slept, uncomfortably tracing the edges of the Spiral with his subconscious. But I have yet to show you what was transpiring on my side that same Solstice eve.

Yes, that is *exactly* where I was. Here we go . . .

On my side, literally on the edge of the Knot, the eddy of Time collapsed into the canyon. The Gypsy couple slept. I changed from H. Toad to H. Coyote. The cougar Yau, who had been observing us so quietly that her presence was almost forgotten, sprang to action.

I shuddered when I felt Yau's call go out to the Coven. (In your tongue, something like: "We will get them now.") The Familiars and their mistresses had more often been my adversaries than allies, even when we worked for common cause, and my hackles rose. Having decided that the Master Seers must not return to Caliente, I felt quite capable of calling them back. Why Yau would think her help was needed— Or had she been instructed to take charge of me and my duties?

Despite my confusion and resentment, Yau easily coaxed me into the hunt. The corralling of Varluft and Malcom felt more like play than duty to Cougar and Coyote, at least at the start.

Working together, we stalked the two Master Seers through the murk of No Place.

The viciousness of the black dog was requiring old Varluft to muster up all manner of musty magic. Although he strove to constrain the demented embodiment of that delinquent Malcom just as we did, he did not spare his allies. Enveloped in choking white smoke, tripped up by enlivened tree roots, and pelted with a shower of falling stars that looked like hail and felt like embers, Yau and I pressed on.

These mere physical agonies were the least of our problems, as it turned out. We were sidetracked and split up several times by unexpected voices:

"Hullo? What is this place?"

"Oh, m'word, I've just walked into me-self... Where are you, love? Lovey?"

"Hush, now... By the unholy powers that best be not, there's a giant yonder."

"Where? I hear him snoring..."

"Careful, careful. Follow my voice... Take my hand... there we go."

"The book doesn't say anything about a place like this."

(There it is—the book!)

Around and around Yau and I went, trying to locate the mouths from whence this dialogue issued. If it was a trick of Varluft's, it was the most diabolical yet. *"Is the old Master Seer trying to trap us in the Knot?"* Yani-Yau relayed her question mind-to-mind, after we had struggled back along tangled trails and were converging again on the man and dog.

"If so, he is truly mad. Maybe the young one is doing it," I answered.

"Or there really are others here in No Place with us."

That was a troubling thought. But if it was true, our chances of getting them out would be far better once we had the two magicians safely in hand.

Yani-Yau followed my logic, and with renewed effort we tracked, triangulated and maneuvered Varluft and Dark-Malcom through the fearsome twinings of the Knot and into the merely frigid passageways below Goathorns Peak. We drove them toward the lair of the queen of dreams, and herded them down, down into Dremtessa's Ice Caves.

The bear Roth did not show herself until we had the panting pair backed into an icy cleft. We snarled and snapped but did not go closer, knowing to stay within a leap of the path to the surface. Leap we did when Roth sprang from her den in the depth of the caverns to secure the prisoners. Her roar shook the caverns and loosened spears of ice from the rock above. Man and dog were pinned between the frozen cave wall and bars of icicles. Exhausted and numbed by cold, their bodies quickly sagged into sleep.

Roth snuffled at the strangers, then padded away to make room for Dremtessa. The great woman, clad in a woolen jumper over thick red longjohns, poked her nose between the icicles and cooed to the slumbering prisoners. Yau and I began to back away. We ourselves were growing cold, could feel our reflexes slowing. When Dremtessa drew near, preceded by a chilling mist, we fled before we could be frozen by her breath.

"Good work," she called after us, and I could feel needles of cold stabbing my haunches. "Terribly out of place, both of them. I'll keep them on ice until we can put them back where they belong." At that, Dremtessa and her Familiar laughed it up, while the cougar and I sprang through a shower of ice. Cougar and Coyote emerged into the desert night singed, bruised and bloodied.

(Robyn of the soft heart does not care for the image, but I'm trying to impress that the Goathorns is a dangerous place even for the magically endowed.)

This would have been a good time to compare notes with my new compatriot, or at least to sniff out more of Yani-Yau's motives to see if she could be trusted. But Intuisha came sweeping down from the High Caverns in a snit, fussed over her bleeding cat briefly, then snapped her fingers and sent the big baby bounding up to its lair.

No better than a spoiled housepet, that one, I thought, *and I'm in the doghouse again, slinking away to lick my wounds until morning. How am I going to get Robyn to send for the rest of the rugs? Black Star has already tried, and she refused.*

Black Star. Now there was another puzzle. And Oscar Too, too. How did they come to be the ones trading in these wayward rugs that must inevitably end up with Robyn? H. Coyote dragged himself back through the Loophole, where I could emerge as a not-so-scathed Brooks and have a look around for Black Star. The shaman was nowhere to be found.

It was dawn already, and I was looking forward to mooching some grub from the campers, but I got wind of two wayward Time Winders before I got a whiff of any cooking, and I had to hurry after them (the work of a Minder is never done) and further exhaust myself transitioning from a frog to a lizard and back again, while the ninnies poked all around the Knot on one side and then the other—

Ah, but wait. Haven't we been here before? The last time I'd followed Robyn and Faye on their dawn excursion, I'd crossed effortlessly—really unintentionally—into the Knot to join the Gypsies on Intuisha's cliff *the night before*. There we'd had the entire lookback on Malcom's original arrival in Ochersfeldt. Now, here I was right back with Robyn and Faye where I'd left off. If I wasn't careful, I would go around with the entire sequence again, when what I wanted to do was sneak back over *now*, while the Gypsies slept off their strange vision, to see if I could catch that cat for breakfast.

This time I stuck close to Robyn and Faye to make sure they were safely out of the borderlands and heading back to Kestrel Lodge. Then I conscientiously returned via my usual passage through the Loophole, and wended my way up to the ledge where Esmarelda and George were camped. Here was a dawn that synched to Robyn and Faye's dawn on the other side (their Saturday). I forbade myself to contemplate how many such dawns and night-befores might exist in the jumble of the Knot.

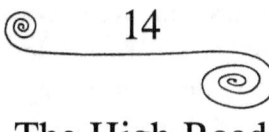

14

The High Road

AFTER THE EDDY OF TIME HAD DISSOLVED BACK INTO THE canyon, Esma and George fell into a deep sleep. Sylvester returned while they snoozed. When I appeared on the scene, I found my prey wedged safely between the man and woman. How warm and happy they all looked. I could've eaten them right up—

George and the cat woke suddenly, and Esmarelda in the next blink. She wrapped her arms around Sylvestor while George bolted up and circled the immediate area protectively. I retreated into some brush and watched. The cat quickly wriggled out of the Gypsy's arms and goaded his Humans to get moving in that annoying cat language. They were groggy after their knotty experiences of the night before. My prey pranced temptingly between the slow-moving couple and the path up to the High Road, howling urgently.

"All right, all right, Sylvestor, I'm as eager to leave this place as you are," George grumbled. "But don't get too far ahead, the forest is hungry."

Indeed it was. Since they were obviously on to me, I had to give up on the cat. While George and Esma scooped up their belongings and hurried up the rocky slope after Sylvestor, I took a detour to hunt. Even so, I reached the High Road ahead of them. I rested in a craggy crevice below the road and listened to their progress as they lumbered up the steep trail. Finally they emerged onto level ground nearby.

Lifting their eyes from the rocky jumble underfoot, George and Esma exclaimed at the vista that rolled out beyond the ridge. The great central plains—the Wide Wilde—stretched to the horizon like a becalmed ocean. Their color this season is mossy green, belying the ruggedness of the high desert terrain. The cloudless blue sky unfurls benignly above the expanse, or so it seems from that vantage. But any who have trekked across the Wide Wilde will tell you that a cloudless sky can be deadly where the landscape offers no cover from the relentless sun. Leave it to a Gypsy to be sentimental about such a place.

"I wonder if our caravans ever come this way," Esma mused, peering into the distance for any sign of movement—a trail of dust or the flash of silver in sunlight. "Their sound carries far across the plain, it's unmistakable. I didn't realize until I had run away. I scurried along all night, and felt I had gotten pretty far from our camp. Then, the next day, the jingle and clatter of the carriages seemed to be right on my heels. But they were nowhere near. The higher I climbed on my way up to a summit much like this one," she jutted her chin toward Goathorns Peak, "the more loudly the bells jangled. I thought I was being followed and would never get away. I think the sound was in my ears long after the caravan could really be heard. I went clear around Andarra to escape them. It added two days to my climb." Esmarelda stood with her hands on her hips and gazed to the east, remembering. What would she have done if Ehrte had not taken her in? Had the Weaver seen, or somehow sealed, her future?

George listened to Esma's reminiscence ruefully. He would gladly rejoin her clan, if that was what she wanted to do after they had returned the magic satchels. But he still dreaded the inevitable encounter. How would the wise women judge his skipping ahead ten years in Time?

The Master Seer, the Witches, the Gypsy sages—he felt

vulnerable to them all. The more he learned about the Spiral Map of Time, the more certain he was that there would have to be some compensation for the liberties he had taken with it. He continued to act innocent and hopeful for Esma's benefit, but her worries had infected him.

"And do you still hear the bells of your caravan ringing in your ears, my Esmarelda?" George asked, putting his arm around her shoulders.

"I'm not haunted by them, if that's what you mean." She put her arm around his waist and leaned against him. "When I traveled back in Time—in time to find you, as it turned out—I was able to reconcile with my people, and to assure them I was and would be safe. Now I only miss them. Too long has passed since we danced together."

"Then let us return that damned Malcom's stolen satchel to the dangerously beautiful Brunagwa, and be quick to find the Gypsies," George offered with bravado. But he jumped like a frightened mongoose in an eagle's shadow when little Nee the Cooper's hawk flapped into view, and he practically fainted when she landed swiftly on the road and took the form of Reta.

"Do not call Malcom damned, and do not call the Red Mountain Witch by name! Remember where you stand, and do not forget your manners, sir."

Esmarelda, once she was certain her big buffoon was not going to fall over, stepped toward Reta for a better look. The woman, petite like herself, backed up a pace.

George, chagrined with himself on several counts, tried to recover. "Well sure, sorry. Aren't you the same girl we saw the other day? You seem more, uhm, something—grown up."

"She is the same," Esma said, offering her outstretched hand to Reta. "But she is with us in our own Time now, aren't you?"

Reta calmly extended her arm and touched Esma's fingertips with her own. She had spent years perfecting her human form and learning to interact with other human forms. At the same time, she had honed her skills as a Minder. With that single light touch of Esmarelda's fingers, Reta instantly knew the Gypsy's character, and she was gratified to find that her younger self had not been wrong. Her trust had not been misplaced.

"Yes, we are together in Time at last. I have waited long for this, we all have."

"You mean the Witches have also been expecting us?" As she said this, Esmarelda realized that quite a lot of time had passed, during which Reta might have told the Coven of an encounter that, for herself and George, had occurred only yesterday.

"The sisters know that the satchel is coming back."

"Well then, why don't you take it now?" George suggested boldly. "What do you think, Esma? Couldn't she simply take the satchel from us now and have it returned all the quicker? I mean, you are, uhm, part of the Witches's, uhm, team, aren't you?"

Esma held her breath and looked at George with wide eyes. She wasn't sure if his suggestion was a stroke of genius or another bad slip of manners.

Reta responded politely. "Coven. And no, you cannot return the satchel to me now. But I can spare you the climb to Red Mountain. The sisters are gathering in Witches Meadow tonight. Take it to them there. They need you, Esmarelda. And you, George Drumm. They need you to lead them in dance."

"Me? Us? Lead the Witches? But why?"

"Because of that!" Reta shivered herself into Nee and took wing toward a fleck of black chasing a wisp of color against the blue sky. The objects grew visible as they neared the ridge—a great black bird and a colorful rippling rug.

Sylvestor, meanwhile, had emerged from his hiding place and transformed into a hawk to join Nee in the chase. The hawks circled wide, herding the strange pair toward the place where Esma and George stood. Then, once the rug was directly over-head, the two hawks charged from opposite directions. The raven peeled off with an angry caw and seemed to vanish into the cloudless sky, as though he had been an illusion—a remnant, perhaps, of the strange eddy of Time.

The rug was quite real. It fell heavily to earth to land with a thud and a cloud of dust at Esmarelda's feet. While Nee and Sylvestor were still flying after the raven, *I* sprang snarling from my hiding place and grabbed a corner of the rug with my teeth. Esma and George gasped in shock. Esma wisely held George back from grabbing another corner and engaging me in a tug of war for the magic carpet. In a blink I had the cursed rug stowed in my burrow under the road.

"Did you see that?" George demanded of Nee-Reta when she alighted and transformed a moment later.

She had, and so had Sylvestor, who circled two times before he risked landing and returning to his feline form. He leapt into George's arms for protection. Reta followed the trail of my pawprints and the rug scraped across the sand; I could hear and smell her as she peered over the edge of the dusty roadway and down the rocky slope. She knew exactly where I was and who I was, I had no doubt.

"Not to worry," she said, moving back onto the road. "It is a good sign, in fact. We have captured a flying carpet. Coyote will take it to the High Caverns Witch for safekeeping. Intuisha's Familiar will stash it in her lair."

Reta spoke in an unnecessarily loud and commanding tone, as though I wouldn't take the hint otherwise.

"Flying carpets, of course." Esmarelda was putting the pieces together. (Are you, Robyn?) "Like the one that brought Robyn into the Coven's circle in our dream last night."

"Not a dream. And yes, just like."

"And how many are out there in the Alternate World?"

"Too many," Reta answered. "A dozen perhaps. Raven has been herding them, but it is not clear if he is friend or foe. He worries me, but we must take advantage of what he has managed to do, which is to keep the rugs from scattering too far. A group of them is nearby, with Robyn, at that camp on the other side. Your dance, your Time Dance, is part of our plan to bring them safely back to this side where they belong. The Witches have been practicing ever since the first time I saw you with the satchel—out of Time, that is, in my Future. I have tried to teach them, but they aren't very good. All they know how to do is dervish and then fall into a heap. "

"And the rest of the flying carpets?" Esmarelda wasn't ready to sanction Reta's plan for the Time Dance and the Witches, she needed to know more.

"They too are in the Alternate World—at The Lost Unicorn with Zeek, who must be persuaded to bring them to Robyn and Faye at this nearby place. Then we can move all of the carpets to this side of the Spiral at once and be done with it. "

"Well, you don't expect *us* to go back there, do you?" George demanded. "None of *us* are supposed to see each other, ever. "

"And yet you have," Reta quipped. She had spent enough time with Oshi at The Top of The World to know that what is, what is supposed, and what is supposed to be, are all subject to interpretation. Her irony was lost on the confused couple, who put their heads close together to whisper about the morning's revelations. I was all ears. Reta, that deceptively obedient changeling, was a stockpile of secrets and secret plans. Her authority came from the entire Coven, as did mine, and yet seemed stronger. Was it because her conviction came from love—her love for that ass, Malcom?

Well, I loved too. I did. I do. And Nee-Reta was the agent for none other than you-know-who—Brunagwa, the object of my attraction. (Reta and I both love jerks, what are we to do?) There and then I chose to put aside my pride, and serve she who serves Her. I would do Nee-Reta's bidding in fealty to her mistress, the Red Mountain Witch.

"Sylvestor, come here," Reta commanded, and the little one also obeyed her. "Wouldn't you like to go back to visit Zeek?"

The cat looked at her expectantly. "It won't be this instant, but soon. And you may speak, just this one more time."

"I will go if I can be sure of coming back to George," Sylvestor said, to allay any worries on that score. But hearing the cat speak did not have a calming effect on George and Esma. They frowned and waited for the next strange thing that would occur. Reta took pity on them.

"Come, there is a place to rest not far along. I will help you find food. You must refresh yourselves today so you will be ready to perform with the Coven tonight. That is all the work you have to do for now, simply rest yourselves. Nothing to worry about. I will send Sylvestor to the Alternate World with my emissary as a sign that the man can be trusted, so that Zeek will cooperate with him and bring the rugs and join Faye at the camp. Your friendly cat will be restored to you as soon as the rugs are brought to the meadow."

What could they do? What could they say? Reta led the weary Gypsies up the road, which allowed me to leave my hiding place at last.

Wrestling the wayward flying carpet to the cougar's hideout, I was irked with myself for having trusted Varluft when he rolled "Arap's" cart back into the enchanted spur of Time. The other rugs had escaped the spell, why assume this one wouldn't? It had taken a day, but apparently it got loose all on its own.

A passing shadow caused me to lift my nose to the sky. I watched two hawks winging overhead in the direction of Piper Canyon. Where was Nee-Reta taking Sylvestor, and to whom? Who was this emissary who was working for her, who would take the cat to The Lost Unicorn and convince Zeek to bring the rugs to the convention? I was as stunned as Esma and George at the morning's turn of events.

My troubled thoughts turned hopefully to Yani-Yau. She had helped me corral the Master Seers. Perhaps now I would have a chance to ask her what she knew of them. I was depleted from days of nonstop minding, and still bristling over Reta's surprising new sophistication in matters of the Knot. I went to Yani-Yau needing and expecting an ally. What I found caught me completely off guard.

Once I had dragged the rather heavy rug to the entrance of Yau's cave, I let out a howl to alert the cougar to my approach. Yau did not answer Coyote's call. When I reached out to her in the Minder way, the sexy grumble of Yani's voice came back in answer. I followed, hackles raised. Something didn't smell right. But then, what did I know of this place? It was the first time I had ever gained admittance to the lair of Intuisha's Familiar.

I trotted into the cool, into the dark, with the rumble of a prowling cat leading me. I felt uneasy and encumbered by the rug, but I knew my duty. I pushed it along as the path narrowed and plunged deeper into the cavern. When I felt fresh air rushing toward me, I nosed the magic carpet into a dark niche and prepared to spring into the chamber from whence this welcome breeze blew. I expected a dusty cavern ventilated by crevasses running through the rocky cliffs above, where I would find that big, lazy, lady-cat Yani-Yau guarding a stash of carpets and perhaps other magical wares that the Coven had confiscated. Yet I also sensed danger, a warning in my gut that Yau or another was waiting to ambush me. I launched myself into the mysteries of Yani-Yau's lair, braced for a fight but not inviting one.

Imagine my confusion upon finding myself in a plush office—carpeted, airy, cabled for electricity, complete with every convenience. A uniformed Yani sat in a swivel chair at a large desk, which was positioned in front of a vast window that overlooked the rolling ranges of the eastern slopes of our Goathorn Mountains. Her telephone, fax machine and computer indicated that this lair faced, or bordered, or perhaps also occupied the Rockies—on the wrong side of the Spiral. I leapt atop the massive desk and breathed fresh mountain air. The window, as I had perceived it, contained no glass. It was the natural exit at the far side of the cave I had entered, sheltered beneath a deep overhang of rock. Below was a sheer drop equal to the height of a tall pine, then swaths of green, soft-looking meadow rolling on toward Kestrel Kamp and Lodge.

I lurched back from the brink and found myself sprawled across the desk—in human form. I peered around the computer equipment, and noticed how the power cords connected to a fat bundle of cables that dropped over the edge of Yani's desk, then down the face of the cliff—directly into the Alternate World, where a generator provided electricity to Kestrel Lodge and a cluster of remote ski chalets. How could it be? The damn cat had her own personal loophole to the Alternate World and was running a home business.

The felinish executive growled at the mess I was making of her papers, and I morphed into Brooks the frog. We were between the worlds, and all manifestations were possible. My Minder mind sought hers: *"What have you done?"*

"That's a question for later," she snapped at me. "Let's talk about what you have *not* done, which is get the magic carpets back. Sending the two magicians for them was a disaster. I helped you get the Master Seers under control, now it is your turn to help me try again for the rugs. Come with me."

She reached for me with cougar speed. Before I could transition to a larger species, she had me in her breast pocket and was winding her way down through a passage within the mountain, relaying instructions to me all the while. Was Yani-Yau following her own plan for getting the rugs from Robyn, or playing along with Nee-Reta and the Coven's scheme? Either way, I suspected she had her own agenda for the magic carpets. I would have to work with her for now yet remain prepared to foil her at the end. No doubt she had the same idea about me.

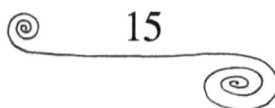

15

Mischief in the Morass

MEANWHILE, BACK AT THE RANCH ... (I'VE BEEN WAITING FOR my chance to write that.)

It was Saturday morning in the Alternate World. After Faye and Robyn returned from their dawn excursion, Faye called a grumpy Zeek, and Robyn called half a dozen friends in Caliente to go keep an eye on The Lost Unicorn. Then they crawled into their beds for a few hours' sleep. While the women snoozed, blissfully unsuspecting of the approach of two Minders from the other side of the Spiral, the vigil for the man and the dog commenced at Robyn's store in Caliente.

Poor Zeek thought that Halloween didn't look so good in the hard light of a summer morning, but the knights, elves, faeries and shamans who had come to protect the rugs brought along plenty of donuts and coffee, for which he was grateful.

The scarecrow man and the black dog were expected at The Lost Unicorn with dread and anticipation, chanting and incense, curiosity, and the unshakable certainty of true believers. Apparently none of the mystics had perceived that the threatening duo was safely on ice in Dremtessa's cave. Zeek munched his third donut, reviewed his photos, which showed nothing much, and listened to his pagan protectors discuss strategy. Should they try to hide the rugs? Should they sit on them? What about a spell? A mark on the door for protection? A mirror in the window facing outwards to deflect black magic? They ignored Zeek completely until he snapped his laptop closed and started gathering his gear.

"What are you doing?" the slight girl named Chrystaline asked in alarm.

"Going home, now that you're all here."

Oh no, they wouldn't hear of that.

"You are the intermediary," Clash explained. "You can't leave."

Zeek liked the kid, who struck him as fairly down to earth despite his unusual get-up. He meant it when he said, "You'd make a better intermediary than me, Sir Clash."

"He wasn't chosen, though. You were."

This was Empire Valerie Mayweather, a matronly transsexual in vaguely priestly robes. She outranked everyone in the room by virtue of both size and age. Zeek chose not to argue the point further. He took another tack.

"I can't stay here all day. Gotta go home and feed the cats."

"We'll go take care of your place." A young woman came forward with a sleepy toddler in her arms. "It's okay." She held out her hand, palm up, and Zeek looked into the clear blue eyes of Marina Gaia. She was the goth Gwenevere to Sir Clash's punked-out Lancelot. The moppet in pink pajamas draped across her shoulders seemed to come from a completely different movie. Zeek rubbed his beard, wanting desperately to escape to the quiet of his own apartment.

"You have to be careful when you go over there, one of the cats will try to get out."

Zeek looked up sharply at Fred, a white-haired man in a brown cassock. He was about to ask Fred how he knew about Dash but changed his mind. Anyone who knew anything about cats could guess something like that.

"It is very important not to let the cat out," Fred continued. "She's gone through the time warp before and will easily go through again. She's drawn to it."

Zeek had never seen the man before this morning, and Faye had not spoken of him. He and his wife Desy had tagged along with Mayweather. That is, they'd all come in together; but when introductions were made, it turned out that no one knew the couple or how they'd known to come. Robyn hadn't called them. They toured the shop with the curious delight of first-time visitors.

"We felt the need to follow the Magus," Fred explained, nodding to Mayweather. His wide-eyed wife kept quiet, and no one questioned them further. Now everyone looked at Zeek to see if Fred had divined the cat situation correctly.

If so, it only made Zeek distrust him more. Marina Gaia was a better bet. He pulled his keyring out of his pocket, separated the house key and dropped it into her hand.

"Just around the corner. Here's the address . . ."

Marina Gaia looked relieved. "We'll go hang out a little bit. I'm good with kitties, aren't I, Naftali?" The boy sighed, she sagged under his sleepy weight. "He needs a nap," the mother mouthed to Zeek, as if it weren't obvious. He smiled and surrendered his home to her. Clash pecked her on the cheek and nuzzled the boy for a moment before seeing them out.

With the exit of the mother and child, the atmosphere in the store changed, as though all that was innocent and pure had abandoned them. Even Zeek could not dismiss the sensation that an unnatural force was concentrated on the rugs and coming their way. His protectors joined hands and formed a circle around him and the rugs. Their chanting gave him the creeps. All he could do was stand glumly beside the pile of rugs feeling foolish.

"Hush," Fred hissed.

Sudden silence. Then the sound of steps approaching the door, and a knock, even though the "Open" sign hung in the window.

"Come on in," Zeek called out in as natural a voice as he could muster.

An enormous form filled the doorway, nothing like the spindly scarecrow man. Shiny black braids cascaded down his barrel chest on either side of a huge silver squash-blossom necklace studded with great chunks of turquoise. His dark leather hat and belt, his wrists and fingers, were similarly adorned in silver and turquoise. The creature at his feet was not a snarling dog but a serene, tiger-striped cat.

"Good work," the man declared to all with a wink. "You have kept the rugs safe. Now let's pack 'em up, Zeek. It's a long ride to Piper Canyon."

The circle parted in dismay at this familiarity. Zeek squinted at the two back-lit figures. "Let me guess—Black Star? My gosh, is that Sylvester?" The cat trotted over to Zeek and hopped into his old friend's arms.

"Correct on both counts, man. I'm serious, we have to get moving. Folks, you're in charge of the store. Except for you two." His gaze fell disapprovingly on Fred and Desy. "You're coming with us."

"We're driving to Colorado? Now?"

"Well, sure. Don't you want to see The Time Winders do their big number? We'll get there in time for it, if we leave right away." Black Star was matter-of-fact. "It's a big stage—they could really use the extra rugs."

"Can I stop at my house for a few things?"

"Uh, no. Look, you don't need anything more than what you have right here, and you've already got it mostly packed up. Time's wasting, man. Am I right?"

Some actually nodded compliantly, and the rest stood gaping. Zeek wondered why they didn't resist, aside from the obvious fact that even if they all jumped on Black Star at once, including Mayweather, they probably couldn't take him down. He was one big dude, and he had come in and taken complete control of the situation. With Sylvestor.

"Who gave you this cat?"

"He's on loan from George Drumm, of course. Aren't you, Sylvestor? But only on condition that we turn right around and go back. Isn't that right?"

The cat, which had been happily purring into Zeek's ear, hopped down and trotted back over to Black Star. He swirled around his new friend's elaborately tooled cowboy boots, then looked back at Zeek as if to say, "He's all right, let's go."

There was a long moment of indecision, and then the tense silence was broken by Mayweather's commanding falsetto.

"Robyn, darling..." She had her cellphone to her ear, "We're at the store, love, prepared for battle, don't you know, but the only chap to show up here is this charming giant named Black Star, and he's all about bringing the flying carpets up to you and the troupe for the performance tonight, and he wants Zeek to come with to see the show. He's got this lovely cat guide, Sylvestor, who seems to think it's all on the up and up, but we just wanted to check in with you, darling, before we let them go... Uh huh. You bet, sweetie.

"She wants to talk to you," Mayweather told Zeek, and as her phone passed from hand to hand, several people spoke into it to confirm that Robyn really was on the line.

"Robyn? Yeah, finally." Zeek was as relieved as the others to hear her voice. "Okay. Cool. We're on our way. Hey, is Faye there? Oh, well tell her I'm coming and I can't wait to see her. You bet."

Zeek stepped over to Mayweather to return her phone, and handed her the keys to the store as well.

"You get the keys, Madame. Clash, can you take my car back to my place and stay with Marina Gaia?" Zeek gave away the rest of his keys. "So, uh, thanks, everyone. Guess I'm ready," he said to Black Star. "You don't mind my bringing all this stuff?" Zeek hoped the recording equipment wouldn't be too obvious amid his overnight things.

"No problem, plenty of room. Can you get it all? Fred and I will get the rugs. Desy, take Sylvestor—and no souvenirs."

That was disappointing, because she had filled her totebag with treasures and was getting out her purse. "Oh, pooh," she sulked, but quickly replaced everything on the shelves and put the cat in her tote instead.

Black Star's harsh attitude toward the couple did not go unnoticed. No one wanted to get on his wrong side. The Lost Unicorn regulars backed off and pretended to shop until the foursome had marched out with Zeek's stuff and all the rugs. Then they gathered at the big window to watch the loading of a dusty, wide, vaguely military-looking van parked at the curb. A couple of brave souls stepped outside to wave to Zeek as the van pulled out onto Fourth Street with Black Star at the wheel.

Those left behind reassembled for incantations over the bare floor where the rugs had been piled. Then everyone had more donuts. Mayweather set up teams to mind the store in shifts until Robyn's return, and all but she and Chrystaline went on their way. It was just after ten in the morning, and the regular Saturday customers were starting to drift in.

Robyn would like me to correct the impression that she was in favor of Black Star taking the rugs, Zeek, the cat and the couple out of The Lost Unicorn and up to the Harmony Convention. She was quite suspicious, to be honest, and only went along with the plan because a scary attractive woman with a badge that read "Agent Yau" was hovering over her during the phone call.

Yau—if that was indeed her name—had been noisily trying to let herself into the suite with what looked like a legitimate keycard, when Robyn, irritable at having her rest disturbed, checked the peephole and yanked the door open.

"What the—?" Robyn had recognized a distraught Oscar Too

standing behind the agent. It was to him she directed her ire, there at the threshold of the suite, until the statuesque Yau regained her balance and advanced on Robyn threateningly, pushing a plastic-sheathed ID close to her face and backing her into the room, while still keeping the trembling Too in tow.

(This was my opportunity to escape from Yani's pocket, check for others in the suite, and make sure no one interfered. I expected to find Faye sleeping, and I did; no one else was present.)

Sharp reflections from the shiny plastic sleeve prevented Robyn from reading the ID card within. She caught the "Agent Yau" part and a seal with an eagle that made it look like a federal issue. Later, when Yau was content to let the badge hang quietly from the lanyard around her neck, Robyn was able to discreetly read: "International Trade . . . Tribal Relations . . . Regional . . ." Everything else was smudged out, sun faded. Yau herself had the look of someone who had been to the far reaches of the earth— tanned, muscular, confident, not entirely polished by American standards but professional.

In an unplaceable accent, Agent Yau informed Robyn that the rugs she had bought from Oscar Too were illegal imports. Every one of them must be returned or herself, her husband, Mr. Too and Mr. Star would be arrested on federal charges. Agent Yau produced some paperwork, which looked fairly convincing. But not entirely. And the coincidence of Black Star showing up in Caliente (he'd have to have driven all night) to get the rest of the rugs and bring them up for the finale—as if he were doing the troupe a favor? When Mayweather called with that news, Robyn became suspicious.

The agent hovered nearby, able to hear every word of the conversation. Robyn tried to exude confidence when she spoke to Mayweather, Zeek, and the others at The Lost Unicorn. To herself, she had to admit that the rugs were becoming more trouble than they were worth. It didn't matter if Yau was a good cop, a bad cop or a fake cop, Robyn was finally ready to be done with the "flying carpets." Besides, Zeek was a good guy. If there was going to be trouble, he might as well be there. He could help the troupe get back to Caliente should she and Ramon end up in jail.

After the call, Yau demanded to see the rugs that Robyn had gotten from Crafts of the World. To Oscar's relief, Robyn didn't deny she had them—that let him off the hook, he hoped. Agent Yau looked ready to turn the suite inside out in order to get her hands on the illegal goods. If she did that to *his* quarters, the unauthorized import citations would be endless.

Robyn had no such worries, but she pleaded for permission for the troupe to use the rugs one last time—all the rugs, including the ones Black Star was bringing. (All *thirteen* rugs, in other words; Robyn had done the math.) Couldn't Agent Yau confiscate them after the performance? It would only be a few more hours.

Oscar thought the agent was acting sly when she seemed willing to grant Robyn's wish, provided she found the rugs to be in decent condition. Whose policy was that? Who was Yau really working for? And hadn't he already encountered this person a while back, skulking around Elk Hollow, that time he'd gone to see Black Star? The uniform had thrown him off at first, but one didn't readily forget a woman of that stature.

Too could tell that Robyn also had doubts about the "agent." He was starting to enjoy the women's match of wits when his own phone chimed, making him the target of Yau's unnerving attention all over again. And speak of the devil, look who was calling—

"Black Star, I thought you told me those rugs were standard imports," he yelled into the device. "Do you have any idea the trouble... Where are you? I've got Customs on my back..."

Robyn rolled her eyes, knowing that Too knew damn well where Black Star was, and that Agent Yau knew he knew it.

Yau snatched the phone away and spoke into it sharply.

"Good of you to check in, Mr. Star. We are tracking your progress. Don't try anything funny. I expect to meet you at the lodge at five p.m., and you'd better have all the rugs." Then she lowered her voice and said something about "the tourists." Black Star's answer seemed to please her. Agent Yau returned the phone to Oscar Too.

"Now don't try to skip out early, Too. We're keeping an eye on you." She allowed him to leave and returned her attention to Robyn.

"The rugs?" The fewer words she spoke, the more menacing she was.

"Okay, okay. They're in Faye's room. She's sleeping, but I'll go get them." Robyn said this loudly, hoping Faye would wake up and come out to witness what was going on.

"Nevermind," Yau said brusquely, sensing me as I passed silently behind Robyn. Agent Yau's golden eyes held Robyn's nervous gaze. "Gather all the rugs together when Black Star arrives, and I will take a look at them all at once. I want to watch your rehearsal. I'm not saying yes to one more show, but if you won't be too rough on them..."

Brooks was in the cuff of her pants; we were out the door before Robyn could choke out a thank you.

"Who was that?" Faye asked groggily, and then crinkled her nose. "And what is that smell? Does this place have mice or racoons or something—feral cats? It smells like pee."

"Probably Oscar Too's flop sweat!" Robyn was exasperated. "I can't believe you slept through all that!"

That Yani-Yau is really something, isn't she? But it wasn't her aroma that lingered in Faye's nostrils, it was mine. While Yani put on one of the greatest Minder performances of all times, I guarded Faye and tried to digest what I had discovered in Yani's lair, and to figure out who else had known about it. How much of this business was Nee-Reta aware of? What about Intuisha? Could Yani-Yau's own mistress be blind to the Familiar's commerce with the Alternate World?

I had some leisure for these thoughts, since my only job was to mind Faye's sleep so that Yani could play out her scene. Before the lovely "Fatima" could wake, Brooks the frog morphed into the other Brooks, stretched out beside her, and mimicked the soothing snore of her man Zeek. It was nearly as impressive as Yani's act, but I hadn't considered the lingering canine odor. At any rate, we Minders soon fled ahead of Robyn's suspicions and Faye's nose, and then had only each other to deal with until the rest of the flying carpets arrived in Piper Canyon with Black Star, Zeek and the others . . .

Zeek knew a thing or two about old cars and vans, but he could not place the vehicle Black Star drove. It had to be a custom remodel of something that was custom to start with. It conjured images of those detective shows, where what looks like a delivery truck is all tricked out inside with a combination office and armory, plus room for a small posse. Black Star's gear was more benign. He had carefully-stowed provisions for camping, partying, and for selling Native American jewelry and crafts. The driver's and front passenger's bucket seats, with cup- and whatnot holders in between, had been swapped out for a full-length banco—fairly recently and at some cost, Zeek guessed. When he asked about it, Black Star just grinned and said, "Better for making out."

The supersized man had settled behind the wheel with obvious pleasure, which was a little surprising considering he'd just driven seven hours to Caliente from Piper Canyon and had the return ride ahead. On Black Star's orders, all four sat in the custom front seat—cramped but tolerable, at least for Zeek, who had the window on the passenger side. Zeek tried to settle down for what was going to be a long ride. The caffeine and sugar breakfast had set his nerves jangling, and sleep was out of the question.

Despite his indignant-ironic attitude toward Black Star—*shaman-businessman with his gas-guzzling urban tank*—Zeek liked his elevated view of the New Mexico landscape. He took breaks from staring out the window to surreptitiously study Black Star and Fred and Desy. His mind seethed with questions about the couple huddling in the middle, silent and expectant. What was their story? They looked old enough to be Black Star's parents, but they deferred to him and acted contrite, like misbehaving children caught in the act.

Not long after they'd gotten up to speed on the interstate, Black Star called Oscar Too but ended up speaking to Agent Yau. Everyone overheard the conversation. They wondered, at least Zeek did, about the strange passivity of Black Star in the face of the federal agent's ultimatum. The big man was imperturbable. He drove a hundred miles before he finally addressed his passengers.

"Do you still play the accordion, Desy?"

Zeek wriggled closer to the door as though to give Fred more room, but really to change his angle so he could see more of the couple's faces when he looked over toward Black Star.

The woman seemed to weigh the possible consequences of her possible answers. "One can always play, once it's learned," she finally replied. "But I haven't an instrument, have I?"

"What about you, Fred, do you still play?"

"I've got me a pipe, it comes along everywhere, and I know how to play it," Fred answered jovially, patting his wife's knee.

That lightened the mood considerably. Black Star chuckled, put his great arm around them both, and squeezed affectionately. "Dear me," the woman gasped, squashed between the men. And they laughed all the louder.

Black Star batted Zeek's shoulder playfully before letting go of the couple. His gestures indicated that they were to dispense with intrigue. He proceeded to regale them with his plans for The Time Winders' performance as if the adventure had been mutually agreed to from the start. They debated Black Star's scheme good-naturedly, and seemed to absolutely fly up the Interstate.

Zeek wished he could peek at the speedometer; instead he busied himself watching the side mirror for flashing red lights. There were always speed traps up this way, and talk about suspicious: Four adults crammed into the front seat of a van loaded with miscellaneous weird gear, tooling up to the border at maybe twenty, thirty miles-an-hour over the limit? But the highway was strangely barren behind them, and the traffic ahead gave way as they advanced. Where the land was undeveloped, a flock of iridescent blackbirds lifted into the sky as they sped past. Further on, several elk looked up from their grazing to stare directly at the van. Zeek had never seen elk so close to the road, and as he gaped at them, he almost felt he was making eye contact. The whole landscape seemed to have come alive, *aware*. He thought of all the things Faye had told him about the Harmony Convention, Robyn, and the rugs—seven of which were piled on the back seat—and struggled with the idea that there was a sort of charm on Black Star, his vehicle, and his passengers. There was no cop stop, there would not be one. He didn't know how he knew, but he knew. Zeek gave up worrying about it.

On up through southern Colorado, the foursome listened to a recording of the troupe's practice tape that Black Star had made on his phone, and discussed the numbers for The Time Winders' performance. Hearing the familiar music, Zeek got excited about seeing Faye again very soon and seeing The Time Winders dance. This would be the big finale for the whole Harmony Convention, and the plan was to use all of the rugs one last time before they were confiscated by the Customs agent. They would put a live band behind the dancers, consisting of Fred on ney, Desy on concertina (Black Star happened to have one among his merchandise), Ramon on guitar, and Black Star on percussion and vocals.

At the next pit stop, room was made for Fred and Desy to sit in the back and practice their instruments. Once they were on their way again, Black Star restarted the tape, and Zeek started lobbying for a part in the show. He surmised that the stage was being set for the flying carpets to fly, or disappear, or dissolve, or do whatever their magic illusion might be, and he wanted to be with Faye and the others when that happened. He hummed along and paddled the dashboard in rhythm, trying to convince Black Star that he knew the music pretty well, from hearing it so many times, and should be allowed to join the band.

Black Star acted noncommittal and asked Zeek to call Ramon and tell him what was up.

"Whoa, you haven't told him he's playing tonight?" Zeek's distrust returned.

"Hey, I wasn't going to ask him until I had a band together. Go ahead, give him a call."

"Shit." Zeek knew he had been played. Now he was working for Black Star. He called Ramon and told him in as few words as possible what was coming his way. Ramon was strangely acquiescent. He'd had the same thought as Zeek—if the dancers were going to disappear with those rugs, he was going with them.

"So, don't you think I could be part of the band? Hit a cowbell or something?" Zeek appealed to Ramon.

"Nuh uh, *amigo*. You should try to take a video of the whole thing on your phone, so we can take a good look at it later."

I can do better than that, Zeek thought. Ramon didn't know he was bringing his good camera, laptop, tripod—his whole kit.

"Okay, if you say so," was all Zeek answered. The others were suddenly quiet and listening intently. "Guess we'll see you in a few hours. Better start practicing."

"Damn, I'll have to re-tune my guitar to play that stuff. What are the other instruments again? Let me talk to those folks."

Zeek passed the phone back to Desy, and she huddled over it with Fred until the mountains blocked the signal. Black Star cruised along smugly, making extraordinary time. Zeek felt suddenly exhausted, and was secretly relieved he would not be on stage with the musicians. He slept until they turned onto the bumpy, switchbacked road to Kestrel Lodge.

Everyone is taking turns sleeping, doesn't it seem? Soon they will take turns dancing. I have the details of Black Star and company's journey courtesy of Zeek's phone. The sly fellow recorded quite a lot of what went on in the van. Maybe Black Star knew about it. Doesn't matter. My skills at hacking are limited, and invariably everything gets deleted after I've had a look and I am trying to exit the program.

Not funny, Robyn says. She'll get over it. This narrative will contain the complete record—everyone's snips and scraps, all pieced together in an entertaining if not chronological sequence. Not a worry, my friend. And see how I've freed you from all that compulsive note-taking, using nothing but thumbs, no less.

Now, while Black Star's van wends its way up to Piper Canyon, let us return to my side.

To say that I was shaken by what I found in Yani-Yau's den when I took the last-first rug to her would be an understatement. Even the second time in the place, when we went back to wait out the return of Black Star to Kestrel Lodge, I was literally beside myself with distress. H. Toad one moment, Frog the next, then Coyote and Man, I was employing my every faculty to search out the nature of this secret niche, or stitch in Time, where the qualities of both worlds permeated. At least this time I was in control of my transitions, and I had a better understanding of where I was.

Earlier, from my undignified but not unpleasant position clinging to Yani's bosom within her shirt pocket, I could not see the route by which we arrived at the back door of Kestrel Lodge. But I was able to observe the landscape on the return to Yau's lair. Once out of sight of the lodge, Yani and I morphed. Coyote kept up easily with Cougar as we sprinted up through cascading ski runs and into the folds of tumbled rock that led to the office-lair. Along the way, I had an eerie sense of recognizing my surroundings, though I had never traveled these paths before. It has pestered the recesses of my mind since. Only whilst I wrote up the origins of the Goathorns Coven did it push forward for a fully focused thought. Now, as I write, all becomes clear (yes, I am having an Aha Moment):

You may recall an unhappy ending for the Redfern clan back in the dramatic finale of the liberation of the taxidermy shop. Gruesome. But the revenge of the forest animals did not come without remorse. When they saw the Minder hawk Ti accept the spirit of Deannalisa Redfern, they did not want her to ever see how they had decimated the family Deannalisa had tried to save. They appealed to Master Seer Varluft for help, and he ingeniously installed a false wall between spiral-turns. Anyone wandering—or flying, or burrowing—in the area, would encounter an imposing barrier literally dividing one side of the Spiral from the other, and so they would turn back before encountering evidence of the massacre. In truth, the barrier was only an illusion, one that degraded over time. Beyond it, the untended swath of no-man's land came to possess some of the properties of both worlds. The old Redfern camp had become a kind of temporal swampland in which elements from both sides combined into an ever-in-flux morass.

Having returned through this wasteland to Yani-Yau's office, which hovered on its brink, I had the advantage over the weary cat. She was no longer in control of me, and I had access to all four of my forms. As a Human, I felt more cogent and less enraged by the civilized surroundings of this place. After H. Toad and H. Coyote had given Yani's hideout the once-over, I confronted her as the man Brooks.

"What are you, Yani-Yau?" I demanded. "What is this place? And what have you to do with him?" I picked up a feather and waved it. In the plastic letter tray atop the desk, I had found something almost as unsettling as the technology—several iridescent black feathers. The raven had been here.

"We are all Minders," Yau answered silently. *"We are all changelings dangling between two worlds. And we all have the same goal, including him—the raven."* Then, wanting to hide something from me that was in her thoughts, the cat shook herself and became the woman Yani. But it was too late, I had seen that there was a connection between the raven and Black Star.

I sensed Yani-Yau's confusion, but my own was even greater. "Are you saying that Black Star also works for you? For the Coven?"

"I don't know who works for who. But Black Star is not from our side. We, well, we had a little business going with crafts and collectibles. Really, it was just for fun. Intuisha can be so slow and boring. But we decided to switch over to e-business— ephemerals, if you will—less risk, more profit."

Yani tried to offer this with a conspiratorial smile, and I believed it to be true as far as it went. But I sensed the troubled feeling that came over her at the naming of Black Star, and it was very much like the fretfulness Reta felt when she thought of Malcom. This Familiar offered up similar defenses, too, in reverting to her animal self Yau and surrendering to her simpler nature. Nee would soar on the wind to soothe herself. Yau would nap. The cougar slunk into a dark corner of her lair beyond the carpeting and laid down on cool dirt to sleep.

I sat at Yani's desk and reviewed recent events. Despite what Yani said, she and Raven were not Minders like me, that much was clear. There was something very different about them both. Yani was more Human when Human than the other Familiars —and experienced in the ways of the Alternate World. Raven,

this raven, had only recently come into the Goathorns—perhaps
he had burst out of Varluft's illusion the way the rugs had. Or
was he Black Star's servant? And what was Black Star? In
business with Yani, and no doubt her lover. Troubles upon
troubles. What other goods had they traded across the supposedly
impermeable boundaries of the Spiral?

The cougar slept. This was my chance to secure the rug I had
left outside her chamber—it was the last to be made and the first
to be found. But, don't you know, the last-first was gone from
the niche where I had stashed it. Yani had been with me all the
while. So, who had taken it? How many accomplices did Yani-
Yau have?

I needed an accomplice too. Before Yani-Yau launched her
scheme, I had intended to enlist Robyn's help in a friendly way.
There was no reason I should not proceed as planned. As A.G.
Brooks, I would offer Robyn my assistance with Agent Yau and
the contraband rugs. Once I had gained her trust and seen to the
return of the magic carpets, I could broach the subject of closing
Kestrel Kamp. Robyn seemed like a more reliable intermediary
for that task than Yani-Yau, and certainly than Black Star. Yani
might help bring back the flying carpets, but then what? What
would we do about the second loophole she practically lived atop
of? And, while Black Star knew how to conduct business in the
Alternate World, he was exactly the sort we did not want to
entrust with our secrets.

Convinced that only Robyn could help me seal up Piper
Canyon, and wanting to speak to her before "Agent Yau" made
another appearance, I postponed further search for the last-first
and returned to Kestrel Lodge.

Robyn had given up on sleep after Agent Yau's intrusion. She
was eating a sandwich on one of several patios when a dapper
A.G. Brooks, Vice President of Deni-Zen, Inc., found her and
offered his services.

Deni-Zen supplied some of the rarer products sold by vendors at the Harmony Convention, Mr. Brooks told Robyn. The company had sent him to rebut allegations of their selling illegal imports—well, knowingly selling them. Unfortunately, Oscar Too's Crafts of the World Ltd. and The Lost Unicorn were both going to be in trouble over the black market rugs. Mr. Brooks assured Robyn that he had plenty of experience with this sort of thing, and access to excellent lawyers. Robyn would have to hand over the rugs, of course, but Mr. Brooks had overheard Agent Yau on a call to her office telling someone that she wouldn't be back until Monday, late. There was still time to work things out.

Robyn didn't believe a word of it, but she wanted the chance to dance on the rugs, and she saw Mr. Brooks as a possible ally. (My plan was working.) There was something familiar about the man. Robyn instinctively trusted me more than she did Yau, but by no means unreservedly. She accused Mr. Brooks of running a scam with Agent Yau, or maybe trying to entrap the merchants with a good-cop-bad-cop routine. (I suppose the latter was not far from the truth.)

Robyn and Mr. Brooks sparred cleverly, but there was never any question of the outcome. She was ready to be rid of the rugs—after the performance. He promised to do his best to persuade Agent Yau to allow the rugs to be danced upon one last time. He would put up some insurance if need be—

And then something horrible happened.

A black cat came out of the shadows below us and hopped up onto the deck. A long, sleek, beautiful black cat. Robyn broke into a smile. She had barely made one little cluck before the cat trotted over to her.

I sensed that it had been making a beeline for her from the beginning, and I had a suspicion—no, a certainty—as to the identity of this cat that made my hackles rise. The business suit was suddenly unbearable. I jumped up and backed away. The prickling sensation told me my body wanted to morph.

Robyn crinkled her nose and looked up suddenly. I read both in her face and in her mind the association to the earlier intrusion by Agent Yau, and Faye's comment about the odor. I could not meet her eyes. My attention was on the cat, and my growing rage was making it difficult to hold my form steady. The infernal beast was rubbing all around Robyn's legs. Its manner was demanding. It was searching for something.

"Ha ha, what have you found there, Mr. Cat?" Robyn teased it. "Aren't you friendly—" And then (*brava*, Robyn, not half bad for an Alternate World girl), she *awoke* to the truth.

"Oh my gosh, you are *the* black cat, Esmarelda's black cat!" The revelation made Robyn forget my presence. Riveted to the cat, she reached into her sock and unclasped the ankle bracelet hidden there. "Audy?"

The cat and I both stared, entranced, as bangle by bangle the charms emerged and caught the light, each silver disk marked with a letter: E-S-M-A-R-E-L-D-A.

The cat reached up a paw as though to bat it playfully. There was no time to wonder who had hypnotized whom, I had to break the spell—

"No-oh-oh-oooooh" I howled, not realizing until too late that I was also under the spell. I lunged at the cat. Robyn screamed. The cat sprang away. A bow sang out, "twang!" and an arrow soared overhead and impaled the wooden rail with a loud "twok!"

People began pouring out of the lodge. A trio of young men with bows and arrows trotted up the hill and hopped onto the deck. Everyone was calling out and talking at once about the black cat that had approached Robyn, and the coyote that had come out of nowhere to pounce on it. They all hushed when the archer himself spoke, and then others also reported what they had seen and heard. And then the conjectures began.

"Strange for the critters to be so hungry at this time of year," someone said.

"Maybe the coyote'd been stalking the cat and didn't see how close it was to civilization," another opined.

"I guess they both got away..."

"Don't see any blood..."

Robyn was still quaking from the shock of the coyote and then the arrow. She clutched Esmarelda's charm bracelet so tightly that she could feel the clasp cutting into her palm. Slowly she slid her hand into her pants pocket and released the bracelet, but she kept her hand there, for fear the thing might jump out and do more damage. She wanted to slip away to look at it again. Were the letters really there or not? The pendants had been blank when Esmarelda gave the ankle bracelet to Robyn the second time; she'd told her the charm was erased. But, since coming to Piper Canyon, Robyn had noticed the letters coming back— How could that be? When she ran her finger over the bangles they were perfectly smooth, with no trace of any design either incised or applied to the surface. Still, just now in the sunlight, the letters had been there clear as day. *Just ask the cat.*

Robyn wanted to ask someone to go get her a Scotch. Instead, she asked, as calmly as she could, "What about that man from Deni-Zen that I was talking to? Has anyone seen him?"

"Here I am, here I am." I came through the crowd brushing the dust off my suit jacket. "I'm afraid I hit the dirt when the fur started flying," I confessed. "Not very brave of me. Are you alright, Miss?"

Robyn clamped her mouth shut and nodded, digging into my eyes with her very knowing baby blues. The others gradually drifted away, alternately commending and chastising the archer. Neither cat nor coyote were sighted. Ramon rushed over from the Drumming & Strumming workshop, where news of the episode had spread excitedly during the break. I retreated while the couple embraced, and then Ramon whisked his damsel away for a debriefing at the bar, leaving me to assess the damage.

The cat: *Was* it the original Audy stumbling into our entangled spiral-turn? And, if not, then what other diabolical creature could it be? My Minder mind sensed it was akin to me. *Had Audy been a Minder from the start?* To be honest, I was so weary at this point that my only wish was for a natural predator of the area to take the devilish thing and spare me the trouble.

The ankle bracelet: I penned a note to Robyn and left it at the front desk. Now that I had been seen by so many, I was obliged to make a rational exit. Out the front door I went, and down the walkway toward the remote parking lot used by the less rugged vehicles. Then, with all eyes out for a hungry coyote, I was forced to work my way back up the slope as H. Toad.

Me: The laborious climb provided time to consider the fact that I had been in the Alternate World and morphed into Coyote. This was something I had never been able to do of my own volition, but here it had happened in spite of my will. Even if this was an isolated incident provoked by Esmarelda's silver anklet, it meant that the Loophole was enlarging and our magic was literally leaking into Piper Canyon.

(Back to) The charmed bracelet: The ankle bracelet ought not to have retained its spells in the Alternate World—it should not even have *been* in the Alternate World. However, once it landed with Robyn, given the nature of the thing, and Robyn's nature, it was always more likely that she would bring it to Piper Canyon than not. How could I have missed its presence at Kestrel Lodge? Because it was a secret, you see. Robyn was hiding it from Ramon, and so she had hidden it from us all. I believe Ramon is still in the dark about the ankle bracelet and the role it played in this incident.

(Our project may spoil his innocence. Are you sure you want to proceed?)

(My Editor says to proceed.)

I decided not to let myself be distracted by either the bracelet or the cat. I would trust that once the rugs were returned, and Varluft's spells were stitched up, all of those miscellaneous misplaced things would also find their way back where they belonged. I was far more concerned about letting the last-first out of my sight. It was the last rug to be made and the first to be recovered, but at this rate it might become the last-last, or the last-never—I had to stay focused on the rugs.

Sigh. If you will forgive another break in continuity, I would like to take a deep breath and detail what had recently transpired in the Ice Caves. *I* was off on the wrong track, but I will put *you*, my Reader, on the right one, so you may see how I erred.

(Please bear with me, Robyn. The retrospective bits are coming closer to the present bits. Soon everything will happen simultaneously. Alas, the human language cannot follow in the same overlapping fashion, so we still have to take it piece by piece. I will do my best to be clear about where each bit fits.)

At about the time Yani and I were making our visit to The Time Winders' suite, Intuisha and Dremtessa took Varluft the Master Seer of Ochersfeldt from his icy cell to a hall of stone located between Dremtessa's Ice Caves and Intuisha's High Caverns—the twins' parlor, if you will. They resuscitated their beloved old mentor, and the pleasure and peculiarity of this unanticipated reunion fully absorbed the three of them for— Time gets so hard to count here. Suffice to say, for at least another chapter or so.

Meanwhile, the wayward soul of the Master Seer Malcom was left to chill in the body of the black dog Dark down in the Ice Caves. Dremtessa's Familiar, Roth-Thea, was ostensibly guarding him, but really she was straining her Minder senses upward toward the happy tea party she would have liked to join. Thus she was not attuned to the gradual waking of Malcom:

. . . The voices of the twins rumbled like a drum-roll. He listened to them for a long time, trying to rally his muscles to turn his head, then lift one eyelid, so that he might catch a glimpse of the legendary women . . .

. . . When he finally remembered that he inhabited the body of a dog, he also realized that the Witches had come and gone from the icy cellar hours, perhaps days, ago. Their visit had stirred him, but it had taken much time for the dim perception echoing through his semi-conscious state to softly pound him awake . . .

. . . He lay still, listening to the bear, while he became aware of something different and possibly glorious about his current canine manifestation . . .

Malcom realized he was attuned to the body of the dog in a way that had not occurred that lifetime ago when he had coexisted in the body of a cat. The cat had been unwilling, but, at least at first, Malcom could control its movements. Sometimes the cat's consciousness took over, and the magician subsided and was not really there—Malcom and the cat were never as one. When he was forced into the black dog's body by that madman Varluft, Malcom had tried to control the dog in the same way he had controlled the cat. And in the same way, but more violently, the dog resisted.

Now, however, after their struggle with Varluft and the Familiars; after their flight, capture and imprisonment in the icy enchantment of Dremtessa's cave; after many half-wakings and drowses; Malcom felt almost whole, almost in control. That he was a dog at that moment did not trouble him. He *was* a dog. The separate dog awareness had receded or surrendered to him. Yes, more like surrendered its consciousness to Malcom's will. And what a consciousness it was. What luck—what absolute genius.

For one thing, this unimpressive black dog had a definite psychic link to that bear-woman. It knew her name—Roth-Thea. It knew where they were—in Dremtessa's Ice Caves. It knew something about alternate embodiments—indeed, this is what accounted for the kinship with Roth-Thea. Was the dog itself a Familiar?

Malcom hid his excitement behind a veil of icicles. If he could feel the bear's mind with his own—with the dog's—mind, then his own thoughts might be as easily exposed. He must contain himself, but he was aroused as he had not been since his scheme-filled youth. Fate had thrust him into the body of a changeling. Just when all seemed lost, he had been given new life—new lives. Malcom monitored the snoring of the bear-woman, who had fallen into a doze. Her resting state was an artfully sculpted blend of Human and ursine. Gently, tentatively, he remembered what the body of Malcom felt like. Through half-closed eyes he watched/willed his furred forelegs to become his own arms clad in his old black tailcoat. He shifted, feeling the return of his legs, feet, knees— *Malcom, my man, you're back!*

"Ouff." The bear's breathing changed. "Are you awake already?"

The black dog lay passively on the rough mats that Roth-Thea had tossed in. Now, more Roth than Thea, she pushed her nose through the icicles and snuffled.

Malcom kept his mind blank while the dog twitched, struggled to stand, swayed, and shook himself half-heartedly.

Boring, Roth-Thea thought, wishing to be with the twins and Varluft. She morphed slightly more toward Human and scooped up a handful of shaved ice from a pocket in the rock wall.

"Sleep, puppy," she cooed, and blew a shower of snow over the dog's muzzle.

Malcom, having seen this coming, was holding his breath. He contracted his nostrils and huffed out with his mouth. He listed to one side and then the other, then back again, and gently toppled over, sighing heavily. He allowed the dog to sleep.

Satisfied, Roth-Thea glided out of the chamber and up a level, the better to overhear the twins' reunion with Varluft.

Unguarded, Malcom now began to remind each cell of his being what it had been like to be the black cat Audy. The black dog, lying at rest, gracefully transitioned into a cat. The cat was Malcom, just as the dog had been, possessed of his own mind and his own will. At a thought, he sprang between the icicles that jailed him and began to prowl his way to freedom.

Malcom navigated by moving always away from the mental or actual echoes of conversation emanating from the twins' parlor. He also steered clear of areas that caused a throbbing sensation in his chest—this was his internal warning of Roth-Thea's proximity. Multiple passageways led down through the rock. The cat followed easily, attracted to the warm zephyrs coming from lower elevations. Soon he noticed slices of sunshine striping the rock overhead. He easily located several chinks in the cavern wall, one large enough to slither through. He found himself on a weedy ledge overlooking a green valley.

The cat blinked in the sun. Malcom felt its urge to lay in the warmth, but he held on to himself and focused his magician's senses. Something was moving in the distance. It was a coyote trotting purposely toward the speck of a settlement.

Why go there, when the hillside is teaming with prey? Malcom wondered. Before the hungry cat himself began to hunt, the newly restored Master Seer morphed back into the black dog. With canine discipline he tracked the coyote. Malcom intuited that it too had come down from the magical ring of mountains. His guess gained credence when the coyote, approaching the open grounds of Kestrel Kamp, suddenly stood on his hind legs and became a *man*—in a *suit*.

Malcom was strongly tempted to do the same. His brief experiment in the ice cave had whetted his desire to again become *himself*. And yet he could not ignore the sensation that his powers were diminishing the closer he got to the small settlement below the mountains. It made that coyote's trick all the more surprising. Malcom cautioned himself not to jeopardize his unlikely freedom by acting brashly. Since the black dog was still being compliant, he would continue on like this.

All this while, Malcom had been gaining on the coyote-man. Now the trees and shrubs that had hidden them from each other and the lodge were growing sparse. In order to continue in stealth, Malcom would have to risk a transition to the cat. With a mere thought, the change occurred. But Malcom immediately sensed that he had achieved the feline form at a cost. In the oddly different energy of this valley it was easy to become a smaller being, but shifting in the other direction was going to be a problem. If he wasn't careful, he could end up as a spider or— Malcom forbade another thought.

Cautious and internally circumspect, the black cat prowled his way toward the building and patio, where the suited man now approached a blond woman. The man sat down at the table with the woman and began to speak to her earnestly. She shifted uneasily as if she was looking for someone who might join her and act as witness to the encounter. She crossed her legs and twisted toward the building to see if anyone she knew would come out onto the patio.

The lady's ankle attracted the cat's attention. In a trice, the feline was at her feet. Malcom was as surprised as anyone. Then the silver charms he himself had commissioned to entrap the Gypsy began to emerge from Robyn's wholesome white sock—

A growl, a gasp, something shot at the railing—

Instinct wrote the rest of the scene. The once Master Seer Malcom shrank into a critter quite a bit smaller than a cat, slipped off the deck, and burrowed under.

It would take hours for Malcom to carefully reconstruct himself in stages. He worked his way back up to the foothills and into successively larger bodies, ever fearful that a predator would take him. He wasn't about to let that happen, not when he was on the cusp of mastering his greatest power. After what seemed an eternity, Malcom finally regained the form of the black dog.

Reaching the shadows of the great cliff from which he had emerged, the magician had no desire to return to the place where he had been imprisoned. In the serviceable body of a dog with excellent olfactory perception, Malcom began to explore north and south along the valley of this cliff. As he went, he cautiously experimented with his powers, which he felt were not only restored but greatly enhanced.

Now you know what I did not, Robyn, in the aftermath of our disastrous meeting. You see, I had never known one like Malcom the Master Seer, who could exist indefinitely on nothing but pride and ironic malevolence. He and I traversed the Morass practically in tandem, yet he did not perceive me within the vast landscape, occupied as he was by his perilous situation. And it was the same for me. I fretted over the cat, and had not the slightest suspicion that Malcom was on the loose again.

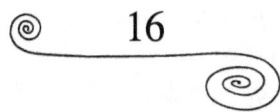

16

Secrets of the Familiars

HAVE YOU NOTICED HOW EVERYTHING HAS TO HAPPEN AT LEAST twice, one way or another—or one way *and* another—in and around the Knot? (And I am the only one who doesn't get to skip even a single iteration?) Yours Truly traversed the Morass yet again and returned to Yani-Yau's office. The cougar was still deeply asleep, exactly the way I'd left her.

How can she be so relaxed? I asked myself, and the logical part of me answered: *Because you are nowhere near her stash.*

A low growl replaced Yau's sleep-breathing. Her whiskered muzzle twitched, showing long fangs. My insight had tickled her Minder mind.

Preferring she not wake, I stealthily left her strange hideout. I maneuvered quickly through the maze of rock and easily followed my own scent back to the ledge where I had entered the cave. Then I sped to the High Road to examine the place where the flying carpet had fallen when the hawks harried it out of Raven's control. Where had the mysterious bird gone after that? I reasoned that if I wanted to recover the last-first, I should learn more about the raven. I trotted up the High Road, dog tired, requiring water and food, but too set on my mission to seek out either.

"Will you not rest now, Minder? I have tucked in the Gypsies.

The sisters are resting up for tonight as well."

"But not their Familiars?"

"No, not all of us," Nee fretted.

"Is there another besides you, and me, poking around in the heat of the day? The raven, perhaps?"

"Ah, so that is who you are looking for."

"And who are you looking for, Nee?" I approached the spindly pine on which the hawk perched, and snuffed around in its scant shade. Nee fidgeted above me. I felt her distress. *"Tell, me, Nee. Maybe I can help you. We can help each other."*

"We are already helping each other, right? We are all working together to get the magic carpets back, aren't we?" She was suspicious, and as tired and grumpy as I was. I was holding back on the black cat encounter, and she sensed my deception.

"I wonder. What do you know about Yani-Yau and Black Star?" I asked to throw her off guard. Plus, I wanted to know.

She ruffled her feathers in irritation and kept her mind a blank.

"What do you know about the magic carpets, how they ended up with Robyn?"

"Everything ends up with Robyn, as I understand it."

"Don't you wonder how the magic carpets could fly out of the Goathorns?"

"And us not see them?"

So, she hadn't known about the rugs' escape either.

When I did not reply, she asked, *"Were you not at The Top of The World with me, Coyote?"*

"I was there, Nee-Reta."

"Did you not see Raven while you were there?"

"That I did not see." This was getting interesting. I scratched away the top layer of hot earth and settled into a less hot hollow.

"It was nearly dusk. I was at the loom with Oshi. Her hands moved so fast, they looked like birds flapping above the yarn. And then it was as if a shadow broke away from the blur—and

suddenly there was a raven winging away so fast that the Weaver never saw it. I shouldn't have, except that I was not looking where I was supposed to, to see how the weft meets the warp. Ever after, I have thought the raven came from The Top of The World, where it has a view of all the Goathorns on both sides of the Spiral, and keeps track of the lost things until the Coven can deal with them."

"You said earlier that you did not know if the raven was friend or foe."

"No, now I don't. That story I made up for myself—why should I have assumed Raven was a blessing?"

"Why, now, do you assume he is not?"

"Because there is one I am missing, and I seek and seek, but he does not come back to me. Where is Raven now, when I need his help?"

"Tell me what is missing, Nee-Reta, I will help."

In her weary, lonely mind, she showed me Dark. I registered suitable surprise but not too much curiosity.

"Well, a canine. Surely I can track him," I boasted. *"And you are certainly better equipped than I to track the raven. What do you say?"*

Nee regretted revealing her secret. *"Do not approach the dog. Only tell me where to find him. I will do the same for Raven. What do you suppose his nature is?"*

"I fear that he is Black Star's tool, an Alternate World version of a Familiar, if that is possible, and has been aiding and abetting that shaman and our Yani-Yau in their trade of goods across the Loophole."

"No, Black Star and Yani-Yau?"

I noted that Nee was already well aware of this character.

"You know as well as I that they work together," I snarled.

"Oh no, I don't. I mean, I know they are—close. Snip-Edie told me how Yani had a lover, and they'd found a place to meet between the worlds. I didn't think there was any harm in it. I

mean, it was so romantic. It seemed fortunate, even. I asked Snip-Edie to ask Yani-Yau to ask Black Star to go to The Lost Unicorn and bring back the rugs. To be honest, I assumed it was Snip-Edie herself who was dealing in them, so here was a way for her to save face and help bring them back. You know how she is. She was supposed to keep Yani-Yau and Black Star's secret, and instead she spilled all, and even blamed those two for taking things. But now you tell me that Yani-Yau and Black Star truly are to blame, which means all three of them are in on it."

To prove the point, I allowed Nee to tour Yani's sophisticated office-lair through my mind's eye, and to find the black feathers on the desk. The hawk lifted off with a cry of alarm, circled above once to calm herself, and then alighted to share her own discovery with me: an image of Snip backing into a burrow on the remote northerly face of Intuisha's cliffs with the last-first flying carpet in her strong jaws. And, before that, Nee had spied the badger with other contraband. That's when Nee-Reta had confronted her. They made a pact of secrecy, provided Snip-Edie would return all the stuff to wherever it came from.

"Are they all in on it?" we asked each other. *"The sisters too? Who can we trust?"* *"Varl—"* *"What?"*

Nee had almost heard me name him in my mind. I quickly closed off the scenes with the black dog, the Malcoms, and the resurrected Master Seer of Ochersfeldt. If Nee-Reta tried to go into Intuisha's caves after them, neither hawk nor woman could survive.

"Enough. We have agreed to a course of action. I will search for the dog. You will search for the raven. And we will both try to discover what the Meadow Watch Witch and her Familiar have to do with all this."

"Very well, Minder. I know you are still keeping secrets from me. But I will trust you, because there is one secret you cannot keep. What you have hidden away from your thoughts reveals itself in your heart."

Nee-Reta had detected my deep affection for Brunagwa. She knew that whatever transpired in the next few hours, I would not miss the opportunity to see Brunagwa when the Coven assembled to dance for the rugs' return. Nee-Reta would escort Esmarelda and George Drumm to Witches Meadow at sunset. I would make my way there as well. We would stick to the plan Nee-Reta and the Coven had devised.

You may have noticed a clever twist in the matters at hand. At least, it would have been clever if what I thought was so, was not so wrong. I had asked Nee the hawk to look for Raven, while I myself looked for Dark. But I already (thought I) knew where Dark was, and (thought I) was free to do other things. Yes, sleep at long last came to mind. But I needed to sniff out the badger Snip-Edie. Why was Hesterluna's Familiar helping Yani-Yau? How much did Hesterluna and Intuisha (and thus Intuisha's twin, Dremtessa) know about the Familiars' business?

From what Nee-Reta had shown me, I guessed that Snip-Edie was a frequent visitor to Yani-Yau. I would start by returning to the High Caverns and conducting a thorough search for Snip's hiding place, where I would surely find the last-first. If I could deal with Snip here on the high ground, I would save myself an ordeal in Witches Meadow, where the badger patrolled all from her subterranean maze.

While I retraced my steps on one of many trails that runs below the High Road, I tried to shake off my unease about confronting Snip-Edie. The woman Edie was sulky and silent, and Snip the badger mean and aggressive. The tricks she played on passing adventurers had come close to outright assault. Hesterluna put Snip up to the pranks at first, but she came to regret it. Word got around, and visitors to the meadow dwindled. This put Hesterluna in a terrible funk. She started venturing down to Ochersfeldt again. Maybe she herself had resorted to smuggling, as Yani had, simply for amusement.

These were my thoughts as I tried to track the badger's movements in and around Yani-Yau's hideout. As a horned lizard I might have entered some of those places that Coyote couldn't, but that would put me at even greater risk if the badger lurked nearby. At some point within the maze of natural tunnels and caverns of this great mountainous divide between one landscape and another, my Alternate World powers kicked in. The passageways opened up, and I was able to morph into Brooks the man. Coming upon a cave-in where forest debris such as pine needles, branches and sap had settled, I made a small torch from these materials and struck a flame to it. Now I could peer into the many hollows without entering them.

Eventually I did find the loot: more rugs; some common forest items like feathers, bark and fallen birds' nests; and crystal formations—from thumb-sized to larger than a winter hare. I suppose these last were the most valuable products of the bunch, but here on our side they are easy to find. Personally, I would rather have had the hare—

"Are you hungry, Mr. Brooks?"

Startled, I nearly knocked myself out on the low rock ceiling. It was Snip-Edie—the woman Edie—and she had me cornered. Any change in my physical form would put her at an advantage in this confined space. If we both morphed, Coyote against Badger would be an even match. A lizard or frog's only chance would be to hide out of reach in a narrow crevice, or possibly choke her going down the gullet—

"Now, now, such unflattering thoughts, Mr. Brooks."

"You know what I'm thinking, even though we are both in our human bodies?"

"I have been long around Humans, as have you. You know as well as I do how transparent their thoughts can be."

"Humans such as Yani and Black Star?"

"Yes, mostly them, when not with Hesterluna and her sisters."

"Why are you helping Yani-Yau? Does Hesterluna know? Does Intuisha?"

"I would like to have you to tea, so we may discuss all of this in depth. I know you are hungry."

"And I know you are trying to trick me. Don't tell me *you* have a full office suite within this mountain as well."

"Actually, I do, and you were about to fall into it."

I held my sputtering torch at waist level and saw a gap in the rock floor ahead of me. When I moved the torch so that my body blocked its light, I could see a faint glow emanating from below. I took a step forward and looked down to see a pleasant sort of study such as can be found here and there in Kestrel Lodge, the kind of place where one might sit on a rainy day.

"Won't you come down? I won't hurt you, Brooks. We are both Minders."

"And yet look what you have done behind my back."

"Yani-Yau paid me well to keep her secrets, but I always urged her to bring everything back to the Goathorns as quickly as she could."

"Why are you so nice here and so cross in the meadow?"

"I do not like that busy meadow. This is more of a place for me."

I stood above the warm glow of lantern light that reached up from her chamber. Edie had slipped gracefully through the portal, and she looked up at me with a sincere expression. I noticed her nice looks for probably the first time; there was no sneer on her lips, and her hair was shaped differently—black and sleek. It was more flattering than the spiky, rust-brown coif she usually donned for her female form.

"Do you have a lover on the other side as well?" I guessed.

Edie chuckled ruefully. "Oh no."

"But you help Yani-Yau because you think it's romantic."

"I guess you have it all figured out already. My neck hurts. Are you coming down? You look tired."

I was tired. Dog tired. I lowered myself into the small den and sank into an extraordinarily soft chair. Edie gave me water and meaty things to eat.

"Why are you being so nice?" I asked her again.

"You rescued someone who is important to us," she said, and I assumed by "us" she meant herself and her mistress Hesterluna; and I assumed by "someone" she meant either Varluft, Malcom or Dark, and I was curious to know which. Before I could ask, she presented me with an irresistible offer.

"Why don't I tell you the story of Yani-Yau and Black Star while you rest. The night's work that awaits will take all of our wits. And this is ever such a good story, the way I heard it told in Yani-Yau's own words, and also saw it in the Minder way. It won't matter if you sleep. When you wake and examine your dreams, you will remember. Hesterluna taught me this skill."

The food and drink, the soft chair, Edie's gentle eyes and voice, and a promise of delicious gossip—I figured if it was all leading to a blade through my heart, it would still be worth it—a fine way to die.

"You've convinced me," I said. "Tell me what goes on here." And I closed my eyes to listen.

Edie began in a philosophical vein that immediately lulled me to something like sleep . . .

YANI-YAU'S ORIGINS

"It seems to me that not many Minders really know where we came from. Once we discover our Minder natures, we quickly part ways with our birth parents and begin to look for others like us. After a time, we may no longer distinguish our kin from the others of their species with certainty; and after more time, those who bore us perish in all the ways that creatures do. But with our Minder nature comes longevity. On and on we go, finding companionship among the magical races and species, and forgetting our own.

"Yani-Yau is rare indeed. She does know who her mother is, because her mother is a woman, and Yani was born a baby girl and expected to grow up to be like her mother." (Startling news, but I was absorbing all of this into my dreams while I snoozed. There will be few interjections on my part while the curious tale continues.)

"Yani's father was likely one of those settlers who tried for a time on the far side of the pond. The village never took. Maybe the Crone herself jinxed it. The Crone of Foster Pond likes to be left alone. Yani never met another Human in all her growing up, and, as best we can tell, not another soul knew of Yani's existence. And so, for fifteen years, two women lived at Foster Pond, and they saw no one and were never seen. Well, with one exception, which we already know well: Our Witches flew as cranes over Foster Pond, and the Crone came out and cursed them. After that, the Crone of Foster Pond became an object of reverence for the sisters, despite her ire, because she was one of few witnesses to their astonishing feat.

"Little did the Goathorns Coven know that there was one other observer at Foster Pond that day. It was young Yani hiding in the woods, where she had fled when she heard her mother shouting angrily. Yani watched the five cranes wheeling overhead with a surge of delight. Whoever, whatever these beings were, they held some kinship to herself and her mother. There were potential other companions in the world.

"The Crone had sometimes spoken of her encounters with others in a place she called 'the astral plane.' Until this day, Yani thought it was all made up in her mother's imagination. Now, however, she was ready to pay attention. When Yani questioned her mother about what they had both seen—five sandhill cranes flying in formation, one or more of which periodically flashed into the form of a laughing woman—the Crone said that she and her astral friends had discussed nothing else since the episode. Theories abounded as to what the sisters had actually done. Was it magic or illusion? Some had even overheard the Goathorns Witches themselves bragging about what they had achieved.

"And so Yani came to believe that indeed there were other people in the world besides herself and her mother, and that under the right circumstances some of them really did gather together by meeting within their minds within an agreed-to visualized landscape. Her mother and the Goathorns Coven might easily have met, astrally or actually, to the benefit of all. But the Crone of Foster Pond thought the Witches of the Goathorns were brash interlopers who had let their magic and curiosity get away from them. She firmly resisted their overtures, and maintained a strict boundary between her turf and theirs, while hiding her little daughter from them.

"Had the Crone ever been able to take her daughter along on her astral adventures, perhaps open-hearted Yani would have brought everyone together. Sadly, that was not to be. To mother and daughter's great disappointment, Yani couldn't do it— couldn't make the astral trip. When she reached the age when a girl starts maturing and manifesting any magical powers she may have, Yani showed no promise whatsoever. She would rub the magic balm on her legs and try to spin into a trance—but then, nothing. The girl would fall deeply asleep and not even dream. Her mother was dismayed.

"Yani did not want to let her mother down. And there was one thing that she could do that seemed special and magical. It started to happen naturally at certain times when she was walking in the woods. Because nothing in nature frightened her, this did not frighten her either. She noticed what happened and how, and she slowly learned how to manage the magic change. When she had full control over it, Yani showed her mother how she could transform into a cougar."

I awoke briefly here because Edie's narrative had stopped. Men wake groggier than coyotes, and so Amos Goathorn gazed confusedly at the young Familiar whom he knew but did not recognize in her much-altered human version. Tears streamed down Edie's pretty, newly-mild face. Her pity for Yani-Yau further unsettled my mind, because that clever cougar certainly seemed to have it made with her lair that straddled the two worlds. The entire matter was exhausting. While Edie composed herself, I set my own thoughts aside and drifted back to sleep for the next installment. (I'm glad to have been able to memorize the tale by this ingenious method. What Edie related next holds a far deeper meaning for me now, as I write it, than I could have imagined at the time.)

"The hurt is with Yani still, you know, from the way her mother reacted with horror and denial. She forbade her daughter to make the change, ever, and she began to plot how to marry off Yani and get her away from the Goathorns.

"You see, by this time the Coven was well installed here, and relations were beginning with the Minders. The Crone could not accept what she heard about us—shape-shifting supernatural animals that lived in the Goathorns. And here was her daughter apparently one of them or some other horrible hybrid. Yani said that what outraged her mother most of all was the thought of her daughter becoming a 'servant' of the Goathorns Coven.

"Poor Yani. With her Minder powers coming into play, she was able to read her mother's thoughts. They provided the information and motivation she needed to make her break, but oh, the cruelty of having to experience so complete a rejection from the one who had been her only friend.

"The Crone plotted, and Yani plotted, ever one step ahead. Try as she might, Yani could not contain her ability to change form. Now she would need it to survive. Yau the cougar would go where even Yani the nature girl could not. She readied herself to live as Cougar for days, weeks and months. When she had learned to hunt, find safe shelter, and prowl at night, Yani-Yau left Foster Pond and loped southward toward the Goathorns. There she would find others of her kind and other Witches, different from her mother, who might accept her.

"Naturally, Yani-Yau was not prepared to reveal herself right away. She had no experience making friends. First she would explore everything and learn the workings of the Goathorns community. There would be caverns aplenty in which to hide. She craved them—this was the landscape the cougar Yau instinctively sought.

"And so we come to the time of the struggles between the Minders and the Coven, of which you and I had our part. That is, H. and Snip. Yau stayed out of it. We knew of her presence but not where she came from. In those times, before the sisters structured everyone's thoughts around their own, I suppose you could say we Minded mindlessly. See how the words pour out of me, as if only in the telling will events be made real and ideas bear fruit? But Coyote and Badger know what reality is, whether they can say it or not."

I had to grumble my approval here. (Haven't I said as much to you, Robyn, about the obsession of Humans with language?)

"Yani-Yau kept to herself all the while Ti the hawk tamed Brunagwa—it certainly wasn't the other way around—and the sisters taught the Minders about Human ways. She saw the thing happen that her mother had feared: magical animals transforming into young women helpers for the Witches. But it didn't look so bad to her—to again have an older woman as her friend, protector and teacher, and to be surrounded by other such pairs—family. Still, it troubled Yani-Yau that none were truly like herself. The Familiars struggled into their womanly forms, and then sprang back into their animal shapes with relief. None had been born Human as she had. How would she bear it if these women also rejected her? She vowed that they would never know, and she watched and waited for her chance to be taken in by the Goathorns Coven."

Edie paused for so long that I opened one eye, "What?" It was hard to read her expression.

"It's funny how you can know and not-know at the same time," Snip-Edie said at last. "Yani has never said what led her to finally reveal herself to Intuisha. I remember when she was introduced to the rest of us, and I can put myself in mind of those times with Hesterluna, which were my early times in the meadow. I know that there was a rift between the three older sisters and the twins. Hesterluna, Brunagwa and Sestorina were having difficulties settling in, while Intuisha and Dremtessa immediately felt at home. The twins' combined powers, which had always outstripped their sisters', seemed to have no limit once they came to the Goathorns. The balance shifted when Sestorina tamed a herd of wild horses and found Flame-Mari; the twins rescued Roth-Thea; Ti-Wyan, and later Nee-Reta, became Brunagwa's Familiar; and then Hesterluna found me." (I noted that Snip-Edie omitted any additional details about herself and Hesterluna.)

"Anyway, something happened that gave Yani-Yau the courage to show herself—her selves—to Intuisha. For Intuisha's part, she had not been in any rush to find a Familiar. But now she needed someone to strengthen her place in the Coven's circle. If each of the other sisters had a Familiar behind her, Intuisha must have one too. It pleased her that Yani-Yau was already able to become a woman and wouldn't need to be trained. If Intuisha and Dremtessa knew that Yani-Yau had *started* as a woman—and how could they not?—they kept that detail a secret from their older sisters. I imagine they had their reasons."

"What are we talking about now? Where does Black Star come in?" I growled.

"Gently, gently, Coyote. How about if we have Mr. Brooks back?"

"Oh, sorry." Irritated, and groggy from her storytelling spell, I had morphed.

"No, the fault is mine. I dwell on vague things instead of forging ahead with actual events."

I was confused by how gracious Snip-Edie had become, and how pensive. I almost wondered if I was dealing with the same being whom I knew as Hesterluna's Familiar. But the nose knows, as they say, and I settled back into semi-slumber to let Edie continue to share her thoughts.

"Yani-Yau became Intuisha's Familiar during turbulent times in and around the Goathorns. But these troubles passed and a new pattern of life took hold, one in which each of the five sisters ruled a section of the Goathorns, aided by a Familiar, and overseen by free Minders like yourself and Ti-Wyan."

"Hmmph." I did not consider myself to have any sway over what the Witches did—let alone imagine I had been overseeing their Familiars, all of whom were in on more secrets than I. But Edie had used the word "free" of me and Ti, as though she and the others were not. This would be something to ponder later on; Snip-Edie was finally getting to the part about Yani-Yau, the second loophole, and Black Star.

YANI-YAU IN THE ALTERNATE WORLD

"Oh, the length of the days here below The Top of The World when our hearts are becalmed, and therefore Time as well," Edie mused. "The five sisters made peace, and they made peace with the Minders. There were secretive but regular exchanges between the Coven and Varluft the Master Seer of Ochersfeldt. Life rolled on uneventfully. Yani-Yau became bored. Intuisha had kept on doing her own slow thing, she never really took her Familiar to her heart to guide and train her. The cliff quarters—and I am speaking of Intuisha's—were primitive, more suited to the cougar than the girl. To this day the High Caverns Witch sleeps on a pile of furs, eats nothing cooked, and bathes but twice annually, in the spring runoff and during the late summer rains. Yani could have taught Intuisha more about being a woman than the other way around.

"Intuisha's Familiar took advantage of her frequent solitude to do what she pleased. For adventure, she prowled as Yau deeper and deeper into the caverns. She eventually found her way through to the other face of the mountain and the high chamber that overlooks the eastern ravine. Here in the big chamber she could be Yani and stand and stretch. She began to arrange the rocks and rubble into something like furniture, and to gather pine needles and cottonwood fluff for cushions.

"Over time, she smuggled in more provisions from Ochersfeldt. She got into the habit of collecting odds and ends to barter. These things were of no consequence until she touted them as magical objects from the magical Goathorns. Being naturally a Human, Yani had quickly overcome the limitations of her upbringing and learned how to deal with Humans. She knew the attraction of stories and magic, of wishes and anything that stirred the imagination. With the right backstory, even an old piece of birch bark was worth something. The problem was, anyone of any species was likely to espy Yau loping down to the outskirts of Ochersfeldt, or Yani coming back again laden with the stuff of civilization; so she was unwilling to tote anything up from Ochersfeldt but small, easily hidden objects.

"One day Yani stood at her great rock ledge and looked across the expanse at a trail of smoke wafting upwards in the distance. It came from one of the ski cabins. Where were *they* getting all *their* stuff? Hunting as Yau the cougar, she had been down the hill almost to the back door of those domiciles. What if Yani were to go there. Or, better still, *beyond*, to wherever the shops and village might be?

"And so began Yani-Yau's adventures in the Alternate World. She proceeded as she had when she first went to the Goathorns, with secrecy and vigilance until she had learned the ways of the new place. The sense of it being across the Spiral in the Alternate World was a long time coming. After all, how much of the world had Yani seen? What did she know of these things?

"Below the ski cabins was Kestrel Lodge, south of which lay

a big town, bigger than Ochersfeldt. The people were very strange, but she recognized the mix of local business folk and tourists. The shops were full of bric-a-brac such as was found in the Ochersfeldt markets. She began to make careful trades of pretty rocks and fossils for the foreign money with which to buy the items she coveted.

"Still, Yani-Yau was limited by whom she dared to interact with, and what she could wrestle up to her lair. And it was a long way, all the way to that town and back again, through a fluctuating temporal terrain that sometimes swept her up or down the slopes with miraculous ease, and sometimes fought her the whole way. The objects themselves proved to be the source of the resistance. When she carried nothing out of the Goathorns or into them, she practically flew down and up again, either with the long-legged strides of Yani or the strong, bounding leaps of Yau.

"Yani-Yau took the hint and deemed her hideout comfortable enough. She would ration her remaining wad of paper money, so that any time she wanted some entertainment she could lope down to the curious town to window shop and have a snack on an outdoor patio. But she was done bringing things back and forth—or so she thought.

"After a time, Yani-Yau noticed that another went frequently through the Morass." Here I awoke and cast a questioning glance toward Snip-Edie. "Yani didn't call it the Morass, but she had noticed its properties."

I was surprised that Snip-Edie of Witches Meadow knew even more about the borderlands than Yani-Yau of the High Caverns (or me, for that matter), but the former was continuing her recounting of the latter's dealings on the other side, and again I closed my eyes to dream along.

"Yani noticed how a raven flew at dawn. It came out of the northwest, from beyond Kestrel Kamp, soaring very high and winging ever higher. The determined strong flap of its wings and the angle at which it rose told Yani-Yau that it aimed for The Top of The World. Was it a game, she wondered, or a trial? She began to watch for the raven and try to anticipate its appearance. However, Yani-Yau still had duties for Intuisha and the Coven. She could not always be present to see if her guesses about the raven's schedule were correct.

"Yani-Yau supposed that the raven commenced its ascent at dawn, flew as long and hard as it could until the sun had crossed its zenith, and then returned. It would play on the air as it descended, then strike out toward its point of origin as the day's heat broke. As far as she could tell, this occurred only twice monthly, after the quarter moons. Yani decided she would go into town on one of these quarter-moon days to test her theory. She would time her trip so she might see the raven dance homeward on the updrafts.

"Some of the shop owners in the town that called itself Elk Hollow had begun to recognize Yani and greet her warmly. They guessed she was one of the rental cabin dwellers in the far reaches of the woodlands, one of the reclusive types, and they never pestered her with nosy questions. The cafe staff didn't mind her sitting for long hours on their patio nursing a hot chocolate—her usual, even in summer. She gave the place a 'local favorite' feeling because she looked like she came right out of the woods, maybe on horseback, in her rugged clothing and furry boots and vest—yes, even in summer. This particular place on the outskirts of town was convenient for her and, when the weather was clear as it was on this day, she could see a piece of the sky path that the raven took on its long journey.

"However, she had not expected to find two men sitting at *her* table. One was small, bookish, and nonthreatening. Had he been alone, she might have scared him off with a look. But his companion was the opposite—enormous, boistrous and colorful. He had shiny black hair, and was laden with silver and turquoise jewelry. The men were comparing a page of pictures and numbers to some samples of bead- and leatherwork. Why had they decided to sit there, if they weren't even going to be quiet and look out at the mountains? Everything about each of them, and the two of them together, offended Yani. She went right up to the men and said, 'If you don't mind, this is my regular spot.'

"Whether because of her wild beauty or her outfit or her rudeness—or perhaps her smell—the men were shocked speechless. The big one finally said, 'Why don't you join us, we're almost done. Pull up a chair.' But Yani said, 'Just finish and go.' And then she stood right there looking over their shoulders while they gathered up their stuff.

"So the men got up, but they weren't really done with their business, and they talked for a while on the steps of the patio before the small one took all the papers and samples and went off. The giant went back and sat down at the table with Yani. He stared at her while she watched for Raven.

"'You are awesome,' he finally said. 'My name's Black Star, and you are?' 'Yani-Yau.'"

I grunted here, and Edie said, "Yes, I know—she hasn't any imagination at all. If it hadn't been for Black Star, she really couldn't have caused much harm."

That jab notwithstanding, Edie was clearly impressed by Yani-Yau's exploits. She continued recounting Yani and Black Star's first meeting in tireless detail.

"Black Star said, 'You like this table because you watch for something. What?' 'The raven,' Yani answered, and then she had to look away from the sky, because she could feel the man start to shake—the vibration was traveling across the little table on which they both rested an elbow. 'You have seen the raven?' she asked. 'Yes,' he sort of choked out. The cat had got his tongue.

"Yani turned her eyes back to the horizon. 'But it doesn't look like he's coming today. I had the idea that I would see him, because last night was the quarter moon.'

"Black Star was clearly distraught and trying to recover. 'How do you know it's a He? You must be quite a birdwatcher.'

'I am,' was all she answered. She continued to study the sky and, out of the corner of her eye, Black Star. At last she said, 'No, not going to see Raven today. Oh well.' And she gave her full attention to the man. 'Sorry if I upset you.'

"'You have, I confess. Do you mind telling me how long you have watched the raven, and where else you have seen him? And then, because you are clearly a woman of significant insight, perhaps you will let me tell you why it concerns me.'

"So began the relationship of Yani-Yau and Black Star."

Here, Snip-Edie fell silent again, but I sensed it was not due to emotion or brooding. She was listening, and I lent my ears to hers. With Minder discipline we dispensed with our own thoughts and opened our sensory and extrasensory channels to the minds of any others who might have their thoughts on *us*. We traced the scraping and chittering of simple creatures above and below ground, assessed the snap and flutter of vegetation in the valleys, and probed the rock itself for any telling reverberation. Though I do not recall either of us doing so, I assume we morphed. As I said, our awareness was not on ourselves or each other. Yet we did behave in unison, as Minders often do. As one, we completed our psychic sweep, and concluded that there was no sign that either of us were being summoned or tracked. Our *tête-à-tête* could continue.

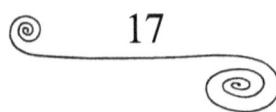

17

The Commerce Between the Worlds

ALLOW ME TO CONDENSE THE REMAINDER OF THIS TALE, WHICH was so elaborately and romantically told by Snip-Edie there in her study. Honestly, I would never have thought that pesky badger sentimental. She near to made us miss the very important dusk doings of the Coven, she spun out her story so hypnotically. But I suppose it is worth a reminder here of how near we were to the queen of the trance, Intuisha. Certain influences were bound to be felt within the slumbery rock. For better or worse, the inter-Spiral affair of Yani-Yau and Black Star is now part of me like a vividly recalled dream.

SALVADOR, BLACK STAR, AND THE RAVEN

There at the cafe on the edge of Elk Hollow, Black Star and Yani entered into deep and surprisingly honest conversation. Yani, without revealing her location or travels exactly, told as best she could the times and places she had seen Raven and all she had noticed about him. And then Black Star, in a state of near-shock, related that each of these incidents coincided with one of his own vision quests.

Black Star explained that he had been retreating to a remote camp twice per month to pursue the shamanic study he had been engaged in for the past seventeen years. It had taken him all over the world, and finally brought him back to the Southwest through dreams and visions of a mountain he recognized from his youth. But the mountain in his dream was far higher—so high, it was called The Top of The World. He came back to this area to see if he could find out what the dream was all about.

He settled in the next town up from Elk Hollow. He knew of a remote camp on its outskirts where he could build a sweat lodge and make a sacred circle in which to carry out his psychic journeys. This he did, and here he meditated on the images he remembered from his dreams. When he was able to visualize the mountain exactly as he had dreamed it, he felt an urgent need to ascend to its peak, The Top of The World.

From long practice, Black Star had learned to call down the spirit of the raven to lift him into the divine sphere and carry him through his inner journeys. That is, the raven came to him and he joined his spirit to it, leaving his body behind in trance. For five months he had gone into retreat, practiced the rituals, joined with Raven spirit, and attempted to ascend to The Top of The World, getting a little closer each time, but never really very close at all.

"And now you, strange beautiful barbaric woman, tell me you have seen my vision as though it were solid reality—a raven who flies up toward that mountain peak every quarter moon."

"But not today."

"Because I am here today to meet with my business partner, and could not go on my vision quest as I would have liked— Unless I really did go, and am in it now and dreaming all of this, in which case I have finally gone mad." The enormous man appeared to be shrinking as his sense of reality wavered. "Might I touch you to assure myself you're real?"

Yani extended her hand. When Black Star grasped it in his, many emotions and visions passed between them. They gaped at each other with awe and desire.

"Come, Raven." Yani finally spoke. "I will take you to a place where your true nature is available to you without such odd preparations. You will see what I am, and I will show you what you are. For many years your quest only took you further from the source of your power. Now you are very nearly home. I feel that I have found an answer to my restless spirit as well, and the reason I have been loitering here where I don't belong."

Yani had by now deduced the nature of the Morass, and elicited information about the Spiral Map of Time and the Alternate World from members of the Coven. So she knew she was in forbidden territory, and she assumed Black Star the Raven had fallen through the cracks somehow and was tortuously living out his life on the wrong side of the Spiral. She was going to rescue him and take him home, and in a blink all of her transgressions would be converted into a heroic mission.

The Morass was kind to them, and this reinforced her theory of things. They sauntered up the trail until out of sight of the cafe. Then they loped/ran/flew up to Yani-Yau's den through a long twilight in which their bodies felt like liquid spilling one shape into the next and then back again.

Breathlessly they sprang into the great den. There was a moment of panic as Cougar and Raven confronted each other in mortal fear. But here they showed the primacy of their human origins, because stress sparked their return to human form, which they had been unable to get a firm grip on within the Morass. They were on our side of the Spiral now, each in the state most comfortable to them—which was Human—and about as hearty and agile as Humans get, and very much alone.

Yani and Black Star abandoned themselves to a lust each had doubted could ever be fulfilled, and found in each other the partner of ultimate desire. There was a good deal of lovemaking, not to mention a long sleep, before they spoke again about their origins and present circumstances.

(*Wasn't Yani missed?* Robyn wants to know. Of course she was. But she was known to go into hiding deep in the caverns, where no one wanted to wander, and Intuisha was too huge to follow, and so she got away with lots of missed summonses and "oversleeping.")

Yani told her story to Black Star. As we have seen, though Yani-Yau could keep things to herself, she was not good at dissembling once a tale had to be told. So her heart was completely open to Black Star. And he, being a trader in esoteric goods in the Alternate World, was keenly interested in all that might be at his disposal within this new magical dimension.

His own story as told to Yani-Yau was murky. While she did not know her father, he did not know his mother—and he wasn't entirely sure about the man who raised him. Black Star called the man Grandfather, and Grandfather called him Son. Others called the boy Salvador and his guardian Uncle Sylviano. Sylviano had an abundance of relatives, most of whom treated Salvador as the old man's unwanted foundling or bastard. (Robyn already knows some of this, because we are speaking of Ramon's Uncle Sylviano—a man who seems to have always been old yet gets no older.)

The boy was trouble. He was tall for his age and growing. In the early days he was a skinny kid, hunched over protectively, trying to blend in. He was both taller and darker-skinned than the rest of the old man's family. One of Sylviano's cousins took it upon himself to foot the bill for a boarding school for the boy in the midwest. Salvador was kicked out before the semester ended. He had that look about him (I should say, that complexion) that (to some) spelled trouble; and so if there was trouble, he was the one accused.

Grandfather had other cousins, more remote ones, and he appealed to them to take in the maladjusted youth. This is how Salvador found himself banished to one of the nearby Pueblos, where he was put to work chopping wood and hauling water for the elders.

Here, finally, was a home that suited Salvador. He showed an interest in the Native customs and was soon on his path to becoming Black Star—artisan, trader, and shaman. His training on the Pueblo made him tall and straight and proud. He learned to run long distances. He learned many things that may not be told here. In time, the ways of the Pueblo were too small for him; he had vast ambitions both spiritual and material. His quest took him to the Navajo Nation next, then up to the Utes in central Colorado. The Utes, so it was told, had been placed in those mountains by the Creator to exist there for all Time.

Black Star was inspired by the lore of the tribes, but aggrieved at how the indigenous nations and their traditions had been undercut by outsiders and modernity. He set out to explore all corners of the world where he might find people who still followed the old ways. He was dividing his time between the big city and a tiny village in central Mexico when the dreams of The Top of The World began. He had been living two lives—that of a wheeling and dealing businessman and that of a solitary seeker of enlightenment.

The dreams brought Black Star back to the Rockies, but he continued to support himself by finding exotic merchandise for Oscar Too's stores. His interest in business was waning as his vision quests took on a new intensity. This is what had prompted Too, who had grown dependent on Black Star, to come find him and urge him to put in more effort for Crafts of the World.

Years before, when Black Star began to master the method of meditation that brought him his power animal, Raven, he had noticed that although he sat in relaxed attention for hours while his mind wandered, afterward his body was terribly depleted from the sessions—more like he had run a marathon. And so he added endurance and strength training to his program and began to fill out his tall frame. That habit was serving him in good stead now. The more he achieved in his meditations, the more strength he needed. He had joined a gym in town, and the training seemed to increase his shamanic range proportionately. Black Star felt he was very close to a breakthrough.

But he could never have anticipated Yani, or how his carefully controlled vision quest would crash through into his waking world. No—how his waking world would crash through into an utterly new Universe. But no—which was it? Black Star made love to Yani, and still was not convinced he wasn't in a dream or trance.

To summarize: There was the first flight up through the Morass to Yani's den, then the lovemaking, then the sleeping, then the telling of more personal history. Then more lovemaking, as you might imagine. Then more questioning from Black Star, and a more cogent explanation of the Spiral Map of Time from Yani (she got it mostly right). Now Black Star wanted to cross back through the Morass again to see if the "reality" of the other side was still possible for him, and if so, how time might have passed there, and what would happen the next time he attempted a new vision quest, and . . .

Yani tried to be patient with Black Star's attachment to the place and method that made magic so ridiculous and laborious —he had never known another way, after all. But she had been away from Intuisha and the Coven far too long. And it still wasn't clear where this Minder—*what else could he be?*—had come from or where he belonged. If he belonged in the Goathorns, why was she so reluctant to bring him through to the domain of the five sisters and their Familiars? His desire was so strong, she feared for any it fell upon. Except herself. She wanted it all for herself.

It was dawn, another dawn. Black Star sprang to the rocky ledge of Yani-Yau's overlook, looked back at her with a confident smile, and with a deep intake of breath shivered himself into Raven. She was thrilled to see him take control of it so. This seemed like confirmation that he belonged on her side of the Spiral and would come settle there in due course. Feeling her own confidence surge, she sped away as the cougar Yau to perform her duties for Intuisha.

Raven launched himself northward—he was going to try for The Top of The World from Yani's side. But the Morass wouldn't have it. He was battered by turbulent gusts, slapped back to earth to catch the ground at a stumbling run and continue the rest of the way on foot as Black Star.

The time that followed was full of discovery for the new lovers. What were the boundaries of their powers? As Black Star explored his, so Yani-Yau experimented with hers. How far from the Goathorns could Yani travel? Was she able to transfrom into Yau on the other side? As the cougar, she had often prowled down the hillside as far as the ski cabins. But when she began to venture all the way into town as the woman Yani, she felt that both the desire and the ability to morph had stayed behind in the wilds. Now that she felt safe with Black Star, Yani-Yau thought it would be interesting to test her Alternate World powers.

And what about Black Star's vision quests? Would he now wakefully become Raven and fly from his camp, across the divide, and up to The Top of The World? Perhaps he could find a place to fly up and over the high cliffs to meet Yani-Yau on the other side of the mountain within the ring of the Goathorns, for neither Black Star nor Raven could travel through the rocky chasms that Yau used. These and other esoteric and practical questions were posed and puzzled out amid much lascivious fun. I leave the frolic to the Reader's imagination, so we can focus on the puzzling out:

In the Alternate World, Black Star had been, apparently, *actually* transforming himself into Raven. But he didn't know it. He had thought it was all a psychic journey. There were no witnesses, since he was unwilling to descend to the necessary depths of meditation when others were present. After his encounter with Yani-Yau, Black Star attempted to make his transformation from a wakeful state, the way he had on the ledge of Yani's overlook. This time he would start at his own camp and try to fly back to Yani's ledge. He fell into a trance in spite of himself and tried for The Top of The World as always. He had indeed flown as Raven, but without conscious control. Further experimentation confirmed that he had to be within the Morass or on Yani-Yau's side of the Spiral to wakefully direct the activities of Raven.

Their next experiment was to bring Yani-Yau to the secluded camp. That entailed her traveling through Elk Hollow and riding in a vehicle some fifty miles. Yani met Black Star at the cafe as arranged, and strode confidently to his car. She'd gotten used to seeing these machines and was curious about the ride. Nonetheless, once they had passed all of the places that Yani had come to know, and they were heading out of town in the opposite direction of her home, our intrepid Familiar started to tremble and whimper with fear. The only way to calm herself was to press against Black Star, which was difficult given the van's configuration. Unable to transform into Yau, the lanky Yani twisted around the bucket seats and scrambled from front seat to back seat, and around again, in her attempt to make as much bodily contact with Black Star as possible while he drove. It was an excruciating hour-long ride.

Finally they came to a country road with a scenic turn-off. Here Black Star parked, loaded them both with packs, and set forth on a trail that dropped off steeply. Out of sight of the road, Black Star struck out from the path and led them through rocky, scrubby terrain to his camp.

Yani was calmed by the exertion and being in the open air, but it still frightened her not to have access to Yau, and to be so deep into a place where not even Nature spoke her language.

They came to the wash and small grove of trees where Black Star had built his sweat lodge. The property was owned by a developer friend who had no immediate plans to develop, since there was no road to the place and no utilities. To Black Star, this was holy ground; but Yani couldn't hide her distaste for the concept of a "sweat." She wanted to become Yau and hunt, but she was still firmly trapped in her human form, and had to make do with gritty nut bars and sticky dried fruit. Her discomfort, her very presence, was a distraction for Black Star, and he regretted bringing her.

Well, they were here, and the limits of Yani-Yau's Alternate World powers were clear. Now it was time to see what was really going on with Raven. Black Star had already discovered that he did not require a lot of rituals to put himself in mind of Raven and sink into that state where he and the bird would be one. He only needed space and quiet. He appealed to Yani to watch carefully and silently while he meditated.

Yani settled down at a distance and gazed at her lover with pleasure. She was at risk of dozing off in the morning sun when a commotion around Black Star startled her to attention. To her amazement, a larger than average raven was sort of bursting out of Black Star, as if it had been hidden under his worn leather vest and now struggled free. Yani, moving with the stealth of Yau, approached on hands and knees while the bird extricated itself completely and took flight. It was away before she could reach out to see if it was substance or illusion. Black Star still sat cross-legged, leaning against an ancient tree stump, his hat tilted low to shade his eyes.

This was not the Minder way. Yani watched the raven fly out of view. Then she inched closer to the man and reached out to touch him, fearful that if she shattered his concentration he and the raven might be split apart never to reunite. They had discussed this possibility over and over, to the point of the first harsh words passing between them. In the end, Yani had agreed that certain questions must be answered. Now she was in tears as she forced herself to touch Black Star's sleeve. She felt the substance of the fabric against her skin, but Black Star did not wake and the raven did not return.

Yani was about to withdraw her hand, when something within directed her to press a little more firmly. She put her whole hand on Black Star's marvelously muscular arm and squeezed gently. The sleeve, then the shirt, then the entire form collapsed into a heap of clothing. Black Star actually had shape-shifted and left only this illusion behind!

Now came a terrible time of waiting. Yani huddled beside a large rock with her nuts and raisins, wondering how long it would be before the raven returned. What would she do if Black Star did not reappear to take her back to Elk Hollow and the Goathorns? She swore never to come away this far again. It would be exactly the banishment her mother had intended for her, to live among the unmagical, without access to Yau.

Black Star had always started his quest at dawn. He figured that Raven would not try for The Top of The World once the sun was high, and fortunately he was correct. By starting late in the morning on this day, he succeeded in keeping his flight brief and local, so that Yani was not alone for more than half an hour. But it felt like forever to her. Our wayward Familiar was near hysteria by the time Raven flapped back into view, came winging to earth, and reanimated the crumpled clothing with the person of Black Star in a sort of explosion of black feathers.

Yani was too distraught to speak. After clutching each other briefly to assure themselves of Black Star's substance, they jogged back to the van in silence, each focused on locking their experience into memory. They exchanged their discoveries in breathless bursts while Black Star sped back to Yani-Yau's comfort zone. Whenever they fell silent, Yani made worried mewing sounds.

Black Star drove all the way up to Kestrel Camp and around to the back road that wound toward the ski cabins. This was as close as he could get to Yani's lair. Yani gave him a half-grateful, half-angry squeeze before tumbling out and loping into the woods. His last glimpse of her was the flick of a long, golden, black-tipped tail. Black Star closed his eyes, rested his head on the steering wheel, and asked himself, "What am I?"

Here, Snip-Edie's once-removed recounting of Yani-Yau's story came around to herself and her own part in the High Caverns intrigue. Her torrent of words seemed to dry up, now that Badger was in the spotlight. Edie's soothing voice fell silent. I awoke and immediately felt her discomfort.

"We could morph," I suggested as gently as I could, for I was impatient to get to the business that was my main concern—the rugs. This was no time for Snip-Edie to clam up. To my relief, she agreed to let the remainder of the story unfold mind to mind.

We moved away from the furniture and a little bit apart from each other. As Badger and Coyote, her memories could play out to my mind's eye. I could see her doings and read her thoughts. Turns out, Snip-Edie had been present when Yani-Yau returned from her harrowing adventure to Black Star's camp . . .

The long absences of Intuisha's Familiar had finally prompted action. Snip the badger was the only one equipped to follow the cougar's trail through the High Caverns. She was waiting in the secret space overlooking the Morass when Yau leapt over the rocky ledge. Snip confronted the cougar with teeth bared and furious thoughts. But after everything Yani-Yau had been through, she was utterly relieved to see her fellow Familiar. The cougar immediately transformed into Yani, so as not to be a threat to the badger, and knelt submissively.

Snip transformed into Edie and plopped to the ground, grudgingly allowing her beleaguered friend to embrace her and cry on her shoulder. Gradually the entire story spilled out, and eventually a deal was struck between the women: Yani-Yau could keep her lover, and Snip-Edie would keep their secret. It was apparent to Snip-Edie that Yani would not willingly go farther than Elk Hollow ever again. In exchange for keeping Yani's secrets, Snip-Edie demanded her own private study within the High Caverns.

This is how Black Star came to be tasked with bringing in a variety of furnishings from the town below to equip both hideouts. Piece by piece he carried everything up through the Morass on his strong back. The Morass, strangely, never denied Black Star, no matter what he carried with him. And Raven flew freely over the foothills that created the border between spiral-turns, though he was limited to a very few places where he could cross over. The three conspirators concluded that Raven was a being whose life, for whatever reason, came from and belonged to the Morass—the place between two worlds.

For Black Star, this felt like progress toward the knowing he had always sought. But the knowing in no way changed his agenda. He reminded Yani that all of the nice furniture and fabrics cost money. Thus began their business, with Snip-Edie ostensibly cooperating while secretly doing her best not to let any Goathorns treasures get too far afield.

The limitations on the trade of objects out of the Goathorns quickly became apparent to Black Star. He perceived the Familiars' ambivalence, and suspected that Yani-Yau and Snip-Edie intentionally or unintentionally sabotaged the operation. The women acted innocent. They suggested that it must be the nature of the magical forest that anything removed would rapidly deteriorate. Who could have guessed that all of the charming crafts they made from bark and pine needles and feathers would rot or mold or (I kid you not—customers in two different cities claimed it) combust within just weeks of purchase?

Black Star was desperate to find a way to bypass his crafty intermediaries and trade directly with the magical town of Ochersfeldt for higher quality goods. As Yani had described it, the town lay to the southwest. He ventured on foot to the southern reaches of the Morass but could never break through.

On the other hand, when Black Star flew high in the opposite direction as Raven, he felt he was getting closer to The Top of The World. At a certain altitude, he could circle round the narrowing peaks to peer over the High Caverns, out toward the High Road, and across Witches Meadow. This is how he came to espy an escaping flying carpet. Raven shepherded it over the caverns and into the Alternate World, where it plunked to earth. Black Star searched the area later, and eventually found the marvelous little rug. He stopped setting his sights for The Top of The World and only sought more of the rugs.

When Oscar Too showed up to complain about the latest batch of spoiled goods and demand replacement stock, Black Star was ready for him. Too, of course, was not going to believe that the rugs could actually fly. His offer was far less than Black Star had in mind, but they struck a deal. Then Black Star insisted that Too make The Lost Unicorn his first sales call with the rugs, so that Robyn would have first pick. How fortuitous (or inevitable) that she took them all.

Yani-Yau never knew what had transpired. One day, Black Star announced that their returns and outstanding bills had finally been settled, and he was done trading in unreliable Goathorns goods. For a second time Yani-Yau felt relieved to be done with such business. From her now well-appointed office, she and Black Star turned their attention to Internet schemes and various intangibles they could more safely trade for fun and profit.

Snip-Edie didn't know about the rugs that went to the Alternate World either. After she had retrieved the first batch of experimental flying carpets that had escaped Varluft's illusory spur of Time, she found no more. She kept her own secret stash in her lovely new lair in the High Caverns to use for ransom or blackmail, as might be required for her long-term plans.

Snip-Edie was pretty sure that her wayward rugs were related to the malicious magic of Malcom the satchel thief, which Nee-Reta had reported foreseeing from The Top of The World a long while back, and for which the Coven had been preparing ever since. Edie figured that as long as she held on to the rugs they couldn't cause any problems, and no one would be the wiser. The sisters could continue to have fun dancing and preparing for an occasion perpetually in the future. But when Robyn from the Alternate World dervished a *second* time into the middle of the Coven's circle in the middle of Witches Meadow, the jig was up.

By the time the last-first fell from the sky, and Yours Truly did everyone the favor of bringing it to the caverns, all of us were aware that the events of which Nee-Reta had warned were unfolding. But these events had snuck up on us, and on none more so than Yani-Yau, so often absent from the work of the Coven. I'm not sure that she ever did fully gather Black Star's role in the escape of the carpets. Her motive in working for their return had nothing to do with either avarice or contrition. It was love. Had I known this from the start, I would never have doubted her commitment to the cause.

Are you sorting it out, Robyn? Where had Raven actually flown, but out of the Morass and into Varluft's illusory spur of Time.

While I'm making asides, I think it worth pointing out that none of these misbehaving souls was inherently inclined to greed and rule-breaking. We mustn't forget that the Morass had its origins in a tragedy of great proportions, beginning with the Redferns' cruel murder of the forest dwellers, and ending with the forest dwellers' cruel murder of the Redferns. Under a blanket of secrecy, a mourning spirit swirled and swelled with no escape—until the ancient spell was pierced by Yani-Yau and then Black Star passing through. It is little wonder that the unhealthy pall, unwittingly inhaled by the trespassers and slowly leaking into the surroundings on both sides, had a corrupting effect.

As for the rugs that Black Star set loose in the Alternate World, I believe they were relatively benign while in Caliente. All of the times that you, Robyn, and others dancing with you, felt as though you were flying, or traveling as it were, on those rugs, your destination was Varluft's illusion or somewhere else within the Knot. But once you brought the rugs to Piper Canyon, the "real" adventures began to play out. Wednesday night you spun yourself all the way back to the Coven's grieving circle for the fake-dead Varluft, where Intuisha—a mystic who lives half the time outside of Time—snapped your photo (so to speak) so that the Gypsies, and especially myself (and even yourself and Faye) might someday witness it via the retrospective eddy of Time we recently watched from her cinematic cliffs.

Thursday night you spun again, and the rugs brought you back to Witches Meadow, to a more recent Coven's circle. Hard to say which one exactly, but I'll venture a guess that Snip-Edie was present and Yani-Yau was not.

That makes two trips clear across the Spiral for Robyn and the rugs. Well, third time lucky, as they say. The trick will be to keep the rugs and not their rider.

And so we reach, at long last, the time of the Harmony Convention, Fifth Annual, et cetera, when the whole mess comes to a head, and everyone who has been sleepwalking toward this moment must wake up and make up and take up their appointed roles in the elaborate plan to gather in the Master Seer Varluft's wayward magic.

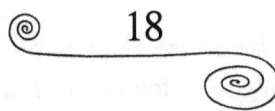

18

The Time Winders Redux

SATURDAY EVENING IN THE ALTERNATE WORLD, THE TIME
Winders and most of the others at the Harmony Convention were
resting or having a light meal before gathering for the big final
show and banquet. Black Star, who has been the object of our
curiosity, was driving back up to the convention with Zeek and
the last of the rugs from The Lost Unicorn, plus the two
mysterious tourists, Fred and Desy, and the cat Sylvestor, on
loan from Esmarelda and George Drumm.

On my side, the Gypsies were also resting up for a big night,
and the Witches were doing the same in their respective encamp-
ments. Presumably the Familiars were resting too, though I can't
vouch for Flame-Mari and the herd. I had left Yani-Yau snoozing
in her loopy lair. Nee-Reta was ostensibly out looking for Raven
in the same way I was ostensibly off looking for Dark (and
should have been)—so she might have been doing anything. I
assumed that the bear Roth-Thea was guarding the Ice Caves and
the two magicians—Varluft the Master Seer of Ochersfeldt who
had been presumed dead until he emerged from his enchanted
spur of Time, and Malcom the disembodied Master Seer now
housed within the strange dog Dark. So, three strikes for me on
that score, but at least my ignorance on one front resulted in new
knowledge on another, for my sojourn with Snip-Edie had been

enlightening.

While dusk settles over Piper Canyon, nestled into the eastern slopes of the Alternate World's Rocky Mountains, let us linger here on my side, where daylight lasts a bit longer . . .

The road beside which the Gypsies rested was bathed in a golden glow. The High Road follows the ridge that connects The Top of The World (from, say, about the knees of Goathorns Peak) to Red Mountain (roughly to the old lady's waist, if you will) mid-way up from the valley floor.

There is a particular place along this road, a natural scenic overlook, where the ridge widens and a tree has taken root. Many a traveler has stopped in its shade to look out across the Wide Wilde to the north or the valley of the Goathorns to the south, or simply to shelter from the sun that loiters overhead during our high country's relentlessly long afternoons. Few have been as rudely awakened from their siesta as George and Esmarelda, who were treated to a low fly-over from Nee-Reta, and her sharp staccato cry, *keh-keh-keh-keh-keh*.

"Come, come! This way!" The Familiar, now taking the form of the woman Reta, rallied the Gypsies. They rubbed the sleep from their eyes and stumbled around groggily, trying to gather their gear. They missed Sylvestor, and had to be reminded of his mission to the Alternate World.

"I'd rather be there than here," George whispered to Esma, as they clambered over the rocky lip of the dusty road and followed Reta to a narrow but well-worn footpath. It twisted to the west, and suddenly Red Mountain loomed above them. Its shadow grew darker and more ominous as they descended to the meadow.

Thinking about the return of Brunagwa's magic satchel and the return of the magical rugs, the couple could not help but fear for their future. Would the Witches demand that George also be returned to his proper Time? They each worried over the problem in their private thoughts as they staggered after Reta.

Nee-Reta skipped ahead gracefully, but equally gloomy. She had not seen Dark in a long day and night. What had become of him? The fact that the Minder of the Knot and the Loophole (Yours Truly) knew, or at least knew where to look, and couldn't tell her was not encouraging.

The magician Malcom had never been far from Reta's mind since that moment at The Top of The World when his consciousness had tried to hijack her human body. She had forgiven him long ago, and had learned patience. While she had not seen exactly what was to come, she understood that all of Malcom's devilish magic would have to be nullified before the Witches would consider reuniting his body and soul, one or both of which were stuck in the Knot in the interim. And in the interim she—that is, Nee—had Dark. What had become of him? What irony if Reta were to gain Malcom, only for Nee to lose Dark. She knew that the fates of both had everything to do with the business at hand, which was the gathering back of the flying carpets, but her glimpse of the Future had been confined to what she was looking for—Malcom, and Brunagwa's satchel—the continued presence of Dark had been assumed.

"Uhm, Reta?" Esmarelda called gently.

Reta paused and looked back. "Oh, sorry." She had gotten too far ahead, and the shadows were deepening. "Are you afraid of the forest, Gypsy?"

"This one, yes. But we're more worried about something else." In a few steps they had caught up to their guide.

"Oh? What?"

"That George might get sent back in Time."

George nodded guiltily.

Reta cocked her head and bit her lip. She'd forgotten that these two had reason not to want the sisters to successfully undo *every* glitch in the Spiral Map of Time.

"Sending George back in Time is not part of the plan. Moving the rugs and putting everyone on the correct side of the Spiral will be magic enough for one night. I think that the more helpful you are in this, the more likely the sisters will be to let you go on your way without interference."

"Fair enough," George said, and put his finger to his lips so Esma wouldn't ask any more questions.

They entered the wood that surrounds the meadow. Here the shadows of dusk gave way to the dark of night. The snickering of nocturnal animals mingled with high-pitched laughter and something repeatedly snapping and breaking with a sharp crack. Then, rising above these nearby sounds, a long eerie howl floated out of the mountains. It sent shivers up their spines. Even the Familiar seemed nonplused.

"Go on, now, straight through," Nee-Reta commanded, ushering them ahead of her and pointing out the beaten path, pale against the deeper undergrowth. Then she was gone.

The scene that greeted George and Esmarelda beyond the grove was terrifying—not for its darkness, but for the great tongues of flame shuddering upward from a tremendous bonfire in the center of Witches Meadow. The Gypsies were blinded by unexpected gashes of light, while their ears were confused by the roar of the fire combined with another kind of clamor coming up behind them. Gradually they were able to make out the silhouettes of five tall forms backlit by the flames.

"What's that?" George stepped closer to Esma and hooked his arm through hers. "Do you hear that? Sounds like—"

"Horses!" They were suddenly surrounded by a curious herd. "It's alright, let them sniff." Esma had learned the art of empathizing with wildlife as a girl. Still, the sensation of being nosed and breathed on by half a dozen or more large horses was disconcerting. And overhead, more unsettling activity. They supposed it was Nee-Reta who circled above, since a bird flying around a fire at night was completely unnatural.

"They're kind of nosing us forward."

"I noticed that. I'm getting out the satchel."

Esma stopped, cringing at the horses' prodding muzzles, and carefully untied the magic satchel from her belt. George stood stubbornly beside her, resisting the pressure of the herd until she was ready to go forward. She held the small woven bundle clutched to her chest. When, as one, the couple began to advance toward the fire, their equine escort immediately swept them forward at a run, until they stumbled and fell at the Witches' feet.

The horses took their time ambling out of the way. Esma and George huddled together while the big hooves moved off. Then they cautiously shifted into a more dignified posture from which to address the Red Mountain Witch.

"I'll take that." Brunagwa the Red Mountain Witch extended her hand to the Gypsy Esmarelda...

. . .

Sorry, I was transfixed by the memory of that recent encounter: H. Coyote had just arrived on the scene. I know that everyone felt my presence. I was part of the plan, if not in on it completely. When I emerged from the wood and saw her in all her glory, my racing heart stopped mid-beat. I willed the moment to be frozen in my mind's eye, perfect and timeless forever. Oh, what beauty. My lady Brunagwa. The fire raged behind her and lit her in a golden aura. Her cape dropped away from her alabaster arm as she reached for the satchel with that exquisite hand. A loose braid cascaded over her bosom, the fine tresses escaping and lightly lifted by the breeze. Brunagwa, Brunagwa, my heart stops when I see you, time stops each time I call up thy memory...

. . .

Where was I?

Esmarelda handed over the satchel with a shy, hopeful smile. Fortunately for her, the Red Mountain Witch—in a state of deep displeasure—did not look into her face.

Brunagwa unfurled the battered net-like bag, turned it inside out, sniffed it, leaned over to sniff Esma and then George, handled the sad object some more, and then turned and flung it into the fire.

"Fie!" she cried.

"Fie! Fie!" her sisters echoed, then chanted in glee, "There's one trouble gone! Gone! Gone!" All five sisters now pranced around George and Esma, who cowered in terror.

"All right, already!" The circling bird of prey had landed with a shriek and transformed into a woman.

It was not Reta. The Witches stopped cavorting, and each put a hand to her heart and extended the other, palm up, then bent a knee—the ultimate show of respect in these parts. Esma recognized the gesture and nudged George. The Gypsies struck the same pose.

Ti-Wyan, as you may recall, had taken in the departing spirit of Deannalisa Redfern. Thereafter, the Witches never failed to honor her as they would have honored their own mother. This makes Ti-Wyan the only individual to whom the sisters are submissive, as though the mere memory of Deannalisa returns them to a state of childlike obedience. Quite a nice trick on Ti-Wyan's part, which is one reason the rest of us Minders also revere and obey her.

The woman Wyan's appearance was not as regal as that of Ti the red-tailed hawk. Wyan wore an old-fashioned belted wool jacket over what looked like a long sheath made of feathers; above her plain features, reddish locks of wavy hair escaped a felt hat adorned with a single striped feather.

"Wyan, welcome," the Witches cooed in unison.

"There are many to be welcomed this night. Here's another." With a brusque gesture, Ti-Wyan released the assembled from their curtsies and summoned a man to come out from the shadows.

"Ladies."

"Varluft!" "Master Seer!" "He lives!"

The three older sisters fell upon the assumed-dead Varluft with such excitement that they practically buried him in ample bosoms, flowing fabrics and long tresses. Fortunately, he had already been welcomed back by the giant twin baby sisters, and they did not pile on as well. Dremtessa and Intuisha smiled benignly at the scene, standing back a bit and making an effort to contain their size, so that puffs of fog rose from their chilled bodies from the effort. The stout woman wearing bearskins who had escorted Varluft to the meadow now transformed into an actual bear.

George and Esma quickly backed away. The hawk-woman whom the others called Wyan nodded curtly in their direction and then ignored them. She was calling the herd back to the fire. The horses approached in a neat line, circled the fire as though in dance, spiraling in closer and closer. The closer they came, the lower the flames dwindled, until only a small campfire was left, and the surrounding ground had been trampled smooth and flat.

Suddenly chilled, the Gypsy couple would have liked to move close to that little flame, but they found themselves guarded by a smirking badger. To make its point, the animal briefly transformed into a fur-clad woman. She said, "Prepare your instruments and wait." In a blink, the woman was gone and the badger was back, teasing them by darting away and diving out of sight, then popping up near enough to nibble their ankles if it chose. She repeatedly made them hop all about, then hissed at them to be still, while the Witches continued to fuss over Varluft.

Ti-Wyan dismissed the horses. This time, instead of dispersing haphazardly, the herd marched smartly toward the wood and stayed together in a cluster when they reached its border. Beyond them, the bear lurked amid the trees. She could be heard thrashing through the undergrowth and roaring from time to time.

I trotted into the clearing, avoiding the bear and the horses, and sat in plain view, not too close. I wasn't trying to make a statement, I just wanted to see Brunagwa, and for her to see me. Varluft, the old goat, was somehow managing to endure the frenzy of hugs and kisses. I put an end to that with a spine-tingling howl.

The sisters looked up, noticed the preparations, and took their traditional positions around the fire, the five points of a pentacle. Each in turn flicked a stern expression my way. I nearly caught Brunagwa's eye, but she dropped her lids.

Varluft, the resurrected Master Seer of Ochersfeldt, went over to Ti-Wyan, who had once been Brunagwa's Familiar, but before and after that, maybe for all Time, acted as the Minder of all Minders. The two stood together near the small fire with the sisters circling them. The Goathorns Coven had not been this strong for many a spiral-turn.

We all waited. Quite a while. I was not impatient. I kept my eyes on Brunagwa, and assumed that time had stopped only for me . . .

A commotion of female, feline and avian sounds brought us out of our reveries. Yani and Reta burst into the meadow, each struggling with an armload of colorful rugs. They staggered over to Varluft and Ti-Wyan, and dropped their burdens at their feet.

"What's this?" Ti-Wyan demanded, while at the same time, Varluft exclaimed, "These too?" Ti-Wyan and the magician glared at each other, then confronted Yani-Yau angrily.

The woman had quickly transitioned into the cougar. She slithered over to Intuisha to sit at her protector's feet calmly licking a paw.

Nee-Reta put some distance between herself and the big cat. As she did so, she gave an encouraging nod to Esma and George, frowned at the badger, and said, "Thank you, H." to me, which did not escape the others' attention.

In anticipation of my Editor's query, allow me to explain: After hearing the over-long confessions of Snip-Edie, I needed to secure her additional cache of rugs. This involved a tiring job for Coyote and Badger. Together we dragged the rugs through those narrow tunnels. As soon as it was done, Snip-Edie hurried away to Witches Meadow, for Hesterluna was by now looking for her.

I howled to summon Nee-Reta. She came quickly, no doubt assuming I had found Dark. When instead I showed her the surprising second batch of flying carpets, she was doubly upset. Yani-Yau had heard my call too, and also some of my mind-to-mind conversation with Nee-Reta. She bounded out of the cave and onto the ledge.

The two Familiars immediately morphed into their human forms and began quarreling. (I'll grant this about the human language—it is truly the best vehicle for argument.) While Yani-Yau disavowed any knowledge of these additional rugs, and Nee-Reta berated her for not minding the High Caverns properly, Coyote sprang away and raced at top speed to Witches Meadow so as not to miss a glimpse of Brunagwa.

Nee-Reta and Yani-Yau followed to the meadow less swiftly, lugging a bunch of rugs . . .

"Are you telling me that these are all of the rugs, and we are done?" Wyan asked Reta with a dubious grin. "I thought we had only captured the last-first so far."

"There were more than we imagined," Reta reported, shooting an accusing look at Master Seer Varluft. "But at least Snip-Edie found and hid some of them before Yani-Yau's *friend* could trade them out of the Goathorns, isn't that right?"

The badger transformed into spiky-haired Edie long enough to bow sarcastically, then became the snarling Snip once more. Yani-Yau posed in restful inattention, a typically aloof feline.

"Anyway," Reta continued, "these rugs will be a help now, stronger than the one alone."

"We must make sure none gets away."

"Yes, Ti-Wyan, we will be extra watchful. Let us count them

while we prepare for the dance."

Through all of this, the sisters held their positions with surprising discipline. Hesterluna was still agog at her old friend Varluft's return. Brunagwa ignored me. She was squinting over at Esmarelda and George Drumm, perhaps regretting having had to dispose of the magic satchel and calculating a revenge. Sestorina, on the far side of the fire, paced impatiently; each time she came close to the fire, it seemed to flare up in reply. The Ice Caves Witch, Dremtessa, was focused on her twin, Intuisha, while Intuisha spilled cold tears over the secret doings of her delinquent Familiar, Yani-Yau.

Reta, Wyan, and Varluft unrolled one flying carpet after another, counting out as they went, "Eight, nine, ten, eleven, twelve—and the last-first makes thirteen."

Yau, unwilling to morph, sent a thought to Nee-Reta, who added, "And still another thirteen on the other side."

At this, Intuisha's hurt turned to ire. The tears steamed off her face, and she herself seemed at risk of dematerializing into a cloud of outraged vapors. She pointed with one long arm at Yau, and with the other at me. "Go get the rest of them," she commanded.

"Go," Dremtessa echoed, and Cougar and Coyote raced ahead of the icy shrapnel of her breath exactly the way we had run from her cave the night before.

The plan was unfolding, but Nee-Reta was unhappy. I had sensed her disappointment when she arrived in the meadow and again did not see Dark waiting with me. Did she sense my own confusion that the badger had been praised and not accused?

Both Snip-Edie and Yani-Yau were being trusted to play out their parts to help bring back the rest of the rugs. I supposed there was no other choice. Badger was not my worry, and so far she had been cooperative. I was still mystified by the suave creature I had found in the caverns, who bore so little resemblance to the brat that snickered around the meadow. I wondered if the other Minders also had secret lives. Didn't I, A.G. Brooks?

All of this went through my mind as Yau and I sped away, along with other disturbing thoughts. While I was loitering in Snip-Edie's secret cubby, I had avoided thinking about my meeting with Robyn and its devastating interruption. Now the worries simmering in the back of my mind threatened to come to a full boil. Was the black cat really Esmarelda's Audy? And what about the ankle bracelet—how would I retrieve the thing when I didn't dare get near it?

I wasn't inclined to share any of this with Yau, whom I had left napping through the whole business, so I quickly put a lid on my mental stew lest she try to listen in while we loped through the Morass. Best to let her focus on her upcoming command performance in the Alternate World.

Agent Yau slipped into Meeting Room 3 in the new wing of Kestrel Lodge to watch the troupe rehearse. She shook her head disapprovingly when she saw the thirteen rugs laid out in a near-square formation—three rows of three lengthwise, and one row of four laid perpendicular to the nine. The musicians had set up folding chairs on this last row of rugs, and were tuning up while the dancers swirled in front of them. Black Star noticed the agent and called out a greeting. Everyone froze.

"Those chair legs might damage the rugs. You'll have to stand," she told the musicians curtly. They jumped up and moved the chairs aside. The agent's alarm only increased. "What have you done with the *fringes*?" The last word was practically hissed, Yau was so mad.

"They're just tucked under," Robyn assured her, pulling up a corner of a rug and shaking out the fringe. "So we don't trip on them. Only, it's hard to get them neat now that we have so many."

Robyn could see why Yau was upset. With some strands

poking out halfway, it looked like the fringe had been cut.

"Well, that's not the way to do it at all," Yau huffed. But she appeared to be satisfied after she had poked around the rugs and lifted an edge here and there.

Everyone waited for the agent's permission to continue practice. She had stepped back a few paces to survey the swath of flying carpets. She seemed to be reviewing something in her mind. For a long minute her lips moved slightly and her head nodded gently up and down, as if counting. Finally, with her eyes still focused on the rugs, Agent Yau spoke.

"It bothers me to see you dancing barefoot on these artifacts. Don't you have dancing slippers?" The Time Winders' rumble of protest rekindled the agent's ire. She straightened to her full height and lifted her glaring golden eyes to the five women. They shut up and nodded obediently.

"I'll be with you throughout your performance to ensure the rugs' safety. I have been checking things out backstage. There's not much room in the wings, so let's be organized about this. Ladies, you can go change into costume, and then watch the other groups from out front somewhere. Practice if you must, but there's no point treading on the rugs more than necessary. The musicians and I will take them backstage, and lay them out *properly* when the time comes."

Agent Yau's golden eyes were spooky. The dancers gladly hurried away to get into their costumes. Zeek, neither musician nor dancer, was following Faye—they'd had no private time at all since he arrived—but the agent stopped him and told him to roll up the rugs while the musicians finished practicing. (I trust that the attentive Reader can easily intuit Zeek's unkind thoughts about the rugs as he performed this chore, so that I need not transcribe. We are tying to keep this epic family friendly.)

Agent Yau and company brought the rugs and instruments to the auditorium. The harried stage manager was put out by the sight of the additional troupe members and all their gear. The other troupes had also brought extra props and supporters for the final round of dancing, and the backstage area was becoming dangerously crowded. Agent Yau sent Zeek out front.

Zeek hastened away with relief, wondering if Yau was going to monitor him. *Apparently not.* When he looked back, he saw her conferring with Black Star over what looked like a page of music. *Black Star seems to have an angle on everything.* Zeek pondered this while he worked his way to the front desk, where he had left his gear for safekeeping. People were now streaming into the auditorium, but he managed to get out and back in again, and to set up along the side aisle without interference. No one noticed Sylvestor peeking out of the camera bag, or really registered Zeek at all. But Faye spotted him immediately when she came out from the wings wearing a long, filmy caftan over her costume. She hurried over and they embraced carefully.

"I thought that Agent Yau would be out here." She looked around.

"No, I figured she stayed backstage with you guys."

Faye and Zeek stood with their arms around each other and their heads close. They savored being together, and kept their suspicions to themselves. Sylvestor kept out of sight. The auditorium buzzed with activity and anticipation.

I was back in my trail guide togs, loitering at the bar and taking in the circus-like atmosphere. With the marvelous communicating device Brooks had snagged from Yani's desk and hidden at the lodge, I would be able to intercept the whole of Zeek's digital recording, as well as all messages he exchanged, while my coyote nose was tuned to the scent of that cat Sylvestor. I would have no trouble keeping track of those two. Yani-Yau was in charge of all the others.

And so the stage was set, literally, for the return of the rugs. We had only to endure the competitive routines of Exotíque, The Mustaphas, and (I kid you not) The Bedouin Belles of Tulsa before implementing our plan. That is, some of us had to endure, but you, my Reader, do not. While the show goes on, I shall use my literary magic to continue the scene on the other side, where the five sisters were going through their paces with Esmarelda. (I am now accused of being ungenerous to the Alternate World ladies, so let me be clear—the Witches' dancing was far worse.)

Under the Gypsy Esmarelda's direction, the Witches arranged themselves on the rugs. Esmarelda positioned herself behind them with her tambourine. George stood beside her with his fiddle. Varluft stood next to George, warming up on a great brass oompah that he had somehow produced from within his cloak.

Ti-Wyan and Nee-Reta reverted to their hawk forms, Ti the red-tailed and Nee the Cooper's. They flew to the tops of the two tallest trees in the wood to watch Yani-Yau and I lope away to the Loophole. When they turned their attention back to the meadow, things were not going well. The Gypsy was discovering for herself why Nee-Reta had been so frustrated with the Witches. The sisters seemed to be immune to rhythm, hardly able to hear the beat of the tambourine at all.

The once Master Seer of Ochersfeldt asked to join in, pointing out that he was not only rusty, but recently iced, and had been stuck in an enchanted spur of Time before that. (Thanks to the twins' pampering, he looked remarkably hale; his white beard was neatly braided down the front of a fresh, colorful caftan, and his recently shaved head was starting to sprout a halo of white fuzz.) When Varluft huffed and puffed into his oompah, the sisters responded to the low throbbing beat as they had not to the tinkling tambourine. After they'd gotten the hang of stepping in time to the beat, George employed his fiddle, and they all worked their way through a semblance of the Time Dance.

Ti-Wyan and Nee-Reta fluttered down from their perches, the better to observe and comment as women. They conferred worriedly. Finally, Nee-Reta called out, "Esmarelda, you will have to dance with them. Sestorina, you can join the band and sing with me."

Their only hope was to have the Gypsy herself dance. Esmarelda might be able to pull off the magic with or without the others, but the Coven certainly couldn't do it without her. And Sestorina, in her breeches and boots, looked exceptionally out of place and awkward. She could keep the beat well enough—too well, in fact. She kept blindly knocking into her slower sisters.

The Six Hills Witch gratefully left the dancers and marched over to the Minders. "Sing what?" She stood dutifully before the two smallish women, Wyan in her dowdy jacket and cap, and Reta in her feathered mini-skirt.

"The song George wrote about the Spiral Map of Time." Reta began to sing the tune and words she had first heard years before—or two days ago, depending how you count.

"No!" The objection escaped Esmarelda's lips before she could censor herself. But she had no trouble keeping silent after that, with the five Witches and two hawk-women glaring at her. She shrugged her shoulders at George. The Gypsies would do as they were told.

The Witches, recognizing the song from their practice, danced to it enthusiastically and, with Esma dancing in front of them while she played the tambourine, even somewhat artfully. The oompah began to play, and then the fiddle. Reta started the verse again. Sestorina joined in, improvising deep harmonies that gave an eerie edge to Reta's light soprano. When the patterns on the rugs began to waver, Ti-Wyan raised her arms.

"Enough. Excellent. Stop and rest. I'll tell you when it's time." The Minder fluttered up into the trees as the red-tailed hawk.

"I will never get used to that," George muttered.

Everyone laughed and laid down on the rugs. Esmarelda and Reta interposed themselves between George and the flirtatious Witches. When the sisters had fallen into a heavy sleep, Nee-Reta quietly moved off to watch for a sign.

George and Esma remained wakeful, their ears perked to the sounds of horses' hooves, the growling of a bear, and the chittering of the tricky badger. The peculiar old man Varluft gave them some courage. He was also on alert, though he paced the perimeter of the rugs more like an inspector than a guard, periodically stooping low to examine the fibers and weaving.

When the right amount of time had passed, here and there, the howl of a coyote floated eerily out of the distance. Nee swooped out of her tree and dive-bombed the sisters until they were all on their feet. Varluft clapped delightedly. George and Esma stood up stiffly and shook out their achy limbs.

"Just like playing the last round at McQuire's on Sumweir Isle after a long nap in the cloakroom," George joked.

"Let's go, let's go," Reta urged. "It's going to be their first number. Too bad they won't get to show off at all, but they'll get a show when they arrive at Witches Meadow!"

Nee-Reta was surprised at how she felt—not nervous, but happy. She sensed how the Witches cared for her, and Ti-Wyan trusted her, and George and Esma respected her. She had become someone apart from a Familiar of Brunagwa's creation. She was a true Minder, doing what truly needed to be done. She was a force among forces, a catalyst—not a magician, but a magical being. Tonight she was excited and not afraid, and so the others were uplifted by her spirit as they took their positions.

Snip the badger, Flame the horse, and Roth the bear came forward and sat at attention in front of the rugs to monitor whatever crossed the Spiral. Under their unsettling gaze, Esmarelda raised her tambourine and beat out the rhythm. Master Seer Varluft came in with his steady oompahs, then George began to slowly spin out the melody on his fiddle. The second time through, he and Esma picked up the tempo a little. Nee-Reta and Sestorina came in with the vocals:

"Oh, the Spiral Map of Time / Unfurls from Nowhere to Forever / And returns upon a mirror path / From Everywhere to

Never..."

With sinuous movements, the petite Gypsy Esmarelda and the tall and even taller Witches—Hesterluna and Brunagwa, and Intuisha and Dremtessa—began to dance along the path of the swirling spiral patterns of the carpets.

The auditorium at Kestrel Lodge was packed. The judges had retired to a meeting room to score the three finalists in the belly dance competition. The contestants, still in bangles and veils, were drifting out from backstage to watch The Time Winders' finale. In the wings, Robyn and her troupe fussed with their costumes and went through their warm-up routine. They shook their arms and wrists, made gentle circles with their hips, and bounced lightly on their toes.

Robyn felt the delicate pendants of Esmarelda's charm bracelet tickle her leg. It moved freely but invisibly within the folds of her harem pants, which were gathered at the ankle. A cheap strand of tiny bells was wound around the outside cuff on each leg, and their rattle covered the surprisingly loud jingle of the hidden silver charms. The letters E-S-M-A-R-E-L-D-A had indeed returned, either before or because of the black cat's appearance. Once again, Robyn possessed physical evidence of the Gypsy and her magical world. If only someone else had also seen the Before, After, and Now pendants—first with the etched letters, then without, and now with them again. But Ramon was the only person she had shown the bracelet to after her first encounter with the Gypsy. His reaction had suprised her. She thought the gift was marvelous, but it bothered Ramon. He told her to send it back to Esmarelda and get something with her own name on it. He didn't exactly insist, but Robyn could tell that keeping the bracelet would cause a conflict. That's why she got rid of it the first time. But when Esmarelda brought it *back*, and showed her that the letters had been erased— Well, Robyn simply kept the trinket but kept it hidden. Were she to show the ankle bracelet to Ramon now, with the letters visible, he would suspect she had never sent it back in the first place. For better or worse, she was stuck with her secret.

Under guise of stretching her neck and back, Robyn was watchful of the backstage shadows, where she assumed Mr. Brooks was lurking. *"Your bracelet is another illegal import and very valuable. I recommend leaving it in the hotel safe. Cannot guarantee your protection if it's lost. Brooks."* That's what his note had said. *To hell with that,* Robyn thought when she read it, squelching the fear his words were meant to provoke. She *was* going to wear the magic ankle bracelet, which had been given to her by *the* Gypsy Esmarelda—*twice*—and she would do so *on the flying carpets.* Robyn easily converted her anxiety to anticipation. It was like a magical, mystical dream come true.

And here she was, lined up with her troupe in the wings and ready to fly. The ankle bracelet seemed to have a life of its own. She felt it straining toward the stage, as though it were as anxious to dance as she. No one would stop her now.

The musicians and Agent Yau were already on stage behind the lowered curtain. The rugs were still rolled up, and Yau was conferring over them with Black Star, Desy, and Fred. Ramon had not been invited into the huddle, and he kept back, plucking his guitar and wondering what was holding them up. He could hear the click and hum of the emcee's mic being turned on. The Time Winders would be announced any minute.

As if responding to the same cue, Yau's foursome sprang into action: They each took a rug, then stood in a row at the back of the stage, facing front. At a nod from Yau, they unfurled the rugs in unison, abutting them side by side, fringes flowing behind and in front. Then, following Yau's directions, Black Star, Desy, and Fred grabbed three more rugs and quickly laid them end to end to end in a horizontal row that covered the front fringes of the first set of four. They did not concern themselves with these rugs' fringes, for where the ends of two rugs met, their fringes reached for each other and intertwined, locking together in a solid mass. Two more horizontal rows were laid out in the same manner.

Ramon watched aghast. The patchwork of small rugs had— *like magic*—knitted itself into a single large carpet figured with a mesmerizing spiral fractal pattern.

"C'mon, cuz." Black Star was summoning the musicians to take their places while Agent Yau went to round up the dancers.

Ramon shook his head. The spirals had sent him into a sort of waking dream.

Out front, the emcee stepped up to the mic. Those still returning from the bar and the restrooms hurried to their seats.

"What a great night. Everyone went all out. And in case you thought The Time Winders didn't have any more tricks up their sleeves, they have brought a live band to play for them tonight. Check it out folks, The Disappearing Black Star Band and The Tiiiime Wiiiinders!"

The crowd roared. The curtain went up, revealing the dancers, with the musicians behind them, arrayed on the larger surface of carpets. The band, what could be seen of them, provoked a mixed response. Many recognized the huge man with the tambourine, the shaman Black Star, with varying degrees of admiration and loathing. Others had met Ramon at the Lost Unicorn booth, and they clapped supportively when they recognized him with his guitar. The older couple in hippie garb had shown up with Black Star that afternoon. They seemed familiar, but no one could pin down exactly how they knew them.

The audience quieted when a tall woman took the emcee's place at the mic off to the side. She was not "Yasmine," who had lined up with her troupe. The Time Winders' costumes had been spruced up, but not over-spangled, and the dancers looked like goddesses. (At least Zeek and I thought so.) The one at the mic wore something tight and almost flesh-colored, with a fur vest and fur-trimmed boots. She leaned toward the mic, and the audience leaned toward her with curiosity.

"Oh, the Spiral Map of Time / Unfurls from Nowhere to Forever..." Yani sang softly and surprisingly well into the microphone, while The Time Winders began to sway. "And returns upon a mirror path / From Everywhere to Never."

The choreography for their original opening number somehow fit this new tune. Robyn led the troupe confidently through the familiar routine.

"The coils of the Spiral / Trace a ceaseless path / And the End meets the Beginning / Where the First will meet the Last."

Now Black Star joined in with Yani, his voice rumbling below hers without need of amplification.

"Out and out the Spiral curls / From the point where All commences / And the Time it keeps is merry / Full of Magic, spells, and da-a-nces..."

Here, where the usual accompaniment picked up speed, the musicians did too. Black Star began to tap the tambourine; he was joined by Ramon, Desy and Fred, on guitar, concertina and ney. The crowd loved the odd tribal-Semitic sound. They began to rock and sway in their seats. The dancers swirled around in a snaky path, following the shape of the patterns that flowed from one rug to the next.

"Winding in and in upon itself itself / A second second world created / A spiraling of other other Times / Where Magic Magic is abated / These Alter-alternating Worlds / of the Spiral-spiral Map of Time / Are like ph-ph-phrases of a poem / It takes the two to to to rhyme."

Each measure was a beat faster than the one before. The Time Winders faced front, posed, and went into their routine of shakes and shimmies, while the singers riffed percussively:

"Each world's a shadow shadow of the other other other / Within alter-alter-alternating rings / Yeah, alternating rings / Jump over over over in a Witch's, in a Witch's satchel / Over over over over / Jump over in a Witch's Witch's satchel / See what the Future, what the Future / See, see now, see!"

The female singer's vocals escalated to a raspy, punky, demanding chant. Audience members were jumping to their feet, the whole auditorium was rocking out.

"What the Future / See what the Future / Brings Brings Brings! / Or dream dream dream your way / dream your way across a-c-c-cross a-c-c-c-cross the c-c-coils / the c-c-c-c-c-c-c-coils / On the psy-sy-sy-sy . . ."

Yasmine began her spin, and the vocalist started scat-screaming like a real rock star, higher and louder. Yasmine spun faster and faster. The lights started strobing, catching her yellow veil, then casting it into darkness, then setting it ablaze again with each quickening beat.

The stage manager was racing around backstage hollering for whoever was screwing around with the lights to cut it out. But no one could hear anything over the band, the audience shouting and stomping, and the scream-singing siren . . .

". . . Psychic spirit psychic spirit / The spirit travels spirit travels travels / Spirit t-t-t-t-t-t-t-t-travels / Tra-vels tra-vels / Spiral travel spiral travel t-t-t-travel / Here and There / Yeah baby! Here and There / Here Here, There There, Yeahhhhhh, Yeah, Ayeeeeeeee, Ayeee, Yeah Yeah Yeah Yeah, Ti-yim, Ti-yim, Ti-yim, Ti-yim, Ti-yim, TI TI TI TI TI TI TI TI-YUHM, TI-YUHM, TI TI TI TI, TI-YUHM, TI-YUHM!"

Whomp. Total black-out. Shocked silence. Then spotlight up on the veiled figure lying at the front of the stage.

Oddly discordant strains of the previous tune were wafting out from a different blend of instruments and voices:

"The coils of the Spiral / Trace a ceaseless path / And the End meets the Beginning / Where the First will meet the Last."

A different dancer fluttered to life under the purple veil—

"But hadn't it been yellow?"

It fell away to reveal the small, dark-haired dancer—

"But wasn't she in a plainer costume—how'd they do that?"

The dazzlingly bedecked dancer's trembling tambourine half

hid her face as she gracefully rose to her feet.

The lights came up on the rest of the troupe, and they all looked different too. The other four were taller—really tall, in fact—their gauzy costumes replaced by mismatched layers of clingy silks, rough linens and flapping furs. A bluish smoke rose out of their midst.

In back, the stage manager was near hysteria trying to locate and disable the unauthorized fog machine. One of the black-clad stage hands, a nurse by profession, took the man aside to cool down before he collapsed. "Almost over, almost over. We'll take it from here," she assured him, putting a cup of water to his lips.

Out front, the audience buzzed with confusion, *"But that's not who—" "Those aren't the—"* that quickly turned to annoyance at the ear-spitting band.

". . . Yes, the Spiral Map of Time / Unfurls from Everywhere to Never . . ."

Two women sang out in close, cringe-inducing harmony over the maniacal, polka-like medley issuing from a red-bearded man's fiddle and a white-bearded man's tuba. The audience hooted with displeasure.

Standing to the side of the stage, Yani-Yau snapped to. Her astonishment at the scene was all the greater for knowing what had really transpired. She had never doubted that the plan would work—until it actually did work. Now the implausibility of it washed over her. She was almost sickened by the shock of seeing the Goathorns Coven all in disarray and on stage in such an undignified fashion, there in the wicked, unnatural Alternate World. And *she* was their Minder, *she* was supposed to protect them. Yani-Yau slipped backstage, where she found the volunteer crew in a state of befuddlement.

However, pulling the curtain was a union job; a hefty man sat placidly on a stool waiting for his cue. He'd figured the crowd for a bunch of looney tunes from day one of the convention, so the current weirdness seemed to him all of a piece. He held his position proudly, the one professional in the house.

"Pull the curtain!"

That crazy sexy singer was suddenly at his side giving directions.

"You ain't the stage manager."

"Pull the curtain now!"

"Says who?"

Their voices rose, but the cacophony on stage drowned out their argument.

". . . And returns upon a mirror path / From Nowhere to For-eh-eh-ver." After one last horrific chord, the dancers and musicians bowed to boos and hisses.

"Now!"

"But. . ." The man's cue sheet showed two more numbers for The Time Winders.

In one swift motion Yani-Yau pulled a knife from her furry boot, sliced the rope, then held the blade to the man's throat. She put her lips seductively next to his cheek, and spoke with quiet, professional calm into his headset.

"House lights, please."

Out front, the nervous emcee was relieved to see the curtain drop with finality on The Time Winders' act, and the houselights come up. He hopped onto the stage and called loudly for Ms. Caper to come give the judges' decision.

Something like a riot seemed about to break out at the Harmony Convention. The Time Winders' performance had stirred people to ecstasy and then revulsion so quickly that the room roiled with emotion. Ms. Caper quickly announced the third, second and first place winners, and then everyone fled. Some went directly to the banquet hall, others to the bar—where the union man was already warming a seat.

Zeek quickly gathered his equipment and watched for any sign of Faye or the others. He worked his way toward the stage against the current of exiting conventioneers, and went up the

steps and behind the curtain into the wings unhindered. The band
and the troupe had rolled up the rugs and were rushing into the
depths of backstage, with that bizarre rock-star-customs-agent
Yau hissing instructions: "Go back, all the way past the dressing
rooms, there's a stage door. George Drumm, you lead the way,
the others are useless!"

"George Drumm? George, George!" Zeek called, but the man
had already disappeared into the shadows. "Faye, Faye! Wait for
me! Faye, is that you?" The dark-haired, glittering woman never
looked back, but hurried after the others even faster. Distraught
and tangled up in his gear, Zeek tripped and sprawled painfully
on his stomach. He found himself eye level with Ramon's guitar,
which lay abandoned in the middle of the stage. Ramon had done
it, he'd gone with them!

Sylvestor leapt from the camera bag and scampered after the
troupe.

"*Et tu?*" Zeek groaned, defeated.

"Heads up," someone growled, "you will soon be needed
here."

Zeek saw the fur-trimmed boots spring away to follow the
others, and he heard their voices fading out of earshot. The crew,
the audience, the dancers, had all gone. He was alone on a dark,
silent stage. For the first time in days, he could think in peace.

"Dammit, Faye. Where are you?"

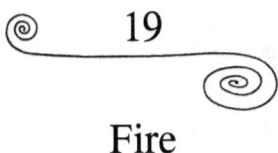

19

Fire

ROBYN SHIVERED UNDER HER VEIL. SHE ASSUMED THE ROARING in her ears, like the sound of the ocean, came from the crowded auditorium. They must be cheering for her. The musicians had resumed a more traditional rendition of the new song, gentle and folksy, with Black Star cooing the last verse in his rumbling bass. She rolled to her knees, letting the veil slide away from her face, and noted the sudden freshness of the air, the softness of the carpets . . .

"Robyn?" Faye whispered from nearby.

"Faye?" That was Sharon. "Alice? Paulette?"

"What? What's happened?"

It wasn't part of the choreography for all of them to do the Turkish Drop, but here they all were, spilled onto the ground with a pounding in their ears and spots in their eyes, as though they'd witnessed an explosion. The women crawled and stumbled toward the sound of each other's voices, and clutched one another in fear. The music continued without Ramon or Agent Yau. Fred, Desy and Black Star played on, and the troupe held onto the tune as to a lifeline. The booming slowly subsided, and their vision cleared.

"Ramon?" Robyn called out weakly as they stood, noticing they were in a field, under a night sky. Were those the gleaming eyes of wild animals drawing near? The women shook with fright. The panting and snuffling sound of—something—grew louder.

"I'm here, babe," Ramon called. "What the hell. I just about lost my lunch."

"Be careful, there's animals." Robyn's eyes were getting used to the dark. She reached out to the shadowy figure coming toward her. She and Ramon fell into each other's arms. Faye and the others stayed near.

"We need to go closer to the fire," Alice said. "I think that will keep the animals away."

"Yes, that's good," Sharon agreed. "And let's stay on the rugs. They brought us here, hopefully they will take us back."

"Is that what it was, you think?" Paulette asked. "These really are flying carpets?"

"Why do they just keep playing?" Faye wondered. The fire danced behind the trio, who played their instruments as though in a trance.

"What happened to that Agent Yau?" Alice asked.

"Those are not your worries, my darlings," a soft voice crooned. A tall woman with long auburn hair stepped out of the shadows. "Your job is done, and we are grateful for your help. The rugs have come home now, and you are free to return to your side. I have brought horses to take you back. Come."

There was nothing to do but go with her. Cautiously, the five women and Ramon stepped off the carpets and onto the meadow grass. Six horses stood at the ready, but with no saddles or reins. The tall leather-clad woman helped each one aboard their mount and gave brief instructions, mostly to the horses. There was none left for her, but she seemed unconcerned as she smacked the rear of the first horse, which held Paulette.

They all moved as one into the wood, where their riders had to duck low to avoid being hit by branches. After a few tense minutes, they emerged onto sandy, high desert terrain, and were joined by a riderless brown mare with a long rust-colored mane. This one took the lead, and they traveled at a swift trot over undulating ground for miles—or so it seemed to those who held on anxiously to those poor horses' necks.

Left behind in the meadow for purposes yet unclear, Black Star quickly took stock. The beat of horses' hoofs was fading into the distance, and the oddly harsh, mechanical music of Fred and Desy rang out eerily into the night. Literally entranced, they played on like wind-up toys even after he quieted his tambourine.

Yet he, Black Star, was not bewitched, at least he didn't feel so. This was his moment to break free, but discipline was crucial. He held his place, his ears alert to the presence of wild animals, his nostrils twitching. A bear had been nearby, recently. That would be Roth-Thea, Yani-Yau's near neighbor in the caverns, but he did not detect its presence now. And the badger—well, he knew her all too well. They were hardly allies, but he did not think she would do violence. He sensed her skittering here and there in her tunnels below. The horses were away. Yani-Yau had not been standing on the rugs during the dance; she must have been left behind at Kestrel Lodge. Any other sort of creature that might be afoot at night had doubtless been scared away by the fire and commotion.

As for other occupants of the meadow, besides himself and Fred and Desy, Black Star observed only one. An older woman stood protectively beside the carpets. Her garments had a historical look. She appeared attentive and yet at the same time passive, as though someone had pressed "pause" so that now she must wait for a cue to resume. At least, that's how she appeared.

Black Star decided to test his ability to move, and hers to notice. He crouched down and laid his tambourine on the ground. She did not react. So far, so good. Rather than stand with the same slow movement, he launched himself into a sprint. He ran swiftly and silently, the way his cousins had taught him, speeding toward the shadows along the downward slope of the earth.

This she noticed. Her shouts rose above Fred and Desy's weird duet. Black Star was fast, but the vibrations he felt under foot told him something was coming even faster. He looked over his shoulder in time to see the badger burst out of the earth and hurl itself at him, teeth glinting like knives. *And after all I've done for you, Edie.*

Summoning all his strength, Black Star thrust himself into Raven and shot upward into the moonlit night. But he was not safe yet. A large hawk was winging hard toward him. The image of the woman who had stood guard and then raised the alarm flashed in his mind. *So, you are also a changeling.*

Raven rose into open air above the trees. He knew he was physically stronger than that aged hawk, but her telepathic powers were almost crippling. She shrieked into his brain. Although no call floated on the air to be perceived naturally, his whole skull was ringing. He sought to answer back, to cajole, or appease, or fend off—anything to silence her. But it was youth and muscle that prevailed, not his psychic will. Raven simply flew the hawk in circles until she dropped back toward the meadow. He himself was exhausted and only able to fly for a few more wing-flaps. Without consciously willing it, he returned to the form of Black Star.

The big man's momentum took him into the woods at a jog. He came to a stop under an ancient pine, leaned his back against the tree trunk, and slid down to a crouch to catch his breath.

In the distance, the music was getting shaky. Perhaps the players were distracted by the loud exhortations of angry women that wafted out of the meadow. Once again Black Star called up techniques he had learned as a Pueblo youth and perfected as a shaman. He identified all of the forest and meadow sounds, and one by one lowered their volume in his perceptions. Now he could make out what the Familiars were saying.

"We must get him. He will be needed on the ridge."

"That one will not get far. But just in case, you go to the ridge and be ready to take his place."

"Me? I am supposed to guard these two. It is my duty to guard Witches Meadow."

"Ah, so it pleases you to tend to your duties now, does it? I wonder if your disobedience has rubbed off on Roth-Thea. Where did *she* go? We could have used her help just now."

"I think she had a worry about the black dog with the magician inside him."

Snip-Edie had so many of her own worries, she'd barely noticed when Roth shifted to Thea during the Witches' dance and slipped quietly out of the meadow.

"Hmph. I don't like it. But I must start out for the ridge now, so I will be there to meet the others. Let us reach out to Roth-Thea in our minds and ask her to bring the magician to the meadow. She can guard him here, along with the tourist couple, so you can help with the rugs if need be. Yes, we must alert Roth-Thea. Perhaps she will locate the intruder along the way."

Wyan trudged out of Witches Meadow using a walking stick. The old Minder was tired, and Ti was not ready to fly again just yet.

"Play, you idiots," Snip-Edie snapped.

The music picked up again with renewed vigor. Black Star guessed she had morphed into Badger.

Black Star noticed himself trembling. Mention of the changeling bear had unsettled him. Roth-Thea was not someone he wanted to meet in this woods. He steadied himself and quietly got to his feet. A few tense moments passed. Nothing happened. Black Star concluded that he had evaded his pursuers for the time being, and his anxiety gave way to elation.

The flying carpets had brought him through the Morass—he had made it! He began to cautiously explore the hillside.

There was a moment, only a moment, when no one and nothing existed but Robyn and Ramon. Riding side by side under a full moon, attuned to their horses and all of Nature, they were at home in the vast landscape, akin to the wind. All the craziness that had brought them here, all the mystery of what was to come, meant nothing. Their recent nauseating gyration across Time was forgotten. *This* was the real magic carpet ride, this dream of a legendary, passionate existence come true. They were the first and last couple on earth, the very inventors of romantic love. For a moment, it felt like a lifetime.

Suddenly, the riderless horse that had been leading them reared up with a snort. The other horses also reared, and a huge black cat streaked between Robyn and Ramon, sending them in opposite directions.

Though an experienced rider, Ramon could do little without bridle and reins. The maddened horse dumped him and galloped after the others. Everything around him seemed to be mad. There were even birds careening crazily overhead, their shadows darting this way and that across the moon.

"Get back! Get away!" Robyn had also been separated from the group, and she was being stalked by the giant black cat. She clung to her horse, tucking her feet up as far as she could without losing her balance. "Oh, dear Goddess, don't hurt the horse." She was carefully backing the horse toward some trees. The sensation of the silver charm bracelet, now jingling freely on her ankle, told her what the cat was after. *Is it a mountain lion? Pure black? It looks like a giant version of Audy. Maybe if I toss it the bracelet, it will go away.*

This was not how Robyn wanted her adventure to end, but she was certain that she had really made it into the Gypsy's magical universe—with Ramon! That would have to be enough.

Resolved, Robyn reached toward her ankle. The jaguar—yes, that's what it was, a black jaguar—immediately halted its advance and sat on its haunches expectantly. Robyn struggled with the clasp for what seemed an eternity. It was stuck. She had never had trouble opening it before. *Just nervous, c'mon—* She pulled her leg up and balanced precariously, trying to work the clasp with both hands, not fall off the horse, and not let the jaguar out of her sight. "Come on, come on—come *off* already."

The bangles caught the moonlight like bright teeth in a laughing mouth. The jaguar tipped itself forward and began to slither toward her. Her horse shifted nervously, ready to bolt. Unable to remove the ankle bracelet, Robyn remembered Mr. Brooks' warning: *Cannot guarantee your protection if it's lost.* She became even more frightened. She needed an escape route. Her eyes darted here and there, and back to the animal whom she was certain was about to pounce and pull her from the horse.

Something moved a few yards off. The cat's ear twitched.

"Oh, no—please, no." Robyn murmured. Horrified, she recognized the figure. *Ramon, you mustn't.* But of course her knight in shining armor would throw himself at the beast of unknown powers to save her. She must prevent that at all costs. She knew what the cat wanted, and she would give it up one way or another, hopefully without her foot attached.

The cat was now fully aware of Ramon, so Robyn called to him, "Go back, Ramon, go back! I know what this is!"

Ramon popped out from behind a rock with an improvised slingshot. He looked determined and dangerous and, to Robyn, very handsome in the moonlight. He mouthed the words "I love you," then readied his assault.

The jaguar zeroed in on the man. Ramon had a true shot, perfectly aimed to strike it between the eyes.

"No! No! Please!" Robyn cried, desperately trying to disrupt them both. "Here kitty, here, *Audy*—I have what you want." Robyn kicked her heels into the horse hard, and they charged. Exactly as she expected, the horse reared up short of the snarling feline, and she slid down its back and off its rump, rolling quickly back toward the trees. She hoped the horse would run the other way and not trample her.

"Robyn! Robyn!"

Ramon's cries raked her heart. She could not go back to him enchained in Esmarelda's charm. She would endanger them all.

"Robyn! Robyn!"

The jaguar must have fled. At least Ramon was safe. Perhaps she could risk one last embrace before she sent him back to Piper Canyon—*if he can find the way*—while she ditched Esmarelda's bracelet once and for all.

Robyn was about to call to Ramon, when another voice rang out. She recognized it at once: Black Star.

"Yani? Yani-Yau? Is that you? What are you doing?"

"What are *you* doing, Sal?" Ramon shouted. "Agent Yau isn't here, but I've lost Robyn somewhere. A black panther almost got us. Good thing you're here, come help me look. Robyn, Robyn! Come out now, it's safe!"

"No, cousin, it is not safe at all," Black Star muttered, approaching Ramon with a reassuring smile. The men took each other's right arm in a strong clasp—and Black Star had Ramon pinned in a jiffy. "You've got to go back, cuz. Seriously, man, just shut up and listen. We have gone down the rabbit hole here, and nothing is what it seems. That jaguar was Yani-Yau, I swear it. She can be a cougar, a woman, anything she wants to be. It's magic, dude. I'm gonna get Robyn back, I promise, but you gotta get out now while you can."

Ramon was hardly in a position to argue. With Black Star sitting on him, he could barely take a proper breath. He half-suspected that he had fallen backstage at Kestrel Lodge, knocked his head, and all else was delirium. He heard Black Star give a piercing whistle, then the drum of hooves. The horse Robyn had been riding came to them. Black Star jumped up and tossed Ramon on its back.

"Hurry, you can still catch the others." Black Star gave the horse a smack. "I'll bring Robyn—I know the way." The animal was already practically flying toward the Loophole.

Robyn, having observed all from her shrubby hiding place,

was no more inclined to be tracked down by Black Star—*of all people*—than the nasty cat. *Why does he think the jaguar could be Agent Yau? Does he know about Audy? Are they one and the same?* This was no time to mull over such questions. Black Star could track a white hare in the snow. How would she get away from him?

Befuddled as she was, Robyn was not afraid of Black Star, a.k.a. Ramon's cousin Salvador. She was grateful to him for sending Ramon to safety. Now her adventure across the Spiral might continue. In fact, while the men had been talking, her fears subsided and her faculties returned. She continued to finger the ankle bracelet, half-hoping that the clasp would let go as magically as it had locked. And half-hoping it would not. (Let's be honest, Robyn.)

The charmed bracelet seemed to whisper to Robyn, to remind her of the tale Esmarelda had told—how Malcom the Master Seer had commissioned it in a place called Ochersfeldt; how, when Esmarelda tried to escape Malcom's thrall, the charm had deposited her in that city. Robyn had memorized Esmarelda's description of Ochersfeldt: . . . *known for its artisans . . . metal workers, glass blowers and crystal cutters . . . many shops not unlike The Lost Unicorn . . . a popular place for Witches, Seers, and Magicians . . . you would fit right in there . . . the local people are blond like you . . .*

Robyn had dreamed of going to Ochersfeldt. Now that she had made it across the Spiral, she was certain that Esmarelda's ankle bracelet would take her there. She didn't have a time-and-space-traveling magic satchel like the Gypsy, but the bracelet itself contained the spell—the bracelet *itself* told her what to do. It whispered, *Use your veil.*

"Why do you hide, Robyn?"

Black Star had sniffed her out and was striding toward her.

"I'm not hiding. I, uh, I think I passed out." Robyn emerged stiffly from the weeds. "Wait a sec, okay? I have to pee."

Black Star stopped. He crossed him arms and politely inspected the fancy silver toe-tips of his tooled leather boots. A flash of yellow caught his eye.

"Hey!"

Robyn had not stepped behind the trees, but pranced forward to unfurl her yellow veil. "Ochersfeldt!" she sang, twirling once around fast, so that the veil swirled around her body. Then she bent double, grasped the silver bracelet, and tumbled to the ground. "Ochersfeldt," she breathed within her cocoon.

Black Star stood transfixed for one second too many. When he threw himself at the yellow mirage, he landed hard, empty-handed.

"Women."

The steed was well away. Black Star's promises trailed after him into the night. Ramon hoped to catch up to the others and turn them back to rescue Robyn, but they were moving too swiftly. It was all he could do to keep them in sight. By the time he passed through the jumble of boulders, he could already hear their horses returning. Speeding through the treacherously winding passage, his own mount miraculously avoided colliding with rock and horse flesh. They had barely rounded the last boulder when the horse bucked nastily, sending its rider aloft, and turned to follow the herd home.

Ramon's painful landing conclusively answered the question of whether he was dreaming. He sprawled on the rocky plateau above Piper Canyon trying to catch his breath. He could hear the beat of the horses quickly receding in one direction, and the exclamations of his friends drifting toward him from the other.

"Robyn! Ramon! Where are they?" "Is everyone else here?" "Is anyone hurt?"

Ramon forced himself to his feet and began to stagger toward their voices. But he was sent reeling again when the riderless chestnut horse came roaring past, as though it had ridden far ahead of the others and was now racing to catch up to them. Ramon saw sparks flying from its hooves, the air smelled charred.

Black Star rested his cheek on Mother Earth and contemplated his predicament. He may have slept. The rumble of horses' hooves roused him. Flame-Mari and the herd were returning. The Witches and Familiars would soon be gathering on the High Road. He had gleaned much about their plans while in the meadow, where he had been able to read snippets of thoughts from one or the other. But why had Yani-Yau subverted the plan and attacked Robyn? Would she join the others on the High Road as though nothing had happened? Then, when no one would miss her, would she hunt Robyn again in the guise of the black jaguar?

Black Star could think of nothing else to do but go up to the ridge and see what he could find out. Perhaps there was still a chance of getting into the Witches' good graces. He had valuable information about Robyn, and legitimate concern for her welfare. Yes, he would play his part in the Witches' scheme. Then he would convince them to send him to Ochersfeldt to rescue Robyn. Who better to locate her than another Alternate Worlder? And once he found Robyn, the two of them could do a little shopping before heading home. What a coup that would be for Crafts of the World and The Lost Unicorn.

I ask you, what is one to do with people who think they know everything? The shaman was all wrong about the black jaguar being another version of the golden cougar. Shame on him for suspecting such a deception from Yani-Yau, even as she valiantly led the sisters back to their own domain. And though Robyn correctly connected the jaguar to the black cat that had approached her at Kestrel Lodge, her decisions from that point on were not nearly as smart as her deductions. While Black Star plotted to cozy up to the Coven, and Robyn plunged into

misadventure, our Goathorns troupe returned across the Spiral
with their flying carpets . . .

Backstage at Kestrel Lodge, Esmarelda forbade herself to
look back at Zeek. A chill had gone up her spine when he called
after her thinking she was Faye. Then Sylvestor dashed past her
and ran to George, who squatted down by the stage door to let the
cat hop onto his shoulder. Esma caught up to him, and they ran
out into the night together.

Esma and George each carried one flying carpet. The twins
each carried several to lighten the load for their older sisters. The
Witches staggered along in long gowns, capes and vests,
swearing colorfully. Spritely Nee-Reta, bringing up the rear with
the first-last carpet cradled in her arms, urged them onward.
Beyond the building's lights, the moon lit the way for the fleeing
imposters—so bright, George noticed, that birds could fly. He
saw one in the distance silhouetted against the moon;
another—nearer, larger—circled above, in and out of view.

Esma kept her eyes on the trail ahead. It was easy to follow
through the campgrounds, but then the land began to slope
steeply upwards, and shadows played tricks on her. She was
about to tell George to release Sylvestor to see if he could find the
way, when a much larger cat sprang past and began to trot lightly
up the path, staying in the open. Here was their guide.

They hurried to keep up with the graceful beast, gasping as
the air thinned. Stealth was not in their repertoire this night. The
Gypsy's tambourine, hastily tied to her sash, rattled and jingled,
while George Drumm clomped noisily alongside her. The
Witches of Goathorns Coven, unaccustomed to traveling in this
manner—that is, in their bodies—kept up a steady stream of
curses. The great bird shrieked overhead. And Nee-Reta, last in
line, laughed giddily and sometimes sang out a series of sharp,
inhuman calls—keh keh keh keh keh—rising in pitch.

The horses were almost upon them before they heard the

thunder of hooves over their own commotion. The ground had leveled, and they were moving in a tighter group. Suddenly, the mountain lion who guided them leapt to the top of a boulder and snarled a warning. Everyone froze, detected the approach of the herd, and scurried behind the great rock. Moments later, several horses and riders raced past. Esma and George watched, wide-eyed. The Witches cackled nervously.

The riders turned their heads in surprise. Eyes locked for an instant, and then the vision slipped away with the distance that the horses rapidly put behind them.

After the horses had passed, Yau bounded back onto the trail. Her clutch of Witches and Gypsies followed more quietly. Nee-Reta was electrified with excitement. She urged Yani-Yau onward with her thoughts, making it impossible for the Familiar to think her own. *Something was not right with the herd, it seemed like someone was missing . . .*

"Keh keh keh keh keh!" Reta called exuberantly into the night, trotting lightly at the rear of the line. The Witches cursed her and stumbled on. Varluft also struggled, but laughingly. His was the delighted rumble of a magician who had pulled off an excellent trick. To conserve energy (or for the sheer fun of it) he let himself be carried along amongst the fuming Witches.

Esma carried a rug under one arm and locked elbows with George with the other. Sylvestor nestled into the rug that George carried. When the cougar took the lead, the Witches surged forward, and the Gypsies gladly put the sisters between the big cat and themselves. They held this position, keeping pace easily. Nee-Reta skipped up close on their heels and then dropped back impatiently, and then went through the pattern again and again. She could have been on the ridge by now, even on foot, but it was her job to guard the rear.

At last they reached a place everyone recognized. They were very near the High Road. The cougar was suddenly gone. The group stood exhausted on a ridge overlooking the bowl of the

Goathorns. A thin tendril of black smoke spiraled upward from a flickering speck of light in the center of Witches Meadow.

"Now what?" Esma sighed. "We're back where we started."

"Come!" Nee-Reta called the weary Witches to the overlook. "The hard part is over. You will like this." They snarled at her but obeyed. "Wyan, are you ready? Black Star? Come quick and help! Varluft! Yani-Yau! Sylvestor, we need you too."

"We are short one," Wyan snapped in exasperation. She was limping slightly as she picked her way along the ridge. "The raven has flown, Roth has not come, Snip has stayed to guard the meadow."

"Raven? Flown?" Yani's heart began to break, her mind was racing. "Oh, no—he is not the only one who is miss—"

Raven? Does she mean Black Star? Or could she mean Dark? Nee-Reta's thoughts were also in turmoil. Unformed premonitions converted her exhilaration to dread.

"Raven? What raven?! What is a Black Star?" The Witches fretted and fussed, feeling confused and out of their element.

The sisters' perturbation drowned out Yani's alarm call. She tried to send the image to Nee-Reta mind-to-mind, a playback of the horses passing: the first with Paulette, the second with Alice, then Sharon, then Faye, then one *riderless* who was not Flame-Mari, and the sixth missing altogether—

"No time, no time!" Reta hurled back. *"Look at the twins— this will never work if we don't go soon."*

Intuisha and Dremtessa had successfully held themselves to human proportions thus far, but these upsets were testing their endurance. They were already noticeably growing.

"Well, who can wrangle two at once?" Wyan demanded, catching the Familiars' thoughts.

"I'm coming!" The message rang out to the Minders clearly, and a moment later—really, only seconds had passed since Wyan's original report—Black Star bounded over to the group, too winded to speak.

"Then we can do this. Now!" Reta took firm control once more, allowing no time for explanations verbal or mental. "Open the carpets and get on them quick."

As each carpet was dropped to the ground and unrolled, it immediately began to float upward. The two Gypsies, the five Witches, the three Minder-women—Yani, Reta and Wyan, the Master Seer Varluft, the spunky little cat Sylvestor, and the mighty big shaman Black Star, each threw themselves upon a flying carpet and were lifted upward. The carpets flew easily, regardless of the weight or grace of their riders, and like a flock of birds they soared out over the rocky ledges of the high caverns and above the treetops of the woods that encircled Witches Meadow. The sisters whooped in delight. Their shouts mingled with a terrified cry rising up from the other side of the Loophole.

"Fire!"
"Fire!"
"Fire!"

The cry carried through Kestrel Lodge like the flames licking through the campground. Zeek found his way to the stage door and raced out into the night. He soon encountered Faye and the others rushing toward the lodge to sound the alarm and find water and tools. Zeek and Faye fell upon each other with relief and wonder as a bright line of flames advanced up the hill. Campers were pouring up to the lodge for safety, and lodgers were pouring into the night with shovels, fire extinguishers, and buckets of water. A fire engine came clanging out of the service garage, and a certain wiry figure you might recognize by now followed in an open jeep; he quickly organized crews to dig firebreaks and hose down the buildings.

The Time Winders, tumbled out onto the ridge above the campgrounds, had been among the first to see that one blaze was out of control in the valley dotted with many small campfires and two big bonfires. Our poor troupe was still reconstituting themselves from their sickening time-warp and bone-shattering ride when Alice raised the alarm.

"Look at that bright line—I thought it was a stream at first, but it's fire, that flame is running—it's not supposed to do that."

Similar cries were going up from campsites on the lower foothills. Ramon had barely caught up to them and got out two words about Robyn. They pulled him along and started scrambling down to the campgrounds, shouting warnings.

I have to hand it to those Harmony folks, they can and do step up when action is needed. The last night of the Fifth Annual Harmony Convention was no party, but they saved the lodge, without a single severe injury. The smoke was bad, though, and many complained of grogginess and confusion. Loss of memory, like. Thank Flame-Mari for that. She had carried the spell from Sestorina.

And that spell. Well, let us attribute it to that spell. What happened next. That is, what happened while we were fighting the fire. The Coven had just sent whole gaggles of people and animals one way and another across the Spiral and through the Loophole. The magic of our side tracked back and forth with them like muddy pawprints. And so, what oughtn't to have happened—what ought never to happen—happened. If it was "for the best," that was only because we had already provoked the worst. I would write the following in a whisper, if I could. I would like to not write it at all.

Because it is one thing to tell a jaunty tale of the Gypsies Esmarelda and George Drumm playing hide and seek with their doubles Faye and Zeek in the Alternate World and even making unwitting contact with their Future/Past selves, and quite another to describe my own knowing encounter with my own parallel self. I am not supposed to know him, or him me. The smoky spell that prompted *his* epiphany blessedly erased it as quickly. But I fear I am destined to be ever haunted by forbidden knowledge. (*We* are, Robyn.)

I was directing the containment of the fire. There was a great deal of smoke and commotion. I was dimly aware of several Time Winders in the mix—Alice, Sharon and Paulette in one of the bucket lines, Faye and Zeek going from tent to tent to make sure no one was passed-out inside—but I was also still faintly in contact with the minds of Yani-Yau and Flame-Mari, and trying to remain so. I sensed trouble, more than one glitch developing in our elaborate plan. And as I probed for clues, a very big glitch stuck his face right into mine.

"Robyn got left behind. I don't know how it works over there. You do. You have to get her. You have to go there and be me and rescue her, because we love her. I mean, if *you* love someone *there*, don't let *me* lose *Robyn*. Black Star is going after her. Or maybe he'll go for *your* girl."

That got my attention. I wanted to bite his face off. We stood nose to nose, the same height, scruffy, sooty, weary, two men looking in a mirror and hating themselves.

Sure, it's laughable now, Black Star going after Brunagwa—

(By the Firsts, I did not want to write that! Where was I?)

"I know what we are," Ramon goaded me. "Why are you waiting? Give me those. This is my place. Go to yours *now*. Go as fast as you can."

We both knew what he meant. He snatched the shovel and pick out of my hands and snarled much like a wild dog. I turned from him, and for the second time Coyote showed himself in the Alternate World. The fastest way to the Loophole was on four paws.

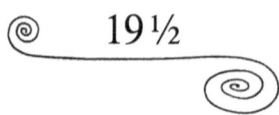

19½

Down the Rabbit Hole

MY NUMBERING OF THIS CHAPTER HAS GOT MY EDITOR'S GOAT, but I think the title makes clear my meaning. I number this the way they do the components of Ochersfeldt, where, by division and division and division, a virtually infinite quantity of everything can be made to fit. And so it is with our tale. Here I was, plowing my way toward a tidy resolution of the rug escapade, and a certain someone had to venture into the infinite town, thus provoking all manner of new activity and encounters, most of which do not fit neatly into the time or space allotted to even a lengthy chapter. Like it or not, this tale is taking a major detour into a place that can't be measured. Our story has not gotten longer at the end, but here in the crack between Chapters 19 and 20. Robyn will have to live with it, it's her own fault.

The transfer to Ochersfeldt via the enchanted ankle bracelet was even more sickening than the flying carpet trick. Robyn suddenly found herself staggering along a town lane, tangled in her veil. She wrestled herself out of it like a drunk, and might have been taken for one, for there was a busy tavern on the corner. To avoid it, she stepped into a small courtyard. There was less bustle here than on the street. At first it seemed like a private residence, and she was about to leave, when a neon sign flashed on the other side of the small, brick-paved square.

Neon, really? Well, why not? Robyn took a few steps forward and ducked between a couple of topiary shrubs in pots. Now she had a clear view of the building opposite. Beneath the sign that alternately lit up a red "RED" and a green "FERN" ornate double doors stood open. She thought she saw movement within. Then several people stepped into the courtyard from other side streets and proceeded into the building. Robyn crossed the courtyard and went inside.

And immediately regretted it. The place was full of hunting trophies, mounted fish, bearskin rugs, and taxidermied mammals and birds. Salespeople kept popping out from behind every display and treating her as if she were a royal visitor. More customers streamed in. People whispered to each other in strange languages, nodding toward her. One word was being repeated over and over. It sounded like "Brownie." No, "Brunie." Someone touched her hair. She felt a strand pulled, and she jerked away looking for an exit.

The place was dimly lit. Antlers, fangs and claws loomed out of the shadows. She thought she heard someone calling to her in a high, chuckling voice. People were crowding in, pushing her into a corner crammed with huge specimens. Human hands reached toward her from one side, and furred paws with sharp claws blocked her escape.

Protect me. Robyn didn't know what prompted her to appeal to those gruesome carcasses for help. The words came into her head as she hid among them, and almost at once she noticed a shadow within a shadow behind the giant stuffed grizzly—a passageway. *Thank you.* She slipped around the bear and down a deserted, dusty hall. A waft of fresh air directed her attention to an outer door, half off its hinges. The same breeze moved a single, creaking, rocking chair.

"And thank *you*." Robyn nodded to the chair as she passed, and a shiver went up her spine. She gave the door a push with her foot. It swung open and she rushed through.

Hurrying to put as much distance as she could between herself and the RED/FERN establishment, Robyn crossed one street after another. She forbade herself to look over her shoulder, or even right or left, lest she catch the eye of someone who might try to question her. The distressing episode in the taxidermy shop was forgotten as she continued to stride along. For a good many blocks, she hadn't a thought in her head.

After a while, Robyn noticed there were rows of small shops along all of the side lanes. She turned down one to have a look. When her nostrils caught the scents of patchouli and amber, she was herself again. The curiosity that had brought her to this place returned. The RED/FERN compound had been a gateway, she decided, a test she had to pass to be allowed into the magical city. And now, after a sort of dream journey, here she was.

The stores did remind her of The Lost Unicorn. A full block of them would be too much competition for her in Caliente, but here business was thriving. Many couples and small groups were out shopping and enjoying the night air. Their costumes were varied and colorful, but few were as eye-striking as Robyn's spangled yellow vest and billowing harem pants. Robyn wrapped her veil around herself like a sari, and felt that she looked fairly respectable. Maybe it didn't matter, though, because no one was paying any attention to her.

Robyn had no money on her, so it was just as well she was being ignored. She was glad the clerks and shopkeepers were not aggressively trying to sell her stuff. She could look to her heart's content without being approached. She began exploring the shops in earnest. There seemed to be no end to them. They all had several levels, courtyards, and inner passages that connected one to the other. The place was a labyrinthine mall, and each collection of wares was more amazing than the last.

(Sorry, but I am refusing my Editor's request for details. Where would one begin and where would one stop? I have already described Ochersfeldt and its arts in an early chapter, plus I have described the sort of merchandise Robyn sells in The Lost Unicorn. Put the two together, enhance by a power of ten, multiply by a gazillion—give or take—and use your imagination. I am confident that the clever Reader will get the gist of it.)

For long periods Robyn forgot entirely about Esmarelda's ankle bracelet, and everything else. She was again entranced, as were those around her. She was following her nose mostly, navigating by comforting scents like pinon, leather, lavender, and, after a time, coffee, baked goods, savory skillets— She had reached the food kiosks.

Now, quite belatedly, certain dilemmas presented themselves that caused our wayward Time Winder to assess her situation: She was hungry. She was lost. She had no plan at all for disposing of the ankle bracelet, which was probably still acting as a beacon for Audy, or Yau, or whatever that cat was, not to mention for Black Star, and maybe that Master Seer creep, Malcom, who had started the whole cat business to get back at Esmarelda. Meanwhile, Ramon and her troupe must be very worried about her, and who knew what had become of *them*.

Fatigue and worry washed over her. Robyn staggered out of the mercado where she had been wandering. The night air was refreshing. She decided that some food would help. She could go back in and see if she could finagle a bite of something. Maybe she could dance for her supper. If only there were a more sit-down sort of restaurant with a little floor space, like the Casa Blanca in Caliente where she sometimes performed for fun and tips. She looked up and down the street, but could not tell what sorts of businesses were housed in these bigger, blockier buildings. Maybe they were all full of stalls and kiosks like the one she had come from.

Suddenly, in the large window of a drab building directly across from her, a sign lit up. A bold-type message began scrolling through while she watched:

HUNGRY?

LOST?

HAVE NO PLAN?

LEFT SOMEONE YOU LOVE BEHIND?

STEP INSIDE—WE ARE AT YOUR SERVICE.

ALL FORMS OF PAYMENT ACCEPTED—CASH, BANGLES, DANCES.

Robyn lost her appetite. This was not good. She was being spied upon. Of course they could read minds here. Anything was possible. But was anyone really so foolish as to walk right into a trap like that? These people didn't know anything about Alternate Worlders if they thought *she* would fall for it.

(One does what one can to buck oneself up, eh, Robyn, after blundering into exactly the trouble one has been given every opportunity to avoid?)

(No, I am not over it.)

And so Robyn stands on one of an infinite number of nearly identical loopy lanes in the Gold Quarter of Ochersfeldt. She is frozen in fear at the sinister message. And you know what? I think we should leave her here. It's going to take a major effort by the Goathorns Coven to rescue her. By now, Coyote is on his way to the meadow to sound the alarm.

WITCHES MEADOW

Roth-Thea and I watched the thirteen flying carpets sail back to the meadow. We had a good vantage, there on the rocky hillside that fell away from the cliffs and caverns. Dremtessa's Familiar was as distraught as I was. Fortunately, our desperate thoughts had reached each other before our wild selves could clash. The rampaging bear Roth became stolid Thea, and H. Coyote, to my own surprise, gave way to the groundskeeper Brooks. The boundaries of the Spiral had become blurred in every direction.

Thea and Brooks exchanged worst-case scenarios, cursed ourselves, and dreaded telling the Witches that we had misplaced two (or three, depending how you count) for whom we were responsible—Robyn, and the black dog Dark now burdened with the soul of the dastardly Master Seer Malcom; and it was probably the latter who had hijacked the former, and even now might hold her captive.

"We may as well let them savor their ride," Thea said.

"Yes, and let them get the rugs squared away before we set them another task."

"True, the rugs could still cause trouble. Ah, look at them."

It was a wondrous, fearful sight, that armada of flying carpets laden with cackling Witches and kindred characters swooshing around under the full moon. Thea and I stayed back and watched them land.

You know by now, dear Reader, as Thea knew, that I only had eyes for Brunagwa. The Red Mountain Witch was glorious, windblown and laughing happily as I have not seen for ages. The twins too, all of the sisters, were almost girlish again. Once they had returned to solid ground, they waved their fingers at Fred and Desy to re-energize the enchanted duet. They wanted to keep dancing the Gypsy dance that had led them on such an adventure. Varluft pranced around them, and we Minders had a fleeting vision of the Time before our Time, when the Coven was new.

But the sisters had not forgotten themselves. They began to cock their heads and look around as though homing in on our presence—or rather, the proximity of bad news. Noticing this, Varluft grew serious and shooed everyone away from the rugs, which now lay in a disheveled heap. The music box couple still stood on one untrampled rug playing their tune over and over. Varluft produced a wand, which he waved like a baton to get Fred and Desy's attention. They marched off of the rugs after him. Stopping a few steps away on a patch of ground padded by meadow flowers, the old magician sent the bewitched pair to Nod with two taps of his wand; they crumpled to earth like rag dolls.

The once Master Seer of Ochersfeldt raised his arms again,

and the flapping sleeves of his robe became wings. The Witches clapped with delight as the scary ten-foot-tall eagle appeared before their eyes. With its wings spread above the flying carpets, the eagle emitted an ear-splitting cry. Each of the twenty-six rugs rolled itself up, then they all rolled themselves into a stack like logs readied for the fire. The eagle flapped his enormous wings twice and settled back into the diminutive magician. Then Varluft waved off the sisters before they tackled him again. He was lucky to have survived the first such welcome.

"I demand to know what was going on while I was stuck in the spur of Time trying to save the soul of that fiend, Malcom."

"I do, too. And he is not a fiend." The emboldened Reta stepped forward. Her garment of feathers had become longer and more refined. It was noted mind to mind that "little Nee-Reta" had even grown in height. "Where is Dark?"

"Dark?" Brunagwa, Hesterluna, and Sestorina acted like they didn't know what she was talking about. The twins remained inscrutable.

"Dark? What? What I want to know is, where is Roth? She's been missing since before *he* bolted." Wyan pointed her long nose at Black Star, who was edging over to Yani-Yau. The elder Minder's composure had been tested to the limit. For a split second Ti the red-tailed hawk flashed out, her feathers literally ruffled, and then Wyan was back, stoic in her cap and jacket even while tufts of down were still settling around her.

"Roth-Thea is guarding the black dog, of course," Dremtessa pronounced icily, giving off her own white puffs. "She's not missing at all, and it is not her fault that this intruder got loose."

"Whatever." Ti-Wyan, a Minder and semi-retired Familiar, was above arguing with Witches.

"Come, time's wasting," I hissed at Thea, prompting her shift. As the bear Roth, she galloped into the meadow. Coyote followed. We morphed back to human form when we neared the fire, and all gathered round nervously.

"I have not been guarding, I've been hunting. The dog still had his magician's tricks— Tricks, stronger than my own— It was too late by the time— I sensed his absence, but too late— I looked and looked— I failed."

It was pathetic to see Thea start crying in anticipation of the Witches' wrath. Before they could react, I hit them with my news about Robyn. My very appearance as Brooks the man had already unhinged them. I revealed that Robyn was at large on our side of the Spiral, likely in Ochersfeldt, wearing the Gypsy's charmed ankle bracelet. And Malcom was on the prowl for her—not necessarily in the body of a black dog, but perhaps manifesting any form he chose. He'd already been a housecat and a jaguar—

The whole crew erupted at that point, as: Black Star learned that the black jaguar had *not* been Yani-Yau; Nee-Reta realized that her precious Malcom was endangering her precious Dark; Esmarelda registered that Malcom was not done with her yet, and now Robyn was in trouble too; all the rest of us became painfully aware that our work was far from finished.

Varluft's eagle reappeared briefly to restore order under his massive wings. He flapped once, blowing away our jumbled outbursts, and returned to his sage self.

"Recriminations will have to wait. What now?"

"I'll track her," Black Star offered.

"How?" several laughed.

"The black cat—dog—whatever—is after her. I'll track *it*."

The obviously ill-informed intruder was brushed off, and more savvy minds went to work.

"What if she gets the bracelet off?" "She could, you know, someone there will know how to do it." "The one who made it certainly will." "Only Malcom knows who that is." "There are scads of able silversmiths who might have done it." "I bet I could narrow down the list if I could see the thing."

The sisters had a way of all talking at once, asking, answering and listening simultaneously.

"How could we ever hope to find the shop in time, even if we knew?" "It could take forever." "And if she takes the charm off, no way to trace her." "Ochersfeldt's a big place." "Some would say infinite."

"She'll blend right in there." Yani asserted loudly from her place near Intuisha. Yani-Yau was no stranger to Ochersfeldt; and, as Agent Yau, she had taken a good look at Robyn and noted her resemblance to our local townsfolk, and in particular to . . .

Everyone fell silent, envisioning the five robust young women with flowing blond hair who once worked behind the counter at the old Redfern place. The site now sported a haunted house and museum complex. So, Robyn would likely land there. But where would she go next? Malcom was the wild card, and the ankle bracelet was the wrench in the works.

"It's not enough to find her," Varluft said. "We have to get her out. Who knows the way out?"

"You do, Master Seer of Ochersfeldt." Hesterluna reminded him.

"Unlikely, after all this time, my sweet."

"Maybe I can help," Esmarelda spoke up. She showed them her magic satchel, which was tied to her sash and hidden in the folds of her skirt.

"Well, I don't see how—" George spluttered.

"You only have one of those things now," Brunagwa, who had thrown the other into the fire, pointed out.

"Oh, but Geor—"

"She's right. What good is just one?" George cut her off. He had no intention of surrendering his own—his *stolen*—magic satchel for this dubious scheme. What if it got lost—or also ended up in the Witches' fire—before he could return it to the Gypsies? He pulled Esma close and bent his head to hers.

"*Hush, will you.*"

"*But it's my fault she's lost there.*"

The Witches went back into a huddle to continue their own

argument. Varluft paced around them, catching snippets and tossing in a word of approval or disapproval here and there. The Familiars arrayed themselves by habit around the Coven's circle, itchy to begin the search.

Black Star gaped this way and that, observing the changes: Thea to the bear Roth, Edie to Snip the badger, Mari to the horse Flame, and Yani—whom he had completely misjudged—to the beautiful tawny cougar Yau. Then he noticed the startling resemblance of Esmarelda and George Drumm to Robyn's friends Faye and Zeek. He looked for the man Brooks among the assembled—where had he gone? There had been something familiar about that guy, too—

A coyote parked himself very near, and Black Star's nerves interfered with his train of thought. The big man was not afraid of being mauled by the relatively small canine, but exposing Raven was another story. It had been Black Star's plan to also morph, but the coyote's posture warned him not to try it. (I'm no spring chicken, but I can sense a fellow Minder's intent before any physical changes occur. Coyote could nab Raven out of the air the very instant he shifted, you better believe it.)

After long minutes, the sisters' five-layered conversation ceased. "We have a plan," they announced in unison; and they arrayed themselves in their usual five-pointed configuration.

Hesterluna spoke: "Esmarelda, we have learned your dance, now you will learn ours. You will dance your way to Robyn on the astral plane. The charmed bracelet will lead your spirit to her, so you can instruct her and deliver our spells. Magic will lead her back to us, but she must not let go of the bracelet. Time is of the essence, we must get started. George Drumm, we think it will help if you play your fiddle. Varluft, wake the tourists and give them a tune for finding things. George, follow along with them."

You can imagine the many questions that poised on the tips of tongues at that moment, but the Meadow Watch Witch inspired obedience. Her satiny purple and orange gown glimmered in the

strange light of this long night. Indeed, Hesterluna, standing in
the center of her meadow, appeared to be in command of the very
moon that hung overhead full and bright. She raised her arms and
lifted her face to it, murmuring a secret mantra.

"Lil, lil, lil, lil, lil . . ."

Black Star observed that the moon had not budged in all this
time since he had been transported into the meadow—surely
hours had passed by now. What was Hesterluna chanting? The
shaman strained to hear. The other Witches were also chanting
now; they had dropped to their knees in postures of supplication
to the moon.

"Just a little little little longer now . . ." Hesterluna sang.
Black Star made it out clearly, as though he had finally tuned in
to the right frequency. "Just a little longer now!" Hesterluna
finished, stretching her arms upward as high as she could, lifting
up on her toes, and . . . Did she really leave the ground? Nothing
would shock Black Star at this point. The moon seemed to pick
her up and then let go. She landed in a crouch, her wide skirt
spreading around her like a rippling pool.

"It is good," all the sisters sighed. They stood, and the moon
lowered visibly in the sky, yet not in the setting way—it dropped
directly down a degree and brightened Witches Meadow.
Hesterluna had turned up the lights the way you would adjust a
chandelier. Varluft saluted them. The rest of us waited,
awestruck. Anything was possible. Even the Gypsies bit their
tongues and prepared themselves to do the Witches' bidding.

"Sister, the balm." Hesterluna reached toward Brunagwa,
who produced a tin from a pocket in her sleeve.

"Master Seer, we are taking Esmarelda to the astral plane, the
better to find Robyn. How shall the Gypsy's aura make herself
known to Robyn without others in Ochersfeldt also seeing her?"

"Not to worry. Robyn herself is barely visible in Ochersfeldt.
Two who are out of place will see each other, yet not be seen."

"Ah, Varluft, how we have missed you," the tempestuous

Sestorina piped up, and there was a brief, happy rumble of assent among the Coven.

"Can we start now?" Intuisha asked. She and her twin had already been too long away from their quiet, chill caves.

"Yes, let's begin. Esmarelda, if you would."

The frightened Gypsy was brought into the center of the Witches' circle. They closed in around her and went to work. Esma's outraged protests could be heard in between the sisters' castigations and instructions. Snip kept George at bay. George, holding Sylvestor protectively in his arms, kicked at the badger. In his concern for Esma, he squeezed the cat so tightly it yowled, and then all the rest of the animals joined in.

"Hey! Stop that! Enough!" Esma lent her voice to the choir.

The Witches hissed and leapt back, revealing our poor Gypsy. Esmarelda had been stripped down to just her chemise and a light skirt, and greased up in magic balm. Her modesty was mainly protected by her magnificent long black hair, which had been let out of its braids. It rippled over her shoulders and down her back nearly to her knees.

Sestorina placed a bundle of Esmarelda's possessions and garments on the ground not too far from where the Gypsy would dance, then she called to Sylvestor with a quiet "snick-snick." The orange tabby hopped down from George's arms and happily planted himself in the middle of the soft, spice-scented pile.

Now Intuisha, who had been protecting the cat (and how many others?) all along, came forward and sprinkled some glittery granules over him. As the sparkles landed, my coyote nose ceased to smell the cat. Sylvestor had become invisible to the forest. I supposed this was how Dark had been hidden from us.

Seeing that Sylvestor was safe, Esma and George nodded their approval. They exchanged brave looks, and Esmarelda motioned for George to place his belongings with hers. He did so, taking out his violin so he would be ready when called upon to play. He warmed up with a tune he'd learned across the Spiral, a song

Robyn always sang while she dusted the sparkling treasures displayed in The Lost Unicorn's long glass case.

The sisters passed Brunagwa's tin among themselves and painted their legs with ointment. At a sign from Hesterluna, Esmarelda presented her slippery left ankle to Varluft. He knelt and bowed his head in meditation, then he gently traced a circle around her ankle with a crooked finger. His muttered words were indecipherable, but the spell he conjured gifted Esmarelda with an awareness that had eluded her all the while the bracelet had been coming and going from her life: The anklet's charm had never been broken. Even when it lay on the workbench of the deceased Master Seer Malcom, with the letters of her name seemingly erased, it still had the power to make her reach out and take it at the last. When she had found it among her possessions later, Esma was horrified. An error, she thought, a childish obsession with glittery things that overtook her in the strangeness of that moment. At least it was de-charmed, or so she'd hoped.

"So mote it be." Varluft completed his incantation.

"So mote it be," The sisters repeated.

"So mote it be," Esmarelda breathed, praying that if she cooperated the Witches would free her from Malcom and his wicked magic once and for all.

Varluft went over to Fred and Desy and waved his arms over them. They rose mechanically. Desy took up the concertina and Fred the ney. Before Varluft could give them the magic song for finding things, they began to follow along with the tune George was playing. The Master Seer listened thoughtfully. The five sisters were humming along. The Gypsy was swaying, making lotus blossoms with graceful gestures of her hands.

"It is good," Varluft decreed. "Go on."

Everyone took their places. The Witches and the Gypsy began to turn in circles, slowly walking around in place, then speeding up until they were spinning—pushing off with one foot to propel themselves while bouncing lightly on the other. Faster, faster.

They spread their arms. Their hair whipped wildly around them. One by one the sisters collapsed to the ground. They lay as they fell, like splatters of paint. Their breathing quieted, they seemed to sleep.

Esmarelda was the last to drop. She knew this technique of whirling, and she was fit as a fiddle and happily aware of George's music. The balm with which they'd anointed her legs, arms and scalp tingled erotically. She felt herself being lifted up, almost like being swept up in the swirls of the magic carpets, but more disembodied. Yes, her body was bursting with sensation, and yet not there at all. She was twirling herself up to the moon. Up, up— She fell to the ground with a sigh.

"Welcome, Gypsy." "Welcome." "Welcome." "Welcome." "Welcome."

Five glowing emanations greeted her. Esmarelda stood with them in a place sort of like the meadow, but turned upside down —blue beneath her feet, a greenish-gold mist all around them.

"Oh my."

"Are you ready?"

"I guess. Am I?"

The women's astral selves were less severe, their garments light and filmy like the Gypsy's own. Released from the rigors of gravity and softly translucent, they were now all of similar size, perfectly matched and perfectly in sync. Experiencing them combined in this way, Esma was impressed by their power as she had not been during their actual physical encounters, when the sisters seemed overblown and almost silly. She surrendered herself to their magic scheme.

While the six women appeared to slumber under the paralyzed moon, Ti-Wyan sent the Familiars Nee, Roth, Flame and Yau to watch for Robyn on the perimeter of Ochersfeldt, that they might guard her hike back to Witches Meadow.

"What about me?" Black Star asked, seeing the animals move off toward the south. Coyote's proximity still constrained him from following.

"Go with them, Raven-Man," Ti-Wyan answered. "I can't hold you. Maybe you can be useful." She sent me the message to back off, and we pretended not to notice how Black Star watched Yani-Yau loping down the hill. "Go now." He flew off as Raven.

Wyan turned to Varluft. "Why are the rugs still here? I thought they would go into the fire."

"No, that would not be a good idea. I created a spur of Time, and a spur there shall always be. That is where these rugs belong. The question is, what else got out that belongs there? I will wait to see what becomes of Malcom before I deal with the rugs and secure the spell that was meant to contain him."

"And what will you do in the meantime, Master Seer?"

"I will guard the rugs while I sit right here with the Coven and follow along on their adventures. I may not be on the astral plane with them, but I do hold one end of the invisible thread that I tied to the Gypsy's ankle," the old magician confided with a self-satisfied smile.

Overhearing this, George faltered in his playing. The aurically traveling women stirred.

"That won't help!" "Play, play!" Wyan and Varluft chided him, and Snip burst out of nowhere, fangs bared.

George quickly found his place and bowed his fiddle valiantly.

"He is right to be worried," Wyan whispered to Varluft. "You and the Coven are vulnerable here. And, with all due respect, I don't trust these rugs to stay put. We Minders are spread thin. Snip cannot manage all of this business alone, and I fear I'll not be much help." She was still chastened from being out-flown by Raven.

"Coyote—" I trotted over, having heard every word and virtually every thought. "I think I should go stand watch at the Loophole, while you stay here and guard Witches Meadow. You have more weapons for protecting the Coven and Master Seer Varluft than I. I can call you to the Loophole if needed. "

My smooth shift to the wiry and rugged trail guide, then back to Coyote, then back to Man again inspired confidence and, dare I say, even awe in those assembled—well, those who were conscious. (I confess, I was still surprised and relieved each time I found all variations at my disposal). I bowed gallantly, my gaze on the lusciously sleeping Brunagwa.

"I will guard the meadow and its occupants with my life. "

"Thank you, Minder. "

Wyan took a step toward the fiddler, whose ears has been trained on the conversation, while his eyes were riveted to the limp figure of Esmarelda. With her hair snaking around and over her oiled body, his beloved looked like a castaway mermaid slowly dying on dry land . . .

"Don't be so melodramatic. " The voice was in his head, the words unspoken, like his own thoughts. Then Wyan said aloud, "No one is dying, but you had better play like your life depends on it until it is time for them to wake. "

"My life does depend on it, until Esmarelda wakes, " George answered without missing a beat.

I waited for Wyan to soar into the moonlit night as Ti, and for Varluft to settle himself between the rugs and the sleeping Witches, then I shifted back to Coyote. As soon as I did so, I detected the presence of another watchful one—someone other than Snip the badger, who was back to her subterranean patrol. I trotted lightly in a wide loop around the entranced Coven.

"Is that you, Nee-Reta? Why have you not gone with the others to stake out Robyn?"

"Yani-Yau has gone to those places along the river and the trails to Red Mountain that I normally watch. Roth-Thea is able to cover all of the routes to the Ice Caves as well as Yau's High Caverns, because anyone coming from Ochersfeldt has to pass through the one to get to the other. And Flame-Mari has the herd

to help patrol all the places around the Six Hills. So, I have decided to stay here and provide another pair of eyes for you and Snip. Perhaps we may converse to keep ourselves alert."

I felt her anger, and read all of her worst fears concerning Dark and Malcom: If the magician's ego had entered Dark and then transformed the black dog into a black cat, a jaguar, and who knew what else—then what of the dog? Was he also present within each of those incarnations? Or had he been destroyed? Poor Nee-Reta was in a tumult of confusion and worry.

"Me too." I confided to her in my mind. *"And our trying to work it out will not make us more alert, only distract us from perceiving the unexpected. What brought us to this business, and what will come of it, is not like anything we have seen before. And you and I have seen much, have we not?"*

"You saw what happened to Dark. You knew where he was, up until he escaped the place. You put him there! But you kept that from me. You learned that Black Star and the raven were one, but hid that from me, too. Why should I believe anything that comes from you, Coyote?"

"This train of thought is distracting us from our duties, I tell you. To start, I can see you clearly against the moon. Hide yourself, Minder."

The silhouette of a hawk perched high in a tree beyond the meadow vanished, and so did the thoughts of Nee-Reta.

Yani-Yau loped toward the southeast, paused briefly, then turned west and made a wide loop around the Six Hills. Raven detected faint snippets of her thoughts. She was coordinating her movements with other Familiars. He shadowed her until she dove into the woodlands bordering Red River. Black Star would have to follow here on foot, where the canopy of trees was dense. He did so easily, calling softly to Yani.

The man reached the path across which Brunagwa had built her warning wall. It was suddenly apparent that he was standing on the road to Ochersfeldt. His objective changed. He was going to Ochersfeldt! The shaman set out jauntily down the well-worn trail that glowed brightly under the suspended moon. At last he would enter the magical city where he had dreamed of expanding both his psychic and material enterprises. He began to jog, eager to get there before any of the magic ones could interfere.

"I know what you're thinking!"

The cougar had hurled itself out of the shadows and pinned him in a blink. In the second blink it had morphed into Yani, and now she lay atop him, her lips to his ear. Black Star embraced her. They held each other. It felt good.

"Oh, stop it," Yani chided him when it began to feel too good. "This is not playtime." She got up. "We were told to watch for Robyn, not to go into Ochersfeldt."

"Those other ones were. But, you told me yourself, we're different, *Human by first nature*, no reason for us to fear that town."

"You don't know anything about Ochersfeldt."

"So, help me out. Why are you afraid for me to go? You go there yourself." Black Star was now on his feet and holding Yani's hand. He began to gently lead her down the hill, as though they only ambled the better to think and talk.

"It's not good to venture far from Ochre Bridge. That's like the pin that holds the town in place. The further you go from the center of town, the more convoluted and unstable the Quarters become. I would not want to be lost there."

"The four quadrants—you told me about them. Which one is Robyn likely to end up in?"

"Well, the bracelet was made by a master crafter from Gold Q—that was everyone's guess after they had a good look at it. The shop will be very near the center of town, because the more skilled the artisan, the closer in they get to be."

"They looked at it? How? When?"

"After they slept, in their un-bodies. In that place, the bracelet is back on Esmarelda's leg; Varluft secured it with his spell before she danced. Her spirit self will find Robyn and convey the spell, so that the 'real' bracelet will be attracted back to the 'real' Gypsy's leg—with Robyn in tow."

"And they think Robyn will end up where the bracelet was made?"

"Enough!" Yani shook her hand away from Black Star's. He was pumping her for information so he could invade Ochersfeldt with his manipulative, mercenary ways. True, *he* would be in personal danger, and she did care for him, and would like to stop him from hurting himself. But he was not stoppable, and she could not spare the time to watch over him. There was more at stake than a couple of fools gone missing on one side or the other—the precarious balance of the the Spiral itself was in jeopardy. She had her instructions.

Tawny Yani-Yau, movie star beautiful, stood on the moonlit path and refused to take another step toward the labyrinth of Ochersfeldt. Black Star moved away from her, then turned back, torn. *What a—Being!* How could he defy her? On the other hand, how could he be sure she was his perfect mate and not his bewitching nemesis? Did Raven and Cougar really belong together? Was any of this even real?

"I'm already lost," he said quietly. "Why shouldn't I go to Ochersfeldt? Maybe I'll find myself there."

Yani felt for him but, much as she loved him, she had no guidance to offer. "I thought if I sent you into the Goathorns, you would stay with me. I wasn't sure the flying carpets would bring you with the others, but they did. It was a good sign, I thought. But you will do as you please. I regret bringing you here. You upset Ti-Wyan greatly."

"But I'm the one who brought the carpets back from The Lost Unicorn for you."

Yani hissed, suspecting if not knowing that he was the one who sent the rugs to Robyn in the first place.

"Hey, I would've had to go to The Lost Unicorn anyway to get those folks who were out of place, right? I've done everything you asked. *And*, I saw what happened to Robyn, *and* when I was needed to fly the carpets, I was there, wasn't I?" Yani growled. Black Star tried again. "You have to agree that I have a part to play here. Let's see how we come out when it's all done. I really am sorry that I suspected *you* were the one hunting Robyn." He reached for her hand.

"But now *you* are hunting her."

"To bring her back. I promised Ramon—"

"As if. You want to stay and so does she—not out here in the wilds of the Goathorns, but there in that foolish town. How do you say it, 'to make a buck.' Well, do what you will. I suppose Raven can always fly out of the maze—if one of the peddlers doesn't snare you first."

Yani spun away from him and effortlessly flowed into the graceful cougar. She slid into the woods and was gone as quickly as she'd appeared.

Black Star accepted Yani-Yau's verdict. He was on his own. But she had not tried to stop him. And she had given him vital information. If he could find Robyn, he could help her get rid of the bracelet before the Witches reeled her in. The way to do it was to find a silversmith, one of the best there near Ochre Bridge, who could safely take it apart. Then, in the reasonably orderly vicinity of the bridge, they would explore the wares of the magical four quadrants. When they'd had enough, Black Star would lead them out of town, down and around to the valley that was the no-man's land between Yani's world and Piper Canyon. He had crossed the divide there many times. He was confident he could get them home—well, fairly so.

The immediate problem was, how to find Robyn and protect her? Would he even recognize that magician they'd been so upset about? In what form would this Malcom manifest next? Black Star considered becoming Raven and making a quick survey of the foothills for a black cat, dog, or jaguar, but his feet were carrying him to Ochersfeldt and not inclined to stop. (Such is the nature of all paths to Ochersfeldt.) He jogged on, his excitement building.

EVERYONE ARRIVES IN OCHERSFELDT

Malcom sat pensively on the low wall at the foot of Red Mountain. He had observed the entire scene between Black Star and Yani-Yau, and so shared the important knowledge that Yani had revealed. Still, there were a good many things he was confused about. Being back in the magician's body, while reassuring, was not affording the clarity of mind he had expected. Nor the rush of vigor he used to feel when one of his goals was in reach. He told himself it was weariness, nothing more. He would claim his prize and be re-established as a Master Seer, and the old spunk would return. Look how close he was:

The charmed bracelet was his own creation. He was being drawn to it without effort. The bracelet was still tied to Esmarelda's psyche—if he found Robyn and followed her, she would lead him to the Gypsy. Better still, if he found Robyn and took the bracelet himself, he could rework the spell and let it draw the Gypsy to *him*. Esmarelda would find her old admirer miraculously rejuvenated, for Malcom the Master Seer was now able to present himself at any age as easily as he morphed into animal forms. All that time in the void with the demented old Varluft had not been wasted, as it turned out. It had given him the template on which to base his new, young physical self.

My patience has paid off, Malcom told himself. *The game is on.* Yet he wished he felt more enthusiastic about the game. Maybe he was also under a spell, or the bracelet's charm had soured and was draining the will out of him.

Malcom slid off the wall with the resignation of a man going to a necessary but unrewarding job. He morphed naturally, almost automatically, into the black dog. But the dog did not want to go down to Ochersfeldt. It had a different attraction that perplexed Malcom. The magician willed himself into the form of the jaguar, and felt comforted by the creature's contained aggression. As soon as he was certain Intuisha's Familiar was well away, he stealthily followed the stranger with the black braids and big boots.

When the jaguar reached the place where the woods thinned out, Malcom compressed himself into the form of the housecat Audy. He did not follow Black Star, who had continued down the trail that became the road to Ochre Bridge, but struck off into the outskirts of Blue Quarter. Malcom had known this place well as a young man, and he quickly wound his way around and over the canals to Gold Q. He trusted that instinct and magic would lead him to Robyn. If he could make contact with Robyn *after* the Gypsy's auric visit, when the two women's psychic connection had been secured, the charmed ankle bracelet must inevitably return to Esmarelda. Malcom would reclaim one and then the other, and then all of Ochersfeldt.

In Varluft's spur of pretend Time, Malcom had succeeded the old magician as Master Seer of Ochersfeldt. Now he would do so in reality. If Robyn and Black Star got stuck in his domain, all the better, he figured. He could use them as leverage when the Goathorns Coven tried to interfere. Perfect. Malcom the Master Seer would have the last laugh.

Robyn had a bad feeling about the sign blinking at her from the store window across the street. Its message continued to scroll through like movie credits:

DREAM TURNED INTO A NIGHTMARE?
TRYING TO WAKE UP?
HAVE TO PEE?
ITCHY LEG SYNDROME?
YOU HAVE COME TO THE RIGHT PLACE.
OF COURSE YOU CAN TRUST US!

Robyn bent down and scratched her left leg violently. The charm bracelet had become terribly uncomfortable, but she still couldn't get it off. At least the itch had broken her trance. She crouched there, half hidden by the wide set of steps that led into the big mercantile behind her, and considered going back in to beg for food at one of those good-smelling kiosks.

The reflections on the cobblestones dimmed. Robyn glanced up. With relief she saw that the sign had gone dark. She stood stiffly. Her legs ached from dancing and running. The burning-itching in her left ankle increased. Then, to her dismay, her left leg stepped into the street, and her right leg followed.

Robyn thought she was about to be drawn against her will into that blocky building with the weird sign. It was lit up again, but the message was nonsensical:

HAIR FALLING OUT?

LOST YOUR TURTLE?

PIXIE MAD AT YOU?

A sad-looking man had stopped to study the window. He approached the door, which was quickly opened for him by the proprietor. "Come in, come in!"

"Couldn't help but notice the brilliant signage."

"Works like a charm—you're the proof."

"I'd say."

"And what business might you be in..." The door closed behind them.

Magical marketing—how do you like that? Robyn's terror of the sign subsided, but a new fright was upon her. Her legs had now taken charge of where she was going. She suppressed her panic at the feeling of losing control by reminding herself that she was seriously lost, and her brain was utterly befuddled—she might as well let instinct, or whatever this was, carry her along.

By now she had already crossed the street and was moving swiftly along the narrow lane. She would have liked to take in her surroundings, but she had to face front and assert what will she could to keep from stumbling and knocking into things. One block after another passed by, and every two or three blocks she turned one way or another, crossed the street, and started down another road. It was a lot like running a maze.

A maze in a daze, Robyn giggled to herself, feeling light-headed. And that was the last thought she had for many blocks.

After some time letting her legs lead her while she drifted in and out of awareness, Robyn came to with the sudden realization that she could *die*. Tripping down the street like this, she might as well be lost at sea. She was at the mercy of nature—no, of the supernatural—and had let go the reins of her own fate. She'd had no food for who knew how long, and a force beyond her control was propelling her on and on through increasingly crowded streets in which no one even noticed her. If she was invisible to this world, then who would help her? She had to gain control.

Robyn reached for one of the lamp posts that were rushing by with increasing speed. She jerked to a stop. Immediately, her left ankle started itching, almost burning. She hooked her left arm securely around the pole and slid to a crouch to work on the bracelet with her right hand.

"I'm so sorry, Ramon. What an idiot. Why didn't I listen? Why did the Gypsy leave this thing with me? This is horrible. What was I thinking?" The litany of self-abuse soothed her. At least she had some possession of her thoughts, her language, past and present. With these, she could attempt to make a plan. Now, what had Esmarelda told her about Ochersfeldt—about how *she* had gotten away when the bracelet brought her here?

"She was afraid to go anywhere by magic. She said she went to a place called Sky by mule, and it was really nice. But maybe I can just ask the bracelet to take me, like I asked to come here. Maybe I'm following the Gypsy's path." Robyn wrapped her fingers around the ankle bracelet. She was not aware that she had been speaking out loud; no one passing by paid any notice. "Yes, I'll just follow Esmarelda's path—she eventually did get to

Caliente." Robyn tightened hold of the silver bangles and took a deep breath, imagining the friendly country Esmarelda had described to her.

"Oh, no you don't!"

Robyn jumped. She nearly lost hold of her anchoring lamp post and went sailing down the street again.

"Esmarelda?" The Gypsy wavered in front of her, ghostlike. Robyn sagged, swooning from the shock.

"Robyn, please hold on. Stay with me."

Strains of a familiar song pulled Robyn back to herself.

"Ramon? Ramon, are you here?"

"That's George Drumm playing. Ramon is waiting for you on the other side. Come, we can do this."

The ghost of Esmarelda settled at Robyn's feet and motioned for Robyn to present her foot with the ankle bracelet. The Gypsy's emanation reached over and easily released the clasp. She put the glimmering trinket around her own left ankle and stood. Robyn stood too, noticing that she and the translucent Gypsy were at the same eye level, though the flesh and blood Esmarelda was a good deal shorter.

Or perhaps she never was flesh and blood?

Robyn looked down to see Esmarelda's feet hovering well above the ground. The sound of laughter that seemed to come from just above her head drowned out the distant melody played by George's fiddle. Robyn looked up to find herself ringed by five pairs of translucent bare feet. She started to pass out again.

"Honestly!" Esmarelda scolded the sisters. Their auras floated upward. She extended her arms pityingly to Robyn. "Come, Robyn, let go and go where you are led. Follow the music. All is well now. Your friends are leading you. I will tend to the bracelet. I will send you home." The Gypsy spirit twirled once and began to skip lightly through the streets of Ochersfeldt. Robyn let go of the lamp post and followed, feeling relief at having surrendered the ankle bracelet to its rightful owner.

Sailing back to Witches Meadow in her astral body, Esmarelda shuddered at the unwelcome sensation of the silver bangles bouncing against her ankle. She tried not to think about how Malcom's spell continued to ensnare her, and focused instead on the pull of Varluft's magic thread. The old magician sometimes tried to lead Esmarelda where Robyn would not be able to follow, but for the most part they agreed on the route. The astral Coven sailed above, holding the inexperienced Gypsy's aura close.

"She's not keeping up," Esmarelda warned the sisters, when she noticed how Robyn was slowed by her tired physical form.

"It's alright. She is connected—she will follow the thread that is spooling out as you lead the way. And the music will help guide her to the meadow."

Hooray, Esmarelda thought, *then let's go faster*.

Robyn was running. She looked down and saw that the bracelet was still on her ankle. Her heart sank. Of course the Gypsy had been a vision—hopefully a genuine visitation and not the onset of delirium. Esmarelda's appearance was a sign, at any rate, and all Robyn had to go on. But she couldn't keep up this pace. She called to Esmarelda to please slow down, but the vision was long gone. Still, Robyn's legs did slow, and she found herself mostly in control of them, even though they were still leading the way. No, Esmarelda was leading. *All is well . . . I will send you home*, the Gypsy had promised.

Robyn walked at a more comfortable clip, her long strides carrying her along with elegant efficiency. Her composure returned; now she could observe her surroundings. She had entered a busier place, a town center bigger than the one where she had first landed. She identified the arch of a bridge in the distance, and then suddenly it dominated the scene. She soon arrived at a heavily constructed riverfront mall, over which the bridge loomed just a few blocks away.

Robyn thought she was dreaming again when she gazed across the river and saw a glimmering green cityscape that looked like it was right out of *The Wizard of Oz*. She would not have been a bit surprised to see the silhouettes of winged monkeys flying across that obscenely pregnant moon.

"Don' ye be moonin' o'er Green Q, m'lovely, we've got all ye 'arts desires rights 'ere in Gold."

"Aye, an' in Silver! Les'av'alookydere."

The couple surrounded Robyn like a swarm. She was completely unprepared, having gone unnoticed through miles of streets and past hundreds of people. Now these two, as well as some others, were able to see her. Everyone here looked livelier, more aware. Curious passers-by stopped at discreet distances to watch the blond, yellow-clad goddess fend off the gatherer gnomes who had been commissioned to get the silver anklet.

"Stop it! Get away! It's not for sale!" Robyn did not want to do violence. There was no point calling for help, because people were standing there watching and not helping already. "Shoo!" The man and woman, both very short, were clad in gray hooded capes, beneath which folds of bright colors flashed. They really seemed to be made more of cape than anything else.

Robyn shook them off and employed a variety of balletic moves to scoot free. She plunged into the crowd surrounding a flower stall. The little couple did not follow, but their voices wafted after her.

"Ah me, no' our day, Missus."

"Don' say, Snooky? Why lookydere—'tis a magic puss."

Robyn looked back and saw the couple stooping toward a black cat. *It can't be—*

"Lovely bracelet, that. Might I have a look, er, Esmarelda— may I call you Esmarelda?" The merchant was already bending down and reaching toward her ankle.

"No!" She hurried through the crowd and over to a bakery.

Please, please, where to now? In all the commotion, Robyn had lost her sense of Esmarelda guiding her. The noise of the shops and shoppers drowned out the lifeline of George's fiddle. She needed to steady herself, but there was no safe place. Here, all eyes followed her. Any time she stopped, someone tried to talk with her. And always, out of the corner of her eye, she spied the black cat.

Robyn wished she could stop to hide the charm bracelet under the cuff of her trousers, but everyone's attention was on it already, and to even acknowledge its attraction might be dangerous. The smells of the bakery beckoned, but she dared not risk being trapped inside. She worked her way back over to the riverwalk, where she could not be pushed unwittingly into a dark shop. The crowd had thinned here because of the chill. A wind blew ever more sharply off the river, which seemed to roil angrily in its too-small channel.

That river frightened Robyn, as did the moon that hung over it so brightly that the street lamps were hardly needed. She pulled her flimsy yellow veil more closely around herself and implored her legs to stop moving. They complied, and she sank onto a bench. She heard laughter in the splashing of the churning water. "I know, I'm an idiot," Robyn muttered, leaning down to push the strand of silver bangles under the cuff of her harem pants. The letters glared out at her; she averted her eyes while she tied the drawstring tighter around her ankle.

"Hiding it won't do any good, let me take it off you."

Black Star sat at Robyn's side.

"You again! Get away from me!" Robyn sprang from the bench. Black Star jumped up and grabbed her before she could be propelled down the esplanade by the charmed bracelet, or carried off by the menacing wind.

"I said get away! Let go! Let go!" All of Robyn's fear and fury erupted at this man she knew but didn't know, welcomed as a possible rescuer and hated for his intrusion into her mystic voyage. "Damn you! Get away!" Black Star held her upper arms while she pushed at his barrel chest and made futile attempts to hook her ankle around his to trip him backwards, a move she'd learned in self-defense class. "Damn you, damn you!" She twisted out of his grip and crumpled onto the bench.

Black Star sat down again, near but not touching, and waited for her to stop weeping. He could sense the black cat waiting with him, just below or behind the bench. It had managed to find Robyn and follow her to the center of town, whereas all Black Star could do was find the bridge and stake her out. So far, no harm had come from the cat, and Black Star considered whether it might be Robyn's totem or spirit guide—not an enemy at all.

The imposing shaman sat placidly and observed the rushing river, the glowing green towers rising up beyond the low waterfront warehouses on the far side, and, looking upstream, much excited bustling across Ochre Bridge a few blocks off. He didn't mind the slicing wind, the mischievous torrent, or the abnormal moon. He felt at home here. He wished Yani were with him. He almost forgot about Robyn.

"What the hell are you doing here and what do you want?" Robyn asked.

"I might ask you the same."

"I got here on the flying carpets, like you did—those rugs *you* sent to me. I got stuck here because of the ankle bracelet—"

"Yes, and we have to get rid of it, or it will trap you here."

"No, now it's leading me back. Esmarelda promised."

"Why would you trust her?"

"Why would I trust you?"

"Because we're two peas in a pod, Robyn. We're in the same business. This place fascinates us for the same reasons. We *know* things, and the proof of what we know is— All of *this*. Of course we want to have a look around, and what's the harm? That bracelet is pulling you out of Ochersfeldt because *they* don't want us here. But then what? Listen, I can get that thing off of you, and we can shop a little bit—right here, with the bridge in sight so we don't get lost—and then I'll take you home."

"I don't get it, I just don't get it." She had used up her store of surprise.

"Me either. But here we are. I mean, how cool is this?"

"Cool? It was cool at first. Then it was terrifying. And I don't *know* anything, and *you* don't either—if I've learned anything here, I've learned that. The longer I'm here, the more I wonder what's even real—forget about how to explain it. Besides, what makes you think you can get the bracelet off? And how do you plan to find your way back?"

"You're not the only one who has a friend on this side," Black Star smirked. "I know my way around. And Ochersfeldt— well, you can get anything here. Look."

Robyn stared at the small silver object in Black Star's palm. It consisted of a stubby silver chain, about half the length of the bracelet itself, with a charm on either end: a silver arrow pointed outward in one direction, and a silver hand pointed a tiny index finger toward the other.

Why did such a small and artfully crafted object make Robyn's skin crawl? Her ankle began burning and jerking. She had a very sick feeling, on top of the very empty feeling, in the pit of her stomach. It occurred to her that Black Star might really be from *this* side of the Spiral. She wondered if he might even be that magician Esmarelda had been running from. But if that were so, then what or who was the black cat and the jaguar—and what about that coyote, and the strange Mr. Brooks? Another panic attack swept over our unfortunate Time Winder.

I have to get away.

"I had it made at the silver shop over there," Black Star was saying. "It's a key to unlock the ankle bracelet. That's why the shopkeepers were on to you, though, they were on the look-out. I should've been more discreet."

Robyn slid down the bench and got to her feet while he

bragged. There was still a lot of activity around the shops behind them on the other side of the street, and much traffic on and around the big bridge nearby, but she and Black Star were alone, their little piece of the quay a private island. No, more like a stage—with a bench, potted shrub and street lamp for the set, and the moon as spotlight. Black Star was still delivering his self-satisfied monologue to the chuckling river. Robyn was poised to sprint away—

"Oh!" A black cat darted out from behind the potted plant and attacked Robyn's left leg.

"Hey!" Black Star was on his feet and lunging for it. The cat leapt away, tearing Robyn's pants and scratching her foot in the process. The huge man took hold of Robyn's arm and brandished the magic key with the arrow end between his fingers, and the tiny silver hand—they both gaped—the miniature hand was now waving to Robyn on the end of its chain.

"C'mon, we can ditch that charm bracelet and the cat at the same time," Black Star cajoled. The tiny hand gave the plan a thumbs-up.

"No! Let go!" Robyn struggled and raised her voice, hoping to draw some attention that might embarrass him into backing off. But the form that suddenly loomed up behind him made her fear for him as well as herself.

"Oh, shit! Get away—quick!"

Black Star turned and saw the black jaguar already mid-air and hurtling toward him. He pushed Robyn aside and took flight, squirting skyward before the razor claws could reach him. The jaguar landed on the bench, leapt snarling into the air as it tipped over, and bounded after the raven.

Robyn hesitated before picking up the glinting silver key that had fallen out of Black Star's hand. Its magic terrified her—a silver hand that really worked like a hand, that behaved as though it were aware? Whose side was it on? Before her eyes, the tiny appendage twitched and made the peace sign. Robyn gulped, snatched it from the ground, and ran, letting her legs lead her. Cold air blew against her ankle where her trousers were torn, and she could feel the wetness of blood dribbling down her foot. The silver bangles around her ankle jangled freely.

George Drumm's fiddle played on the wind. Hearing it again, she breathed a sigh of relief. As she ran after the sound, she began to sing along:

"I'd like to be under the sea / In an octopus's garden..."

... In the shade ...

George led Fred and Desy through verse after verse, chorus after chorus, ornamented instrumentals, and jazzy improvisations of the Alternate World classic. As he played, he kept his eyes always on Esmarelda, who lay in the center of the ring of Witches. Her long black tresses seemed to turn into the tentacles of an octopus, and even to float freely in an unseen current.

George blinked hard and looked again—now all of the women had turned into sea creatures, with their limbs, gowns and locks of hair swirling languidly slightly above the ground.

This time he blinked hard twice, and now the air around the Coven had taken on a blue-green tinge, as though they swam in a bubble—as though Witches Meadow had become a giant aquarium. Even the old magician Varluft, sitting cross-legged between Esmarelda and the stack of rolled-up carpets, swayed weightlessly in time to the music.

... We would be warm below the storm / In our little hideaway beneath the waves ...

The lyrics of the song were coming back to George while he played. He smiled, remembering how absurd they had once sounded—a rather naive effort at whimsy from the oh-so-logical Alternate World. But after this night, should it ever end, nothing would be absurd or impossible again.

I might as well be from the Alternate World as from little Sumweir Isle, for all I ever knew of Witches and Gypsies and changelings and such. George hoped fervently that he would survive all this magic and return to his island to tell the tale, with Esma by his side. And so he played on determinedly, though his arms felt like they would fall off. He did not notice the Red Mountain Witch begin to twitch and flinch—something was disturbing her ease.

Brunagwa suddenly sprang to her feet. The fiddler's bow screeched to a stop, and his heart nearly did too.

THE BUBBLE BURSTS

The bubble burst. The moon was sucked back into the sky. The ground actually dampened with dew, and the dwindling fire spluttered out. The Wings were so startled, they threw their instruments into the air and fell into each others' aching arms. The Witches came to with outraged curses and flailing limbs. They were speaking in tongues, all at once. H. Coyote lent his eerie howl to the pandemonium, and a stampede of horses could be heard racing up the hill. Only Varluft held his place.

George found himself cradling Esmarelda in his arms, as she wakened with the gasp of one who has almost drowned. Sylvestor had startled out of his spell and leapt upon him, clinging painfully to his thigh. While chaos raged around them, George reached for their gear and began to urge Esma into her outer clothes and cape, while he stashed his fiddle in its case. When they stood, the old magician snapped to. A bejeweled claw darted out of a floppy sleeve and grasped the Gypsy's left ankle.

"Ouch!" It wasn't only his steely grip that made Esma exclaim, but sharp, slicing pains—like little cuts from fine silver bangles breaking the skin.

"If you run off now, you'll miss your chance to get rid of it," Varluft chided Esmarelda. "Of course, if Robyn is lost because we have broken the link, there may be no hope anyway."

"Then do something!" George reached for his fiddle.

"No, too late for that. Listen—" Varluft clapped twice. The

Witches' language became comprehensible.

"Not to the meadow! *Not* to the *meadow*, you ninnies!" Brunagwa berated us, looking from one to the other to the other until her eyes met mine. Did no one understand but we two?

I let out a howl that did not end until everyone was silent. When I morphed into Brooks, the look of longing mixed with repulsion that crossed Brunagwa's face nearly derailed my sanity and my resolve. But in our crisis was a whiff of something like hope, or so I imagined. Anyway, we had everyone's attention.

"Tell them," I demanded.

"I did not intend to wake, but all at once I realized we were leading Robyn back to the meadow, to us—to me." The last word was whispered, and at last it came clear. Robyn and Brunagwa ought not be allowed to meet.

"But the link to Robyn is broken now," Varluft complained. "And I am done in." He had not been able to conjure his Eagle to bring order to the assembled. He nodded to me. "You get her. You know Ochersfeldt, and you know her."

"But—"

"Coyote can do it. Find her and lead her to the Loophole. The horses can carry the Gypsies there to meet you. The charmed bracelet is still looking for Esmarelda. Let her take it from Robyn and bring it here to us, while you return Robyn to her side."

"The Raven-Man must go back, too."

Our Minder of Minders had perceived the commotion and was on her way, her thoughts flying ahead.

"Ti-Wyan . . ." The now organized and very serious Coven offered their traditional salute to Wyan when the red-tailed hawk alit and settled among them in her female form.

"Enough of that. Get moving, all of you. Raven must also be found and sent back to the other side. He causes trouble wherever he goes. I will go back to watch the Loophole, since Coyote's work here is not done. You all know what to do." Wyan cast her eyes skyward, huffed unhappily, and set out wearily on foot.

"Wait." Sestorina led a horse to the visibly aged woman, and helped her aboard. "Donnie will carry you until there is light in the sky, Mother-Minder," the imposing Witch murmured respectfully. Then she stomped back into the middle of Witches Meadow, where she re-lit the fire by striking the heel of her scuffed boot to one of the encircling stones.

The Gypsies were mounted on two more of the horses. The herd bucked and shook their manes, eager to follow Donnie, but George was holding them back. He wanted Sylvestor to be handed up to him.

"The horses are well trained, but do not expect any of them to carry a cat." Flame-Mari huffed. Sestorina's Familiar tossed her long hair once and became a horse again.

"Sylvestor will stay here to insure your return," Sestorina avowed. "Snick-snick," she told the cat, and he bounded into Varluft's lap and hid himself in the Master Seer's robes.

"Go now," the Six Hills Witch told her Familiar. The herd galloped off with Flame-Mari in the lead. George and Esma's mounts followed as fast as they could without unseating their clumsy riders.

I strode over to Brunagwa, knowing that she would have the strongest link to Robyn. Nee, the Cooper's hawk, was perched on her shoulder. The Familiar was inscrutable, the Witch all too obvious. I could tell how Brunagwa loathed and feared my power to morph—the power she had never mastered.

"Show me where you last saw Robyn."

"It isn't right. It should not be you."

"It will be Coyote."

The Red Mountain Witch turned her face from me. When she turned back she had regained her composure, and H. Coyote sat obediently where the man had stood. Brunagwa tilted her head toward the hawk on her shoulder, and mind to mind Nee relayed the last known location of Robyn, there on the quay in the middle of Ochersfeldt.

I loped swiftly out of the meadow and down to the city, following my secret trails. The moon had set. It was that darkest time before the dawn.

Robyn ran faster, fearful that the cat—the cat that might turn into a jaguar at any moment—would return. Or Black Star would. She was nearly at the bridge when the music stopped, and the link to Esmarelda was severed with such swift finality that she almost toppled over. Instead of tripping along with a purpose, she found herself frozen in place with dread and indecision. Lost and alone. Bleeding, even. Hunted, by who knew what or for what reason, and back to thoughts of impending death. In short (as they say in the Alternate World) she was not in good place.

(Isn't that right, Robyn?)

(Ah, I have been testily reminded that she can't remember, which is why I have to write this.)

Robyn continued determinedly on toward the bridge, which Black Star had implied would point the way out of town. It had appeared to be very close, but now it seemed to scoot further out of reach with every block she passed. Fewer and fewer people noticed her—she was falling back into that "maze in a daze" state. She unwound the veil from her torso to be able to move more freely, and wrapped it around the creepy silver key.

Clutching the crumpled yellow ball of chiffon in one hand, Robyn started to jog. She began to gain on the bridge, but the streets were ever more crowded the nearer to it she got. People pushed by mindlessly, no more aware of each other than they were of her. She made herself keep going despite her aching feet and gnawing stomach.

All at once, Robyn was at the foot of Ochre Bridge. She needed to pass on by it and find the road that exited town. But she was caught up in a veritable river of pedestrians, all going over the bridge. She was being carried across with them.

"Excuse me. Pardon—" They seemed not to hear. "Please let

me pass. Not going that way—" They only pressed in closer and pushed her along faster. She raised her voice and pushed back. "Hey! I do not want to go across!"

Nothing. No reaction. The crowd shoved forward. She could feel the rise of the bridge under foot—they were forcing her over. Robyn's heart was pounding. There were too many people, too close, if she stopped she could be trampled. But she feared she would be lost in Ochersfeldt if she crossed the bridge. Panic rose within her along with a growing certainty that just a few more steps would put her on the other side of an invisible but terrible divide. She must make her stand before her feet, and her luck, tipped decisively in the the wrong direction.

Robyn took a deep breath, brought her elbows in close to her sides, made two fists at chest level, and lurched around in a sharp u-turn to face the wave. She had readied herself to weave through the surging crowd, but the instant she turned, everything came to a crushing halt. Apparently, everyone who had been crossing the bridge in front of her had also changed their minds, and now they all bore down on her from behind, while the throng that had been pushing her across still charged forward. Their progress blocked, the crowds pummeled Robyn from both directions.

Summoning her strength, Robyn tried to maneuver through the mash of bodies. *Step to the side, now turn to the side . . . Suck it in, girl, just squeeze on through . . .*

She stumbled over a tiny elf-like person who was also trying to negotiate the hubbub, causing a chain reaction: The wee one's shoulder caught the knee of a fellow carrying a heavy sack; the lad was knocked off balance; the sack punched Robyn in the gut, and the wind was knocked out of her. She did not fall, could not in the thick of the crowd, but bobbed along limply in the midst of the suffocating confluence.

This is not looking good, kiddo. Am I just going to let myself be crushed?

Blessedly unburdened by complaints of the flesh, Robyn

observed herself being held aloft by the mash of humanity, the loose ends of her filmy yellow veil lifting up eerily above the scene like smoke. She watched the thrashing and jostling, with no one getting anywhere, and more coming all the time from both directions. Shifting her attention to see where these streams of people originated and how they came to be in such a muddle, she was transfixed by the view of the four quadrants laid out with the vivid, colorful precision of a board game.

Seeing all with her second sight as her spirit hovered above the apex of Ochre Bridge, where a metaphorical (or metaphysical) pin holds the infinite town of Ochersfeldt in place, Robyn paused in the becalmed eye of a storm. Her desperation subsided. Now she could rationally assess her situation—

Oh crap. With a jolt, Robyn realized that she was out of body, and, from the looks of the body she was out of, almost out of time. *Think, think!* But the necessary idea did not come from Robyn's clever brain. It just came.

Like magic, Robyn's physical and mental operations resumed their collaboration: "Oh, the Spiral Map of Time—" she gasped, struggling for breath. There was a slight let-up in the pressure of the people pushing in.

"Oh, the Spiral Map of Time / Unfurls from nowhere to forever—" If she could just remember what Agent Yau had sung. The frenzied movement of the crowd was definitely slowing.

"Oh, the Spiral Map of Time / Unfurls from nowhere to forever / D'dada dada dada da from everywhere to never—"

C'mon, you can do better than that! Robyn sensed the magic ebbing away. *There is no spell that goes, D'dada dada dada— Duh!* She began making up her own words.

"Oh, the Spiral Map of Time / Takes us where we want to go—" Everyone around her froze. *That's more like it.* "And sometimes where we shouldn't / But we follow even so—"

Robyn was now able to push through. Still singing, she squirmed around the statue-like bodies.

"Oh, the Spiral Map of Time / Took me to a magic city / If it doesn't take me home again / That will be a pity—"

In this way, Robyn laboriously returned to the foot of the bridge. She kept singing until she was well beyond the street that led back to the quay and the shops where everyone was after her. Her song trailed off when she confronted a complicated intersection with the following signposts:

"To The Fairgrounds"

"To The Top of The World"

"To The Open Road"

"To Ochre Bridge (right behind you—you can't miss it)"

C'mon, Esmarelda, come back and get me out of here.

Beyond the circle of street lamps that illuminated this crossroads, the world had become very dark. The shadows were full of animal sounds. Robyn's confidence faltered. She had found a signpost, now what? She waited there, hoping for a sign.

"Yeeeaaauuuu!" On the outskirts of Ochersfeldt, Yani-Yau intercepted the black jaguar. She had trailed it long enough to see that the animal was addled. Now, confronted by the cougar Yau, it morphed subserviently into the black dog we know as Dark— the original hijacked vessel for the soul of Malcom the Master Seer of Nowhere.

Before Yau could try to address the dog with her mind, Black Star burst out of the woods. At this intrusion, the dog growled and poised to attack. Yani-Yau sent the dog a silent Minder command. When it did not heed her, she quickly took female form and told it, "Stay!" It did. Yani patted the dog's head while she offered the man an exasperated scowl, feeling deeply confused about both these dark creatures.

"Come, Yani-Yau, didn't you catch wind of the upset in the meadow? Robyn's going the wrong way. Let's go get her. This one will lead us. He's found her once already. And *we* know how to get across the Spiral." Black Star was exhilarated from his exploits and eager to be back in Yani's good graces.

"Not us. Others will see to her, and to him. I will see to you."

"How do you plan to stop me, love? Are you able to fly? Have you been holding back a secret avian self?"

Yani smiled and shook her head. He was outrageous. How she loved him.

"You are not the only one who knows how to transact business in Ochersfeldt." The golden woman Yani flowed into the golden cougar Yau. The big cat stretched its jaws wide, contracted its belly, said "ack," and slowly regurgitated a slimy black feather. While Black Star stared at the feather in horror, Yau again gave way to Yani. The lanky woman bent and gingerly picked up the feather. "As I was saying—" Black Star froze.

In his prime, Malcom the Master Seer would have delighted in this performance. But Malcom was not in his prime. He was in a dog. And even though he possessed the ability to be in a cat or a jaguar instead, he did not feel the power of a Master Seer. He did not feel much like a magician at all. He felt . . .

A lot like a dog. He would like something to eat and drink and some comfort. A kind word. The woman Yani offered that, and so, against all reason, he sat like a pup at her feet. But his senses were perked up to another, another who was like this one in some ways but was his true friend. Yes, someone from the distant past, a nymph of the woods, a glorious striped bird in flight. At the same time, there was still that place in Malcom's being to which the enchanted ankle bracelet beckoned, drawing him both toward Robyn who wore it, and toward Esmarelda whose spell it held. Pulled in so many directions at once, he stayed put, hoping for another pat on the head.

Here, Yours Truly came upon the scene. It was not the high drama I expected. In fact, they were all frozen in place. Yani was stuck there because of her unwillingness to leave the magician unattended while she returned Black Star to the Alternate World. She held the man in thrall with the raven feather, but could not bring herself to begin their trek. The dog was also motionless. The sky was turning indigo. I called for Roth-Thea, and soon heard the bear approaching.

It was Roth in the form of the mighty grizzly who swung into the clearing to confront Dark. Yani jumped out of the way, and Black Star jumped in synchrony. So long as she held the feather, he would follow her every move. The bear reared up and bellowed in rage at the whimpering canine.

"Keh-keh-keh-keh-keh-keh!" Nee screeched in the distance. She had overheard the activities of the Familiars, but it was too dark for her to fly. At the sound of her call, the black dog leapt, only to be caught up by the scruff of the neck.

"No, Thea! No, Roth!" Reta cried. "Keh-keh-keh-keh-keh-keh! Dark! Dark!"

Heedless, the bear lumbered back to her cave with the dog swinging limply from her jaws.

In quick succession there was a crash, a cry, and a thud as Nee-Reta fell out of the sky.

"Ah-oooooo!" Coyote called again for help. Daylight was now coming at its usual pace, which meant that time was growing short to get Robyn across the Loophole.

Fweeet! Fweeet! Fweeet! Three sharp whistles alerted us that Sestorina was on her way.

"It's Nee-Reta, Nee-Reta! Watch for her, don't trample her!" Yani sang out to the woods. Then, to me, "Go, Coyote!" She began to walk Black Star quickly toward the east, where she would circle below the Ice Caves and take him back to Piper Canyon via the Morass.

Both of us would have rather gone to Nee-Reta. We could hear her calling weakly in response to Sestorina, and the crunch of boots as the Six Hills Witch picked her way through the woods on foot. The cry Sestorina made when she found Nee-Reta did not bode well. Would the Coven heal her? I forbade myself to think otherwise as I raced toward Ochersfeldt. My full attention must be on the business at hand. I had promised Brunagwa that I would not let Robyn see me on our side as Brooks, but I dared not enter town as Coyote. Fortunately, I had a plan.

Robyn felt like she was trapped in a revolving door. She had been circling the signpost indecisively. She was exhausted, but afraid to stop. For to sleep, or possibly go out-of-body again, would leave her terribly vulnerable. She kept pushing one foot in front of the other, around and around. She was near the point of collapse when she heard it. The song was back. Someone was whistling.

Robyn stumbled away from the crossroads to follow the music. She began to sing, hoping that whoever was there to save her would appear and take her by the hand. But the music moved off; she followed again. Each time she came close, the whistler receded to a more distant place. In this way, Robyn was led away from the bridge and out of Ochersfeldt.

When the town structures had dwindled, and nature appeared before her with the dim sunrise, the whistling ceased. She expected to see her rescuer at any moment. And so she did. It was a coyote. He sat at attention on a grassy slope. She moved toward him, and he led her up the hill a short way. Our tattered dancer could hardly walk by this time. The soles of her thin slippers were worn through. She staggered along in tears.

A horse appeared out of the dawn mist and bowed to her.

"Oh, bless you." She struggled aboard. "I'm an idiot." It was the same horse that had been carrying her out of the meadow with her troupe.

"Hang on, Robyn." Another of the horses came out of the woods carrying the fiery woman who had helped them earlier— No, that one had auburn hair, and this one's long locks were blond, almost white. "Heey-yahh!" the rider called, and both horses set out at a fast clip. Robyn swung her veil around her horse's neck and tied herself into it before she passed out.

There was a moment, only a moment, when no one and nothing existed but Esmarelda and George. Riding side by side at sunrise, they felt as one with all of Nature, akin to the wind. The mysteries that had brought them here, the dangers yet to come, meant nothing. They were the first and last couple on earth, the very inventors of romantic love, and this exuberant unfettered flight across the vast landscape was their eternal existence. For a moment, it felt like a lifetime.

Suddenly, the rust-colored horse that had been leading them reared up with a snort, forcing their own horses to a jolting stop. Flame conveyed something in horse language before racing back toward the meadow, and soon the Gypsy couple was hurtling onward again. But the enchanted memory of Sestorina's true love had been interrupted, and they clung to their horses with the panic of the inexperienced riders they were, their anxiety compounded by the unexplained urgency of Flame-Mari's u-turn.

Now they recognized that they were being carried swiftly back the way they had come from the Alternate World. Up ahead was the boulder where they had hidden to let the returning Time Winders pass. A red-tailed hawk perched on the rock.

The hawk screeched at the horses. They stopped with another sudden jolt that knocked the wind out of George and Esmarelda, and nearly made them fall off.

"No, do not dismount or they will not stay to take you back." The hawk Ti had become the worried Wyan. She sat atop the boulder holding her jacket closed at the throat, cold and tired.

"What's happened?" Esma gasped.

"Nee-Reta has been hurt. Badly. The Coven and Varluft would normally be able to fix her, but look, the sun rises. This night's magic is nearly done. Until the moon comes round again, there is little anyone can do. She will have to hang on. Look, the twins are turning in. Oh dear."

George and Esma maneuvered around to see the view to the

south. At first they thought the very mountains were on the march, but then they made out the silky sheen of one giantess's blond hair, bound around the forehead with a colorful braided cord, and then a second, similar figure. One turned more southward and one more to the north, and they disappeared within the knobby landscape around which the icy dawn mist descended. The Gypsies shivered and encouraged their horses to move closer together while they waited for Robyn to arrive.

"Thank you for taking care of all my stuff," Esma said softly to George. Everything had been thrown on haphazardly, and backwards in some cases, but it was all there. She fidgeted atop the unhappy horse, taking inventory. She was especially glad to locate the hand-shaped pouch slung around one shoulder and hanging heavily between her chemise and blouse—or maybe between the blouse and the vest. She couldn't quite get her hand on it without stripping down, but at least it was there. The magic herbs she carried within its many compartments didn't need the moon or the Witches' astral powers to make them work. She wondered in what form Nee-Reta had been injured. If the Familiar was in her human body, the Gypsy felt certain she would be able to heal her.

"They're coming!"

Two speeding horses pulled up hard, raising a cloud of dust. Coyote bounded along after them. He raced around the boulders and through the Loophole to the other side without stopping.

Sestorina led Robyn's horse over to Esmarelda. Without being told, the Gypsy reached for Robyn's foot.

"Look, she's bleeding, and she's passed out. Do you have water?"

"Get the bracelet off her," Sestorina commanded, but she did pull a canteen from her shoulder and, maneuvering her horse close, pour some liquid down Robyn's gullet. (Imagine if you will a rag-doll Robyn splayed across her horse, sandwiched between Esmarelda on horseback on one side, working on her leg, and Sestorina on her steed on the other, sloshing her with drink—which, Robyn tells me, based on her later laundering difficulties, definitely was not water.)

"I can't get it. Why won't it open?"

"Tsk tsk. That has been the problem right a long," Ti-Wyan grumped from her high perch. "Any ideas, Six Hills Witch?"

"Well, actually— Gypsy, what is that thing?"

"Hullo! Esma, watch out!" George shouted, making the horses start. There was a strange object or possibly animal squirming within Robyn's twisted and knotted yellow veil.

"Silence." Sestorina pointed a finger at George, and his cheeks and lips sucked inward as though he had just eaten a lemon. Then she pointed the same finger at the thing, and it stopped squirming.

"Come, my lovely, let us see you." The Witch pulled a short knife out of her belt, reached over, and slashed apart layers of cheap chiffon to reveal the silver object.

As soon as it was released from the tangle of fabric, the silver arrow shot towards Robyn's foot, the silver hand waving like a fin on the other end of the chain. Everyone cringed, but it did not impale Robyn's already wounded foot, or Esma's hand as she held it. Instead of an anguished cry, there was a light plink as silver met silver.

"Curious." Sestorina set Robyn upright on the horse, and leaned over her to assess the bracelet situation. The arrow had propelled the key to Robyn's ankle and looped its chain around the chain of the bracelet. The tiny silver hand now reached up and began to fiddle with the locked clasp.

Esmarelda stopped taking inventory of her fingers to gawk. She had withdrawn her hand in time, but the speed with which the dart flew at Robyn's foot had given her a scare. Now she wondered if she were in shock and only dreaming this marvel.

George was still all eyes for the Six Hills Witch. Her trousers and billowing peasant blouse enhanced rather than disguised her womanly figure. With her long, sun-bleached hair flowing around her, she reminded him of a mermaid, and in his mind he replayed the scene in the meadow, with the moon almost touching the magic astral fishbowl full of Witches and his own Esmarelda. Then came that eternal dream of riding free in another's life, and now this—Witches' spells and magical change-lings at the very fault line between one side of the Spiral and the other. Having been to the Alternate World and spent some time there, George could smell it faintly on the wind coming through the rocky chasm; he had an unexpected yearning to go through.

"Time is wasting, Gypsy!" (George would swear later that he had seen sparks fly out of the Witch's mouth.)

Esmarelda swallowed the fear she felt rising as she watched the key do its work. She knew it only awaited a sign from her. The bracelet had been made for her, and she must have the trouble of it. She bent toward Robyn, her rescuer from the Alternate World, who had saved her and befriended her when she was in trouble. Robyn, the one soul she had confided in, had not broken her trust. And yet Esma had repaid her with a pretty gift that was really a nasty charm she was trying to ditch.

"I'm sorry about all of this," the Gypsy told the unconscious woman. As soon as she cupped her hands around Robyn's ankle the clasp flew open. She caught the key in one hand and the ankle bracelet that bore her name in the other.

The strand of silver disks quickly slipped between her fingers, slithered along her leg, and wound itself around her ankle. One by one, the bangles caught the light so each letter flashed brightly: E-S-M-A-R-E-L-D-A. And then the wicked thing secured itself with a decisive click.

Esmarelda still held the silver key, it tingled in her hand. But now that the bracelet was on her own ankle, the key was repelled by it rather than attracted. She strained to reach down to her foot with the key, but her muscles could not overcome the magic force that had attached itself to her. Malcom's wretched gift had come back more powerful than before.

"Give that to me." George avoided looking down at Esma's lovely, sparkling ankle. He kept his eyes on the key in her hand, and his emotions steady. He reached over and was able to gently extract the key from Esmarelda's grip. Determined to keep the key safe until the time came to release Esma from the charm, he slipped it into the leather tube that was slung across his shoulder and quickly replaced the cap. He could feel the frightful object slide down to the very bottom within the cylinder of rolled-up papers, and then begin to rustle around angrily. He was concerned for his manuscripts, but he did not dare peek inside lest the key escape. Esma was more important than his songs.

Esmarelda fidgeted, unsettling her horse. The bangles around her ankle jingled seductively. She had an intense urge to jump down and dance.

"Enough. Back to the meadow with you two," Sestorina decreed. With a short whistle, she sent the Gypsies' horses on their way. Then she clucked to the horse that was bearing Robyn, and it followed her own between the boulders and on into Piper Canyon.

Robyn awoke briefly when she hit the ground rather hard at the north end of the smoldering campgrounds of Kestrel Kamp. But she did not come to when a scrappy maintenance man checking the firebreaks found her and called in for help. He did not try to revive her. When he saw the lights of the first-aid jeep bouncing toward his flare, he retreated to the high ground, moving quickly in the opposite direction of Kestrel Lodge . . .

Ti-Wyan continued to guard the slot between the two tallest boulders. I was on my way back to Witches Meadow when I heard her hawkish shriek. I stopped. We spoke in our minds across the divide.

"Is your work in the Alternate World done, H. ?"

"No, but I— Nee-Reta—?"

"Not at all good. But do not pass through now, I beg you. There is little you can do here, and much you must do there. If you do your work well, then your next time through the Loophole will be your last, don't you think?"

"Well—" Really, I hadn't thought. But now that I did, I found I had some regrets about losing my Alternate World privileges.

"Not privileges, duties," Ti corrected, spying on my innermost thoughts. *"Once completed, it will be your reward to let them go."*

"Nee-Reta?" I asked again to take my mind off my own future.

"Not good at all," Ti sighed. *"But all the forces of the Goathorns are focused on sustaining her. You must settle our business with the other side and gather our power back in. Do whatever you can to put a period on this episode, and then roll up the mat and bar the door when you return."*

"Closing the Loophole is not in my power."

"It will be done, one way or another. Your next time through these boulders will be your last."

"You said that already."

"Then mind me well." She turned her thoughts away from me, but I felt her deep concern for Nee-Reta.

I would not disobey Ti-Wyan. She was right that I had much work to do in the Alternate World. However, it was barely dawn there, and everyone was out of it, one way or another, and when they came to it would be Sunday—not the best time for transacting business. If I could not return to Witches Meadow to lend my strength to Nee-Reta, then I would pursue another avenue of investigation.

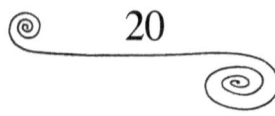

20

Lost and Found

H. COYOTE EASILY MANEUVERED AROUND THE EASTERN RIDGE that overlooks Piper Canyon. I was alert for any sign of Yani-Yau and Black Star below, perhaps even now winding their way back to Kestrel Lodge via the Morass. I entered the web of chambers within the mountain from the Alternate World side and worked my way to Yani's illicit lair. There I caught wind of her recent presence.

Advancing cautiously, I determined that Yani had already ushered Black Star to Piper Canyon and then raced back through to join the others in the meadow. I figured I would have Yani's office to myself for a while, and I commenced my search. This time I was looking for something specific. I believed that the object of my quest would have been confiscated by Yani from Fred and Desy, and most likely hidden here, in her . . .

Desk?

Yes. There it was in the top middle drawer. Not what I had envisioned, but unmistakable. Allow me to explain:

My recent encounters with the conveniently placed, or misplaced, tourist couple suggested the answer to a lingering puzzle. When Yau and I chased the two magicians through the Knot, we overheard the voices of a man and a woman; they spoke of a book. I had recognized those voices by now as belonging to Fred and Desy. Yani-Yau must have traced them to The Lost Unicorn and asked Black Star to bring them back to our side. Really, she would hardly have had to track them—it was a pretty good bet that the intrepid pair would break through in exactly the same place as the scarecrow man and the black dog, and also end up at The Lost Unicorn. (For that matter, it would not be far-fetched to assume that any of us who broke through anywhere would end up at The Lost Unicorn.)

What I sought was Fred and Desy's guidebook to the Alternate World. What I found was none other than that purple-bound wonder, *The Time Dancer*. Desy had even written her name on the first page. I sat in Yani's swivel chair and read it cover to cover. I cannot describe how irritated I was by the time I got to the end. But I felt I could use the book to my advantage in negotiating with Robyn.

Robyn's next memory (or first, depending how you count) was of waking up in a soft bed. Ramon was perched by her side, and she could hear the chattering of her troupe in the next room.

She woke several times after that to gentle ministrations and welcome spoonfuls of soup and such. (Really, Robyn, your friends have been too modest about how they cared for you, especially given their own sorry state. I want you to take everyone out to dinner someplace posh—they do have such establishments in Caliente, do they not?—compliments of Mr. Brooks.)

Sorry, where was I?

Right. Robyn returns: At last Robyn woke and stayed awake. Faye was changing the bandage on her foot.

"Hi there. Are you back for real?"

"What happened?"

"We're not exactly sure. The fire alarm must've sounded during our performance—none of us remember finishing, or dealing with the rugs, or any of that. I sure hope that Agent Yau picked them up, 'cause no one's seen them. Or her. She really couldn't sing—I guess she got to live out some great fantasy or something."

Faye babbled happily. Now that Zeek had joined them, and the performance was over with, she didn't mind staying on. There was a lot to do, and the lodge had discounted their room rates. There were rumors that something toxic had been buried in the mountains, and the fire, or fighting of the fire, had caused release of a bad substance. Basically, everyone who had been in Piper Canyon that night was pretty sick and woozy all night and the next morning.

"Just as well you've been passed out most of the time," Faye was saying. "We've been fighting over the bathrooms, and everyone's just been generally in a bad way."

"You seem chipper enough."

"Well, Zeek's here."

"Oh, right. Black Star brought him."

"Yeah, and was Black Star ever relieved when he heard we'd found *you*. Ramon was totally pissed at him. Maybe because he didn't see him helping put out the fire. Or maybe he's jealous." Faye gave Robyn a meaningful look. Robyn rolled her eyes. "But the cousins had to kiss and make up, because Ramon had to hitch a ride to Denver to meet up with his band. Remember? That was the plan—we would drop him in Denver and then take the van back to Caliente? Only, no one's fit to go yet."

"What day is it?"

"It's Sunday afternoon—well, almost evening."

Robyn tried to remember what had happened. Saturday night the performance . . . a black jaguar . . . She raised her left leg and looked. Circling the leg above the ankle was a series of small moon-shaped cuts, greasy and vivid under Faye's salve.

"I know, weird, huh? From your ankle bells, I guess. But the other leg is alright."

"Hic, ewww, urp . . ."

Faye grabbed a nearby wastebasket, and Robyn sat up and heaved. (No, not a pleasant scene, I agree, but we are using this as a teachable moment.)

(Nope, I still have not gotten over it.)

"Anyway," Faye resumed, after she had matter-of-factly tended to Robyn and her mess. "I heard that Oscar Too left, and someone said he had the Wings with him and was dropping them off in Durango, but I didn't see them. Maybe they're just too sick to be out and about. This sure has turned into a mess for the owners of Kestrel Kamp. They're blaming the fire on the campers, and the Harmony Collective by extension. But the Harmony folks are saying that the site wasn't fit for camping on, and the whole place had been misrepresented—for all five years! But, get this, there's a guy here who's talking about buying up the property *and* paying off everyone's claims. He thinks all the participants are due some reimbursement, and he wants to talk to you. Wouldn't that be awesome? He's been by asking for you a couple times already. Here's his card with his room number. Mr. Brooks. Really nice guy. Horrible cologne, though."

Robyn grabbed the freshly lined wastebasket and puked again.

"Oh, brother. I told Ramon that when you said you were starving, *heuvos rancheros* was probably not what you had in mind. But then you snarfed it up like— You don't even remember, do you?"

Robyn shook her head weakly. Faye frowned, and her chirpy mood subsided. She bustled around Robyn and the bathroom, sprayed some air freshener, and sat down again to look at Robyn's feet.

"Where's Ramon?"

"I told you, he had to get a ride to Denver with Black Star. They left a while ago, remember? You woke up and he brought you lunch, and then he got all his stuff? He said to call him any time—here, your phone's right here."

Faye put the phone near Robyn's hand. Robyn stared at it like she had never seen such a thing.

"You know, we probably should get out of here as soon as we can. Something is definitely in the air. It's like mass amnesia. You wouldn't think it possible, but everyone's been even more spaced out than usual. You want to try to get out of bed?" Faye was considering Robyn's feet. There was a bad scratch on the top of her left foot, and the soles of both feet were tender and raw in places—not burnt, pockmarked—like she'd been running on gravel.

"I guess it was a good thing we were wearing our ballet shoes," Faye continued. "I can't remember why we decided to, unless it had something to do with Agent Yau. Huh. See? I've got it too. Anyway, we'll all need new ones after running around outside in them Saturday night. And yours are completely shot. You were pretty far up the canyon when we found you, almost to where we'd climbed the other day— Oh my gosh, I *am* losing it. I almost forgot the coolest thing—"

Faye jumped up, went back into the bathroom, and returned with an old plastic tub. It had obviously been left outdoors for a long time. Brittle and sun-faded on one side, dark and mildewy on the other, it didn't look like much of a prize to Robyn. Not until Faye put it into her hands did she see that it once had a blue and yellow handle, and that it still bore traces of its vivid pattern: blond mermaids floating on blue-green waves.

"They found you holding it, like maybe you had gone back there looking for it, or saw it exposed from down below and went to get it. Robyn, could it really be the toy pail you lost back when your mom thought she had lost *you?*"

When their eyes met, both women were flooded with vivid recollection of their hike up the trail, and the mist that greeted them at the top with mystic disembodiment and farsightedness. Around the edges of this scene, glimpses of a meadow, a herd of horses, and a mountainous passage teased at their memories. They directed their attention to the mermaid pail, which had been buried on that hilltop for— Decades?

Faye felt her stomach flip and flop. She ran to the bathroom. Robyn picked up Mr. Brooks' card and reached for the phone.

I had returned to Kestrel Lodge to find the Fifth Annual attendees in the process of packing up and leaving—in many cases a departure delayed by the fire and its aftermath. I checked in as A.G. Brooks, using my cover as a Deni-Zen, Inc. executive. I shared my concern for the peace-loving and not very business savvy New Agers with the gentleman at the front desk. I told him I was working on arranging payment of the Lodge's claims, in hopes of preventing any legal action against the Harmony Collective, and I expected that the Collective would withdraw any claims against the Lodge in turn. This news circulated quickly.

Yes, rather to Robyn's surprise, Faye's story checked out. Deni-Zen was even going to pick up the tab for their suite.

Deni-Zen, Inc. certainly does exist. Yani-Yau and Black Star saw to that—very conveniently for me, as it turned out. But then, most problems do come packaged with their own solutions, at least on my side. (Perhaps on your side too, if you would look.)

(Robyn has had enough of my finger-wagging, and says to get on with it. And so I shall. We have come to my Editor's pivotal moment.)

Ah, Robyn. She bounced back to health the minute her relentlessly curious mind perceived a chink in the wall of charms and will that shields one world from the other. The scratch on her foot proved (and continues to prove) problematic with respect to the efficacy of Sestorina's spell. Robyn's blood was spilled on our side, after all, and the venom of a strange being, passing as the housecat Audy, returned to the Alternate World with her.

Robyn called my number. I asked her to meet me in the reading nook on the east side of the lodge. I said I had some business to complete before I could join her, but meanwhile she might want to go there to peruse a certain book. If she took a good look in that case beside the bay window, on the second shelf from the top, she would recognize which one I had in mind.

I did not doubt she would go at once. I actually had nothing going on—nothing but worry for Nee-Reta. I waited in my room for two hours with vain hope of detecting some message from the other side, and I readied myself for the confrontation to come.

Robyn is a fast reader. I entered the makeshift library to find that she had finished *The Time Dancer* with time to spare for her own thoughts and recollections. She looked up at me with a wry smile and asked if we ought to move outside, in case Coyote made another appearance. It took some discipline for her to maintain her bemused manner, but truth was she still hadn't the strength to get terribly agitated.

As for me, it took a heroic effort to suppress the desire to see, in Robyn, Brunagwa. I needed to shut down all desire, now that any desire triggered my obsession with the Red Mountain Witch. It was my greatest trial yet. Robyn looked up at me with the eyes of my beloved, and I hid my feelings within the guise of that strange, powerful but sexually neutralized Alternate World creation: the Executive.

"I assure you that the coyote will not appear today," Mr. A.G. Brooks said confidently. Still, the suit was hot. I sat down in the shadowed alcove catty-corner to Robyn, who lolled in the sunlight-bathed bay window with *The Time Dancer* in her lap.

"Did you write this book?"

"No. I'd like to know who did."

"Do you know if it's all true?"

"I believe it is."

"Even the part about that black cat having the Master Seer Malcom inside it?"

"Troubling but true."

Robyn pursed her lips, wondering which of many questions

to ask next. I gazed at the landscape beyond the window, so as not to think about lips.

"Are you a coyote?"

"Do I look like a coyote?" I hoped I didn't smell like one, though the musky cologne I'd dowsed myself in didn't smell any better.

Robyn supposed she could be dreaming, maybe still knocked out from the misadventures of Saturday night.

"Why are we here?"

I don't think even she knew how she meant that. I used it as an opening to discuss our problems with the Spiral Map of Time.

"You and your friends are here because there has been a leakage between the two sides of the Spiral. Those on your side who are open to such things have been attracted to our magic. You in particular, Robyn, have an affinity for our side. That is why the Gypsy found you. That is why the rugs found you. That is why I have found you. It is my task to repair the rift between the worlds, and I need you to be my helper on this side."

"Am I awake?"

"Yes."

"Are you a coyote?"

"Do I look like a coyote?"

What's wrong, Robyn? Aren't you relieved to finally get back to things you remember? Why would you want me to breeze through this scene with a snappy summary? I cannot tell you how anxious *I* am to finish this treatise, but if we are to maintain this fiction I must devote some space to the details of our second meeting—the face-to-face *aware* dialogue between two beings from opposite sides of the Spiral. It was your own intention, your genius brainstorm at this very juncture, to secure my testimony as to the existence of the parallel universe on the flip side of Time—just as it was my intention to zip up the seam that would have allowed anyone else to cross through to see for themselves.

Knowing what you know now, you think our dialogue here seems foolish, but your Readers (we might at least pretend) are curious. They are asking themselves, "How would I react if I found myself in the presence of Magic? What would I do with absolute proof positive that a parallel universe exists, and that certain people—actual changelings—are able to cross over?" You are their hero, Robyn, brave and true. Look:

Robyn dispensed with the idea that she was dreaming or hallucinating when another lodger—not even someone from the Harmony crowd—came into the room and, seeing us, quickly selected a book and went out again. The aroma of *carne adovada* that wafted in each time the door opened additionally conveyed a sense of physical reality in the way it caused Robyn's recently filled then purged stomach to churn unhappily. She gazed down at the book, then looked up at me defiantly as she dropped it into her tote bag.

I shrugged. I knew that look. I would not be getting the book back. I had figured as much.

"Is it from my side or your side?" Robyn asked.

"Not sure."

"The woman named Robyn in the book is me. I mean, really me. I know *that* part really happened. That's *my* story."

"That's our story. Interesting that all of the names on your side have been changed, but not the names on our side." I was as eager to pursue the mystery of *The Time Dancer* as Robyn (I had even been wondering if she herself was the author) but I had a more important mission. "You are keeping the book, so let's just say it's from your side. It is no longer my concern," (I lied). "I am here to ask you to help me buy up and close up this lodge, so that your people will never again come so near this part of the Spiral."

"Help you buy up the whole lodge?"

"The whole mountain, actually."

"What? Do you think I'm made of money?"

"No. *I* am made of money. You, my sweet, are made of sugar and spice and everything nice." (I confess, and I apologize, I may have leered here.) "And I am certain you have connections with all sorts of business people, people who can help, people who *will* help—if *you* ask. A.G. Brooks is very real here on your side, he is 'on the books' as you say, and flush with cash. But I need an agent to handle, well, everything. Someone who can be trusted."

Robyn looked at me dubiously. "Trusted with what? Maybe you're the one who can't be trusted."

"I fear that will be the case. The original Brooks' identity and origins were quite humble. Anyone looking at that and at my current circumstance might have cause to wonder where I came by my fortune—how I rose in the ranks of Deni-Zen, Inc. Then they'd want to look into Deni-Zen, Inc. itself. I would prefer certain questions not be asked."

"Why?"

"Even by you."

"I won't do it if you won't answer."

"We're wasting time," I growled at her. She was angering me. I'm sure I gave off a whiff of riled coyote.

A tense silence ensued in which I was able to follow Robyn's thoughts, memories, fears and calculations fairly easily. And— the damnedest thing—in her own way, she was able to follow mine. Of course, not very much of what was in my mind was rational or recognizable to Robyn (or in some cases even myself). Still, feelings were shared. Feelings of longing and worry, of the pressure of great responsibility.

"Tell you what," she finally said, taking her totebag into her arms protectively and pushing the purple book under her rolled-up sweatshirt. "You write me another book like this one, and I'll help you."

"But I told you, I didn't write that one."

"That's okay. Just write what happened after this one ended—plus all the stuff that came before, and everything about the Alternate World. I mean, everything that's been going on here at the Harmony Convention—the rugs and the ankle bracelet, and your being here—it's all somehow the result of what happened with the Gypsy and the Master Seer, right?"

Now I was the one feeling disoriented. I supposed what she said was true. It seemed true. But you must remember that everything I have written thus far resulted *from* this conversation and did not *precede* it. Yes, the events (the facts) were as they were (and are as they are), but the understanding—the connections—have only come clear since. When Robyn told me to write a story explaining what had brought us all to this crossroads, my curiosity was suddenly as great as hers. Everything everywhere was in a stew, especially my heart. Why?

"Not right?" she pressed, for I had not responded. My attention was many spiral-turns away.

I stared at Robyn. She was not Brunagwa. I did not belong here. If I ever hoped to be in Brunagwa's good graces again, I had to do my job now and do it well. For that I needed Robyn's help. All she was asking in return was that I tell her what was going on, what had gone on. I wanted to know that too, I really did. And even more, I wanted to know how it was that Robyn and Ramon came to such a happy union here in the Alternate World, while Brunagwa and I had (and have) thus far been denied. (Yes, I am still trying to write my way into Brunagwa's heart. You give me hope, Robyn—you and Ramon.)

Robyn asked me to write a "sequel" to *The Time Dancer*, and I agreed. I had my reasons to take a whack at it, as I have explained. As for the technique, I had been observing it right along, had I not? Reading the novels at Kestrel Lodge, even learning the typing and transmitting technology that allowed me to eavesdrop on the Alternate World, and then gradually begin to participate in it. For better or worse, with the discovery of *The*

Time Dancer I had plunged fully into the world of the written word. Now I would have to attempt a sort of literary mind-meld with Robyn if the Spiral, and Nee-Reta, were to be healed.

(Robyn does not appreciate my portraying her as somehow holding Nee-Reta and Time itself hostage because she *requested* this written testimony. While I concur that she had no idea about Nee-Reta's life hanging in the balance—where would I have begun to explain *that* in our brief encounter?—I dispute the "requested" part. She made a non-negotiable *demand* for this document. I'm not faulting her. We made a deal and we are keeping it, aren't we? No shame in that. Now let's get on with it. Hope makes me grumpy, especially when time is crawling so. Better to forget my personal wishes and focus on facts.)

Robyn and I agreed on our cover stories. Robyn would have to disguise the truth of my identity and motives, while I attempted to encode proof of the Spiral Map of Time in a work of fiction. My objective, after all, was to keep people away from "Piper Canyon," not to draw them here. I wondered at Robyn's willingness for me to fictionalize the information she was so determined to obtain. But she was keen on continuing in the vein of *The Time Dancer*, and, quoting my own words, she said she was certain that those "who are open to such things" would know the truth of it when they read it. Not to mention, she added, the many people who had attended the convention and would recognize the events, the same way she easily recognized herself and her activities as portrayed in *The Time Dancer*.

I refrained from bringing up Sestorina's smoky spell and Robyn's singular exception to it. Her bubble would burst soon enough. I repaired to my room with one of the lodge's loaner laptops and immediately began to write.

Robyn returned to her suite and told her crew that she was facilitating important arrangements between the Harmony Convention organizers, Kestrel Lodge, and Mr. Brooks. Since she is a natural leader, no one doubted her. The Time Winders were strangely complacent about staying over one more night while the business was transacted. But then, everyone at the lodge was still in a dreamy fog from the after-effects of the magical blaze. Even Faye's brief jolt of awareness had dissipated like a dream.

Monday morning came, as Monday mornings (on your side) always do. The lawyer and the insurance adjuster for the lodge showed up, as well as a business partner in the Harmony venture. Robyn managed to reel in some high rollers for my side of the table. We commandeered a meeting room and went to work. As soon as I felt assured of my agents' skills, I returned to my room to field questions by email—you know, playing the part of the rich recluse. Mainly I busied myself continuing to write chapters to send to Robyn as a sign of my good faith. (She was miffed that already no one remembered "anything about anything.")

The wheeler-dealers had a long lunch on Mr. Brooks' tab, nailed down some numbers, transmitted their data to each others' devices, and went their separate ways. Meanwhile, I churned out more chapters for Robyn, sent them through email, and she emailed back her questions and comments. By tacit agreement, there would be no further in-person contact between us.

When there was nothing more for Robyn to do at Kestrel Lodge, The Time Winders loaded into the van and hastened home, Zeek at the wheel. I waited until they were safely away, and then I checked out. Before returning the laptop, I sent one more message to Robyn to assure her that I would resume contact as soon as I could. She had no choice but to trust me. Besides, reception down through Colorado was spotty. She pretended to sleep, and did off and on, while the others conversed quietly.

The troupe's group memory of the weekend was that Saturday night they had not given a very good performance, and then they'd fought a fire, and then they'd all been sick. In the women's minds, Agent Yau had indeed confiscated all the lovely rugs; and in their hearts, some inexpressible delight to do with dancing had faded. Zeek wished Ramon were along to share his pleasure at how things had turned out: The rugs were gone. The troupe was finished. Even if the women did want to keep dancing and working on routines, word around the Harmony crowd was that The Time Winders had blown it—just a bunch of klutzy wannabes.

Robyn says I have made my point, and I should explain how A.G. Brooks came by all his money.

Well, I thought the money part was obvious. I electronically hijacked all of Yani-Yau's and Black Star's misbegotten gains. Remember how I dallied in their office-lair Sunday morning? After I found *The Time Dancer* in Yani's desk, I took a peek at her computer. Turns out Deni-Zen, Inc. had been highly profitable. A quick meeting was held, and all present (*moi*) voted to reward the Vice President (*moi*) with a huge bonus.

I decided to use it to buy a mountain.

Imagine that. You do have magic on your side. You call it money—the stuff with no particular substance and no consistent value. It certainly appears to be controlled by an unnatural force. Money magically makes things happen. It fixes things. You just need enough of it and enough people to believe in it and perform the right rituals. I clicked here and I authorized there, and *voilà*, the mountain was mine.

If only the troubles on my side could be remedied with cash. On my side of the Spiral, as you recall, Nee-Reta had been badly injured right before I left. Other loose ends were also dangling over there like the frayed fringe on a flying carpet. Having set my Alternate World plans in motion, I rushed back through the Loophole wondering if things had unraveled completely.

They had not. There had not been time.

NEE-RETA

I crossed the Spiral to find myself almost exactly where I had left off. Only minutes had elapsed since I had raced into Piper

Canyon, become Brooks, and stationed myself where I could discover Robyn and call for help. It was as if my sojourn in Yani-Yau's office and my twenty-four hours of transacting business from Kestrel Lodge had taken up no time at all. I counted this a good sign. Spell by spell, the leakage between the worlds was healing, so that time was again moving at its own pace on either side. Here, it was still the day-before-yesterday's dawn.

Coyote loped to Witches Meadow and nearly caught up to Esmarelda and George, who were returning on horseback after freeing Robyn of the ankle bracelet. Sestorina had already overtaken them. The scene that took shape up ahead when the dust of her galloping steed settled was alarming: The three elder sisters knelt together near the small fire, Sestorina still breathing hard from her ride. The Familiars Ti-Wyan, Snip-Edie, and Flame-Mari circled around them, periodically morphing into Hawk, Badger or Mare, and then back to Human again.

Fred and Desy reclined against the stack of magic carpets while they slept off their spells. Varluft, with the cat Sylvestor in his lap, was now seated on top of the pile. Someone had produced a floppy hat for the old man, and he repeatedly twisted his head to the side and up to peek around its brim and curse the sun. The carpets, so surprisingly sedate through the whole long night, rustled underneath him.

The atmosphere was unsettled, the mood despondent. The Gypsies' horses pulled up ahead of me. Esmarelda, bravely but stupidly, I thought, dove from her horse. She knew what she was doing, however, and she executed an acrobatic tumble to land on her feet. When she plunged into the Witches' huddle, her cry of dismay made my blood run cold. I morphed instinctively into my first male form, Amos Goathorn, and followed her.

Nee-Reta lay in Brunagwa's lap. There is no better word to describe her condition than "broken." Our little one was recognizably Nee, but oddly contorted, as though someone had taken her apart and snapped the pieces back together in all different directions. She was breathing. She was a bird. She was not bleeding. It could have been worse. But efforts to dribble water and crumbs into her beak had been futile.

The Gypsy knew immediately that there was nothing in her bag of tricks to cure such a condition. Esmarelda stumbled back through the circle of Witches and Familiars, and fell into George's arms. The hard-worked horses were wandering away to graze. Varluft slid off the carpets, gave the Gypsy couple their cat, then hurried back to sit on the now disheveled pile of rugs. It was taking all of his concentration to keep the flapping flying carpets in check.

"Bring the magician already," the old Master Seer demanded querulously. "What is taking so long? We must deal with at least some of this mess. If it must be noon and not the full moon, then so be it. Until I see the Malcom complete, I cannot put away these blasted things."

"Urrrr." At the name Malcom, Nee-Reta uttered a pathetic moan.

Ti was already winging toward the Ice Caves to hurry along the frozen ones. There was none closer to Nee-Reta than she, not even Brunagwa. Ti felt responsible for Nee becoming a Familiar, and in a way responsible for all the Familiars. She vowed—and we Minders heard her—that whether or not Nee-Reta survived, just as she Ti-Wyan had been Brunagwa's first Familiar, so Nee-Reta would be the Red Mountain Witch's last.

"Good news! We are no longer synchronized with the Alternate World." Before despair could sweep us away utterly, I made my announcement. "It is now almost two days hence on the other side. The fabric of Time is mending and our magic is no longer leaking out. Look, I have Amos, H. Toad, Coyote—all of my forms—at the ready. Surely all of you will find your own energies enhanced as well, so that you will have the power to save Nee-Reta." I looked each of the sisters in the eye, and they did not turn away. Brunagwa held my gaze an instant—or a lifetime—longer. For the Familiars' sake, I tried to keep my thoughts as upbeat as my words.

"Well!" Fred woke with a start and addressed us jovially. "We'll be off now, I think. Sorry to have taken the wrong turn and ended up on the wrong side of the Spiral. But all's well that ends well, as they say. You've gotten your intrepid tourists back, and we thank you for it. And we did our part too, didn't we?" He patted the stack of rugs. "Delighted to be of service. Desy, dear, shall we?" He looked around, alert for any signs of a trail that might take them down to Ochersfeldt.

"Shan't go just yet," Varluft corrected from his perch above them. "Fred and Desy— That wouldn't be Wing, would it? Frederick and Destiny Wing? Adoptive parents of one baby Malcom?"

"Urrghhh." Nee-Reta gurgled again. Everyone watched her eagerly for signs of recovery, while the Master Seer's revelation bounced around our brains.

"Ahem," George took advantage of the uncomfortable silence. "What about us? I think our business here is done. Returning the magic satchel and all that. Esma, let's give over the enchanted things and be off." He uncapped his leather tube and dumped the peculiar silver key onto the ground.

Esmarelda pouted, for she had no desire to leave Nee-Reta in this sad state. The silver bracelet tormented her ankle. She was eager to be rid of it. But she did not want to distract the Witches from the more important task at hand. Now all eyes were on her—actually, on the ground at her feet. The key was quickly walking away from her on two tiny fingers, dragging the miniature chain and arrow behind.

"If you would, Snip-Edie," Hesterluna said matter-of-factly.

Scrappy Snip-Edie marched over to the charm, hunkered down, and slid a twig under the center of the short chain, then lifted the key from the ground. Both arrow and hand gyrated angrily from either end of the chain as the Familiar carried them over to the Meadow Watch Witch.

"Behave now." Hesterluna took the object from the twig with her long pinkie fingernail and dropped it into her cleavage.

The Gypsy couple and their cat were not going anywhere yet. They huddled together. Edie stomped over to them, muttering under her breath, and turned back into the badger Snip. The ferocious Familiar assumed an inscrutable pose, watching the distance, and her sudden stillness was even more disconcerting than her frenetic circling and chittering.

When the badger raised herself up to stand on her hind legs and watch the horizon, everyone looked to see who was coming. At first all we could see in the distance was the head of the brown bear, but soon a large black dog appeared. It was running into the meadow ahead of Roth-Thea, frost still dripping from his muzzle, and his coat sleek with moisture.

The sun was casting strong warming rays on us by now. The bedraggled canine reached the meadow, shook violently, then rolled in the grass to dry himself. The bear, who had stopped within the ring of trees, emerged from the wood as Thea. We felt her beneficence for the creature that had tricked her, and we wondered what had changed.

Lanky Yani-Yau came out of the woods next and stood beside Thea, petite by comparison. Then the ground shook, and the inevitable wave of mortal terror at the twins' approach washed over the meadow, but as quickly passed. There are certain times when one's instinct for self-preservation outweighs all intellect, and the nearness of two giants is one of them. Even Sestorina and Hesterluna jumped up and backed away when Dremtessa and Intuisha strode into the clearing.

Brunagwa kept her place in the center of Witches Meadow between the dwindling fire and the unruly stack of flying carpets, atop which Master Seer Varluft sat pensively under his wide hat. I quelled my jitters and stayed nearby, ready to serve the Red Mountain Witch. Wyan came and stood beside me. Something

Snip-Edie had said in her study about Ti-Wyan and me tugged at my heart.

The black dog was still rolling around excitedly under the watchful eyes of the Witches and their Familiars. After one more exuberant shake that ruffled his short coat in waves from head to tail, he trotted over to our unhappy group. I felt his mind, unfocused, friendly. He approached Nee-Reta with curiosity. I did not sense distress. He lay down in front of Brunagwa with his chin on her crossed ankles, and his breath gently lifted the speckled breast feathers of the small, malformed hawk.

When Reta failed to respond, the dog's passivity gave way to whimpering. He nudged the broken bird with his nose. He yelped sharply, and though the rest of us startled, Nee-Reta lay still. Dark got up and circled Brunagwa, who sat stoically with the dying bird in her lap, while the dog growled and bared his teeth in agitation.

"Is that the best you can do?" the Red Mountain Witch spat back at the half-mad dog. Even in her grief, she seethed with a terrible magical force. The dog slunk back to its position at her feet.

We Minders sensed what Dark was about to attempt. Resolve, fear and doubt commingled as he recalled how he had managed to become a cat and later a jaguar. But this— The memory of his exploits in Piper Canyon flashed across our minds: Under attack, he'd shifted into something small so he could hide, but his vulnerability only added to his terror. The return to his full self was time-consuming and arduous, and all the while he was at risk of attack.

"That was in the Alternate World, " we assured him. *"You are safer here, and your magic is stronger—you can do this. "*

How did we know? We didn't. But we would have happily sacrificed this unsettling stranger for our own Nee-Reta. So, we thought, let him try.

The dog, lying at Brunagwa's feet, slowly, painfully,

morphed into a state similar to Nee-Reta's. It was appalling to watch. He held himself in that twisted, half-alive state for what seemed an eternity. Though he gradually came to mimic her physical condition with excruciating success, he could not make his mind touch hers. Nee-Reta only sagged more heavily, her breath became more labored. Would they both die like this? We Minders, in sympathy, began to feel our own life force draining away. I caught Wyan before she collapsed.

"Make him stop," I hissed at Brunagwa.

"You make him," she hissed back through clenched teeth. "He is one of you!"

Her words pierced like a blade in my heart. I wanted to lower Wyan to the ground, lay down beside her, and die.

"Look, he shifts." The alert from Roth-Thea restored our will.

Dark was now putting himself together the way we hoped Nee-Reta would. In form he transitioned into a healthy hawk, a good imitation of Nee. But all he could do was sit unnaturally in the grass, grounded—an apparition only.

Nee-Reta did not respond, but Ti-Wyan did. The elderly woman came to and shrugged off my supporting grip. Wyan shook herself into Ti—but not Ti the red-tailed hawk, Ti as a Cooper's hawk, like Nee. She fluttered onto Brunagwa's shoulder, in Nee's place, and she and the Red Mountain Witch drew strength from each other. Together with Dark, who flowed gratefully back into the body of a black dog, they sent the injured Familiar mental images of her healthy self, the beautiful Cooper's hawk Nee. But still she did not respond.

Now the most remarkable feat of all was performed by the four other Familiars. Snip-Edie, Yani-Yau, Flame-Mari, and Roth-Thea transitioned to their human forms. Then each in turn reconfigured herself as best she could from her own unique female being into Reta—petite, feather-clad, Reta. Even Roth-Thea achieved a fine if oversized approximation. It took my breath away. Four Retas arrayed themselves around Brunagwa and the broken one to ask their friend to come back to them.

The sisters five were humbled to see this. Master Seer Varluft, still astride the pile of unruly magic carpets, was inspired. He tossed aside his floppy hat and appealed to the sun.

"Zia! Star of the blue sky! Single eye of the perceivable soul! Wake us! Warm us! Make us whole!" He fell back limply on the pile of rugs like a puppet that had been briefly animated.

The Familiars, quickly wearied by their effort, flowed back into their animal forms. Ti flew from Brunagwa's shoulder, shifted from the Cooper's to the red-tailed hawk, and landed gracefully as the woman Wyan. I was hard pressed not to join in with all this morphing. I had a strong urge to retract into my original H. Toad self, but I held steady for Brunagwa. The black dog was again sprawled in front of her with his chin on her crossed ankles, panting onto the broken bird in her lap.

The others present—Esmarelda and George Drumm, and the tourists Fred and Desy—had been watching these events in horror, until Varluft's supplication to the sun stirred them. In unison, without plan or collaboration, the four began to sing:

"Oh, the Spiral Map of Time / Unfurls from everywhere to never..."

"And returns upon a mirror path / From nowhere to forever," the Witches joined in.

I do not know why they sang to Nee-Reta. The sun told them to, I guess. I did not sing. I watched the dog Dark, troubled. Now, as he breathed on the crooked hawk, she visibly took strength from him. The sun, the song, our love—something was working. Before our brimming eyes, the little being in Brunagwa's lap melted, morphed, and reshaped itself into a small, perfect, feather-clad woman. She slumbered peacefully in the lap of the Red Mountain Witch, breathing in time with the dog, heedless of our exclamations of relief. Brunagwa's tears of joy splashed onto her brow.

Reta's eyes flew open. The dog bounded away. Sestorina and

Hesterluna came forward to help Brunagwa to her feet, and Brunagwa set a child-sized Reta on hers.

Our restored Familiar had no memory of her accident or our attempts to heal her. Her only thought was of Dark, who had returned to her at last. He stood apart, waiting for her, and she pushed past all of us and rushed toward him, feeling herself in a dream. She approached cautiously, preparing herself to meet the dog for the first time in her human form. How strange that she was no bigger than he.

When our miniature Reta reached out and touched the dog, and actually felt his fur, not just a spark of electricity, her surprise was so great that she flittered into Nee and soared overhead. Dark jumped up and ran below her, and they frolicked all around the meadow in their way, with Nee dipping down to bat the dog's head with her wing, and the dog leaping into the air to bark happily for more.

We watched in wonderment. The emotion that grew in our hearts at the scene shifted from joy for Nee-Reta's restoration to dread at what we would learn about Dark. Why had he been hidden from us for so long? Why had we not seen him until the diabolical Malcom had taken him over? And where was *he*? I wasn't sure I wanted to know the answer. Instinctively I stepped over to Brunagwa and took her hand. She was worried also, and she squeezed my hand.

(Yes, time stopped, definitely, but my Editor has requested no further interruptions of that sort.)

The sun was at its zenith. Nee and Dark ceased their frolic to rejoin our exhausted and confused party. Our dark secrets would be revealed in the light of day.

The sisters three trembled. Behind them, the little fire, no longer needed, sputtered out. Before them, the hawk Nee floated lightly to the ground and took shape as a perfectly intact and full-sized Reta. The Witches offered thanks to the Firsts, and a formal welcome to the restored Familiar.

Reta curtsied slightly, still unaware of her recent grave condition. Then she turned and reached out to the black dog, who had stayed back from the group. He bounded toward us in a blur, and came to a stop at Reta's side wearing a black suit and cape—a man, the magician Malcom. He touched Reta's hand and... Well, we know what happened for *them*—time stopped. But it was not nearly enough time for some of those present, including myself, to gather our wits.

The oddly young Malcom pressed his lips to the fingers of the ever young Reta, then he approached Frederick and Destiny. He touched his cheek lightly to first hers then his. My coyote ears could hear what he said to them, I'm not sure how much the Witches heard.

"Mother, Father, you only got the weakest half of me. You did your best for your adopted son. I did my worst. You cut me loose long ago. I release you now." Destiny wept against her husband's chest. It was a pretty scene, fit for the melodrama at Taverna Red. Sestorina put a stop to it.

"Mari, please show them the way to The Open Road. By no means send them to Ochersfeldt. They have no more business in the Goathorns." To the couple she said, with an edge of threat in her voice, "Perhaps it's time to settle down, dears."

Sestorina's Familiar trotted over and nudged the couple away from the group.

"Mari, not Flame," Sestorina snapped.

The Familiar shook her head imperiously and changed into the tall red-haired woman in leathers. "Oh, all right." She shooed the protesting couple toward the south side of the meadow. They were looking all around and calling for Black Star.

"I'll give him your regards," Yani-Yau said dryly as they passed. "And, no, you may not keep the concertina." She snatched Black Star's instrument away from Desy.

"Wait!" Everyone froze.

"Tell me where you got that book that led you to the Alternate

World," I demanded of the Wings—as if I didn't know the answer already, and how useless it would be.

"Ochersfeldt," they pronounced in unison.

"Where in Ochersfeldt? How many copies were there?"

A low growl issued from Yani-Yau. *"Have you been snooping in my office?"*

"By the Firsts, 'Agent' Yau, I'll have my answers one way or another."

"Come, come." The sisters fumed impatiently at our silent undercurrents.

"Get those two out of here," Brunagwa scolded. She had been spooked by the couple from the start, and had not hidden her distress very well when Varluft identified the Wings. Now she was staring at the restored and rejuvenated Malcom with an emotion that was surely half-dread, and might have been half-hope.

Mari led the Wings away, and I could feel all three of the elder sisters' relief. We turned our attention back to the magician. He watched his adoptive parents leave the meadow without emotion. Then he approached Varluft, who was still grappling with the impatient rugs.

Malcom locked the Master Seer in a determined stare. Neither blinked for some minutes. The rugs quieted. Varluft broke the spell by hopping to the ground and taking the man in his arms.

"Yes, my boy. I see that you are whole now," he declared.

"You saved me. Thank you."

"I thought I was saving us *from* you."

"You did that too."

"I'm an old fool. Will you let me go now? Everything I have is yours, though I doubt you'll want it."

"You've died twice, you can die as many times as you want," Malcom answered cheerily.

"So long as you never go away like that again," Hesterluna warned.

Varluft blew her a kiss, then shot straight up into the air. The great eagle flapped at the rugs, and one by one they launched into the air and flew in a line up through blue sky, through an invisible slot, into Varluft's enchanted spur of Time.

The eagle circled the meadow once to scattered applause before settling, now normal-sized, on a high, bare branch of a lightning-split tree.

Malcom came over to Brunagwa and me. My beloved nearly broke the bones of my hand in her anxiety. The pain made time start up again for me, and I belatedly wondered what we two had to do with all of this. (Yes, Robyn, I am that stupid. Obviously.)

"I am your son."

He looked from Brunagwa to me. The shock was more than I could bear. H. Coyote took over, hackles up and snarling. The Red Mountain Witch was also snarling.

"You see why we couldn't allow it. He's not Human!"

"He's a Minder, and you loved him, and you love him still," Malcom said calmly. "You had a child together, and that child was me. When you told your sisters Hesterluna and Sestorina, they agreed with you that it was a travesty, dangerous. The three of you worked a wicked spell while your twin sisters slumbered. You cast out the animal part of me, and gave the baby Malcom to the tourist couple. My Minder soul was left behind, a force with no form. A shadow. A spark. Dark. Intuisha saved Dark by giving him something to love, Nee." Malcom looked over his shoulder to Reta, who wept tears of compassion. "Nee-Reta saved Dark's soul. When the time came, Dremtessa saved Malcom's body." He turned to the twins. "Thank you, Ladies of Dreams. And thank you, Roth-Thea. I deserved to be eaten."

Thea sighed, "Too bad, you are one of us." But there was a twinkle in her eye.

Dremtessa and Intuisha nodded approvingly, while their three older sisters stared at them in shock.

"You are surprised?" Dremtessa scoffed. "The Master Seer

Malcom knew all about the Goathorns, and he had learned a few things about the Spiral Map of Time from Esmarelda. He sent his body into the Knot for the first time when he put his consciousness into the black cat. He did not know exactly what he was doing. He followed his instincts. In fact, he has resided on the edges of our domain ever since he passed through here as a young man. Malcom came and went while Intuisha and I slept, but some threads of the Knot attached themselves to him, like the filaments of a spider's web. Later on we perceived him, and we have reeled him in, more than once, hoping to one day make him whole. Ah, Thea, would you?"

Her Familiar finished the story, for Dremtessa had not strung together so many spoken words in ages and was exhausted. Whereas the ursine-looking Thea, thanks to Hesterluna's tutelage, spoke as though she had spent time at university.

"Malcom's physical essence came to the twins emptied of that great striving ego he had acquired to make up for the missing piece of his being. The ego inhabited the unfortunate cat Audy, and later chased the illusion of Malcom's young self into the spur of Time—the trap that Varluft had set—and finally in desperation entered Dark, where two aspects of the Minder battled. Varluft held things together until H. and Yau bravely brought them all to the caves. There our good Master Seer Varluft could rest and recover from his long ordeal. And there the ego, spirit, and body of Malcom were finally made one, though it did take two tries. How do you feel, Malcom?"

"I feel—better. As I said, Nee-Reta saved Dark's soul. In the Ice Caves, Dark took substance and was joined to Malcom's mind. Dark's innocent spirit softened the man's bitterness. The old Malcom orchestrated the escape from Dremtessa's cave, but along the way to fulfilling his futile plan, the parts continued to merge, to make peace, to become whole. I have had to forget some of Malcom the Master Seer's magic and his reasons for wanting it. Now I will be a Minder as I was born to be, not a magician. Now I only know one trick—but it is a good one."

The man swirled his cape up into the air, into—nothing. While all eyes were upon it, he transformed into Dark. He was now much bigger than Coyote, feeling the strength of his new embodiment. We chased around the meadow together, father and son, to escape the weeping of the Witches.

Through all of this, the Gypsy Esmarelda and her husband George Drumm fended off the sneaky nips of Snip the badger. Sylvestor clung painfully to George's shoulder. They had no idea if they had been forgotten or were being kept there for a purpose. Nee-Reta was saved. The dog and the coyote romped. Three of five Witches wailed. An eagle watched. A bear snuffed all about. The badger was obnoxious. The once proud Yani-Yau wound around Intuisha's legs like an overgrown lost kitten. It all made for a mess they didn't want any part of.

If they could only be rid of the ankle bracelet, they could go. That's why they had not slipped away already during the sisters' melodrama—the Witches held the key to Malcom the Master Seer's infernal charm. Surely one of them, or even this restored version of Malcom himself, could remove it. If they would only regain their wits—

Esmarelda could not contain herself any longer. She addressed Brunagwa, Hesterluna and Sestorina testily:

"I don't see why you three are so upset. Reta's a hawk, and Wyan's a hawk, and Mari's a horse, and Yani's a cougar. Brooks is a coyote. So that one's a dog. Why is that wrong? I thought it was awful that Malcom the Master Seer had found a way to use a magic satchel to turn himself into a cat, but that was different. He went into the cat, he took it over. Now we know that he was naturally prone to do that—I mean, there was a part of him that was supposed to *be able to be* an animal. Maybe he didn't even need the satchel—or the cat. But the cat survived, and so did Malcom, finally put together the way he should be. I don't see what the issue was in the first place, but I wish you would let

George and me go away from here. I was glad to be rid of the old Malcom, and I don't care to linger here with this one—no offense."

The Witches three stared stonily at the air above the petite Gypsy's head.

"Couldn't someone take the ankle bracelet off me before he changes back?" Esma appealed to Reta, whom she knew would not want the old Malcom's old love interest loitering around.

"She has a point."

"Well, sister?" Hesterluna asked Brunagwa after another uncomfortable silence. "Her business was with you." She drew the silver key from her cleavage and tossed it to her younger sister. Brunagwa snatched the trinket from the air.

(Throughout the ensuing exchange, George would keep his eyes on Brunagwa's fist, and pray that the key to their release would not be a useless mash of metal when the incensed woman finally opened her hand.)

The Red Mountain Witch glared at Esmarelda. "Minders are animals. People are people. It is unnatural for the two to mate. That coyote tricked me and got me with child. Who could know what its powers might be? How could I have raised such a thing?"

"Tell her." Intuisha pushed Yani-Yau out from under foot. "Tell her, Yani."

The golden cougar Yau flowed into beautiful Yani. The way everyone suddenly surrounded her caught the attention of Coyote and Dark. As Amos G. and Malcom we rejoined the cluster of unhappy Humans to hear what Yani had to say.

"Minders are special beings. Special members of their species who have the ability to change into other species. We all start as something. A hawk, a frog, a cat, a dog—a man, a woman. In and around the Goathorns all of this is possible. And so some of us have Human parents and were born Human ourselves. Life is hard for us but we have learned to make our way."

"So we have seen," I declared. "Intuisha, did you know about her business with Black Star? Hey, where's Intuisha?" The twins were already retreating to their caves.

"Don't worry, we're listening," they assured us from their minds.

"Too hot for them," Roth-Thea explained. "They were positively melting."

Yani-Yau ignored my accusations and continued her story.

"When I was just new in the Goathorns, I observed those three and their magic without really understanding, until it was too late. I had been watching all of you. Ti-Wyan, well, I didn't think she would approve of me. I went to Intuisha. She had no Familiar. I told her what I'd seen. And I told her the way it was with me. Maybe Brunagwa's child was—could have been—as whole and natural as me. The twins took things from there, they have helped Dark whenever they could."

"How did you manage not to give Dark away all this time?" I butted in again. I knew the twins had plenty of powers to shield the creature, and that Roth-Thea had the discipline to keep a secret. But how had the curious Yani-Yau managed to keep her thoughts away from this dreadful deed?

"To tell you the truth, I forgot all about him."

Intuisha chuckled in the distance, thus confirming my suspicions about her involvement. Ti-Wyan and I took small comfort that we Minders had not deceived each other—Ti had also been unaware of Dark for all this time. We were dismayed to learn that the twin Witches had put one over on us. But Yani-Yau, simple child, didn't care that her knowledge of the origins and continued existence of Dark had been blocked. Her memories were suddenly back, and they helped her understand her own behavior.

"I knew the twins could help Brunagwa's child because they have a way with lost things. But, later on, that was why I was afraid to ask their advice about Black Star. If he did not belong here, they would expel him."

"So you joined him in the Alternate World," Roth-Thea chided. "Where do you suppose he came from?" She wrinkled her nose as though she could still detect the intruder's lingering odor.

"We think he was born on the other side, or perhaps in between. But he never had proper instruction, and he serves no one. Not even me," Yani said sadly. "Black Star will only come back here if he is allowed to come and go freely. He has a life on the other side. He would be missed."

Ti-Wyan looked toward Hesterluna, Brunagwa and Sestorina. The three elder sisters of the Coven clung to each other like bad little girls. They were too upset about Malcom-Dark to deal with Black Star.

"You decide," the Familiars told Ti-Wyan in their minds. *"If he is one of us, it is for you to decide."*

"So be it," Wyan answered aloud. "Tell Black Star that if he has a way to cross over that does not damage the Spiral, he may come to us for the friendship of his own kind. But you, Yani-Yau, must not cross. The rift in your den will be repaired. The twins are seeing what can be done about it."

Yani-Yau growled at that. "How am I supposed to relay the message to Black Star?"

"He will have to return to you to get it."

"If he can," Yani sighed. "He travels easily through the Knot and the Morass. But it was only the flying carpets that allowed him to cross over all the way. I thought I could keep him here, but of course it is not up to me."

There was a long pause in the meadow while everyone watched the sky, as if the raven might suddenly appear, alight as Black Star, and answer all our questions. Brooks gave way to Coyote the better to perceive Raven, but the blue sky remained a blank even to we Minders.

Malcom approached the Gypsies.

THE TWO MAGICIANS

"One shouldn't regret the painful past that brought us to a pleasing present," the smart young fellow said.

"I suppose not," Esma conceded. "You are not anything like the man I knew, anyway, so the pain he caused is not yours to apologize for. But I wish you would take back this thing." She shook her ankle, and the liveliness of the bracelet almost caused her to spin. George took her hand.

"As I said, I am no longer a magician. I do not remember how to cancel the spell."

That was the last straw. Esmarelda began to shake. Her feet wanted to break out into dance, her fists wanted to pummel something, and her head wanted to explode. George squeezed her hand hard.

"M'lady?" Esmarelda directed this to Brunagwa, but kept her eyes lowered.

"What say you, friends?" George, looking pointedly at the white-knuckled fist that held the key to their freedom, appealed to the group at large. "Time for us to hit the road, wouldn't you say? Me-self and Esma, that is. We have business with the Gypsies yet."

"I think we should let these two go," Nee-Reta chimed in. She went to Brunagwa and said, "I did sort of promise that if they helped with the rugs, the Coven wouldn't get involved with—you know what."

Brunagwa was angry and looking for someone to take it out on. Hesterluna and Sestorina would have been the obvious targets, since they'd encouraged and abetted her in her folly. If it was folly. Yes, cruel. But she was not won over to me or to Malcom. Something bothered her very much. And her sisters looked miserable. She actually spoke to them kindly.

"Peace, sisters. You have done well. We've taken care of the satchel and the rugs, and our dear Varluft is back. I don't hold the past against you. I am the one at fault. I am the one who is punished." She waved them back, then folded her arms and glared at H. Coyote. I had moved off to a respectful distance and was sitting at attention. I admit that my coat was more neat and glossy than usual. I wanted to impress. The pain in her eyes made me tremble.

"So, anyway—" The Gypsies worried that if this went on much longer they would be forced to spend another night in the Goathorns, with Esmarelda encumbered by the infernal ankle bracelet. What would happen when she could no longer resist the urge to dance? Where would she go? How would George find her? They clung to each other, fearful that the object still had the power to tear Esma away.

"Please let them go," Reta pleaded.

"Don't you see?" Brunagwa snapped. "Don't you see? You two," indicating Esma and George, "are people, two people. You travel, you dance, you sing. You know a little magic. You are always yourselves and united." Suddenly, as if she'd read their thoughts and taken pity on them, she hurled the silver key onto the ground near Esmarelda's left foot. This time it darted toward the ankle bracelet and wound itself around. Esma and George stood frozen in place, waiting for their moment to flee. The Red Mountain Witch raged on.

"You two," now she cast an agonized look at Reta and Malcom, who stood with their arms around each other. "You each have two forms—your human form and your animal form. As Minders your minds may join as one, as Humans you belong to each other body and soul. All that was denied you is given back today twofold. But me—and him?"

I cowered. Had she no heart to comfort me?

"I am only this. But he is—what? More? Because he is Minder? Or less, because he is half the time not Human? Either way, it is not a match for me. That is not a partner I can ever know or trust."

I howled in agony to hear her pain, her yearning for what seemed impossible. Yau and Roth joined in with their roars.

Even Snip added a chittering lament. Brunagwa fell to the ground and wept. Sestorina and Hesterluna followed suit.

Master Seer Varluft wished everyone would quiet down so he could think. While the Witches fumed over the ancient escapades of H. Coyote, there were more serious matters to consider. The soul-stunted Master Seer Malcom had probably left all kinds of bothersome magic dangling, like that foolish ankle bracelet. So, there would be all of that to deal with, plus the problem of George being out of place in Time, and no way to return him without separating him from Esma or putting *her* out of sync.

I wonder... Varluft covered his ears with his hands and pondered. *Yes, that would be a good trick.*

There was no time for the old magician to develop his germ of an idea into a proper plan. All he could do right then was to (hmm, how to describe this, let's say) insert a bookmark.

Amid the frenzy of the Witches' sorrow, Esma leaned against George, her left leg outstretched, and they both stared down at her ankle. The silver hand on the silver keychain had begun to work the clasp of the bracelet. The nine silver disks bearing the letters of Esmarelda's name jangled angrily. Then the arrow end of the key began to sway gently. The charms calmed and matched its tempo. The hand began to conduct them. When they were all swinging back and forth in unison, the clasp opened. The bracelet, with the key still looped around it, hit the ground.

They were free! George lifted Esma in a bear hug while she kicked her liberated legs ecstatically. Sylvestor, who had been hiding in the Gypsies' gear, pounced on the squirming chains and bangles.

"Quick, take your things." Reta and Malcom were there, pushing packs and fiddle case into the Gypsies' arms, and hustling them toward the northerly trail through the woods. "By the Firsts, the cat!"

Sylvestor was tossed after the couple not a moment too soon. As they turned back to grab him, they saw the huge eagle dive at the objects the cat had just been playing with. The Gypsies shrank back, then turned and ran before some other magical event could trap them in the domain of the Witches.

Reta spoke into Malcom's ear. He transformed into Dark, and she into Nee. The black dog and the Cooper's hawk overtook the Gypsy couple with cat and led them up to the High Road.

The eagle's cry was barely audible above the ear-splitting chord of the three sisters' keening, which went on and on. The magical objects were cast into the ring of stones in the center of Witches Meadow, where a fire had recently burned. Here the charms began to melt. As the bangles dissolved, the nine fancy letters remained, floating atop a small pool of silver. The chains and arrow melted next. The hand was the last charm to go. It thrust out of the silver puddle and snapped its tiny fingers before becoming one with the shimmering blob. Then nine inky letters rose up, slid away from the carnage, and slipped single file through the blades of meadow grass to follow the trail of Esmarelda, spelling her name as they went.

Varluft rejoined those in the meadow, too depleted to brag about his latest feat of magic or, for that matter, even to get the attention of the still-raving Witches. He understood that the emotion was being wrung out of them, and they were winding up the episode, but he was darn tired and wished they would shut up.

Before too long, his wish was fulfilled, because a shaking and quaking alerted all that the twins were returning. The three older sisters hushed up and jumped to their feet, sensing that a new trouble was upon them. Varluft retrieved his floppy hat and scurried out of the way. We Minders, having been incapacitated by the sisters' shrill cacophony, tried to gather our wits.

Intuisha and Dremtessa trounced back into the meadow, panting and red-faced, literally growing and shrinking with every inhale and exhale. They had been all over and around the cliffs, but could not find a way into Yani's secret office without taking off the top of the mountain. They looked steaming mad enough

to do it, too. No one had seen them so nonplused since they were
girls, and the frightening prospect of the twins throwing a
monumentally destructive adult tantrum tumbled through our
already tumultuous thoughts.

With great effort, I pulled myself together. The Loophole and
the Knot, and now the Morass, were mine to Mind. I realized that
until my bargain with Robyn was fulfilled, I could not allow the
twins to destroy the office between the worlds. We were lucky
they hadn't done so already.

I hurtled my intention into the minds of Ti-Wyan, Snip-Edie,
Yani-Yau, and Roth-Thea. They heeded me and added their wills
to mine. I was surprised at how powerful I felt in the face of
Brunagwa's scorn and others' betrayals. The knowledge of Dark,
my son, my legacy, made me strong. That, and the role I had
assumed in the Alternate World. Mr. A.G. Brooks, if only
briefly, had come into his own. I was a high-roller and a mover
and shaker as well as a Minder. I was a Man.

One by one, the sisters quieted and noticed someone new
amongst them. That was not earthy Amos Goathorn in the place
of H. Coyote, but Mr. A.G. Brooks in full executive regalia—

(By the First Minder's pawprints, she has been asking this
question since Chapter 1: *How do the Minders "do" clothes?*
Here I'm reaching the culmination of an entire compendium of
magical lore, and my Editor cannot get off this ridiculous subject.
That's an Alternate Worlder, for you. Not a peep as to how a
horned lizard no bigger than a potato had sufficient substance to
become a coyote and then a man, but she is obsessed with the
properties of the Familiars' garments and now my business suit.
Didn't we agree that it was magic, pure and simple, every bit of
it? I didn't promise to tell you how it *works*, only that it *is*.)

Actually, the suit worked like a charm. They all gathered
round and lent me their ears. I explained the arrangements I was
making on the other side to prevent further trespass across the
Spiral, and I described the deal I had made with Robyn. That was

not met with enthusiasm, but everyone deferred to my authority over the borderlands. I laid out exactly what must happen next: "I will go to Yani-Yau's office to finish my work with Robyn. Yani-Yau and Snip-Edie can claim their personal things and all that belongs on this side, and then everything else will go over the ledge into the Morass. I will see to it. How do you plan to clean up that mess, Varluft?"

"It shall be done, it shall be done." The old Master Seer stroked his beard thoughtfully.

"You will have help," Hesterluna promised. To me, she said, "Go, see to your work."

But I had one more message for the Witches. A strong appeal from Snip-Edie had come into my mind, and again I remembered her words from our time together in her hideaway.

"Take note, sisters. It has come to my attention that your Familiars do not consider themselves to be free. This is surely the reason for their transgressions. We will remove their Alternate World contraband, but what will you do to make things right for them here? It was never intended that Minders would be your unwilling servants."

Without waiting for a reply, I motioned to Yani-Yau and Snip-Edie, and we began to march stoically out of the meadow—a wiry, well-groomed man in a gray suit; a towering, tawny-haired rock star in fur vest and boots over a tight, tan jumpsuit; and a small, sleek woman in a plain black dress, black boots and black gloves. Our haughty comportment belied our roiling emotions.

I wondered if anyone besides me and Yani-Yau had ever seen this version of Snip-Edie. In the sunlight, I noticed the bright silver streak that shot through her black hair and striped the shiny ponytail spilling down her back. A bright knowing streaked into my mind. Thea received it too. She was following behind us, staying in her human form so long as we did in a show of solidarity. Her sympathetic thoughts reached out for us, and her kind manner was a comfort to three forlorn souls.

Out of range of Brunagwa's glare, I took to four paws for the climb ahead. The others morphed too. Badger, Cougar, Coyote, and Bear sprang toward the cliffs.

The shadows were already lengthening within the bowl of the Goathorns when Esmarelda and George Drumm reached the ridge, but the Wide Wilde beyond was still aglow in the slanting sun. Somewhere along the way, Nee and Dark had slipped back into the woods.

"Listen." Esma quieted her breath. George followed suit.

"Yes, I hear it." Wafting across the Wide Wilde came the faint jingle of bells dancing merrily as Gypsy wagons bumped along in search of a place to camp.

Esma and George sighed with relief and hugged each other. Sylvestor sprang from his perch on George's backpack and led them forward to a split in the ridge where the road divided. One branch rose steeply to Red Mountain, the other took a hairpin turn and descended into the plains. The Gypsies hastened down the latter in the last rays of the setting sun, leaving the realm of the Witches behind.

And so we have seen our intrepid travelers all the way into and all the way out of the Goathorns. Naturally, Robyn wants to know more about the letters of the charm bracelet that were sent after Esmarelda by Varluft. I have nothing to offer on that score. All of those characters have left the building, as you like to say. The Gypsy and her crew are off my radar. Besides which, we are about to run out of time in a whoosh, like the last bit of sand in the hourglass. I had better wrap up.

In the span of my one long, long evening in the dreamy depths of the twins' domain overhanging the muddling Morass, days, perhaps weeks, have passed in the Alternate World. It feels quite distant to me already. While I have sat here at Yani-Yau's desk writing and exchanging emails, Robyn has seen to a number of tasks on my behalf. I'm surprised she found time to do all of that and still read the installments of this epic with such a critical eye. The work stands as a monument to her inquisitiveness.

Nee-Reta and Ti-Wyan, the present and previous Familiars of Brunagwa, have remained in Witches Meadow to monitor the Coven's doings. It is no accident that these two are beloved and obeyed by all the Familiars and Minders, and the Witches as well, for they have the disarming power to show you to yourself, to reveal the truths you wear on your sleeve. (Hawk is the messenger of the obvious, as Robyn and her customers know from all those animal totem products they so enjoy.)

(Yes, and Coyote is the trickster. *Touché.*)

Roth-Thea guards the entrance to this place; she is too big to come through but able to reach us with her mind. She has been our link to the Coven. Flame-Mari and the herd have had to watch over all of the other doings around the Goathorns whilst I dwell here uneasily with Yani-Yau and Snip-Edie. Those two have been putting up a stink. All the time I have been writing, they have been dragging their stuff back and forth and bickering.

Soon, with dread and desire, we wayward Minders will return to the meadow to negotiate our fates. What our lives in the Goathorns will be like henceforth is unclear. Writing this chronicle has forced me to contemplate my own options. I confess that after being so eager to finish the chore, I find myself reluctant to set it aside.

Wish us luck, Robyn. My friends tell me it is time to put a period on the Past and pull the plug. This desk and chair, the cables and equipment, are about to go into the ravine along with the planks and spindles of Snip-Edie's modular furniture. Here my narrative meets the Present, and this computer is going over the cliff.

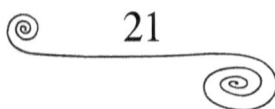

21

The Moral of the Story

IS THERE A MORAL TO THIS STORY? THERE WEREN'T REALLY ANY bad guys—not even the Redferns, who were only creatures of their Time and Place like the rest of us. Yani-Yau, Black Star, Snip-Edie, Malcom the Master Seer—they all behaved badly, self-centeredly. This is often the case with outsiders. Sure, add me to the list. We always have to prove ourselves, or make up for something we feel we've missed. I am a Horny Toad and a Horny Coyote at heart—have been known to do things purely for pleasure, which is the Witches' weakness as well.

There were a lot of heroes, but I can't say any are without blemish, behavior-wise. The twins act benevolent but, whatever their motives, they are highly manipulative. As for the other three—ditto, except without pretending niceness. But we are none of us villains, not among ourselves.

Now, in the Alternate World, A.G. Brooks is the bad guy. He's the one who acted like a hero when he swooped in to keep the Harmony Collective from being sued. But then he bought up Kestrel Lodge and everything around it, and now the whole operation will have to move somewhere else. Not only that, the regular tourist business in that area is finished. Mean old Brooks is claiming dibs on a whole mountainside, and he doesn't plan to share it with anyone. Rich jerk. (Right, Robyn?)

What I'm getting at, trying to get at, is that all the troubles of the world come from feeling divided or incomplete. Varluft had that part right—Malcom, in his pain and frustration, was very dangerous. But we can't always have everything. We can't always be everything. Not even we Minders. Sometimes we have to be satisfied with knowing what the potential is without striving to be, to have, to command all.

If the greatest pain and danger in the world comes from incomplete knowing/being/having, then what is the greatest good? Perhaps to know without having to display. To tread lightly, I'm saying.

Like with Piper Canyon. Your job, Robyn, is to let your friends know that they can cherish the idea of our magical universe without treading into it. Brooks doesn't care about being the bad guy, but the inharmonious demise of the Harmony Conventions would be unfortunate. When the last of the summer reservations have been honored, Kestrel Kamp will close its doors, but the Convention can move elsewhere. The Harmony folks were drawn here for a reason, and for this same reason they should move on. If you could convey to them that they are helping repair something that was ruptured, then all of you could also have a happy ending.

Also? she asks.

I know. Brunagwa was not happy at the end of the last chapter and neither was I. That's exactly my point. If you *don't have* but *want*, that is a problem. But if you *could have* but *don't need*—if you surrender, release, concede—for love, that is a joy.

Brunagwa gave up Nee-Reta, her Familiar, so Reta-Nee would be free to be with Malcom-Dark. To keep Brunagwa's love, I agreed to give up H. Toad, H. Coyote and all other H.s but one. Yes, A.G. Brooks has moved to Red Mountain, and Time has stopped for good. I am now and forever forward Brunagwa's H.usband, and she no longer needs a Minder.

. . .

(I know, Robyn, we agreed. But I thought you might need a moment to contemplate that delicious news.)

Varluft put the rugs back into the spur of Time and stitched up the spell so they won't get out again. He gave up being the Master Seer of Ochersfeldt (again) and moved in with Hesterluna, on condition that snotty Snip the badger would be released from duty.

Having been granted the freedom for which she longed, Snip-Edie then gave up being a pest. She reverted to the form she always preferred but Hesterluna didn't allow her—a skunk. You see, Malcom was not the only one who had been divided from himself. What had happened was this:

Hesterluna, our Meadow Watch Witch, simply never bothered to learn the subtle ways of all the wild things around her. She did not know the ways of the skunk when she adopted Snip. The former professor was attracted to Skunk's sleek look, it went well with her satiny university robes. And a skunk Minder was a rare thing. Having Snip-Edie as her Familiar would be another achievement for Hesterluna, who likes achieving. But the skunk would not do the things that Hesterluna needed done in Witches Meadow. Snip had created Badger for tasks that required aggressiveness. Hesterluna began to call on Badger almost exclusively, and Snip changed her female image to that of the punky Edie in retaliation. Nonetheless, Snip-Edie is another soul who benefited from Hesterluna's tutoring, and she enjoys her liberation all the more for it. A content recluse now, she is far more helpful when you need her than that unhappy badger.

Sestorina and Flame-Mari, Dremtessa and Roth-Thea, Intuisha and Yani-Yau—all went back to their usual routines, though Yani-Yau is encouraged to be Yani more and Yau less, and provided with entertaining tasks and trips into Ochersfeldt on behalf of Hesterluna and Varluft.

Ti-Wyan resumed her retirement, but we know she keeps an eye on us. It was her idea for Nee and Dark to mind the borderlands, since I would be living on Red Mountain, and lacking the necessary power to morph. It turns out that the hawk and the dog can cross into the Alternate World with ease, but in human form—as Reta and Malcom—they must stay here. They have a little camp not far from where the Redferns originally kept their summer ranch. They are helping Varluft clean up the Morass by resettling the lands on our side, while keeping tabs on the Knot and the Loophole.

(We will wait for the Alternate Worlders to clear out of Piper Canyon before initiating the landslide needed to close the Loophole, if indeed it can be closed.)

Black Star was not forgotten. He had to dissolve Deni-Zen, Inc. after that shady Mr. Brooks drained away all the profits. The parties parted ways without recourse to lawsuits. Soon after, Black Star was offered a position with a new nonprofit corporation, Piper Canyon Trust, established to maintain Coyote Mountain as a protected wilderness area. Outwardly his life hasn't changed so much. He has become an even more successful businessman and sometimes shaman.

The Harmony Convention experience did not lead to closer ties between Black Star and his cousin Ramon and cousin-in-law Robyn. Far from it. When Ramon got back to Caliente with his band, he swore to Robyn that he would never ride with Black Star again after their harrowing "road rage road race" from Piper Canyon to Denver. We may recall that at that point Black Star was regrouping from his adventure across the Spiral—one that began in high spirits, but ended with a humiliating betrayal by the woman he loved.

Robyn has her own reasons for not wanting to see Black Star again any time soon—not until this book is published, at any rate, she figures.

(I can tell you now, Robyn, he is not going to acknowledge any part of what happened during the Fifth Annual, no matter what you have in print. The names have been changed, and he will deny everything. Secrecy has always been the prerequisite to his endeavors. Anyway, what makes you think our book will be news to Black Star? Haven't you wondered how I managed to get this last chapter to you *after* we closed Yani-Yau's office? Do you think we have Internet service on Red Mountain? More likely, we have an emissary.)

Sorry, where was I?

Ah, yes. Parting ways. Black Star and Oscar Too also parted ways after the convention, as must I and my Editor.

Robyn has her childhood pail—the one with the mermaids—as evidence of our adventure, as well as a jagged scar on the top of her left foot. She wasn't meant to keep that, just as we probably are not meant to keep the intrepid cat Sylvestor, who started out in the Alternate World and ended up on our side. Maybe that balances things out—a cat for a cat scratch—or maybe the material score is still not settled between one side of the Spiral and the other.

I have in mind the book, *The Time Dancer*. Where did it originate, and how many copies were produced, and where did they all end up? Three big questions. But I have decided not to sweat it. Words are so insubstantial, after all, and what is the rest but ink, paper and glue? A tree here or there, on one side of the mountain or the other, is not such a big deal. It all becomes mulch in the end. And the digital versions—even more transient.

I have eliminated virtually everyone in the Goathorns community from my original list of suspected authors. For one thing, who here knew anything about Esmarelda, or George, prior to their recent visit? Robyn and I have batted this around. We still have a suspect or two, but I do not feel it would be strategic to say more. We are sticking to our plan, which is to appropriate that bizarre *nom de plume* for *this* work, and see if it will flush out the author of the other.

As for the problem of George Drumm being misplaced in Time ever since he leapt ahead ten years to follow Esmarelda, the

Coven has pushed that little squibble on down the Spiral—with a hastily concocted "bookmark" from Varluft trailing behind. To be honest, the lack of attention to the Gypsy couple's ten-years conundrum was more by default than decision. We, or they, or all of us, may yet come to regret it, but for now the couple is safely away. (Yes, "we." I am a member of the Coven now, as is Varluft. The old girls club has been integrated.)

This really is my last installment, Robyn. My view of your little loop-the-loop in the Alternate World, my insightfulness in general, is dimmed without the aspects of my animal forms. My range is limited to Red Mountain plus what can be got second-hand from the Familiars now and then, which will never replace the data from Coyote's nose and ears. Not that I'm complaining. My senses are well pleased here. Call me a Happy Man. (H. will still do for short.)

Farewell, fair Editor. Here is our final scene. If there is a moral to this story, The Top of The World is the place to find it:

"Who goes there?" The Weaver Oshi hobbled out of her yurt. "I hear flapping. Ti, is that you? Nee-Reta? Surely not Varluft—"

A raven landed at her feet, sleek and black.

"Ah, you. Come in." She turned and toddled back inside, pushing aside the heavy hangings.

Black Star had to bend low to pass through, and he could not stand to his full height once within. He sat on the yak wool rug and submitted to the Weaver's near-sighted scrutiny.

"What brings you here, Raven?"

"The mountain called me. I have been trying for a long time to get here. Then something happened that made me dream differently. I took a journey. There have been many animal guides. Recently it was Hawk. When she showed herself, a knowing came to me, and with it the knowledge of how to come to you."

"Is that so. A knowing of what?"

"Where I come from. Everyone should know where they come from."

"I don't know where I came from."

"You came from loving someone. Before that you only spun Time, like the Firsts had taught you. When you fell in love, you became yourself."

"I wasn't supposed to love, I wasn't supposed to be anyone, I was only supposed to spin Time into being. But Time without love—or hurt, or worry, or names, or souls, or pride, or magic, or opposites—what was that? I might as well have been spinning sugar candy without being able to enjoy the sweetness. The Firsts were long gone. Already I was a variation. Once a variation is introduced, more change will follow."

"That is true."

"You act as if you have news for me."

"No, not really. But I bring regards from my father."

"Do you? Should I know him?"

"Yes, I think you should."

"Oh. Well, how is he?"

"Old as the hills yet remarkably spry. Everyone says so."

"Good for him. Whoever he is, I want you to tell your father that he raised you well."

"I will do that, Mother."

"Ah, so that is the secret Nee-Reta told you. I did not realize she had seen so much."

"Now I know why I have the abilities I have, even in the Alternate World. But why was I kept away from this side for so long, and then confined to the Morass and the Knot?"

"The power to go anywhere, to cross between the worlds, is not to be taken lightly. When I ventured to the other side and met your father, I introduced something new into the Future that seemed to have no place in my tapestry of Time. You were born at The Top of The World, my son, and I sent you to your father to see what you would become. Sometimes at day's end I have dozed over my spinning wheel and dreamt of you, and, waking, I have said a prayer that you would be strong and well-meaning, that someday you would reclaim this summit. So long as your intentions are pure, you shall be able to ascend to this place, and from here you may go into the Goathorns. But beware corruption on either side, or you may be tripped up again."

"Is love a corruption?"

"As I said, it is a variation."

"So, I could go to Yani-Yau sometimes, and still find my way back to the Alternate World? They have given me much work there, you know."

"Be your own master, son, and follow your heart's highest purpose. Love will always grant you access to this place. I cannot say about the Alternate World, but if your father still remembers me with fondness, that is a hopeful sign. That you sit before me without anger after your long years of seeking makes me more hopeful still."

"I feel no anger for you, Mother, only awe and gratitude. I will visit with you often now."

The Weaver smiled as she gently put her hand on Black Star's head and chanted a blessing.

"Now, my child, sing me that song about Nowhere to Forever while I finish the day's weaving."

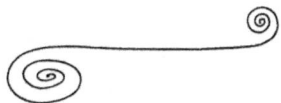

Spiral Map of Time Trilogy Book 1

The adventure begins . . .
THE TIME DANCER
A Novel of Gypsy Magic
by Zelda Leah Gatuskin

Can one really navigate the vast sea of Time? Celtic fiddler George Drumm is intrigued by symbols etched on the cairns of his remote Sumweir Isle home by ancient Wanderer tribes. The closed double spiral is said to depict the alternating timelines of two parallel worlds. When George learns that there are still Wanderer peoples criss-crossing the great continent, he sets out to find them and learn their secrets.

Across the ocean, George soon finds the Wanderers and woos them with his music. He travels with one group after another, at last joining a Gypsy caravan far inland. When time-dancing Gypsy Esmarelda drops in on them from the Future, romance blossoms. But the couple is out of sync in Time. Esmarelda is on a mission to rescue her cat Audy, presumably stolen by her nemesis, Malcom the Master Seer. Her quest takes her, and then George, to the parallel, frighteningly un-magical Alternate World. But in the dusty town of Caliente, New Mexico, the lovers find a friend in Robyn, proprietor of The Lost Unicorn metaphysical shop. As Esmarelda and George leapfrog across the Spiral Map of Time in search of lost cats, missing satchels and each other, they share glimpses of their enchanted universe with Robyn, and confirm what she has always suspected: There *is* a world of Magic just the other side of our dreams.

Spiral Map of Time Trilogy Book 2

The magic dance continues . . .
THE TWO MAGICIANS
From Nowhere to Forever
by Zelda Leah Gatuskin

Esmarelda and George Drumm, with Sylvestor the cat, have their hands (and paws) full when they attempt to find the Red Mountain Witch and return her magic satchel. Drawn into the dangerous doings of the Goathorns Coven, which collects and corrects lost charms and broken spells in their mystical domain, the couple fears the Witches will force George to make up his ten-years leap in Time.

In the Alternate World, the Summer Solstice Harmony Convention in Piper Canyon, now in its fifth year, has been increasing the leakage between parallel timelines. The New Age gathering in the Rockies happens to be a mere spiral-turn away from Goathorns Peak, a.k.a. The Top of The World, where the Spiral Map of Time reverses direction, Future meets Past, and the mundane world turns into a world of magic.

With Robyn and her belly dance troupe joining the Harmony Convention on one side, and the time-traveling Gypsies approaching on the other, the Minder of the Knot and the Loophole must work valiantly to restore order and prevent Time from unraveling. Before he is done, Brooks the Minder will expose the dark history of the five sisters of the Goathorns Coven, the recent transgressions of their shape-shifting Familiars, the secret lives of two Master Seers, and his own deepest desires.

Spiral Map of Time Trilogy Book 3

History repeats itself . . .
THE TEN YEARS
Double or Nothing
by Zelda Leah Gatuskin

Both Past and Future are catching up to Esmarelda and George Drumm, who have taken liberties with Time in order to stay together. Now, fleeing the Goathorn Mountains after their escapades with the two magicians, they find that their lives have been turned upside-down.

Across the Spiral in Caliente, New Mexico, Robyn's universe is also shaken. Her metaphysical shop, The Lost Unicorn, is still serving as a way station between worlds, and the mammoth cottonwood tree in back has become an actual portal. Mr. Brooks, the Emissary, and others she thought she would never see again after last year's Harmony Convention debacle, resurface.

At The Top Of The World, Weaver Oshi contemplates the tangled threads of Fate that have brought together more than one pair of Time-crossed lovers. When all of the Witches', Gypsies' and New Agers' magic has played out, where—and when—will everyone end up?

Here is the passionate, mind-blowing, music-and-dance-filled resolution to the Time Dancer's conundrum.

the Spiral Map of Time Trilogy

The Time Dancer

THE TWO MAGICIANS

THE TEN YEARS

by Zelda Leah Gatuskin